FOR FAITH AND FREEDOM

BY WALTER BESANT

CHAPTER I.

The morning of Sunday, August 23, in the year of grace 1662, should have been black and gloomy with the artillery of rolling thunder, dreadful flashes of lightning, and driving hail and wind to strip the orchards and lay low the corn. For on that day was done a thing which filled the whole country with grief, and bore bitter fruit in after years, of revenge and rebellion. And, because it was the day before that formerly named after Bartholomew, the disciple, it hath been called the Black Bartholomew of England, thus being likened unto that famous day (approved by the Pope) when the French Protestants were treacherously massacred by their King. It should rather be called 'Farewell Sunday' or 'Exile Sunday,' for on that day two thousand godly ministers preached their last sermon in the churches where they had laboured worthily and with good fruit, some during the time of the Protector, and some even longer, because among them were a few who possessed their benefices even from the time of the late King Charles the First. And, since on that day two thousand ministers left their churches and their houses, and laid down their worldly wealth for conscience' sake, there were also, perhaps, as many wives who went with them, and, I dare say, three or four times as many innocent and helpless babes. And, further (it is said that the time was fixed by design and deliberate malice of our enemies), the ministers were called upon to make their choice only a week or two before the day of the collection of their tithes. In other words, they were sent forth to the world at the season when their purses were at the leanest; indeed, with most country clergymen, their purses shortly before the collection of tithes have become well-nigh empty. It was also unjust that their successors should be permitted to collect the tithes due to those who were ejected.

It is fitting to begin this history with the Black Bartholomew, because all the troubles and adventures which afterwards befell us were surely caused by that accursed day. One know not certainly,[2] what other rubs might have been ordained for us by a wise Providence (always with the merciful design of keeping before our eyes the vanity of worldly things, the instability of fortune, the uncertainty of life, and the wisdom of looking for a hereafter which shall be lasting, stable, and satisfying to the soul). Still, it must be confessed, such trials as were appointed unto us were, in severity and continuance, far beyond those appointed to the ordinary sort, so that I cannot but feel at times uplifted (I hope not sinfully) at having been called upon to endure so much. Let me not, however, be proud. Had it not been for this day, for certain, our boys would not have been tempted to strike a blow—vain and useless as it proved—for the Protestant religion and for liberty of conscience: while perhaps I should now be forbidden to relate our sufferings, were it not for the glorious Revolution which has restored toleration, secured the Protestant ascendancy, and driven into banishment a Prince, concerning whom all honest men pray that he and his son (if he have, indeed, a son of his own) may never again have authority over this realm.

This Sunday, I say, should have wept tears of rain over the havoc which it witnessed; yet it was fine and clear, the sun riding in splendour, and a warm summer air blowing among the orchards and over the hills and around the village of Bradford Orcas, in the shire of Somerset. The wheat (for the season was late) stood gold-coloured in the fields, ready at last for the reaper; the light breeze bent down the ears so that they showed like waves over which the passing clouds make light and shade; the apples in the orchards were red and yellow, and nearly ripe for the press; in the gardens of the Manor House, hard by the church, the sunflowers and the hollyhocks were at their tallest and their best; the yellow roses on the wall were still in clusters; the sweet-peas hung with tangles of vine and flower upon their stalks; the bachelors' buttons, the sweet mignonette, the nasturtium, the gillyflowers and stocks, the sweet-williams and the pansies, offered their late summer blossoms to the hot sun among the lavender, thyme, parsley, sage, feverfew, and vervain of my Lady's garden. Oh! I know how it all looked, though I was then as yet unborn. How many times have I stood in the churchyard and watched the same scene at the same sweet season! On a week-day one hears the thumping and the groaning of the mill below the church; there are the voices of the men at work—the yo-hoing of the boys who drive; and the lumbering of the carts. You can even hear the spinning-wheels at work in the cottages. On Sunday morning everything is still, save for the warbling of the winged tribe in the wood, the cooing of the doves in the cote, the clucking of the hens, the grunting of the pigs, and the droning of the bees. These things disturb not the meditations of one who is accustomed to them.

At eight o'clock in the morning, the Sexton, an ancient man and rheumatic, hobbled slowly through the village, key in hand, and opened the church-door. Then he went into the tower and rang the first bell. I suppose this bell is designed to hurry housewives with their morning work, and to admonish the men that they incline their hearts to a spiritual disposition. This done, the Sexton set open the doors of the pews, swept out the Squire's and the Rector's in the chancel, dusted the cushions of the pulpit (the reading-desk at this time was not used), opened the clasps of the great Bible, and swept down the aisle: as he had done Sunday after Sunday for fifty years. When he had thus made the church ready for the day's service, he went into the vestry, which had only been used since the establishment of the Commonwealth for the registers of birth, death, and marriage.

At one side of the vestry stood an ancient, black oak coffer, the sides curiously graven, and a great rusty key in the lock. The Sexton turned the key with difficulty, threw open the lid and looked in.

'Ay,' he said, chuckling, 'the old surplice and the old Book of Common Prayer. Ye have had a long rest; 'tis time for both to come out again. When the surplice is out, the book will stay no longer locked up. These two go in and out together. I mind me, now'—— Here he sat down, and his thoughts wandered for a space; perhaps he saw himself once more a boy running in the fields, or a young man courting a maid. Presently he returned to the task before him, and drew forth an old and yellow roll which he shook out. It was the surplice which had once been white. 'Here you be,' he said. 'Put you away for a matter of twelve year and more and you bide your time; you know you will come back again; you are not in any hurry. Even the Sexton dies; but you die not, you bide your time. Everything comes again. The old woman shall give you a taste o' the suds and the hot iron. Thus we go up and thus we go down.' He put back the surplice and took out the great Book of Common Prayer—musty and damp after twelve years' imprisonment. 'Fie!' he said, 'thy leather is parting from the boards, and thy leaves they do stick together. Shalt have a pot of paste, and then lie in the sun before thou goest back to the desk. Whether 'tis Mass or Common Prayer, whether 'tis Independent or Presbyterian, folk mun still die and be buried—ay, and married and born—whatever they do say. Parson goes and Preacher comes; Preacher goes and Parson comes; but Sexton stays'— —He chuckled again, put back the surplice and the book, and locked the coffer.

Then he slowly went down the church and came out of the porch, blinking in the sun, and shading his old eyes. He sat down upon the flat stones of the old cross, and presently nodded his head and dropped off asleep.

This was a strange indifference in the man. A great and truly notable thing was to be accomplished that day. But he cared nothing. Two thousand godly and learned men were to go forth into poverty for liberty of conscience—this man's own minister was one of them. He cared nothing. The King was sowing the seed from which should[4] spring a rod to drive forth his successor from the kingdom. In the village the common sort were not moved. Nothing concerns the village folk but the weather and the market prices. As for the good Sexton, he was very old: he had seen the Church of England displaced by the Presbyterians and the Presbyterians by the Independents, and now these were again to be supplanted by the Church of England. He had been Sexton through all these changes. He heeded them not; why, his father, Sexton before him, could remember when the Mass was said in the church, and the Virgin was worshipped, and the folk were driven like sheep to confession. All the time the people went on being born, and marrying, and dying. Creed doth not, truly, affect these things, nor the Sexton's work. Therefore, this old gaffer, having made sure that the surplice was in the place where it had lain undisturbed for a dozen years, and remembering that it must be washed and ironed for the following Sunday, sat down to bask in the sun, his mind at rest, and dropped off into a gentle sleep.

At ten o'clock the bell-ringers came tramping up the stone steps from the road, and the Sexton woke up. At ten they used to begin their chimes, but at the hour they ring for five minutes only, ending with the clash of all five bells together. At a quarter-past ten they chime again, for the service, which begins at half-past ten.

At the sound of these chimes the whole village begins to move slowly towards the church. First come the children, the bigger ones leading those who are little by the hand; the boys come next, but unwillingly, because the Sexton is diligent with his cane, and some of those who now go up the steps to the church will come down with smarting backs, the reward of those who play or laugh during the service. Then come the young men, who stand about the churchyard and whisper to each other. After them follow the elders and the married men, with the women and the girls. Five minutes before the half hour the ringers change the chime for a single bell. Then those who are outside gather in the porch and wait for the Quality.

When the single bell began, there came forth from the Rectory the Rector himself, Mr. Comfort Eykin, Doctor of Divinity, who was this day to deliver his soul and lay down his charge. He wore the black gown and Geneva bands, for the use of which he contended. At this time he was a young man of thirty—tall and thin. He stooped in the shoulders because he was continually reading; his face was grave and austere; his nose thin and aquiline; his eyes bright—never was any man with brighter eyes than my father; his hair, which he wore long, was brown and curly; his forehead high, rather than broad; his lips were firm. In these days, as my mother hath told me, and as I well believe, he was a man of singular comeliness, concerning which he cared nothing. Always from childhood upwards he had been grave in conversation and seriously inclined in mind. If I think of my father as a boy (no one ever seems to think that his father was once a boy), I am fain to compare him with Humphrey, save for certain bodily defects, my father having been like a Priest of the Altar for bodily perfection.

That is to say, I am sure that, like Humphrey, he had no need of rod or ferule to make him learn his lessons, and, like that dear and fond friend of my childhood, he would willingly sit in a corner and read a book while the other boys played and went a-hunting or a-nesting. And very early in life he was smitten with the conviction of sin, and blessed with such an inward assurance of salvation as made him afterwards steadfast in all afflictions.

He was not a native of this country, having been born in New England. He came over, being then eighteen years of age, to study at Oxford, that university being purged of malignants (as they were then called), and, at the time, entirely in the hands of the godly. He was entered of Balliol College, of which Society he became a Fellow, and was greatly esteemed for his learning, wherein he excelled most of the scholars of his time. He knew and could read Hebrew, Chaldee, and the ancient Syriac, as well as Latin and Greek. Of modern languages he had acquired Arabic, by the help of which he read the book which is called the Koran of the False Prophet Mohammed: French and Italian he also knew and could read easily. As for his opinions, he was an Independent, and that not meekly or with hesitation, but with such zeal and vehemence that he considered all who differed from him as his private enemies—nay, the very enemies of God. For this reason, and because his personal habits were too austere for those who attained not to his spiritual height, he was more feared than loved. Yet his party looked upon him as one of their greatest and stoutest champions.

He left Oxford at the age of five or six and twenty, and accepted the living of Bradford Orcas, offered him by Sir Christopher Challis of that place. Here he had preached for six years, looking forward to nothing else than to remain there, advancing in grace and wisdom, until the end of his days. So much was ordered, indeed, for him; but not quite as he had designed. Let no man say that he knoweth the future, or that he can shape out his destiny. You shall hear presently how Benjamin arrogantly resolved that his future should be what he chose; and what came of that impious resolution.

My father's face was always austere; this morning it was more serious and sterner than customary, because the day was to him the most important in his life, and he was about to pass from a condition of plenty (the Rectory of Bradford Orcas is not rich but it affords a sufficiency) to one of penury. Those who knew him, however, had no doubt of the course he was about to take. Even the rustics knew that their minister would never consent to wear a surplice or to read the Book of Common Prayer, or to keep holy days—you have seen how the Sexton opened the box and took out the surplice; yet my father had said nothing to him concerning his intentions.

In his hand he carried his Bible—his own copy, I have it still,[6] the margins covered with notes in his writing bound in black leather, worn by constant handling, with brass clasps. Upon his head he had a plain black silk cap, which he wore constantly in his study and at meals to keep off draughts. Indeed, I loved to see him with the silk cap rather than with his tall steeple hat, with neither ribbon nor ornament of any kind, in which he rode when he afterwards went about the country to break the law in exhorting and praying with his friends.

Beside him walked my mother, holding in her hand her boy, my brother Barnaby, then three years of age. As for me, I was not yet born. She had been weeping; her eyes were red and swollen with tears; but when she entered the church she wept no more, bravely listening to the words which condemned to poverty and hardship herself and her children, if any more should be born to her. Alas, poor soul! What had she done that this affliction should befall her? What had her innocent boy done? For upon her—not upon her husband—would fall the heavy burden of poverty, and on her children the loss. Yet never by a single word of complaint did she make her husband sorry that he had obeyed the voice of conscience, even when there was nothing left in the house, not so much as the widow's cruse of oil. Alas, poor mother, once so free from care! what sorrow and anxiety wert thou destined to endure for the tender conscience of thy husband!

At the same time—namely, at the ringing of the single bell—there came forth from the Manor House hard by the church, his Honour, Sir Christopher, with his family. The worthy knight was then about fifty years of age, tall and handsome still—in his later years there was something of a heavenly sweetness in his face, created, I doubt not, by a long life of pious thoughts and worthy deeds. His hair was streaked with grey, but not yet white; he wore a beard of the kind called stiletto, which was even then an ancient fashion, and he was dressed more soberly than is common with gentlemen of his rank, having no feather in his hat, but a simple ribbon round it, and though his ruffles were of lace and the kerchief round his neck was lace, the colour of his coat was plain brown. He leaned upon a gold-headed cane on account of an old wound (it was inflicted by a Cavalier's musket-ball when he was a Captain in the army of Lord Essex). The wound left him somewhat lame, yet not so lame but that he could very well walk about his fields and could ride his horse, and even hunt with the otter-hounds. By his side walked Madam, his wife. After him came his son, Humphrey, newly married, and with Humphrey his wife; and last came his son-in-law, the Reverend Philip Boscorel, M.A., late Fellow of All Souls' College, Oxford, also newly married, with his wife, Sir Christopher's daughter, Patience. Mr. Boscorel, like my father, was at that time thirty years of age. Like him, too, his face was comely and his features fine; yet they lacked the fire and the earnestness which marked my father. And in his silken cassock, his small white bands, his lace ruffles, and his dainty walk, it seemed as if Mr. Boscorel thought himself above the common run of mankind and of superior clay. 'Tis sometimes the way with scholars and those who survey the world from the eminence of a library.

Sir Christopher's face was full of concern, because he loved the young man who was this day to throw away his livelihood; and although he was ready himself to worship after the manner prescribed by law, his opinions were rather Independent than Episcopalian. As for Mr. Boscorel, who was about to succeed to the ejected minister, his face wore no look of triumph, which would have been ungenerous. He was observed, indeed, after he had silently gone through the Service of the day with the help of the Common Prayer-book, to listen diligently unto the preacher.

The people, I have already said, knew already what was about to happen. Perhaps some of them (but I think not) possessed a copy of the old Prayer-book. This, they knew, was to be restored, with the surplice, and the observance of Holy days, Feasts, and Fasts, and the kneeling at the administration of the Holy Communion. Our people are craftsmen as much as they are rustics; every week the master-clothiers' men drive their packhorses into the village laden with wool, and return with yarn; they are not, therefore, so brutish and sluggish as most country folk; yet they made no outward show of caring whether Prelacy or Independency was to have the sway. Perhaps the abstruse doctrines which my father loved to discuss were too high for them; perhaps his austerity was too strict for them, so that he was not beloved by them. Perhaps, even, they would have cared little if they had heard that Bishop Bonner himself was coming back. Religion, to country folk, means, mostly, the going to church on Sunday morning. That done, man's service of Prayer and Praise to his Creator is also done. If the form be changed the church remains, and the churchyard; one shepherd followeth another, but the flock is always the same. Revolutions overthrow kings, and send great heads to the block; but the village heedeth not unless civil war pass that way. To country folk, what difference? The sky and the fields are unchanged. Under Queen Mary they are Papists; under Queen Elizabeth they are Protestants. They have the Prayer-book under King James and King Charles; under Oliver they have had the Presbyterian and Independent; now they have the Book of Common Prayer and the surplice again. Yet they remain the same people, and tell the same stories, and, so far as I know, believe the same things—viz., that Christ Jesus saves the soul of every man who truly believes in Him. Why, if it were not for his immortal soul—concerning which he takes but little thought—the rustic might be likened unto the patient beast whom he harnesseth to his plough and to his muck-cart. He changeth no more; he works as hard; he is as long-enduring; his eyes and his thoughts are as much bound by the hedge, the lane, and the field; he thinks and invents and advances no more. Were it not, I say, for the Church, he would take as little heed of anything as his ox or his ass; his village would become his country; his squire would become his king; the nearest village would become the camp of an enemy; and he would fall into the condition of the Ancient Briton when Julius Cæsar found every tribe fighting against every other.

I talk as a fool. For sometimes there falls upon the torpid soul of the rustic a spark which causes a mighty flame to blaze up and burn fiercely within him. I have read how a simple monk, called Peter the Hermit, drew thousands of poor, illiterate, credulous persons from their homes, and led them, a mob armed with scythes and pikes, across Europe to the deserts of Asia Minor, where they miserably perished. I have read also of Jack Cade, and how he drew the multitudes after him, crying aloud for justice or death. And I myself have seen these sluggish spirits suddenly fired with a spirit which nothing could subdue. The sleeping soul I have seen suddenly starting into life; strength and swiftness have I seen suddenly put into sluggish limbs; light and fire have I seen gleaming suddenly in dull and heavy eyes. Oh! it was a miracle: but I have seen it. And having seen it, I cannot despise these lads of the plough, these honest boys of Somerset, nor can I endure to hear them laughed at or contemned.

Bradford Orcas, in the Hundred of Horethorne, Somerset, is a village so far from the great towns, that one would think a minister might have gone on praying and preaching after his own fashion without ever being discovered. But the arm of the Law is long.

The nearest town is Sherborne, in Dorsetshire, to which there is a bridle-path across the fields; it is the market-town for the villages round it. Bradford Orcas is an obscure little village, with no history and no antiquities. It stands in the south-eastern corner of the county, close to the western declivity of the Corton Hills, which here sweep round so as to form a valley, in which the village is built along the banks of a stream. The houses are for the most part of stone, with thatched roofs, as is the custom in our country; the slopes of the hills are covered with tres , and round the village stand goodly orchards, the cider from which cannot be surpassed. As for the land, but little of it is arable; the greater part is a sandy loam or stone brash. The church, which in the superstitious days was dedicated to St. Nicolas, is built upon a hillock, a rising ground in the west of the village. This building of churches upon hillocks is a common custom in our parts, and seemeth laudable, because a church should stand where it can be seen by all the people, and by its presence remind them of Death and of the Judgment. The practice doth obtain, for example, at Sherborne, where there is a very noble church, and at Huish Episcopi, and at many other places in our county. Our church is fair and commodious, not too large for the congregation, having in the west a stone tower embattled, and consisting of a nave and chancel with a very fine roof of carved woodwork. There is an ancient yew-tree[9] in the churchyard, from which in old times bows were cut; some of the bows yet hang in the great hall of the Manor House. Among the graves is an ancient stone cross, put up no man knows when, standing in a six-sided slab of stone, but the top was broken off at the time of the Reformation; two or three tombs are in the churchyard, and the rest is covered with mounds, beneath which lie the bones and dust of former generations.

Close to the churchyard, and at the north-east corner, is the Manor House, as large as the church itself, but not so ancient. It was built in the reign of Henry VII. A broad arched gateway leads into a court, wherein is the entrance to the house. Over the gateway is a kind of tower, but not detached from the house. In the wall of the tower is a panel, lozenge-shaped, in which are carved the arms of the Challis family. The house is stately, with many gables, and in each are casement windows set in richly-carved stone tracery. As for the rooms within the house, I will speak of them hereafter. At present I have the churchyard in my mind. There is no place upon the earth which more I love. To stand in the long grass among the graves; to gaze upon the wooded hills beyond, the orchards, the meadows, the old house, the venerable church, the yew-tree: to listen to the murmur of the stream below and the singing of the lark above; to feel the fresh breeze upon my cheek—oh! I do this daily. It makes me feel young once more; it brings back the days when I stood here with the boys, and when Sir Christopher would lean over the wall and discourse with us gravely and sweetly upon the love of God and the fleeting joys of earth (which yet, he said, we should accept and be happy withal in thankfulness), and the happiness unspeakable that awaiteth the Lord's Saints. Or, if my thoughts continue in the past, the graveyard brings back the presence and the voice of Mr. Boscorel.

'In such a spot as this,' he would say, speaking softly and slowly, 'the pastorals of Virgil or Theocritus might have been written. Here would the shepherds hold their contests. Certainly they could find no place, even in sunny Sicily or at Mantua itself, where (save for three months in the year) the air is more delightful. Here they need not to avoid the burning heat of a sun which gently warms, but never burns; here they would find the shade of the grove pleasant in the soft summer season. Innocent lambs instead of kids (which are tasteless) play in our meadows; the cider which we drink is, I take it, more pleasing to the palate than was their wine flavoured with turpentine. And our viols, violins, and spinets are instruments more delightful than the oaten pipe, or the cithara itself.' Then would he wave his hand, and quote some poet in praise of a country life—

There is no man but may make his paradise, And it is nothing but his love and dotage Upon the world's foul joys that keeps him out on't. For he that lives retired in mind and spirit Is still in Paradise.

'But, child,' he would add, with a sigh, 'one may not always wish to be in Paradise. The world's joys lie elsewhere. Only, when youth is gone—then Paradise is best.'

The service began, after the manner of the Independents, with a long prayer, during which the people sat. Mr. Boscorel, as I have said, went through his own service in silence, the Book of Common Prayer in his hand. After the prayer, the minister read a portion of Scripture, which he expounded at length and with great learning. Then the congregation sang that Psalm which begins—

Triumphing songs with glorious tongues Let's offer unto Him.

This done, the Rector ascended the pulpit for the last time, gave out his text, turned his hour-glass, and began his sermon.

He took for his text those verses in St. Paul's second epistle to the Corinthians, vi., 3-10, in which the Apostle speaks of his own ministry as if he was actually predicting the tribulation which was to fall upon these faithful preachers of a later time—'In much patience, in afflictions, in necessities, in distresses, in stripes, in imprisonments, in tumults, in labours, in watchings, in fastings,'—could not the very words be applied to my father?

He read the text three times, so that everybody might fully understand the subject upon which he was to preach—namely, the faithfulness required of a minister of the gospel. I need not set down the arguments he used or the reasons he gave for his resolution not to conform with the Act of Uniformity. The rustics sat patiently listening, with no outward sign of assent or of sympathy. But their conduct afterwards proved abundantly to which side their minds inclined.

It behoves us all to listen with respect when scholars and wise men inquire into the reasons of things. Yet the preachings and expositions which such as my father bestowed upon their flocks did certainly awaken men's minds to consider by themselves the things which many think too high for them. It is a habit which may lead to the foundation of false and pernicious sects. And it certainly is not good that men should preach the doctrines of the Anabaptists, the Fifth Monarchy men, or the Quakers. Yet it is better that some should be deceived than that all should be slaves. I have been assured by one—I mean Humphrey—who hath travelled, that in those countries where the priest taketh upon himself the religion of the people, so that they think to be saved by attending mass, by fasting, confession, penance, and so forth, not only does religion itself become formal, mechanical, and inanimate, but in the very daily concerns and business of life men grow slothful and lack spirit. Their religion, which is the very heat of the body, the sustaining and vital force of all man's actions, is cold and dead. Therefore, all the virtues are cold also, and with them the courage and the spirit of the people. Thus it is that Italy hath fallen aside into so many small and divided kingdoms. And for this reason, Spain, in the opinion of those who know her best, is now falling rapidly into decay.

I am well assured, by those who can remember, that the intelligence of the village folk greatly increased during the period when they were encouraged to search the Scriptures for themselves. Many taught themselves to read, others had their children taught, in order that they might read or hear, daily, portions of the Scriptures. It is now thirty years since Authority resumed the rule; the village folk have again become, to outward seeming, sheep who obey without questioning. Yet it is observed that when they are within reach of a town—that is to say, of a meeting-house—they willingly flock to the service in the afternoon and evening.

It was with the following brave words that my father concluded his discourse:—

'Seeing, therefore, my brethren, how clear is the Word of God on these points; and considering that we must always obey God rather than man; and observing that here we plainly see the finger of God pointing to disobedience and its consequences, I am constrained to disobey. The consequence will be to me that I shall stand in this place no more: to you, that you will have a stranger in your church. I pray that he may be a godly person, able to divide the Word, learned and acceptable.

'As for me, I must go forth, perhaps from among you altogether. If persecutions arise, it may behove me and mine to seek again that land beyond the seas whither my fathers fled for the sake of religious liberty. Whatever happens, I must fain preach the gospel. It is laid upon me to preach. If I am silent, it will be as if Death itself had fallen upon me. My brethren, there have been times—and those times may return—when the Elect have had to meet, secretly, on the sides of barren hills, and in the heart of the forest, to pray together and to hear the Word. I say that these times may return. If they do, you will find me willing, I hope and pray, to brave for you the worst that our enemies can devise. Perhaps, however, this tyranny may pass over. Already the Lord hath achieved one great deliverance for this ancient Realm. Perhaps another may be in His secret purposes when we have been chastened, as, for our many sins, we richly deserve. Whether in affliction or in prosperity, let us always say, "The Lord's name be praised!"

'Now, therefore, for the sand is running low and I may not weary the young and the impatient, let me conclude. Farewell, sweet Sabbaths! Farewell, the sweet expounding of the Word! Farewell, sweet pulpit! Farewell, sweet faces of the souls which I have yearned to present pure and washed clean before the Throne! My brethren, I go about, henceforth, as a dog which is muzzled; another man will fill this pulpit; our simple form of worship is gone; the Prayer-book and the surplice have come back again. Pray God we see not Confession, Penance, the Mass, the Inquisition, the enslavement of conscience, the stake, and the martyr's axe!'

Then he paused and bowed his head, and everybody thought that he had finished.

He had not. He raised it again, and threw out his arms and shouted aloud, while his eyes glowed like fire:

'*No!* I will not be silent. I WILL NOT. I am sent into the world to preach the gospel. I have no other business. I must proclaim the Word as I hope for everlasting life. Brethren, we shall meet again. In the woods and on the hills we shall find a Temple; there are houses where two or three may be gathered together, the Lord Himself being in their midst. Never doubt that I am ready, in season and out of season, whatever be the law, to preach the gospel of the Lord!'

He ended, and straightway descended the pulpit stair, and stalked out of the church, the people looking after him with awe and wonder. But Mr. Boscorel smiled and wagged his head, with a kind of pity.

CHAPTER II

IN THE VILLAGE.

Thus did my father, by his own act and deed, strip himself of all his worldly wealth. Yet, having nothing, he ceased not to put his trust in the Lord, and continued to sit among his books, never asking whence came the food provided for him. I think, indeed, so wrapt was he in thought, that he knew not. As for procuring the daily food, my mother it was who found out the way.

Those who live in other parts of this kingdom do not know what a busy and populous county is that of Somerset. Apart from the shipping and the great trade with Ireland, Spain, and the West Indies carried on from the Port of Bristol, we have our great manufactures of cloth, in which we are surpassed by no country in the world. The town of Taunton alone can boast of eleven hundred looms always at work making Sagathies and Des Roys; there are many looms at Bristol, where they make for the most part Druggets and Cantaloons; and there are great numbers at that rich and populous town of Frome Selwood, where they manufacture the Spanish Medleys. Besides the cloth-workers, we have, in addition, our knitted-stocking trade, which is carried on mostly at Glastonbury and Shepton Mallet. Not only does this flourishing trade make the masters rich and prosperous (it is not uncommon to find a master with his twenty—ay, and his forty—thousand pounds), but it fills all the country with work, so that the towns are frequent, populous, and full of everything that men can want; and the very villages are not like those which may be seen in other parts, poor and squalid, but well-built and comfortable.

Every cottage has its spinning-wheel. The mother, when she is not doing the work of the house, sits at the wheel; the girls, when they have nothing else to do, are made to knit stockings. Every week the master-clothier sends round his men among the villages, their packhorses laden with wool; every week they return, their packs laden with yarn, ready for the loom.

There is no part of England where the people are more prosperous and more contented. Nowhere are there more towns, and all thriving; nowhere are the villages better built; nor can one find anywhere else more beautiful churches. Because the people make good wages they are independent in their manners; they have learned things supposed to be above the station of the humble; most of them in the towns, and many in the villages, are able to read. This enables them to search the Scriptures, and examine into doctrine by the light of their own reason, guided by grace. And to me, the daughter of a Nonconforming preacher, it does not seem wonderful that so many of them should have become stiff and sturdy Nonconformists. This was seen in the year 1685, and, again, three years later, when a greater than Monmouth landed on the western shores.

My mother, then, seeing no hope that her husband would earn, by any work of his own, the daily bread of the household, bravely followed the example of the women in the village. That is to say, she set up her spinning-wheel, and spent all the time that she could spare spinning the wool into yarn; while she taught her little boy first and afterwards her daughter—as soon as I was old enough to manage the needles—to knit stockings. What trade, indeed, could her husband follow save one—and that, by law, prohibited? He could not dig; he could not make anything; he knew not how to buy or sell; he could only study, write, and preach. Therefore, while he sat among his books in one room, she sat over her wheel in the other, working for the master-clothiers of Frome Selwood. It still makes my heart to swell with pity and with love when I think upon my mother, thus spending herself and being spent, working all day, huckstering with the rough pack-horsemen more accustomed to exchange rude jests with the rustics than to talk with gentlewomen. And this she continued to do year after year, cheerful and contented, so that her husband should never feel the pinch of poverty. Love makes us willing slaves.

My father, happily, was not a man whose mind was troubled about food. He paid no heed at all to what he ate, provided that it was sufficient for his needs; he would sup his broth of pork and turnips and bread, after thanks rendered, as if it were the finest dish in the world; and a piece of cold bacon with a hot cabbage would be a feast for him. The cider which he drank was brewed by my mother from her own apples; to him it was as good as if it had been Sherris or Rhenish. I say that he did not even know how his food was provided for him; his mind was at all times occupied with subjects so lofty that he knew not what was done under his very eyes. The hand of God, he said, doth still support His faithful. Doubtless we cannot look back upon those years without owning that we were so supported. But my mother was the Instrument; nay, my father sometimes even compared himself with satisfaction unto the Prophet Elijah, whom the ravens fed beside the brook Cherith, bringing him flesh and bread in the morning and flesh and bread in the evening. I suppose my father thought that his bacon and beans came to him in the same manner.

Yet we should sometimes have fared but poorly had it not been[15] for the charity of our friends. Many a fat capon, green goose, side of bacon, and young grunter came to us from the Manor House, with tobacco, which my father loved, and wine to comfort his soul; yea, and clothes for us all, else had we gone barefoot and in rags. In this way was many an ejected Elijah at that time nourished and supported. Fresh meat we should never have tasted, any more than the humblest around us, had it not been for our good friends at the Manor House. Those who live in towns cannot understand how frugal and yet sufficient may be the fare of those who live in the country and have gardens and orchards. Cider was our drink, which we made ourselves; we had some sweet apple-trees, which gave us a stock of russets and pippins for winter use; we had bees (but we sold most of our honey at Sherborne market); our garden grew sallets and onions, beans and the like; skim milk we could have from the Manor House for the fetching; for breakfast we had bread and milk, for dinner bread and soft cheese, with a lettuce or an apple; and bread or bread and butter for supper. For my father there was always kept a piece of bacon or fat pork.

Our house was one of the cottages in the village: it is a stone house (often I sit down to look at it, and to remember those days of humility) with a thick thatch. It had two rooms below and two garrets above. One room was made into a study or library for my father, where also he slept upon a pallet. The other was kitchen, spinning room, parlour, all in one. The door opened upon the garden, and the floor was of stone, so that it was cold. But when Barnaby began to find the use of his hands he procured some boards, which he laid upon the stones, and so we had a wooden floor; and in winter across the door we hung a blanket or rug to keep off the wind.

The walls were whitewashed, and over all my mother had written texts of Scripture with charcoal, so that godly admonition was ever present to our eyes and minds. She also embroidered short texts upon our garments, and I have still the cradle in which I was laid, carved (but I do not know by whose hand) with a verse from the Word of God. My father used himself, and would have us employ, the words of the Bible even for the smaller occasions of daily use; nor would he allow that anything was lawful unless it was sanctioned by the Bible, holding that in the Word was everything necessary or lawful. Did Barnaby go shooting with Sir Christopher and bring home a rabbit?—Lo! David bade the children of Israel teach the use of the bow. Did my mother instruct and amuse me with riddles?—She had the warrant of Scripture for it in the example of Samson. Did she sing Psalms and spiritual songs to while away the time and make her work less irksome and please her little daughter?—In the congregation of Nehemiah there were two hundred forty-and-five singing men and singing women.

My father read and expounded the Bible to us twice a day—morning and evening. Besides the Bible we had few books which[16] we could read. As for my mother, poor soul, she had no time to read. And as for me, when I grew older I borrowed books from the Manor House or Mr. Boscorel. And there were 'Old Mr. Dod's Sayings' and 'Plain Directions by Joseph Large' always on the shelf beside the Bible.

Now, while my father worked in his study and my brother Barnaby either sat over his lesson-book, his hands rammed into his hair, as if determined to lose nothing, not the least scrap of his portion (yet knowing full well that on the morrow there would be not a word left in his poor unlucky noddle, and once more the whip), my mother would sit at her wheel earning the daily bread. And, when I was little, she would tell me, speaking very softly, so as not to disturb the wrestling of her husband with a knotty argument, all the things which you have heard—how my father chose rather poverty than to worship at the altar of Baal; and how two thousand pious ministers, like-minded with himself, left their pulpits and went out into the cold for conscience' sake. So that I was easily led to think that there were no Christian martyrs and confessors more excellent and praiseworthy than these ejected ministers (which still I believe). Then would she tell me further of how they fared, and how the common people do still reverence them. There was the history of John Norman, of Bridgwater; Joseph Chadwick, of Wrenford; Felix Howe, of West Torrington; George Minton, and many others. She also instructed me very early in the history of the Protestant uprising over the best half of Europe, and showed me how, against fearful odds, and after burnings and tortures unspeakable, the good people of Germany, the Netherlands, and Great Britain won their freedom from the Pope, so that my heart glowed within me to think of the great goodness and mercy which caused me to be born in a Protestant country. And she instructed me, later, in the wickedness of King Charles, whom they now call a martyr, and in the plots of that King, and Laud his Archbishop, and how King and Archbishop were both overthrown and perished when the people arose and would bear no more. In fine, my mother made me, from the beginning, a Puritan. As I remember my mother always, she was pale of cheek and thin, her voice was gentle; yet with her very gentleness she would make the blood to run quick in the veins, and the heart to beat.

How have I seen the boys spring to their feet when she has talked with them of the great civil war and the Revolution! But always soft and gentle; her blue eyes never flashing; no wrath in her heart; but the truth, which often causeth righteous anger, always upon her tongue.

One day, I remember, when I was a little girl playing in the garden, Mr. Boscorel walked down the village in his great silken gown, which seemed always new, his lace ruffs, and his white bands, looking like a Bishop at least, and walking delicately, holding up his gown to keep it from the dust and mud. When he spoke it was in a soft voice and a mincing speech, not like our[17] plain Somersetshire way. He stopped at our gate, and looked down the garden. It was a summer day, the doors and windows of the cottage were open; at our window sat my father bending over his books, in his rusty gown and black cap, thin and lank; at the door sat my mother at her wheel.

'Child,' said the Rector, 'take heed thou never forget in thine age the thing which thou seest daily in thy childhood.'

I knew not what he meant.

'Read and mark,' he said; 'yea, little Alice, learn by heart what the Wise Man hath said of the good woman: "She layeth her hands to the spindle ... she maketh fine linen and selleth it ... she eateth not the bread of idleness.... Let her works praise her in the gates."'

CHAPTER III.

THE BOYS.

The family of Challis, of Bradford Orcas, is well known; here there has always been a Challis from time immemorial. They are said to have been on the land before the time of the Conqueror. But because they have never been a great family, like the Mohuns of Dunster, but only modest gentle-folk with some four or five hundred pounds a year, they have not suffered, like those great houses, from the civil wars, which, when they raged in the land, brought in their train so many attainders, sequestrations, beheadings, imprisonments, and fines. Whether the Barons fought, or whether Cavaliers and Roundheads, the Challises remained at Bradford Orcas.

Since the land is theirs and the village, it is reasonable that they should have done everything that has been done for the place. One of them built the church, but I know not when; another built the tower; another gave the peal of bells. He who reigned here in the time of Henry VII., built the Manor House; another built the mill; the monuments in the church are all put up to the memory of Challises dead and gone; there is one, a very stately tomb, which figures, to the life, Sir William Challis (who died in the time of Queen Elizabeth), carved in marble, and coloured, kneeling at a desk; opposite to him is his second wife, Grace, also kneeling. Behind the husband are three boys, on their knees, and behind the wife are three girls. Apart from this group is the effigy of Filipa, Sir Christopher's first wife, with four daughters kneeling behind her. I was always sorry for Filipa, thus separated and cut off from the society of her husband. There are brasses on the floor with figures of other Challises, and tablets in the wall, and the Challis coat-of-arms is everywhere, cut in lozenges, and painted in wood, and shining in the east window. It seemed to me, in my young days, that it was the grandest thing in the world to be a Challis.

In this family there was a laudable practice with the younger sons, that they stayed not at home, as is too often their custom, leading indolent lives without ambition or fortune, but they sallied forth and sought fortune in trade, or in the Law, or in the Church, or in foreign service—wherever fortune is to be honourably won—so that, though I daresay some have proved dead and dry branches, others have put forth flowers and fruit abundantly, forming new and vigorous trees sprung from the ancient root. Thus, some have become judges: and some bishops: and some great merchants: some have crossed the ocean and are now settled in the Plantations: some have attained rank and estates in the service of the Low Countries. Thus, Sir Christopher's brother Humphrey went to London and became a Levant merchant and adventurer, rising to great honour and becoming alderman. I doubt not that he would have been made Lord Mayor but for his untimely death. And as for his wealth, which was rumoured to be so great—but you shall hear of this in due time.

That goodly following of his household which you have seen enter the church on Farewell Sunday, was shortly afterwards broken into by death. There fell upon the village (I think it was in the year 1665) the scourge of a putrid fever, of which there died, besides numbers of the village folk, Madam herself—the honoured wife of Sir Christopher—Humphrey his son, and Madam Patience Boscorel, his daughter. There were left to Sir Christopher, therefore, only his daughter-in-law and his grandsons Robin and Benjamin. And in that year his household was increased by the arrival of his grand-nephew Humphrey. This child was the grandson of Sir Christopher's brother, the Turkey or Levant merchant of whom I have spoken. He was rich and prosperous: his ships sailed out every year laden with I know not what, and returned with figs, dates, spices, gums, silks, and all kinds of precious commodities from Eastern parts. It is, I have been told, a profitable trade, but subject to terrible dangers from Moorish pirates, who must be bravely fought and beaten off, otherwise ship and cargo will be taken, and captain and crew driven into slavery. Mr. Challis dwelt in Thames-street, close to Tower-hill. It is said that he lived here in great splendour, as befits a rich merchant who is also an Alderman.

Now, in the year 1665, as is very well known, a great plague broke out in the city. There were living in the house in Thames-street the Alderman, his wife, his son, his son's wife, a daughter, and his grandson, little Humphrey. On the first outbreak of the pestilence they took counsel together and resolved that the child should be first sent away to be out of danger, and that they would follow if the plague spread.

This was done, and a sober man, one of their porters or warehousemen, carried the child with his nurse all the way from London to Bradford Orcas. Alas! Before the boy reached his great-uncle, the house in Thames-street was attacked by the plague, and everyone therein perished. Thus was poor little Humphrey deprived of his parents. I know not who were his guardians or trustees, or what steps, if any, were taken to inquire into the Alderman's estate; but when, next year, the Great Fire of London destroyed the house in Thames-street, with so many others, all the estate, whatever it had been, vanished, and could no more be traced. There must have been large moneys owing. It is certain that he had ventures in ships. It has been supposed that he owned many houses in the City, but they were destroyed and their very sites forgotten, and no deeds or papers, or any proof of ownership, were left. Moreover, there was nobody charged with inquiring into this orphan's affairs. Therefore, in the general confusion, nothing at all was saved out of what had been a goodly property, and the child Humphrey was left without a guinea in the world. Thus unstable is Fortune.

I know not whether Humphrey received a fall in his infancy, or whether he was born with his deformity, but the poor lad grew up with a crooked figure, one shoulder being higher than the other, and his legs short, so that he looked as if his arms were too long for him. We, who saw him thus every day, paid no heed, nor did he suffer from any of those cruel gibes and taunts which are often passed upon lads thus afflicted. As he was by nature or misfortune debarred from the rough sports which pleased his cousins, the boy gave himself up to reading and study, and to music. His manner of speech was soft and gentle; his voice was always sweet, and afterwards became strong as well, so that I have never heard a better singer. His face—ah! my brother Humphrey, what a lovely face was thine! All goodness, surely, was stamped upon that face. Never, never, did an unworthy thought defile that candid soul, or a bad action cast a cloud upon that brow!

As for Robin, Sir Christopher's grandson, I think he was always what he is still, namely, one of a joyous heart and a cheerful countenance. As a boy, he laughed continually, would sing more willingly than read, would play rather than work, loved to course and shoot and ride better than to learn Latin grammar, and would readily off coat and fight with any who invited him. Yet not a fool or a clown, but always a gentleman in manners, and one who read such things as behove a country gentleman, and scrupulous as to the point of honour. Such as he is still such he was always. And of a comely presence, with a rosy cheek and bright eyes, and the strength of a young David, as well as his ruddy and goodly countenance. The name of David, I am told, means 'darling.' Therefore ought my Robin to have been named David. There were two other boys—Barnaby, my brother, who was six years older than myself, and, therefore, always to me a great boy; and Benjamin, the son of the Rev. Mr. Boscorel—the Rector. Barnaby grew up so broad and strong that at twelve he would have passed easily for seventeen; his square shoulders, deep chest, and big limbs made him like a bull for strength. Yet he was shorter than most, and looked shorter than he was by reason of his great breadth. He was always exercising his strength; he would toss the hay with the haymakers, and carry the corn for the reapers, and thresh with the flail, and guide the plough. He loved to climb great trees, and fell to them with an axe. Everybody in the village admired his wonderful strength. Unfortunately, he loved not books, and could never learn anything, so that when, by dint of great application and many repetitions, he had learned a little piece of a Latin verb, he straightway forgot it in the night, and so, next day, there was another flogging. But that he heeded little. He was five years older than Robin, and taught him all his woodcraft—where to find pheasants' eggs, how to catch squirrels, how to trap weasels and stoats, how to hunt the otter, how to make a goldfinch whistle and a raven talk—never was there such a master of that wisdom which doth not advance a man in the world.

Now, before Barnaby's birth, his mother, after the manner of Hannah, gave him solemnly unto the Lord all the days of his life, and, after his birth, her husband, after the manner of Elkanah, said: 'Do what seemeth thee good; only the Lord establish his word.' He was, therefore, to become a minister, like his father before him. Alas! poor Barnaby could not even learn the Latin verbs, and his heart, it was found, as he grew older, was wholly set upon the things of this world. Wherefore, my mother prayed for him daily while she sat at her work, that his heart might be turned, and that he might get understanding.

As for the fourth of the boys, Benjamin Boscorel, he was about two years younger than Barnaby, a boy who, for want of a mother, and because his father was careless of him, grew up rough and coarse in manners and in speech, and boastful of his powers. To hear Ben talk you would think that all the boys of his school (the grammar school of Sherborne) were heroes; that the Latin taught was of a quality superior to that which Robin and Humphrey learnt of my father; and that when he himself went out into the world, the superiority of his parts would be immediately perceived and acknowledged.

Those who watch boys at play together—girls more early learn to govern themselves and to conceal their thoughts, if not their tempers—may, after a manner, predict the future character of every one. There is the man who wants all for himself, and still wants more, and will take all and yield nothing, save on compulsion, and cares not a straw about his neighbour—such was Benjamin, as a boy. There is the man who gives all generously—such was Robin. There is, again, the man whose mind is raised above the petty cares of the multitude, and dwells apart, occupied with great thoughts—such was Humphrey. Lastly, there is the man who can act but cannot think; who is born to be led; who is full of courage and of strength, and leaves all to his commander, captain, or master—such was Barnaby.

As I think of these lads it seems as if the kind of man into which each would grow must have been stamped upon their foreheads. Perhaps to the elders this prognostic was easy to read.

They suffered me to play with them or to watch them at play. When the boys went off to the woods I went with them. I watched them set their traps—I ran when they ran. And then, as now, I loved Robin and Humphrey. But I could not endure—no; not even the touch of him—Benjamin, with the loud laugh and the braggart voice, who laughed at me because I was a girl and could not fight. The time came when he did not laugh at me because I was a girl. And oh! to think—only to think—of the time that came after that!

CHAPTER IV.

SIR CHRISTOPHER.

At the mere remembrance of Sir Christopher, I am fain to lay down my pen and to weep, as for one whose goodness was unsurpassed, and whose end was undeserved. Good works, I know, are rags, and men cannot deserve the mercy of God by any merits of their own; but a good man—a man whose heart is full of justice, mercy, virtue, and truth—is so rare a creature, that when there is found such a one, his salvation seems assured. Is it not wonderful that there are among us so many good Christians, but so few good men? I am, indeed, in private duty bound to acknowledge Sir Christopher's goodness to me and to mine. He was, as I have said, the mainstay of our household. Had we depended wholly on my mother's work, we should sometimes have fared miserably indeed. Nay, he did more. Though a Justice of the Peace, he invited my father every Sunday evening to the Manor House for spiritual conversation, not only for his own profit, but knowing that to expound was to my father the breath of his nostrils, so that if he could not expound he must die. In person, Sir Christopher was tall; after the fashion (which I love) of the days when he was a young man he wore his own hair, which, being now white and long, became his venerable face much better than any wig—white, black, or brown. He was generally dressed, as became his station of simple country gentleman, in a plush coat with silver buttons, and for the most part he wore boots, being of an active habit and always walking about his fields or in his gardens among his flowers and his fruit-trees. He was so good a sportsman that with his rod, his gun, and his hawk he provided his table with everything except beef, mutton, and pork. In religion he inclined to Independency, being above all things an upholder of private judgment; in politics, he denied the Divine right, and openly said that a Challis might be a King as well as a Stuart; he abhorred the Pope and all his works; and though he was now for a Monarchy, he would have the King's own power limited by the Parliament. In his manners he was grave and dignified; not austere, but one who loved a cheerful companion. He rode once a week, on market day, to Sherborne, where he dined with his brother Justices, hearing and discussing the news, though news comes but slowly from London to these parts—it was fourteen days after the landing of the King in the year 1660 that the bells of Sherborne Minster rang for that event. Sometimes a copy of the *London Gazette* came down by the Exeter coach, or some of the company had lately passed a night where the coach stopped, and conversed with travellers from London and heard the news. For the rest of the week, his Honour was at home. For the most part he sat in the hall. In the middle stands the great oak table where all the household sit at meals together. There was little difference between the dishes served above and those below the salt, save that those above had each a glass of strong ale or of wine after dinner and supper. One side of the hall was hung with arras worked with representations of herbs, beasts and birds. On the other side was the great chimney, where in the winter a noble fire was kept up all day long. On either side of it hung fox skins, otter skins, pole-cat skins, with fishing-rods, stags' heads, horns and other trophies of the chase. At the end was a screen covered with old coats of mail, helmets, bucklers, lances, pikes, pistols, guns with match-locks, and a trophy of swords arranged in form of a star. Below the cornice hung a row of leathern jerkins, black and dusty, which had formerly been worn in place of armour by the common sort. In the oriel window was a sloping desk, having on one side the Bible and on the other Foxe's 'Book of Martyrs.' Below was a shelf with other books, such as Vincent Wing's Almanack, King Charles's 'Golden Rules,' 'Glanville on Apparitions,' the 'Complete Justice,' and the 'Book of Farriery.'

There was also in the hall a great side-board, covered with Turkey work, pewter, brass, and fine linen. In the cupboard below was his Honour's plate, reported to be worth a great deal of money.

Sir Christopher sat in a high chair, curiously carved, with arms and a triangular seat. It had belonged to the family for many generations. Within reach of the chair was the tobacco-jar, his pipe, and his favourite book—namely, 'The Gentleman's Académie: or the Book of St. Albans, being a Work on Hunting, Hawking, and Armorie,' by Dame Juliana Berners, who wrote it two hundred and fifty years ago. Sir Christopher loved especially to read aloud that chapter in which it is proved that the distinction between gentleman and churl began soon after the Creation, when Cain proved himself a churl, and Seth was created Gentleman and Esquire or Armiger by Adam, his father. This distinction was renewed after the Flood by Noah himself, a gentleman by lineal descent from Seth. In the case of his sons, Ham was the churl, and the other two were the gentlemen. I have sometimes thought that, according to this author, all of us who are descended from Shem or Japhet should be gentlemen, in which case there would be no churl in Great Britain at all. But certainly there are many; so that, to my poor thinking, Dame Juliana Berners must be wrong.

There is, in addition to the great hall, the best parlour. But as this was never wanted, the door of it was never opened except at cleaning time. Then, to be sure, one saw a room furnished very grand, with chairs in Turkey work, and hung round with family portraits. The men were clad in armour, as if they had all been soldiers or commanders; the women were mostly dressed as shepherdesses, with crooks in their hands and flowing robes. In the garden was a long bowling green, where in summer Sir Christopher took great pleasure in that ancient game: below the garden was a broad fishpond, made by damming the stream: above and below the pond there were trout, and in the pond were carp and jack. A part of the garden was laid out for flowers, a part for the still-room, and a part for fruit. I have never seen anywhere a better ordered garden for the still-room. Everything grew therein that the housewife wants: sweet cicely, rosemary, burnet, sweet basil, chives, dill, clary, angelica, lipwort, tarragon, thyme and mint; there were, as Lord Bacon, in his 'Essay on Gardens,' would have, 'whole alleys of them to have the pleasure when you walk or tread.' There were thick hedges to keep off the east wind in spring, so that one would enjoy the sun when that cold wind was blowing. But in Somerset that wind hath not the bitterness that it possesses along the eastern shores of the land.

Every morning Sir Christopher sat in his Justice's chair under the helmets and the coats of armour. Sometimes gipsies would be brought before him, charged with stealing poultry or poisoning pigs; or a rogue and vagabond would stray into the parish; these gentry were very speedily whipped out of it. As for our own people, there is nowhere a more quiet and orderly village; quarrels there are with the clothiers' men, who will still try to beat down the value of the women's work, and bickerings sometimes between the women themselves. Sir Christopher was judge for all. Truly he was a patriarch like unto Abraham, and a father to his people. Never was sick man suffered to want for medicines and succour; never was aged man suffered to lack food and fire; did any youth show leanings towards sloth, profligacy, or drunkenness, he was straightway admonished, and that right soundly, so that his back and shoulders would remind him for many days of his sin. By evildoers Sir Christopher was feared as much as he was beloved by all good men and true. This also is proper to one in high station and authority.

In the evening he amused himself in playing backgammon with the boys, or chess with his son-in-law, Mr. Boscorel: but the latter with less pleasure, because he was generally defeated in the game. He greatly delighted in the conversation and society of that learned and ingenious gentleman, though on matters of religion and of politics his son-in-law belonged to the opposite way of thinking.

I do not know why Mr. Boscorel took upon himself holy orders. God forbid that I should speak ill of any in authority, and especially of one who was kind and charitable to all, and refused to become a persecutor of those who desired freedom of conscience and of speech. But if the chief duty of a minister of the Gospel is to preach, then was Mr. Boscorel little better than a dog who cannot bark. He did not preach; that is to say, he could not, like my father, mount the pulpit, Bible in hand, and teach, admonish, argue, and convince without a written word. He read every Sunday morning a brief discourse, which might, perhaps, have instructed Oxford scholars, but would not be understood by the common people. As for arguments on religion, spiritual conversation, or personal experience of grace, he would never suffer such talk in his presence, because it argued private judgment and caused, he said, the growth of spiritual pride. And of those hot Gospellers whose zeal brings them to prison and the pillory, he spoke with contempt. His conversation, I must acknowledge, was full of delight and instruction, if the things which one learned of him were not vanities. He had travelled in Italy and in France, and he loved to talk of poetry, architecture, statuary, medals and coins, antiquities and so forth—things harmless and, perhaps, laudable in themselves, but for a preacher of the Gospel who ought to think of nothing but his sacred calling they are surely superfluities. Or he would talk of the manners and customs of strange countries, and especially of the Pope. This person, whom I have been taught to look upon as from the very nature of his pretensions the most wicked of living men, Mr. Boscorel regarded with as much toleration as he bestowed upon an Independent. Then he would tell us of London and the manners of the great; of the King, whom he had seen, and the Court, seeming to wink at things which one ought to hold in abhorrence. He even told us of the playhouse, which, according to my father, is the most subtle engine ever invented by the Devil for the destruction of souls. Yet Mr. Boscorel sighed to think that he could no longer visit that place of amusement. He loved also music, and played movingly upon the violoncello; and he could make pictures with pen, pencil, or brush. I have some of his paintings still, especially a picture which he drew of Humphrey playing the fiddle, his great eyes looking upwards as if the music was drawing his soul to Heaven. I know not why he painted a halo about his face. Mr. Boscorel also loved poetry, and quoted Shakspeare and Ben Jonson more readily than the Word of God.

In person he was of a goodly countenance, having clear-cut features: a straight nose, rather long; soft eyes, and a gentle voice. He was dainty in his apparel, loving fine clean linen and laced neckerchiefs, but was not a gross feeder; he drank but little wine, but would discourse upon fine wines, such as the Tokay of Hungary, Commandery wine from Cyprus, and the like, and he seemed better pleased to watch the colour of the wine in the glass, and to breathe its perfume, than to drink it. Above all things he hated coarse speech and rude manners. He spoke of men as if he stood on an eminence watching them, and always with pity, as if he belonged to a nobler creation. How could such a man have such a son?

CHAPTER V.

THE RUNAWAY.

Everybody hath heard, and old people still remember, how one Act after the other was passed for the suppression of the Nonconformists, whom the Church of England tried to extirpate, but could not. Had these laws been truly carried into effect, there would have been great suffering among the Dissenters; but, in order to enforce them, every man's hand would have been turned against his neighbour, and this—thank God!—is not possible in Somerset. For example, the Act of Uniformity provided not only for the ejectment of the Nonconforming ministers (which was duly carried out), but also enacted that none of them should take scholars without the license of the Bishop. Yet many of the ejected ministers maintained themselves in this way openly, without the Bishop's license. They were not molested, though they might be threatened by some hot Episcopalian; nor were the Bishops anxious to set the country afire by attempting to enforce this law. One must not take from an honest neighbour, whatever an unjust law may command, his only way of living.

Again, the Act passed two years later punished all persons with fine and imprisonment who attended conventicles. Yet the conventicles continued to be held over the whole country, because it was impossible for the Justices to fine and imprison men with whom they sat at dinner every market-day, with whom they took their punch and tobacco, and whom they knew to be honest and God-fearing folk. Again, how could they fine and imprison their own flesh and blood? Why, in every family there were some who loved the meeting-house better than the steeple-house. Laws have little power when they are against the conscience of the people.

Thirdly, there was an Act prohibiting ministers from residing within five miles of the village or town where they had preached. This was a most cruel and barbarous Act, because it sent the poor ministers away from the help of their friends. Yet how was it regarded? My father, for his part, continued to live at Bradford Orcas without let or hindrance, and so, no doubt, did many more.

Again, another Act was passed giving authority to Justices of the Peace to break open doors and to take in custody persons found assembling for worship. I have heard of disturbances at Taunton, where the Magistrates carried things with a high hand; but I think the people who met to worship after their own fashion were little disturbed. Among the Churchmen were some, no doubt, who remembered the snubs and rubs they had themselves experienced, and the memory may have made them revengeful. All the persecution, it is certain, was not on the side of the Church. There was, for instance, the case of Dr. Walter Raleigh, Dean of Wells, who was clapped into a noisome prison where the plague had broken out. He did not die of that disease, but was done to death in the jail, barbarously, by one David Barrett, shoemaker, who was never punished for the murder, but was afterwards made Constable of the City. There was also the case of the Rev. Dr. Piers, whom I have myself seen, for he lived to a good old age. He was a Prebendary of Wells, and being driven forth, was compelled to turn farmer, and to work with his own hands—digging, hoeing, ploughing, reaping, and threshing—when he should have been in his study. Every week this reverend and learned Doctor of Divinity was to be seen at Ilminster Market, standing beside the pillars with his cart, among the farmers and their wives, selling his apples, cheese, and cabbages.

I say that no doubt many remembered these things. Yet the affection of the people went forth to the Nonconformists and the ejected ministers, as was afterwards but too well proved. I have been speaking of things which happened before my recollection. It was in the year 1665, four years after the Ejection, that I was born. My father would have named me Grace Abounding, but my mother called me Alice, after her own name. I was thus six years younger than my brother Barnaby, and two years younger than Robin and Humphrey.

The first thing that I can recollect is a kind of picture, preserved, so to speak, in my head. At the open door is a woman spinning at the wheel. She is a woman with a pale, grave face; she works diligently, and for the most part in silence; if she speaks, it is to encourage or to admonish a little girl who plays in the garden outside. Her lips move as she works, because she communes with her thoughts all day long. From time to time she[29] turns her head and looks with anxiety into the other room, where sits her husband at his table.

Before him stand three boys. They are Barnaby, Robin, and Humphrey. They are learning Latin. The room is piled with books on shelves and books on the floor. In the corner is a pallet, which is the master's bed by night. I hear the voices of the boys who repeat their lessons, and the admonishing of their master. I can see through the open door the boys themselves. One, a stout and broad lad, is my brother Barnaby: he hangs his head and forgets his lesson, and causes his father to punish him every day. He receives admonition with patience; yet profiteth nothing. The next is Humphrey; he is already a lad of grave and modest carriage, who loves his book and learns diligently. The third is Robin, whose parts are good, were his application equal to his intelligence. He is impatient, and longs for the time when he may close his book and go to play again.

Poor Barnaby! at the sight of a Latin Grammar he would feel sick. He would willingly have taken a flogging every day—to be sure, that generally happened to him—in order to escape his lessons and be off to the fields and woods.

It was the sight of his rueful face—yet never sad except at lessons—which made my mother sigh when she saw him dull but patient over his book. Had he stayed at home I know not what could have been done with him, seeing that to become a preacher of the Gospel was beyond even the power of prayer (the Lord having clearly expressed His will in this matter). He would have had to clap on a leathern apron, and become a wheelwright or blacksmith; nothing better than an honest trade was possible for him.

But (whether happily or not) a strange whim seized the boy when he was fourteen years of age. He would go to sea. How he came to think of the sea I know not; he had never seen the sea; there were no sailors in the village; there was no talk of the sea. Perhaps Humphrey, who read many books, told him of the great doings of our sailors on the Spanish Main and elsewhere. Perhaps some of the clothiers' men, who are a roving and unsettled crew, had been sailors—some, I know, had been soldiers under Oliver. However, this matters not, Barnaby must needs become a sailor.

When first he broke this resolution, which he did secretly, to my mother, she began to weep and lament, because everybody knows how dreadful is the life of a sailor, and how full of dangers. She begged him to put the thought out of his head, and to apply himself again to his books.

'Mother,' he said, 'it is no use. What comes in at one ear goes out at the other. Nothing sticks: I shall never be a scholar.'

'Then, my son, learn an honest trade.'

'What? Become the village cobbler—or the blacksmith? Go hat in hand to his Honour, when my father should have been a Bishop, and my mother is a gentlewoman? That will I not. I will go and be a sailor. All sailors are gentlemen. I shall rise and become first mate, and then second captain, and lastly, captain in command. Who knows? I may go and fight the Spaniard, if I am lucky.'

'Oh, my son, canst thou not stay at home and go to church, and consider the condition of thine immortal soul? Of sailors it is well known that their language is made up of profane oaths, and that they are all profligates and drunkards. Consider, my son'—my mother laid her hand upon his arm—'what were Heaven to me, if I have not my dear children with me as well as my husband? How could I praise the Lord if I were thinking of my son who was not with me, but—ah! Heaven forbid the thought!'

Barnaby made no reply. What could he say in answer to my mother's tears? Yet I think she must have understood very well that her son, having got this resolution into his head, would never give it up.

'Oh!' she said, 'when thou wast a little baby in my arms, Barnaby—who art now so big and strong'—she looked at him with the wonder and admiration that women feel when their sons grow big and stout—'I prayed that God would accept thee as an offering for His service. Thou art vowed unto the Lord, my son, as much as Samuel. Do you think he complained of his lessons? What would have happened, think you, to Samuel if he had taken off his ephod and declared that he would serve no longer at the altar, but must take spear and shield, and go to fight the Amalekite?'

Said Barnaby, in reply, speaking from an unregenerate heart, 'Mother, had I been Samuel, to wear an ephod and to learn the Latin syntax every day, I should have done that. Ay! I would have done it, even if I knew that at the first skirmish an arrow would pierce my heart.'

It was after a great flogging, on account of the passive voice or some wrestling with the syntax, that Barnaby plucked up courage to tell his father what he wished to do.

'With my consent,' said my father, sternly, 'thou shalt never become a sailor. As soon would I send thee to become a buffoon in a playhouse. Never dare to speak of it again.'

Barnaby hung his head and said nothing.

Then my mother, who knew his obstinate disposition, took him to Sir Christopher, who chid him roundly, telling him that there was work for him on land, else he would have been born beside the coast, where the lads take naturally to the sea: that being, as he was, only an ignorant boy, and landborn, he could not know the dangers which he would encounter: that some ships are cast away on desert islands, where the survivors remain in misery until they die, and some on lands where savages devour them, and some are dragged down by calamaries and other dreadful monsters, and some are burned at sea, their crews having to choose miserably between burning and drowning, and some are taken by the enemy, and the sailors clapped into dungeons and tortured by the Accursed Inquisition.

Many more things did Sir Christopher set forth, showing the miserable life and the wretched end of the sailor. But Barnaby never changed countenance, and though my mother bade him note this and mark that, and take heed unto his Honour's words, his face showed no melting. 'Twas always an obstinate lad; nay it was his obstinacy alone which kept him from his learning. Otherwise he might perhaps have become as great a scholar as Humphrey.

'Sir,' he said, when Sir Christopher had no other word to say, 'with submission, I would still choose to be a sailor, if I could.'

In the end he obtained his wish. That is to say, since no one would help him towards it, he helped himself. And this, I think, is the only way in which men do ever get what they want.

It happened one evening that there passed through the village a man with a pipe and tabor, on which he played so movingly that all the people turned out to listen. For my own part I was with my mother, yet I ran to the garden-gate and leaned my head over, drawn by the sound of the music. Presently the boys and girls began to take hands together and to dance. I dare not say that to dance is sinful, because David danced. But it was so regarded by my father, so that when he passed by them, on his way home from taking the air, and actually saw his own son Barnaby in the middle of the dancers, footing it merrily with them all, joyfully leading one girl up and the other down at *John come and kiss me now*, he was seized with a mighty wrath, and, catching his son sharply by the ear, led him out of the throng and so home. For that evening Barnaby went supperless to bed, with the promise of such a flogging in the morning as would cause him to remember for the rest of his life the sinfulness of dancing. Never had I seen my father so angry. I trembled before his wrathful eyes. But Barnaby faced him with steady looks, making answer none, yet not showing the least repentance or fear. I thought it was because a flogging had no terrors for him. The event proved that I was wrong; that was not the reason: he had resolved to run away, and when we awoke in the morning he was gone. He had crept down-stairs in the night; he had taken half a loaf of bread and a great cantle of soft cheese, and had gone away. He had not gone for fear of the rod: he had run away with design to go to sea. Perhaps he had gone to Bristol; perhaps to Plymouth; perhaps to Lyme. My mother wept, and my father sighed; and for ten years more we neither saw nor heard anything of Barnaby, not even whether he was dead or living.

CHAPTER VI.

BENJAMIN, LORD CHANCELLOR.

Summer follows winter and winter summer, in due course, turning children into young men and maidens, changing school into work, and play into love, and love into marriage, and so onwards to the churchyard, where we all presently lie, hopeful of Heaven's mercy, whether Mr. Boscorel did stand beside our open grave in his white surplice, or my father in his black gown.

Barnaby was gone; the other three grew tall, and would still be talking of the lives before them. Girls do never look forward to the future with the eagerness and joy of boys. To the dullest boy it seems a fine thing to be master of his own actions, even if that liberty lead to whipping-post, pillory, or gallows. To boys of ambition and imagination the gifts of Fortune show like the splendid visions of a prophet. They think that earthly fame will satisfy the soul. Perhaps women see these glories and their true worth with clearer eye as not desiring them. And truly it seems a small thing, after a life spent in arduous toil, and with one foot already in the grave, to obtain fortune, rank, or title.

Benjamin and Humphrey were lads of ambition. To both, but in fields which lay far apart, the best life seemed to be that which is spent among men on the ant-hill where all are driving or being driven, loading each other with burdens intolerable, or with wealth or with honours, and then dying and being forgotten in a moment—which we call London. In the kindly country one stands apart and sees the vanity of human wishes. Teat the ambition of Humphrey, it must be confessed, was noble, because it was not for his own advancement, but for the good of mankind.

'I shall stay at home,' said Robin. 'You two may go if you please. Perhaps you will like the noise of London, where a man cannot hear himself speak, they say, for the roaring of the crowd, the ringing of the bells, and the rumbling of the carts. As for me, what is good enough for my grandfather will be surely good enough for me.'

It should, indeed, be good enough for anybody to spend his days after the manner of Sir Christopher, administering justice for the villagers, with the weekly ordinary at Sherborne for company, the green fields and his garden for pleasure and for exercise, and the welfare of his soul for prayer. Robin, besides, loved to go[33] forth with hawk and gun; to snare the wild creatures; to hunt the otter and the fox; to bait the badger, and trap the stoat and weasel; to course the hares. But cities and crowds, even if they should be shouting in his honour, did never draw him, even after he had seen them. Nor was he ever tempted to believe any manner of life more full of delight and more consistent with the end of man's creation than the rural life, the air of the fields, the following of the plough for the men, and the spinning-wheel for the women.

'I shall be a lawyer,' said Benjamin, puffing out his cheeks and squaring his shoulders. 'Very well, then, I say I shall be a great lawyer. What? None of your pettifogging tribe for me: I shall step to the front, and stay there. What? Someone must have the prizes and the promotion. There are always places falling vacant and honours to be given away: they shall be given to me. Why not to me as well as another?'

'Well,' said Robin, 'you are strong enough to take them, willy-nilly.'

'I am strong enough,' he replied, with conviction. 'First, I shall be called to the Outer Bar, where I shall plead in stuff—I saw them at Exeter last 'Sizes. Next, I shall be summoned to become King's Counsel, when I shall flaunt it in silk. Who but I?' Then he seemed to grow actually three inches taller, so great is the power of imagination. He was already six feet in height, his shoulders broad, and his face red and fiery, so that now he looked very big and tall. 'Then my Inn will make me a Bencher, and I shall sit at the high table in term-time. And the attorneys shall run after me and fight with each other for my services in Court, so that in every great case I shall be heard thundering before the jury, and making the witnesses perjure themselves with terror—for which they will be afterwards flogged. I shall belong to the King's party—none of your canting Whigs for me. When the high treason cases come on, I shall be the counsel for the Crown. That is the high road to advancement.'

'This is very well, so far,' said Robin, laughing. 'Ben is too modest, however. He does not get on fast enough.'

'All in good time,' Ben replied. 'I mean to get on as fast as anybody. But I shall follow the beaten road. First, favour with attorneys and those who have suits in the Courts; then the ear of the Judge. I know not how one gets the ear of the Judge'—he looked despondent for a moment, then he held up his head again—'but I shall find out. Others have found out—why not I? What? I am no fool, am I?'

'Certainly not, Ben. But as yet we stick at King's Counsel.'

'After the ear of the Judge, the favour of the Crown. What do I care who is King? It is the King who hath preferment and place and honours in his gift. Where these are given away, there shall I be found. Next am I made Serjeant-at-Law. Then I am saluted as 'Brother' by the Judges on the Bench, while all the others burst with envy. After that I shall myself be called to the Bench. I[34] am already "my Lord"—why do you laugh, Robin?—and a Knight: Sir Benjamin Boscorel—Sir Benjamin.' Here he puffed out his cheeks again, and swung his shoulders like a very great person indeed.

'Proceed, Sir Benjamin,' said Humphrey, gravely, while Robin laughed.

'When I am a Judge, I promise you I will rate the barristers and storm at the witnesses and admonish the Jury until there shall be no other question in their minds but to find out first what is my will in the case, and then to govern themselves accordingly. I will be myself Judge and jury and all. Oh! I have seen the Judge at last Exeter 'Sizes. He made all to shake in their shoes. I shall not stop there. Chief Baron I shall be, perhaps—but on that point I have not yet made up my mind—and then Lord Chancellor.' He paused to take breath, and looked around him, grandeur and authority upon his brow. 'Lord Chancellor,' he repeated, 'on the Woolsack!'

'You will then,' said Robin, 'be raised to the peerage—first Lord Boscorel; or perhaps, if your Lordship will so honour this poor village, Lord Bradford Orcas'——

'Earl of Sherborne I have chosen for title,' said Benjamin. 'And while I am climbing up the ladder, where wilt thou be, Humphrey? Grovelling in the mud with the poor devils who cannot rise?'

'Nay, I shall have a small ladder of my own, Ben. I find great comfort in the thought that when your Lordship is roaring and bawling with the gout—your noble toe being like a ball of fire, and your illustrious foot swathed in flannel—I shall be called upon to drive away the pain, and you will honour me with the title not only of humble cousin, but also of rescuer and preserver. Will it not be honour enough to cure the Right Honourable the Earl of Sherborne (first of the name), the Lord Chancellor, of his gout, and to restore him to the duties of his great office, so that once more he shall be the dread of evildoers and of all who have to appear before him? As yet, my Lord, your extremities, I perceive, are free from that disease—the result, too often, of that excess in wine which besets the great.'

Here Robin laughed again, and so did Benjamin. Nobody could use finer language than Humphrey, if he pleased.

'A fine ambition!' said Ben. 'To wear a black velvet coat and a great wig; to carry a gold-headed cane; all day long to listen while the patient tells of his gripes and pains; to mix boluses, and to compound nauseous draughts!'

'Well,' Humphrey laughed, 'if you are Lord Chancellor, Ben, you will, I hope, give us good laws, and so make the nation happy and prosperous. While you are doing this, I will be keeping you in health for the good of the country. I say that this is a fine ambition.'

'And Robin, here, will sit in the great chair, and have the rogues haled before him, and order the Head-borough to bring out his cat-o'-nine-tails. In the winter evenings, he will play backgammon, and in the summer, bowls. Then a posset, and to bed. And never any change from year to year. A fine life, truly!'

'Truly, I think it is a very fine life,' said Robin; 'while you make the laws, I will take care that they are obeyed. What better service is there than to cause good laws to be obeyed? Make good laws, my Lord Chancellor, and be thankful that you will have faithful, law-abiding men to carry them out.'

Thus they talked. Presently the time came when the lads must leave the village and go forth to prepare for such course as should be allotted to them, whether it led to greatness or to obscurity.

Benjamin went first, being sixteen years of age and a great fellow, as I have said, broad-shouldered and lusty, with a red face, a strong voice, and a loud laugh. In no respect did he resemble his father, who was delicate in manner and in speech. He was to be entered at Gray's Inn, where, under some counsel learned in the law, he was to read until such time as he should be called.

He came to bid me farewell, which at first, until he frightened me with the things he said, I took kindly of him.

'Child,' he said, 'I am going to London, and, I suppose, I shall not come back to this village for a long time. Nay, were it not for thee, I should not wish to come back at all.'

'Why for me, Ben?'

'Because'—here his red face became redder, and he stammered a little, but not much, for he was ever a lad of confidence—'because, child, thou art not yet turned twelve, which is young to be hearing of such a thing. Yet a body may as well make things safe. And as for Humphrey or Robin interfering, I will break their heads with my cudgel if they do. Remember that, then.' He shook his finger at me, threatening.

'In what business should they interfere?' I asked.

'Kiss me, Alice'—here he tried to lay his arm round my neck, but I ran away. 'Oh! if thou art skittish, I care not: all in good time. Very well, then; let us make things safe. Alice, when I come back thou wilt be seventeen or eighteen, which is an age when girls should marry'——

'I have nothing to do with marrying, Ben.'

'Not yet. If I mistake not, child, thou wilt then be as beautiful as a rose in June.'

'I want no foolish talk, Ben. Let me go.'

'Then I shall be twenty-one years of age, practising in the courts. I shall go the Western Circuit, in order to see thee often—partly to keep an eye upon thee and partly to warn off other men. Because, child, it is my purpose to marry thee myself. Think upon that, now.'

At this I laughed.

'Laugh if you please, my dear; I shall marry thee as soon as the way is open to the Bench and the Woolsack. What? I can see a long way ahead. I will tell thee what I see. There is a monstrous great crowd of people in the street staring at a glass coach. "Who is the lovely lady?" they ask. "The lovely lady"—that is you, Alice; none other—"with the diamonds at her neck and the gold chain, in the glass coach?" says one who knows her liveries: "'tis the lady of the great Lord Chancellor, the Earl of Sherborne." And the women fall green with envy of her happiness and great good fortune and her splendour. Courage, child: I go to prepare the way. Oh! thou knowest not the grand things that I shall pour into thy lap when I am a judge.'

This was the first time that any man spoke to me of love. But Benjamin was always masterful, and had no respect for such a nice point as the wooing of a maiden—which, methinks, should be gentle and respectful, not as if a woman was like a savage to be tempted by a string of beads, or so foolish as to desire with her husband such gauds as diamonds, or gold chains, or a glass coach. Nor doth a woman like to be treated as if she was to be carried off by force like the Sabine women of old.

The Rector rode to London with his son. It is a long journey, over rough ways; but it pleased him once more to see that great city, where there are pictures and statues and books to gladden the hearts of such as love these things. And on the way home he sojourned for a few days at his old college of All Souls, where were still left one or two of his old friends. Then he rode back to his village. 'There are but two places in this country,' he said, 'or perhaps three, at most, where a gentleman and a scholar, or one who loveth the fine arts, would choose to live. These are London and Oxford, and perhaps the Sister University upon the Granta. Well, I have once more been privileged to witness the humours of the Court and the town: I have once more been permitted to sniff the air of a great library. Let us be thankful.' He showed his thankfulness with a sigh which was almost a groan.

It was three years before we saw Benjamin again. Then he returned, but not for long. Like his father, he loved London better than the country, but for other reasons. Certainly, he cared nothing for those arts which so much delighted the Rector, and the air of a coffee-house pleased him more than the perfume of books in a library. When he left us he was a rustic; when he came back he was already what they call a fopling: that is to say, when he went to pay his respects to Sir Christopher, his grandfather, he wore a very fine cravat of Flanders lace, with silken hose, and lace and ribbons at his wrist. He was also scented with bergamot, and wore a peruke, which, while he talked, he combed and curled, to keep the curls of this monstrous head-dress in place. Gentlemen must, I suppose, wear this invention, and one of the learned professions must show the extent of the learning by the splendours of his full-bottomed wig. Yet I think that a young man looks most comely while he wears his own hair. He had cocked his hat, on which were bows of riband, and he wore a sword. He spoke also in a mincing London manner, having now forsworn the honest broad speech of Somerset; and (but not in the presence of his elders) he used strange oaths and ejaculations.

'Behold him!' said his father, by no means displeased at his son's foppery, because he ever loved the city fashions, and thought that a young man did well to dress and to comport himself after the way of the world. 'Behold him! Thus he sits in the coffee-house; thus he shows himself in the pit. Youth is the time for finery and for folly. Alas! would that we could bring back that time! What saith John Dryden—glorious John—of Sir Fopling?—

'"His various modes from various fathers follow: One taught the toss, and one the new French wallow; His sword-knot this, his cravat that, designed, And this the yard-long snake he twirls behind. From one the sacred periwig he gained, Which wind ne'er blew, nor touch of hat profaned."

'Well, Ben,' said Sir Christopher, 'if the mode can help thee to the Bench why not follow the mode?'

'It will not hinder, Sir,' Ben replied. 'A man who hath his fortune to make does well to be seen everywhere, and to be dressed like other men of his time.'

One must do Benjamin the justice to acknowledge that though, like the young gentlemen his friends and companions, his dress was foppish, and his talk was of the pleasures of the town, he suffered nothing to stand in the way of his advancement. He was resolved upon being a great lawyer, and, therefore, if he spent the evening in drinking, singing, and making merry, he was reading in chambers or else attending the Courts all the day, and neglected nothing that would make him master of his profession.

And, though of learning he had little, his natural parts were so good, and his resolution was so strong, that I doubt not he would have achieved his ambition had it not been for the circumstances which afterwards cut short his career. His course of life, by his own boastful confession, was profligate; his friends were drinkers and revellers; his favourite haunt was the tavern, where they all drank punch and sang ungodly songs, and smoked tobacco; and of religion he seemed to have no care whatever.

I was afraid that he would return to the nauseous subject which he had opened three years before. Therefore I continued with my mother, and would give him no chance to speak with me. But he found me, and caught me returning home one evening.

'Alice,' he said, 'I feared that I might have to go away without a word alone with thee.'

'I want no words alone, Benjamin. Let me pass!' For he stood before me in the way.

'Not so fast, pretty!'—he caught me by the wrist, and, being a young man so strong and determined, he held me as by a vice. 'Not so fast, Mistress Alice. First, my dear, let me tell thee that my purpose still holds—nay'—here he swore a most dreadful, impious oath—'I am more resolved than ever. There is not a woman, even in London, that is to be compared with thee, child. What? Compared with thee? Why, they are like the twinkling stars compared with the glorious Queen of Night. What did I say?—that at nineteen thou wouldst be a miracle of beauty? Nay, that time hath come already! I love thee, child! I love thee, I say, ten times as much as ever I loved thee before!'

He gasped, and then breathed hard; but still he held me fast.

'Idle compliments cost a man nothing, Benjamin. Say what you meant to say and let me go. If you hold me any longer I will cry out and bring your father to learn the reason.'

'Well,' he said, 'I will not keep thee. I have said what I wanted to say. My time hath not yet arrived. I am shortly to be called, and shall then begin to practise. When I come back here again, 'twill be with a ring in one hand, and in the other the prospect of the Woolsack. Think upon that while I am gone. "Your Ladyship" is finer than plain "Madam," and the Court is more delightful than a village green among the pigs and ducks. Think upon it well: thou art a lucky girl; a plain village girl to be promoted to a coronet! However, I have no fears for thee; thou wilt adorn the highest fortune. Thou wilt be worthy of the great place whither I shall lead thee. What? Is Sir George Jeffreys a better man than I? Is he of better family? Had he better interest? Is he a bolder man? Not so. Yet was Sir George a Common Serjeant at twenty-three, and Recorder at thirty; Chief Justice of Chester at thirty-two. What he hath done I can do. Moreover, Sir George hath done me the honour to admit me to his company, and will advance me. This he hath promised, both in his cups and when he is sober. Think it over, child: a ring in one hand and a title in the other.'

So Benjamin went away again. I was afraid when I thought of him and his promise, because I knew him of old; and his eyes were as full of determination as when he would fight a lad of his own age and go on fighting till the other had had enough. Yet he could not marry me against my will. His own father would protect me, to say nothing of mine.

I should have told him then—as I had told him before—that I would never marry him. Then, perhaps, he would have been shaken in his purpose. The very thought of marrying him filled me with terror unspeakable. I was afraid of him not only because he was so masterful—nay, women like a man to be strong of will—but because he had no religion in him and lived like an Atheist, if such a wretch there be; at all events, with unconcern about his soul; and because his life was profligate, his tastes were gross, and he was a drinker of much wine. Even at the Manor House I had seen him at supper drinking until his cheeks were puffed out and his voice grew thick. What kind of happiness would there be for a wife whose husband has to be carried home by his varlets, too heavy with drink to stand or to speak?

Alas! there is one thing which girls, happily, do never apprehend. They cannot understand how it is possible for a man to become so possessed with the idea of their charms (which they hold themselves as of small account, knowing how fleeting they are, and of what small value) that he will go through fire and water for that woman; yea, and break all the commandments, heedless of his immortal soul, rather than suffer another man to take her—and that, even though he knows that the poor creature loves him not, or loves another man. If maidens knew this, I think that they would go in fear and trembling lest they should be coveted by some wild beast in human shape, and prove the death of the gallant gentleman whom they would choose for their lover. Or they would make for themselves convents and hide in them, so great would be their fear. But it is idle to speak of this, because, say what one will, girls can never understand the power and the vehemence of love, when once it hath seized and doth thoroughly possess a man.

CHAPTER VII.

MEDICINÆ DOCTOR.

Humphrey did not, like Benjamin, brag of the things he would do when he should go forth to the world. Nevertheless, he thought much about his future, and frequently he discoursed with me about the life that he fain would lead. A young man, I think, wants someone with whom he may speak freely concerning the thoughts which fill his soul. We who belong to the sex which receives but does not create or invent, which profits by man's good work, and suffers from the evil which he too often does, have no such thoughts and ambitions.

'I cannot,' he would say, 'take upon me holy orders, as Mr. Boscorel would have me, promising, in my cousin Robin's name, this living after his death, because, though I am in truth a mere pauper and dependent, there are in me none of those prickings of the spirit which I could interpret into a Divine call for the ministry; next, because I cannot in conscience swear to obey the Thirty-nine Articles while I still hold that the Nonconformist way of worship is more consonant with the Word of God. And, again, I am of opinion that the Law of Moses, which forbade any but a well-formed man from serving at the altar, hath in it something eternal. It denotes that as no cripple may serve at the earthly altar, so in heaven, of which the altar is an emblem, all those who dwell therein shall be perfect in body as in soul. What, then, is such a one as myself, who hath some learning and no fortune, to do? Sir Christopher, my benefactor, will maintain me at Oxford until I have taken a degree. This is more than I could have expected. Therefore, I am resolved to take a degree in medicine. It is the only profession fit for a mis-shapen creature. They will not laugh at me when I alleviate their pains.'

'Could anyone laugh at you, Humphrey?'

'Pray heaven, I frighten not the ladies at the first aspect of me.' He laughed, but not with merriment; for, indeed, a cripple or a hunchback cannot laugh mirthfully over his own misfortune. 'Some men speak scornfully of the profession,' he went on. 'The great French playwright, Monsieur Molière, doth make the physicians the butt and laughing-stock of all Paris. Yet consider. It is medicine which prolongs our days and relieves our pains. Before the science was studied, the wretch who caught a fever in the marshy forest lay down and died; an ague lasted all one's life; a sore throat putrefied and killed; a rheumatism threw a man upon the bed, from which he would never rise. The physician is man's chief friend. If our Sovereigns studied the welfare of humanity as deeply as the art of war, they would maintain, at vast expense, great colleges of learned men continually engaged in discovering the secrets of nature—the causes and the remedies of disease. What better use can a man make of his life than to discover one—only one—secret which will drive away part of the agony of disease? The Jews, more merciful than the Romans, stupefied their criminals after they were crucified; they died, indeed, but their sufferings were less. So the physician, though in the end all men must die, may help them to die without pain. Nay, I have even thought that we might devise means of causing the patient by some potent drug to fall into so deep a sleep that even the surgeon's knife shall not cause him to awaken.'

He, therefore, before he entered at Oxford, read with my father many learned books of the ancients on the science and practice of medicine, and studied botany with the help of such books as he could procure.

Some men have but one side to them—that is to say, the only active part of them is engaged in but one study; the rest is given up to rest or indolence. Thus Benjamin studied law diligently, but nothing else. Humphrey, for his part, read his Galen and his Celsus, but he neglected not the cultivation of those arts and accomplishments in which Mr. Boscorel was as ready a teacher as he was a ready scholar. He thus learned the history of painting, and sculpture, and architecture, and that of coins and medals, so that at eighteen Humphrey might already have set up as a virtuoso.

Nor was this all. Still, by the help of the Rector, he learned the use of the pencil and the brush, and could both draw prettily, or paint in water colours, whether the cottages or the church, the cows in the fields, or the woods and hills. I have many pictures of his painting which he gave me from time to time. And he could play sweetly, whether on the spinnet, or the violin, or the guitar, spending many hours every week with Mr. Boscorel playing duettos together; and willingly he would sing, having a rich and full voice, very delightful to hear. When I grew a great girl, and had advanced far enough, I was permitted to play with them. There was no end to the music which Mr. Boscorel possessed. First, he had a great store of English ditties such as country people love—as, 'Sing all a green willow,' 'Gather ye rosebuds while ye may,' or 'Once I loved a maiden fair.' There was nothing rough or rude in these songs, though I am informed that much wickedness is taught by the ribald songs that are sung in playhouses and coffee-rooms. And when we were not playing or singing, Mr. Boscorel would read us poetry—portions from Shakspeare or Ben Jonson, or out of Milton's 'Paradise Lost'; or from Herrick, who is surely the sweetest poet that ever lived, 'yet marred,' said Mr. Boscorel, 'by his coarseness and corruption.' Now, one day, after we had been thus reading—one winter afternoon, when the sun lay upon the meadows—Humphrey walked home with me, and on the way confessed, with many blushes, that he, too, had been writing verses. And with that he lugged a paper out of his pocket.

'They are for thine own eyes only,' he said. 'Truly, my dear, thou hast the finest eyes in the world. They are for no other eyes than thine,' he repeated. 'Not for Robin, mind, lest he laugh: poetry hath in it something sacred, so that even the writer of bad verses cannot bear to have them laughed at. When thou art a year or two older thou wilt understand that they were written for thy heart as well as for thine eyes. Yet, if thou like the verses, they may be seen by Mr. Boscorel, but in private; and if he laugh at them do not tell me. Yet, again, one would like to know what he said; wherefore, tell me, though his words be like a knife in my side.'

Thus he wavered between wishing to show them to his master in art, and fearing.

In the end, when I showed them to Mr. Boscorel, he said that, for a beginner, they were very well—very well, indeed; that the rhymes were correct, and the metre true; that years and practice would give greater firmness, and that the crafty interlacing of thought and passion, which was the characteristic of Italian verse, could only be learned by much reading of the Italian poets. More he said, speaking upon the slight subject of rhyme and poetry with as much seriousness and earnestness as if he were weighing and comparing texts of Scripture.

Then he gave me back the verses with a sigh.

'Child,' he said, 'to none of us is given what most we desire. For my part, I longed in his infancy that my son should grow up even as Humphrey, as quick to learn; with as true a taste; with as correct an ear; with a hand as skilful. But——you see, I complain not, though Benjamin loves the noisy tavern better than the quiet coffee-house where the wits resort. To him such things as verses, art, and music are foolishness. I say that I complain not; but I would to Heaven that Humphrey were my own, and that his shoulders were straight, poor lad! Thy father hath made him a Puritan: he is such as John Milton in his youth—and as beautiful in face as that stout Republican. I doubt not that we shall have from the hand of Humphrey, if he live and prosper, something fine, the nature of which, whether it is to be in painting, or in music, or in poetry, I know not. Take the verses, and take care that thou lose them not; and, child—remember—the poet is allowed to say what he pleases about a woman's eyes. Be not deceived into thinking——But no—no—there is no fear. Good-night, thou sweet and innocent saint.'

I knew not then what he meant; but these are the verses, and I truly think that they are very moving and religious. For if woman be truly the most beautiful work of the Creator (which all men aver), then it behoves her all the more still to point upwards. I read them with a pleasure and surprise that filled my whole soul, and inflamed my heart with pious joy:—

Around, above, and everywhere The earth hath many a lovely thing; The zephyrs soft, the flowers fair, The babbling brook, the bubbling spring.
The grey of dawn, the azure sky, The sunset glow, the evening gloom; The warbling thrush, the skylark high, The blossoming hedge, the garden's bloom.
The sun in state, the moon in pride, The twinkling stars in order laid; The winds that ever race and ride, The shadows flying o'er the glade.
Oh! many a lovely thing hath earth, To charm the eye and witch the soul; Yet one there is of passing worth— For that one thing I give the whole.
The crowning work, the last thing made, Creation's masterpiece to be— Bend o'er yon stream, and, there displayed, This wondrous thing reflected see.
Behold a face for heaven designed; See how those eyes thy soul betray— Love—secret love—there sits enshrined, And upwards still doth point the way.

When Humphrey went away, he did not, like Benjamin, come blustering and declaring that he would marry me, and that he would break the skull of any other man who dared make love to me—not at all; Humphrey, with tears in his eyes, told me that he was sorry I could not go to Oxford as well; that he was going to lose the sweetest companion in the world; and that he should always love me; and then he kissed me on the forehead, and so departed. Why should he not always love me? I knew very well that he loved me, and that I loved him. Although he was so young, being only seventeen when he was entered at Exeter College, I suppose there never was a young gentleman went to theUniversity of Oxford with so many accomplishments, and so much learning. By my father's testimony he read Greek as if it were his mother tongue, and he wrote and conversed easily in Latin: and you have heard what arts and accomplishments he added to this solid learning. He was elected to a scholarship at his college, that of Exeter, and, after he took his degree as Bachelor of Medicine, he was made a Fellow of All Souls, where Mr. Boscorel himself had also been a Fellow. This election was not only a great distinction for him, but it gave him what a learned young man especially desires—the means of living and of pursuing his studies.

While he was at Oxford he wrote letters to Sir Christopher, to Mr. Boscorel, and to my father (to whom also he sent such new books and pamphlets as he thought would interest him). To me he sent sometimes drawings and sometimes books, but never verses.

Now (to make an end of Humphrey for the present), when he had obtained his fellowship, he asked for and obtained leave of absence and permission to study medicine in those great schools which far surpass, they say, our English schools of medicine. These are that of Montpellier; the yet more famous school of Padua, in Italy; and that of Leyden, whither many Englishmen have resorted for study, notably Mr. Evelyn, whose book called 'Sylva' was in the Rector's library.

He carried on during the whole of this time a correspondence with Mr. Boscorel on the paintings, statues, and architecture to be seen wherever his travels carried him. These letters Mr. Boscorel read aloud, with a map spread before him, discoursing on the history of the place and the chief things to be seen there, before he began to read. Surely there never was a man so much taken up with the fine arts, especially as they were practised by the ancients.

There remains the last of the boys—Robin, Sir Christopher's grandson and heir. I should like this book to be all about Robin—yet one must needs speak of the others. I declare, that from the beginning, there never was a boy more happy, more jolly; never anyone more willing to be always making someone happy. He loved the open air, the wild creatures, the trees, the birds, everything that lives beneath the sky; yet not—like my poor brother Barnaby—a hater of books. He read all the books which told about creatures, or hunting, or country life; and all voyages and travels. A fresh-coloured, wholesome lad, not so grave as Humphrey, nor so rustic as Barnaby, who always seemed to carry with him the scent of woods and fields. He was to Sir Christopher, what Benjamin was to Jacob. Even my father loved him though he was so poor a scholar.

Those who stay at home have homely wits; that is well known: therefore Robin must follow Humphrey to Oxford. He went thither the year after his cousin. I never learned that he obtained a scholarship, or that he was considered one of the younger pillars of that learned and ancient University; or, indeed, that he took a degree at all.

After he left Oxford he must go to London, there to study Justice's Law and fit himself for the duties he would have to fulfil. Also his grandfather would have him acquire some knowledge of the Court and the City, and the ways of the great and the rich. This, too, he did; though he never learned to prefer those ways to the simple customs and habits of his Somerset village.

He, too, like the other two, bade me a tender farewell.

'Poor Alice!' he said, taking both my hands in his, 'what wilt thou do when I am gone?'

Indeed, since Humphrey went away, we had been daily companions; and at the thought of being thus left alone the tears were running down my cheeks.

'Why, Sweetheart,' he said, 'to think that I should ever make thee cry—I who desire nothing but to make thee always laugh and be happy! What wilt thou do? Go often to my mother. She loves thee as if thou wert her own daughter. Go and talk to her concerning me. It pleaseth the poor soul to be still talking of her son. And forget not my grandfather; play backgammon with him; fill his pipe for him; sing to the spinnet for him; talk to him about Humphrey and me. And forget not Mr. Boscorel, my uncle. The poor man looks as melancholy since Humphrey went away as a turtle robbed of her nest. I saw him yesterday opening one of his drawers full of medals, and he sighed over them fit to break his heart. He sighed for Humphrey, not for Ben. Well, child, what more? Take Lance'—'twas his dog—'for a run every day; make George Sparrow keep an eye upon the stream for otters; and—there are a thousand things, but I will write them down. Have patience with the dear old man when he will be still talking about me.'

'Patience, Robin,' I said. 'Why, we all love to talk about thee.'

'Do you all love to talk about me? Dost thou, too, Alice? Oh, my dear, my dear!' Here he took me in his arms and kissed me on the lips. 'Dost thou also love to talk about me? Why, my dear, I shall think of nothing but of thee. Because—oh, my dear!—I love thee with all my heart.'

Well, I was still so foolish that I understood nothing more than that we all loved him, and he loved us all.

'Alice, I will write letters to thee. I will put them in the packet for my mother. Thus thou wilt understand that I am always thinking of thee.'

He was as good as his word. But the letters were so full of the things he was doing and seeing, that it was quite clear that his mind had plenty of room for more than one object. To be sure, I should have been foolish, indeed, had I desired that his letters[46] should tell me that he was always thinking about me, when he should have been attending to his business.

After a year in London, his grandfather thought that he should travel. Therefore, he went abroad and joined Humphrey at Montpellier, and with him rode northwards to Leyden, where he sojourned while his cousin attended the lectures of that famous school.

CHAPTER VIII.

A ROYAL PROGRESS.

When all the boys were gone the time was quiet, indeed, for those who were left behind. My mother's wheel went spinning still, but I think that some kindness on the part of Mr. Boscorel as well as Sir Christopher caused her weekly tale of yarn to be of less importance. And as for me, not only would she never suffer me to sit at the spinning-wheel, but there was so much request of me (to replace the boys) that I was nearly all the day either with Sir Christopher, or with Madam, or with Mr. Boscorel.

Up to the year 1680, or thereabouts, I paid no more attention to political matters than any young woman with no knowledge may be supposed to give. Yet, of course, I was on the side of liberty, both civil and religious. How should that be otherwise, my father being such as he was, muzzled for all these years, the work of his life prevented and destroyed?

It was in that year, however, that I became a most zealous partisan and lover of the Protestant cause in the way that I am about to relate.

Everybody knows that there is no part of Great Britain (not even Scotland) where the Protestant religion hath supporters more stout and staunch than Somerset and Devonshire. I hope I shall not be accused of disloyalty to Queen Anne, under whom we now flourish and are happy, when I say that in the West of England we had grown—I know not how—to regard the late misguided Duke of Monmouth as the champion of the Protestant faith. When, therefore, the Duke came into the West of England in the year 1680, five years before his rebellion, he was everywhere received with acclamations and by crowds who gathered round him to witness their loyalty to the Protestant faith. They came also to gaze upon the gallant commander who had defeated both the French and the Dutch, and was said (but erroneously) to be as wise as he was brave, and as religious as he was beautiful to look upon. As for his wisdom, those who knew him best have since assured the world that he had little or none, his judgment being always swayed and determined for him by crafty and subtle persons seeking their own interests. And as for his religion, whatever may have been his profession, good works were wanting—as is now very well known. But at that time, and among our people, the[48] wicked ways of Courts were only half understood. And there can be no doubt that, whether he was wise or religious, the show of affection with which the Duke was received upon this journey, turned his head and caused him to think that these people would rally round him if he called upon them. And I suppose that there is nothing which more delights a Prince than to believe that his friends are ready even to lay down their lives in his behalf.

At that time the country was greatly agitated by anxiety concerning the succession. Those who were nearest the throne knew that King Charles was secretly a Papist. We in the country had not learned that dismal circumstance; yet we knew the religion of the Duke of York. Thousands there were, like Sir Christopher himself, who now lamented the return of the King, considering the disgraces which had fallen upon the country. But what was done could not be undone. They, therefore, asked themselves if the nation would suffer an avowed Papist to ascend a Protestant throne. If not, what should be done? And here, as everybody knows, was opinion divided. For some declared that the

Duke of Monmouth, had he his rights, was the lawful heir; and others maintained, on the King's own words, that he was never married to Mistress Lucy Waters. Therefore, they would have the Duke of York's daughter, a Protestant princess, married to William of Orange, proclaimed Queen. The Monmouth party were strong, however, and it was even said—Mr. Henry Clark, minister of Crewkerne, wrote a pamphlet to prove it—that a poor woman, Elizabeth Parcet by name, touched the Duke (he being ignorant of the thing) for King's Evil, and was straightway healed. Sir Christopher laughed at the story, saying that the King himself, whether he was descended from a Scottish Stuart or from King Solomon himself, could no more cure that dreadful disease than the seventh son of a seventh son (as some foolish people believe), or the rubbing of the part affected by the hand of a man that had been hanged (as others do foolishly believe), which is the reason why on the gibbets the hanging corpses are always handless.

It was noised abroad, beforehand, that the Duke was going to ride through the West Country in order to visit his friends. The progress (it was more like a Royal progress than the journey of a private nobleman) began with his visit to Mr. Thomas Thynne, of Longleat House. It is said that his chief reason for going to that house was to connect himself with the obligation of the tenant of Longleat to give the King and his suite a night's lodging when they visited that part of the country. Mr. Thynne, who entertained the Duke on this occasion, was the same who was afterwards murdered in London by Count Konigsmark. They called him 'Tom of Ten Thousand.' The poet Dryden hath written of this progress, in that poem wherein, under the fabled name of Absalom, he figures the Duke:—

He now begins his progress to ordain, With chariots, horsemen, and a numerous train.[49] Fame runs before him as the morning star, And shouts of joy salute him from afar. Each house receives him as a guardian god, And consecrates the place of his abode.

It was for his hospitable treatment of the Duke that Mr. Thynne was immediately afterwards deprived of the command of the Wiltshire Militia.

'Son-in-law,' said Sir Christopher, 'I would ride out to meet the Duke in respect to his Protestant professions. As for any pretensions he may have to the succession, I know nothing of them.'

'I will ride with you, Sir,' said the Rector, 'to meet the son of the King. And as for any Protestant professions, I know nothing of them. His Grace still remains, I believe, within the pale of the Church as by law established. Let us all ride out together.'

Seeing that my father also rode with them, it is certain that there were many and diverse reasons why so many thousands gathered together to welcome the Duke. Madam, Robin's mother, out of her kind heart, invited me to accompany her, and gave me a white frock to wear and blue ribbons to put into it.

We made, with our servants, a large party. We were also joined by many of the tenants, with their sons and wives, so that when we came to Ilchester, Sir Christopher was riding at the head of a great company of sixty or more, and very fine they looked, all provided with blue favours in honour of the Duke.

From Bradford Orcas to Ilchester is but six miles as the crow flies, but the ways (which are narrow and foul in winter) do so wind and turn about that they add two miles at least to the distance. Fortunately, the season was summer—namely, August—when the sun is hottest and the earth is dry, so that no one was bogged on the way.

We started betimes—namely, at six in the morning—because we knew not for certain at what time the Duke would arrive at Ilchester. When we came forth from the Manor House the farmers were already waiting for us, and so, after greetings from his Honour, they fell in and followed. We first took the narrow and rough lane which leads to the high road; but, when we reached it, we found it full of people riding, like ourselves, or trudging, staff in hand, all in the same direction. They were going to gaze upon the Protestant Duke, who, if he had his way, would restore freedom of conscience, and abolish the Acts against the Nonconformists. We rode through Marston Magna, but only the old people and the little children were left there; in the fields the ripe corn stood waiting to be cut; in the farmyards the beasts were standing idle; all the hinds were gone to Ilchester to see the Duke. And I began to fear lest when we got to Ilchester we should be too late. At Marston we left the main road and entered upon a road (call it a track rather than a road) across the country, which is here flat and open. In winter it is miry and boggy, but it was now dry and hard. This path brought us again to the main road in two miles, or thereabouts, and here we were but a mile or so from Ilchester. Now, such a glorious sight as awaited us here I never expected to see. Once again, after five years, I was to see a welcome still more splendid; but nothing can ever efface from my memory that day. For first, the roads, as I have said, were thronged with rustics, and next, when we rode into the town we found it filled with gentlemen most richly dressed, and ladies so beautiful, and with such splendid attire that it dazzled my eyes to look upon them. It was a grand thing to see the gentlemen take off their hats and cry, 'Huzza for brave Sir Christopher!' Everybody knew his opinions, and on what side he had fought in the Civil War. The old man bent his head, and I think that he was pleased with this mark of honour.

The town which, though ancient, is now decayed and hath but few good houses in it, was made glorious with bright-coloured cloths, carpets, flags, and ribbons. There were bands of music; the bells of the church were ringing; the main street was like a fair with booths and stalls, and in the market-place there were benches set up with white canvas covering, where sat ladies in their fine dresses, some of them with naked necks, unseemly to behold. Yet it was pretty to see the long curls lying on their white shoulders. Some of them sat with half-closed eyes, which, I have since learned, is the fashion at Court. Mostly, they wore satin petticoats, and demi-gowns also of satin, furnished with a long train. Our place was beside the old Cross with its gilt ball and vane. The people who filled the streets came from Sherborne, from Bruton, from Shepton, from Glastonbury, from Langport, and from Somerton, and from all the villages round. It was computed that there were twenty thousand of them. Two thousand at least rode out to meet the Duke, and followed after him when he rode through the town. And, oh! the shouting as he drew near, the clashing of the bells, the beating of the drums, the blowing of the horns, the firing of the guns, as if the more noise they made the greater would be the Duke.

Since that day I have not wondered at the power which a Prince hath of drawing men after him, even to the death. Never was heir to the Crown received with such joy and welcome as was this young man, who had no title to the Crown and was base born. Yet, because he was a brave young man, and comely above all other young men, gracious of speech, and ready with a laugh and a joke, and because he was the son of the King, and the reputed champion of the Protestant faith, the people could not shout too loud for him.

The Duke was at this time in the prime of manhood, being thirty-five years of age. 'At that age,' Mr. Boscorel used to say, 'one would desire to remain if the body of clay were immortal. For then the volatile humours of youth have been dissipated. The time of follies has passed; love is regarded with the sober eyes of experience; knowledge has been acquired; skill of eye and hand has been gained, if one is so happy as to be a follower of art and music; wisdom hath been reached, if wisdom is ever to be attained. But wisdom,' he would add, 'is a quality generally lacking at every period of life.'

'When last I saw the Duke,' he told us while we waited, 'was fifteen years ago, in St. James's Park. He was walking with the King, his father, who had his arm about his son's shoulders, and regarded him fondly. At that time he was, indeed, a very David for beauty. I suppose that he hath not kept that singular loveliness which made him the darling of the Court. That, indeed, were not a thing to be desired or expected. He is now the hero of Maestricht, and the Chancellor of Cambridge University.'

And then all hats were pulled off, and the ladies waved their handkerchiefs, and the men shouted, and you would have thought the bells would have pulled the old tower down with the vehemence of their ringing; for the Duke was riding into the town.

He was no longer a beautiful boy, but a man at whose aspect every heart was softened. His enemies, in his presence, could not blame him; his friends, at sight of him, could not praise him, of such singular beauty was he possessed. Softness, gentleness, kindness, and goodwill reigned in his large soft eyes: graciousness sat upon his lips, and all his face seemed to smile as he rode slowly between the lane formed by the crowd on either hand.

What said the Poet Dryden in that same poem of his from which I have already quoted?—

Early in foreign fields he won renown With Kings and States allied to Israel's crown; In peace the thoughts of war he could remove, And seemed as he were only born for love. Whate'er he did was done with so much ease, In him alone 'twas natural to please; His motions all accompanied with grace, And Paradise was opened in his face.

Now I have to tell of what happened to me—the most insignificant person in the whole crowd. It chanced that as the Duke came near the spot beside the Cross where we were standing, the press in front obliged him to stop. He looked about him while he waited, smiling still and bowing to the people. Presently his eyes fell upon me, and he whispered a gentleman who rode beside him, yet a little in the rear. This gentleman laughed and dismounted. What was my confusion when he advanced towards me and spoke to me!

'Madam,' he said, calling me 'Madam!' 'His Grace would say one word to you, with permission of your friends.'

'Go with this gentleman, child,' said Sir Christopher, laughing. Everybody laughs—I know not why—when a girl is led out to be kissed.

'Fair White Rose of Somerset,' said his Grace—twas the most[52] musical voice in the world, and the softest. 'Fair White Rose'—he repeated the words—'let me be assured of the welcome of Ilchester by a kiss from your sweet lips, which I will return in token of my gratitude.'

All the people who heard these words shouted as if they would burst themselves asunder. And the gentleman who had led me forth lifted me so that my foot rested on the Duke's boot, while his Grace laid his arm tenderly round my waist, and kissed me twice.

'Sweet child,' he said, 'what is thy name?'

'By your Grace's leave,' I said, the words being very strange, 'my name is Alice. I am the daughter of Dr. Comfort Eykin, an ejected minister. I have come with Sir Christopher Challis, who stands yonder.'

'Sir Christopher!' said the Duke, as if surprised. 'Let me shake hands with Sir Christopher. I take it kindly, Sir Christopher, that you have so far honoured me.' So he gave the old man, who stepped forward bareheaded, his hand, still holding me by the waist. 'I pray that we may meet again, Sir Christopher, and that before long.' Then he drew a gold ring, set with an emerald, from his forefinger, and placed it upon mine, 'God grant it bring thee luck, sweet child,' he said, and kissed me again, and then suffered me to be lifted down. And you may be sure that it was with red cheeks that I took my place among my friends. Yet Sir Christopher was pleased at the notice taken of him by the Duke, and my father was not displeased at the part I had been made to play.

When the Duke had ridden through the town, many of the people followed after, as far as White Lackington, which is close to Ilminster. So many were they that they took down a great piece of the park paling to admit them all; and there, under a Spanish chestnut-tree, the Duke drank to the health of all the people.

At Ilminster, whither he rode a few days later; at Chard, a Ford Abbey, at Colyton, and at Exeter—wherever he went he was received with the same shouts and acclamations. It is no wonder therefore, that he should believe, a few years later, that those people would follow him when he drew the sword for the Protestant religion.

One thing is certain—that in the West of England, from the progress of Monmouth to the Rebellion, there was uneasiness, with an anxious looking forward to troubled times. The people of Taunton kept as a day of holiday and thanksgiving the anniversary of the raising of Charles's siege. When the Mayor, in 1683, tried to stop the celebration, they nearly stoned him to death. After this, Sir George Jeffreys, afterwards Lord Jeffreys, who took the spring circuit in 1684, was called upon to report on the loyalty of the West Country. He reported that the gentry were loyal and well disposed. But he knew not the mind of the weavers and spinners of the country.

'Fair White Rose of Somerset, let me be assured by a kiss from your sweet lips.'

It was this progress; the sight of the Duke's sweet face; his flattery of me, and his soft words, and the ring he gave me, which[53] made me from that moment such a partisan of his cause as only a woman can be. Women cannot fight, but they can encourage those who do; and they can not only ardently desire, but they can despise and contemn those who think otherwise. I cannot say that it was I who persuaded our boys five years later to join the Duke; but I can truly say that I did and said all that a woman can; that I rejoiced when they did so; and that I should never have forgiven Robin had he joined the forces of the Papist King.

CHAPTER IX.

WITH THE ELDERS.

So we went home again, all well pleased, and I holding the Duke's ring tight, I promise you. It was a most beautiful ring when I came to look at it; a great emerald was in the midst of it, with little pearls and emeralds set alternately around it. Never was such a grand gift to so humble a person. I tied it to a black ribbon, and put it in the box which held my clothes. But sometimes I could not forbear the pleasure of wearing it round my neck secretly; not for the joy of possessing the ring, so much as for remembering the lovely face and the gracious words of the giver.

At that time I was in my sixteenth year, but well-grown for my age. Like my father, I was above the common stature and taller than most. We continued for more than four years longer to live without the company of the boys, which caused me to be much in the society of my elders, and as much at the Manor House and the Rectory as at home. At the former place, Sir Christopher loved to have me with him all day long, if my mother would suffer it; when he walked abroad, I must walk with him; when he walked in his garden I must be at his side. When he awoke after his afternoon sleep, he liked to see me sitting ready to talk to him. I must play to him and sing to him; or I must bring out the backgammon board; or I must read the last letters from Robin and Humphrey. Life is dull for an old man whose friends are mostly dead, unless he have the company of the young. So David, in his old age, took to himself a young wife. I have sometimes thought that he would have done better to have comforted his heart with[55] the play and prattle of his grandchildren—of whom, I suppose, there must have been many families.

Now, as I was so much with his Honour, I had much talk with him upon things on which wise and ancient men do not often converse with girls, and I was often present when he discoursed with my father or with his son-in-law, the Rector, on high and serious matters. It was a time of great anxiety and uncertainty. There were great Pope burnings in the country; and when some were put in pillory for riot at these bonfires not a hand was lifted against them. They had one at Sherborne on November 17, the anniversary of Queen Elizabeth's Coronation day, instead of November 5, Guy Faux Day. Boys went about the streets asking for halfpence and singing—

Up with the ladder, And down with the rope; Give us a penny To burn the old Pope.

There were riots in Taunton, where the High Church party burned the pulpit of a meeting-house; people went about openly saying that the Roundheads would soon come back again. From Robin we heard of the Popish plot, and the flight of the Duke of York, and afterwards of Monmouth's disgrace and exile. At all the market towns where men gathered together they talked of these things, and many whispered together: a thing which Sir Christopher loved not, because it spoke of conspiracies and secret plots, whereas he was all for bold declaration of conscience.

In short, it was an anxious time, and everybody understood that serious things would happen should the King die. There were not wanting, besides, omens of coming ills—if you accept such things as omens or warnings. To Taunton (afterwards the town most affected by the Rebellion) a plain warning was vouchsafed by the rumbling and thundering and shaking of the earth itself, so that dishes were knocked down and cups broken, and plaster shaken off the walls of houses. And once (this did I myself see with my own eyes) the sun rose with four other suns for companions—a most terrifying sight, though Mr. Boscorel, who spoke learnedly on omens, had an explanation of this miracle, which he said was due to natural causes alone. And at Ile Brewers there was a monstrous birth of two girls with but one body from the breast downwards; their names were Aquila and Priscilla; but I believe they lived but a short time.

I needs must tell of Mr. Boscorel, because he was a man the like of whom I have never since beheld. I believe there can be few men such as he was, who could so readily exchange the world of heat and argument for the calm and dispassionate air of art and music. Even religion (if I may venture to say so) seemed of less importance to him than painting and sculpture. I have said that he taught me to play upon the spinnet. Now that Humphrey was gone, he desired my company every day, in order, he pretended, that I might grow perfect in my performance, but in reality because he was lonely at the Rectory, and found pleasure in my company. We played together—he upon the violoncello and I upon the spinnet—such music as he chose. It was sometimes grave and solemn music, such as Lulli's 'Miserere' or his 'De Profundis'; sometimes it was some part of a Roman Catholic Mass: then was my soul uplifted and wafted heavenwards by the chords, which seemed prayer and praise fit for the angels to harp before the throne. Sometimes it was music which spoke of human passions, when I would be, in like manner, carried out of myself. My master would watch not only my execution, commenting or correcting, but he would also watch the effect of the music upon my mind.

'We are ourselves,' he said, 'like unto the instruments upon which we play. For as one kind of instrument, as the drum, produces but one note; and another, as the cymbals, but a clashing which is in itself discordant, but made effective in a band; so others are, like the most delicate and sensitive violins—those of Cremona—capable of producing the finest music that the soul of man hath ever devised. It is by such music, child, that some of us mount unto heaven. As for me, indeed, I daily feel more and more that music leadeth the soul upward, and that, as regards the disputations on the Word of God, the letter indeed killeth, but the spirit which music helpeth us to feel—the spirit, I say, giveth life.' He sighed, and drew his bow gently across the first string of his violoncello. ''Tis a time of angry argument. The Word of God is thrown from one to the other as a pebble is shot from a sling. It wearies me. In this room, among these books of music, my soul finds rest, and the spiritual part of me is lifted heavenwards. Humphrey and you, my dear, alone can comprehend this saying. Thou hast a mind like his, to feel and understand what music means. Listen!' Here he executed a piece of music at which the tears rose to my eyes. 'That is from the Romish Mass which we are taught ignorantly to despise. My child, I am, indeed, no Catholic, and I hold that ours is the purer Church; yet, in losing the Mass, we have lost the great music with which the Catholics sustain their souls. Some of our anthems, truly, are good; but what is a single anthem, finished in ten minutes, compared with a grand Mass which lasts three hours?'

Then he had portfolios filled with engravings, which he would bring forth and contemplate with a kind of rapture, discoursing upon the engraver's art and its difficulties, so that I should not, as is the case with ignorant persons, suppose that these things were produced without much training and skill. He had also boxes full of coins, medals, and transparent gems carved most delicately with heathen gods and goddesses, shepherds and swains, after the ancient fashion, unclothed and unashamed. On these things he would gaze with admiration which he tried to teach me, but could not succeed, because I cannot believe that we may without blame look upon such figures. Nevertheless, they were most beautiful, the hands and faces and the very hair so delicately and exquisitely carved that you could hardly believe it possible. And he talked solemnly and scholarly of these gauds, as if they were things which peculiarly deserved the attention of wise and learned men. Nay, he would be even lifted out of himself in considering them.

'Child,' he said, 'we know not, and we cannot even guess, the wonders of art that in heaven we shall learn to accomplish'—as if carving and painting were the occupation of angels!—'or the miracles of beauty and of dexterity that we shall be able to design and execute. Here, the hand is clumsy and the brain is dull; we cannot rise above ourselves; we are blind to the beauty with which the Lord hath filled the earth for the solace of human creatures. Nay; we are not even tender with the beauty that we see and love. We suffer maidens sweet as the dreams of poets to waste their beauty unpraised and unsung. I am old, child, or I would praise thee in immortal verse. Much I fear that thou wilt grow old without the praise of sweet numbers. Well; there is no doubt more lasting beauty of face and figure hereafter to joy the souls of the elect. And thou wilt make his happiness for one man on earth. Pray Heaven, sweet child, that he look also to thine!'

He would say such things with so grand an air, speaking as if his words should command respect, and with so kindly an eye and a soft smile, while he gently stroked the side of his nose, which was long, that I was always carried away with the authority of it, and not till after I left him did I begin to perceive that my father would certainly never allow that the elect should occupy themselves with the frivolous pursuits of painting and the fine arts, but only with the playing of their harps and the singing of praises. It was this consideration which caused him to consent that his daughter should learn the spinnet. I did not tell him (God forgive me for the deceit, if there was any!) that we sometimes played music written for the Mass; nor did I repeat what Mr. Boscorel said concerning art and the flinging about of the Word of God, because my father was wholly occupied in controversy, and his principal, if not his only, weapon was the Word of God.

Another pleasure which we had was to follow Humphrey in his travels by the aid of his letters and a 'Mappa Mundi,' or atlas, which the Rector possessed. Then I remember when we heard that the boys were about to ride together through France, from Montpellier to Leyden in Holland, we had on the table the great map of France. There were many drawings, coats-of-arms, and other pretty things on the map.

'It is now,' said Mr. Boscorel, finding out the place he wanted, and keeping his forefinger upon it, 'nearly thirty years since I made the grand tour, being then governor to the young Lord Silchester, who afterwards died of the Plague in London. Else had I been now a Bishop, who am forgotten in this little place. The boys will ride, I take it, by the same road which we took: first, because it is the high road and the safest; next, because it is the best provided with inns and resting places; and, lastly, because it passes through the best part of his Most Christian Majesty's dominions, and carries the traveller through his finest and most stately cities. From Montpellier they will ride—follow my finger, child!—to Nismes. Before the Revocation it was a great place for those of the Reformed Religion, and a populous town. Here they will not fail to visit the Roman temple which still stands. It is not, indeed, such a noble monument as one may see in Rome; but it is in good preservation, and a fair example of the later style. They will also visit the great amphitheatre, which should be cleared of the mean houses which are now built up within it, and so exposed in all its vastness to the admiration of the world. After seeing these things they will direct their way across a desolate piece of country to Avignon, passing on the way the ancient Roman aqueduct called the Pont de Gard. At Avignon they will admire the many churches and the walls, and will not fail to visit the palace of the Popes during the Great Schism. Thence they will ride northwards, unless they wish first to see the Roman remains at Arles. Thence will they proceed up the Valley of the Rhone, through many stately towns, till they come to Lyons, where, doubtless, they will sojourn for a few days. Next, they will journey through the rich country of Burgundy, and from the ancient town of Dijon will reach Paris through the city of Fontainebleau. On the way they will see many noble houses and castles, with rich towns and splendid churches. In no country are there more splendid churches, built in the Gothic style, which we have now forgotten. Some of them, alas! have been defaced in the wars (so-called of Religion), where, as happened also to us, the delicate carved work, the scrolls and flowers and statues were destroyed, and the painted windows broken. Alas! that men should refuse to suffer Art to become the minister and handmaid of Religion! Yet in the first and most glorious temple, in which the glory of the Lord was visibly present, there were carved and graven lilies, with lions, oxen, chariots, cherubim, palm-trees and pomegranates.'

He closed his atlas and sat down.

'Child,' he said, meditating, 'for a scholar, in his youth, there is no pleasure comparable with the pleasure of travelling in strange countries, among the monuments of ancient days. My own son did never, to my sorrow, desire the pleasant paths of learning, and did never show any love for the arts, in which I have always taken so great delight. He desireth rather the companionship of men; he loveth to drink and sing; and he nourisheth a huge ambition. 'Tis best that we are not all alike. Humphrey should have been my son. Forget not, my child, that he hath desired to be remembered to thee in every letter which he hath written.'

If the Rector spoke much of Humphrey, Madam made amends by talking continually of Robin, and of the great things that he would do when he returned home. Justice of the Peace, that he would certainly be made; Captain first and afterwards Colonel in the Somerset Militia, that also should he be; Knight of the Shire, if he were ambitious—but that I knew he would never be; High Sheriff of the County, if his slender means permitted—for the estate was not worth more than five or six hundred pounds a year. Perhaps he would marry an heiress: it would be greatly to the advantage of the family if an heiress were to come into it with broad acres of her own; but she was not a woman who would seek to control her son in the matter of his affections, and if he chose a girl with no fortune to her back, if she was a good girl and pious, Madam would never say him nay. And he would soon return. The boy had been at Oxford and next in London, learning law, such as Justices require. He was now with Humphrey at the University of Leyden, doubtless learning more law.

'My dear,' said Madam, 'we want him home. His grandfather groweth old, though still, thank God! in the full possession of his faculties. Yet a young man's presence is needed. I trust and pray that he will return as he went, innocent, in spite of the many temptations of the wicked city. And, oh! child—what if he should have lost his heart to some designing city hussy!'

He came—as you shall hear immediately—Robin came home. Would to God that he had waited, if only for a single month! Had he not come all our afflictions would have been spared us! Had he not come that good old man, Sir Christopher——but it is vain to imagine what might have been. We are in the hands of the Lord; nothing that happens to us is permitted but by Him, and for some wise purpose was Sir Christopher in his old age—alas! why should I anticipate what I have to narrate?

CHAPTER X.

LE ROY EST MORT.

In February of the year 1685, King Charles II. died.

Sir Christopher himself brought us the news from Sherborne, whither he had gone, as was his wont, to the weekly ordinary. He clattered up the lane on his cob, and halted at our gate.

'Call thy father, child. Give you good day, Madam Eykin. Will your husband leave his books and come forth for a moment? Tell him I have news.'

My father rose and obeyed. His gown was in rags; his feet were clad in cloth shoon, which I worked for him; his cheek was wasted; but his eye was keen. He was lean and tall; his hair was as white as Sir Christopher's, though he was full twenty years younger.

'Friend and gossip,' said Sir Christopher, 'the King is dead.'

'Is Charles Stuart dead?' my father replied. 'He cumbered the earth too long. For five-and-twenty years hath he persecuted the saints. Also he hath burnt incense after the abomination of the heathen. Let his lot be as the lot of Ahaz.'

'Nay; he is buried by this time. His brother the Duke of York hath been proclaimed King.'

'James the Papist. It is as though Manasseh should succeed to Ahaz. And after him Jehoiakim.'

'Yet the bells will ring and we shall pray for the King; and wise men, friend Eykin, will do well to keep silence.'

'There is a time to speak and a time to keep silence. It may be that the time is at hand when a godly man must stretch forth his hand to tear down the Scarlet Woman, though she slay him in the attempt.'

'It may be so, my friend; yet stretch not forth thine hand until thou art well assured of the Divine Command. The King is dead. Now will my son-in-law ring out the bells for the new King, and we shall pray for him, as we prayed for his brother. It is our duty to pray for all in authority, though to the prayers of a whole nation there seemeth, so far as human reason can perceive, no answer.'

'I for one will pray no more for a King who is a Papist. Rather will I pray daily for his overthrow.'

'King Charles is said to have received a priest before he died. Yet it is worse that the King should be an open than a secret Catholic. Let us be patient, my friend, and await the time.'

So he rode up the village, and presently the bells were set a-ringing, and they clashed as joyously, echoing around the Corton Hills, as if the accession of King James II. was the only thing wanted to make the nation prosperous, happy, and religious.

My father stood at the gate after Sir Christopher left him. The wind was cold, and the twilight was falling, and his cassock was thin, but he remained there motionless, until my mother went out and drew him back to the house by the arm. He went into his own room, but he read no more that day.

In the evening he came forth and sat with us, and while I sat sewing, my mother spinning by the light of the fire, he discoursed, which was unusual with him, upon things and peoples and the best form of government, which he held to be a Commonwealth, with a strong man for President. But he was to hold his power from the people, and was to lay it down frequently, lest he should in his turn be tempted to become a King. And if he were to fall away from righteousness, or to live in open sin, or to be a merry-maker, or to suffer his country to fall from a high place among the nations, he was to be displaced, and be forced to retire. As for the man Charles, now dead, he would become, my father said, an example to all future ages, and a warning of what may happen when the doctrine of Divine Right is generally accepted and acted upon; the King himself being not so much blamed by him as the practice of hereditary rule which caused him to be seated upon the throne, when his true place, my father said, was among the lacqueys and varlets of the palace. 'His brother James,' he added, 'hath now an opportunity such as is given to few—for he may become another Josiah. But I think he will neglect that opportunity,' he concluded; 'yea, even if Hilkiah, the priest, were to bring him a message from Huldah, the prophetess; for he doth belong to a family which, by the Divine displeasure, can never perceive the truth. Let us now read the Word, and wrestle with the Lord in prayer.'

Next we heard that loyal addresses were poured in from all quarters congratulating the King, and promising most submissive obedience. One would have thought that the people were rejoiced at the succession of a Roman Catholic; it was said that the King had promised liberty of conscience unto all; that he claimed that liberty for himself, and that he went to Mass daily and openly.

But many there were who foresaw trouble. Unfortunately, one of them was Sir Christopher, who spoke his mind at all times too fiercely for his safety. Mr. Boscorel, also, was of opinion that civil war would speedily ensue.

'The King's friends,' he said, 'may for a time buy the support of the Nonconformists, and make a show of religious liberty. Thus may they govern for a while. But it is not in the nature of the Roman Catholic priest to countenance religious liberty, or ever[62] to sit down contented with less than all the pie. They must for ever scheme and intrigue for more power. Religious liberty? It means to them the eternal damnation of those who hold themselves free to think for themselves. They would be less than human if they did not try to save the souls of the people by docking their freedom. They must make this country even as Spain or Italy. Is it to be believed that they will suffer the Church to retain her revenues, or the universities to remain out of their control? Nay, will they allow the grammar schools to be in the hands of Protestants? Never! The next generation will be wholly Catholic, unless the present generation send King and priests packing.'

These were treasonable words, but they were uttered in the hall of the Manor House with no other persons present than Sir Christopher and the Rector himself.

'Seeing these things, son-in-law,' said Sir Christopher, 'what becomes of Right Divine? Where is the duty of Non-Resistance?'

'The doctrine of Right Divine,' said Mr. Boscorel, rubbing his nose, 'includes the Divine institution of a Monarchy, which, I confess, is manifestly untenable, because the Lord granted a King to the people only because they clamoured for one. Also, had the institution been of Divine foundation, the Jews would never have been allowed to live under the rule of Judges, Tetrarchs, and Roman Governors.'

'You have not always spoken so plainly,' said Sir Christopher.

'Nay; why be always proclaiming to the world your thoughts and opinions? Besides, even if the doctrine of Non-Resistance were sound, there may be cases in which just laws may be justly set aside. I say not that this is one, as yet. But if there were danger of the ancient superstitions being thrust upon us to the destruction of our souls, I say not that we should meekly sit down. Nay; if a starving man take a loaf of bread, there being no other way possible to save his life, one would not, therefore, hold him a thief. Yet the law remains.'

'Shall the blood which hath been poured out for the cause of liberty prove to be shed in vain?' asked Sir Christopher.

'Why, Sir,' said the Rector, 'the same question might be asked in France, where the Protestants fought longer and against greater odds than we in this country. Yet the blood of those martyrs hath been shed, so far as man can see, in vain; the Church of Rome is there the conqueror indeed. It is laid upon the Protestants, even upon us, who hold that we are a true branch of the ancient Apostolic Church, to defend ourselves continually against an enemy who is always at unity, always guided by one man, always knows what he wants, and is always working to get it. We, on the other hand, do not know our own minds, and must for ever be quarrelling among ourselves. Nevertheless, the heart of the country is Protestant; and sooner or later the case of conscience may arise whether—the law remaining unchanged—we may not blamelessly break the law.'

That case of conscience was not yet ripe for consideration. There needed first many things—including the martyrdom of saints and innocent men and poor, ignorant rustics—before the country roused herself once more to seize her liberties. Then as to that poor doctrine of Divine Right, they all made a mouthful of it, except only a small and harmless band of Nonjurors.

At the outset, whatever the opinions of the people—who could have been made to rise as one man—the gentry remained loyal. Above all things, they dreaded another civil war.

'We must fain accept the King's professions,' said the Rector. 'If we have misgivings, let us disguise them. Let us rather nourish the hope that they are honestly meant; and let us wait. England will not become another Spain in a single day. Let us wait. The stake is not yet set up in Smithfield, and the Inquisition is not yet established in the country.'

It was in this temper that the King's accession found Sir Christopher. Afterwards, he was accused of having harboured designs against the King from the beginning. That, indeed, was not the case. He had no thought of entering into any such enterprise. Yet he never doubted that in the end there would be an uprising against the rule of the priests. Nor did he doubt that the King would be pushed on by his advisers to one pretension after another for the advancement of his own prerogative and the displacement of the Protestant Church. Nay, he openly predicted that there would be such attempts; and he maintained—such was his wisdom!—that, in the long run, the Protestant faith would be established upon a surer foundation than ever. But as for conspiring or being cognisant of any conspiracy, that was untrue. Why, he was at this time seventy-five years of age—a time when such men as Sir Christopher have continually before their eyes Death and the Judgment.

As for my father, perhaps I am wrong, but in the daily prayers of night and morning, and in the grace before meat, he seemed to find a freer utterance, and to wrestle more vehemently than was his wont on the subject of the Scarlet Woman, offering himself as a willing martyr and confessor, if by the shedding of his blood the great day of her final overthrow might be advanced; yet always humble, not daring to think of himself as anything but an instrument to do the will of his Master. In the end, his death truly helped, with others, to bring a Protestant King to the Throne of these isles. And since we knew him to be so deep a scholar, always reading and learning, and in no sense a man of activity, the thing which he presently did amazed us all. Yet we ought to have known that one who is under the Divine command to preach the Word of God, and hath been silenced by man for more than twenty years, so that the strength of his manhood hath run to waste and is lost—it is a most terrible and grievous thing for a man to be condemned to idleness!—may become like unto one of those burning mountains of which we sometimes read in books of voyages. In him, as[64] in them, the inner fires rage and burn, growing ever stronger and fiercer, until presently they rend asunder the sides of the mountain and burst forth, pouring down liquid fire over the unhappy valleys beneath, with showers of red-hot ashes to destroy and cover up the smiling homesteads and the fertile meadows.

It is true that my father chafed continually at the inaction forced upon him, but his impatience was never so strong as at this time, namely, after the accession of King James. It drove him from his books and out into the fields and lanes, where he walked to and fro waving his long arms, and sometimes crying aloud and shouting in the woods, as if compelled to cry out in order to quench some raging fever or heat of his mind.

About this time, too, I remember, they began to talk of the exiles in Holland. The Duke of Monmouth was there with the Earl of Argyle, and with them a company of firebrands eager to get back to England and their property.

I am certain now that my father (and perhaps through his information, Sir Christopher also) was kept acquainted with the plots and designs that were carried on in the Low Countries. Nay, I am also certain that his informant was none other than Humphrey, who was still in Leyden. I have seen a letter from him, written, as I now understand, in a kind of allegory or parable, in which one thing was said and another meant. Thus, he pretends to speak of Dutch gardening:—'The gardeners,' he says, 'take infinite pains that their secrets shall not be learned or disclosed. I know, however, that a certain blue tulip much desired by many gardeners in England, will be taken across the water this year, and I hope that by next year the precious bulb may be fully planted in English soil. The preparation of the soil necessary for the favourable reception of the bulb is well known to you, and you will understand how to mix your soil and to add manure and so forth. I myself expect to finish what I have to do in a few weeks, when I shall cross to London, and so ride westwards, and hope to pay my respects to my revered tutor in the month of June next. It may be that I shall come with the tulip, but that is not certain. Many messages have been received offering large sums of money for the bulb, so that it is hoped that the Dutch gardeners will let it go.

'From H. C.'

The tulip, in a word, was the Duke of Monmouth, and the Dutch gardeners were the Scotch and English exiles then in Holland, and the English gardeners were the Duke's friends, and H. C. was Humphrey Challis.

I think that Sir Christopher must have known of this correspondence, because I now remember that my father would sit with him for many hours looking at a map of England, conversing long and earnestly, and making notes in a book. These notes he made in the Arabic character, which no one but himself could read. I therefore suppose that he was estimating the number of Nonconformists[65] who might be disposed to aid in such an enterprise as Humphrey's 'gardeners' were contemplating.

Robin, who certainly was no conspirator, also wrote a letter from Leyden about this time saying that something was expected, nobody knew what; but that the exiles were meeting constantly, as if something was brewing.

It was about the first week of June that the news came to us of Lord Argyle's landing. This was the beginning. After that, as you will hear, the news came thick and fast; every day something fresh, and something to quicken the most sluggish pulse. To me, at least, it seemed as if the breath of God Himself was poured out upon the country, and that the people were everywhere resolved to banish the accursed thing from their midst. Alas! I was but a simple country maid and I was deceived! The accursed thing was to be driven forth, but not yet. The country party hated the Pope, but they dreaded civil war; and, indeed, there is hardly any excuse for that most dreadful scourge except the salvation of the soul and the safeguarding of liberties. They would gladly welcome a rising, but it must be general and universal. They had for five-and-twenty years been taught the wickedness of rebellion, and now there was no way to secure the Protestant Faith except by rebellion. Unhappily, the rebellion began before the country gentlemen were ready to begin.

CHAPTER XI.

BEFORE THE STORM.

Before the storm breaks there sometimes falls upon the earth a brief time when the sun shines in splendour from a clear sky, the air is balmy and delightsome, the birds sing in the coppice, and the innocent lambs leap in the meadows. Then, suddenly, dark clouds gather from the north; the wind blows cold; in a minute the sky is black; the lightnings flash, the thunders roll, the wind roars, the hail beats down and strips the orchard of its promise, and silences the birds cowering in the branches, and drives the trembling sheep to take shelter in the hedges. This was to be my case. You shall understand how for a single day—it was no more—I was the happiest girl in all the world.

I may now without any shame confess that I have always loved Robin from my earliest childhood. That was no great wonder seeing what manner of boy he was, and how he was always kind and thoughtful for me. We were at first only brother and sister together, which is natural and reasonable when children grow up together; nor can I tell when or how we ceased to be brother and sister, save that it may have been when Robin kissed me so tenderly at parting, and told me that he should always love me. I do not think that brothers do generally protest love and promise continual affection. Barnaby certainly never declared his love for me, nor did he ever promise to love me all his life. Perhaps, had he remained longer, he might have become as tender as he was good-hearted; but I think that tenderness towards a sister is not in the nature of a boy. I loved Robin, and I loved Humphrey, both as if they were[67] brothers; but one of them ceased to be my brother, while the other, in consequence, remained my brother always.

A girl may be ignorant of the world as I was, and of lovers and their ways as I was, and yet she cannot grow from a child to a woman without knowing that when a young man, who hath promised to love her always, speaks of her in every letter, he means more than common brotherly love. Nor can any woman be indifferent to a man who thus regards her; nor can she think upon love without the desire of being herself loved. Truly, I had always before my eyes the spectacle of that holy love which consecrates every part of life. I mean, in the case of my mother, whose waking and sleeping thoughts were all for her husband, who worked continually and cheerfully with her hands that he might be enabled to study without other work, and gave up her whole life, without grudging—even reckoning it her happiness and her privilege—in order to provide food and shelter for him. It was enough reward for her that he should sometimes lay his hand lovingly upon her head, or turn his eyes with affection to meet hers.

It was in the night of June 12, as I lay in bed, not yet asleep, though it was already past nine o'clock, that I heard the trampling of hoofs crossing the stream and passing our cottage. Had I known who were riding those horses there would have been but little sleep for me that night. But I knew not, and did not suspect, and so, supposing that it was only one of the farmers belated, I closed my eyes, and presently slept until the morning.

About five o clock, or a little before that time, I awoke, the sun having already arisen, and being now well up above the hills. I therefore arose softly, leaving my mother asleep still, and, having dressed quickly, and prayed a little, I crept down the stairs. In the house there was such a stillness that I could even hear the regular breathing of my father as he slept upon his pallet among his books; it was chill and damp (as is the custom in the early morning) in the room where he lived and worked. Yet, when I threw open door and shutter and looked outside, the air was full of warmth and refreshment; as for the birds, they had long since left their nests, and now were busy looking for their breakfast; the larks were singing overhead, and the bees already humming and droning. Who would lie abed when he could get up and enjoy the beauty of the morning? When I had breathed a while, with pleasure and satisfaction, the soft air, which was laden with the scent of flowers and of hay, I went indoors again and swept and dusted the room. Then I opened the cupboard, and considered the provision for breakfast. For my father there would be a slice of cold bacon with a good crust of home-made bread (better bread or sweeter was nowhere to be had) and a cup of cider, warming to the spirits and good, for one who is no longer young, against any rawness of the morning air. For my mother and myself there would be, as soon as our neighbours' cows were milked, a cup of warm milk and bread soaked in it. 'Tis a breakfast good for a grown person as[68] well as for a child, and it costs us nothing but the trouble of going to take it.

When I had swept the room and laid everything in its place I went into the garden, hoe in hand, to weed the beds and trim the borders. The garden was not very big, it is true, but it produced many things useful for us; notably onions and sallet, besides many herbs good for the house, for it was a fertile strip of ground and planted in every part of it. Now, such was the beauty of the morning and the softness of the air that I presently forgot the work about which I had come into the garden, and sat down in the shade upon a bench, suffering my thoughts to wander hither and thither. Much have I always pitied those poor folk in towns who can never escape from the noise and clatter of tongues and sit somewhere in the sunshine or the shade, while the cattle low in the meadows and the summer air makes the leaves to rustle, and thus alone suffer their thoughts to wander here and there. Every morning when I arose was this spectacle of Nature's gladness presented to my eyes, but not every morning could my spirit (which sometimes crawls, as if fearing the light of day and the face of the sun) rise to meet and greet it, and to feel it calling aloud for a hymn of praise and thanksgiving. For, indeed, this is a beautiful world, if we could always (which we cannot for the earthliness of our natures) suffer its loveliness to sink into our hearts. I know not what I thought this morning; but I remember, while I considered the birds, which neither reap nor sow, nor take any thought of to-morrow, yet are daily fed by Heaven, that the words were whispered in mine ear: 'Are ye not much better than they?' And this, without doubt, prepared my heart for what should follow.

While I sat thinking of I know not what, there came footsteps—quick footsteps—along the road; and I knew those footsteps, and sprang to my feet, and ran to the garden-gate, crying, 'Robin!—it is Robin!'

Yes; it was Robin.

He seized me by both hands, looking in my face curiously and eagerly.

'Alice!' he said, drawing a deep breath, 'Oh! but what hath happened to thee?'

'What should happen, Robin?'

'Oh! Thou art changed, Alice! I left thee almost a child, and now—now—I thought to catch thee in my arms—a sweet rustic nymph—and now—fain must I go upon my knees to a goddess.'

'Robin!' Who, indeed, would have expected such language from Robin!

'Alice,' he said, still gazing upon me with a kind of wonder which made me blush, 'do you remember when we parted four years ago—the words we said? As for me, I have never forgotten them. I was to think of thee always; I was to love thee always. Truly I may say that there is never a day but thou hast been in my mind. But not like this'—— He continued to look upon me as[69] upon some strange creature, so that I began to be frightened and turned away.

'Nay, Alice, forgive me. I am one who is dazzled by the splendour of the sun. Forgive me; I cannot speak. I thought of a village beauty, rosy-cheeked, sweet and wholesome as an August quarander, and I find'——

'Robin—not a goddess.'

'Well, then, a woman tall and stately, and more beautiful than words can say.'

'Nay, Robin, you do but flatter. That is not like the old Robin I remember and'——I should have added 'loved,' but the word stuck.

'I swear, sweet saint—if I may swear—nay, then I do affirm, that I do not flatter. Hear me tell a plain tale. I have travelled far since last I saw thee; I have seen the great ladies of the Court both of St. James's and of the Louvre; I have seen the famous beauties of Provence, and the black-eyed witches of Italy; but nowhere have I seen a woman half so fair.'

'Robin—you must not! Nay, Robin—you shame me!'

Then he knelt at my feet and seized my hand and kissed it. Oh, the foolishness of a man in love! And yet it pleases us. No woman is worth it. No woman can understand it; nor can she comprehend the power and might of man's love, nor why he singles out her alone from all the rest and fills his heart wholly with her, so that all other women are henceforward as his sisters. It is wonderful; it is most wonderful. Yet it pleases us. Nay, we cannot choose but thank God for it with all our heart and with all our soul.

I would not, if I could, set down all the things which Robin said. First, because the words of love are sacred; next, because I would not that other women should know the extravagance of his praise. It was in broken words, because love can never be eloquent.

As for me, what could I do, what could I say? For I had loved him from my very childhood, and now all my heart went out from me and became his. I was all his. I was his slave to command. That is the quality of earthly love by which it most closely resembles the heavenly love, so that just as the godly man is wholly devoted to the will of the Lord in all things great and small, resigned to His chastisements, and always anxious to live and die in His service, so in earthly love one must be wholly devoted to the person whom one loves.

And Robin was come home again, and I was lying in his arms, and he was kissing me and calling me all the sweet and tender things that he could invent, and laughing and sighing together as if too happy to be quiet. Oh! sweetest moments of my life! Why did they pass so quickly? Oh! sacrament of love, which can be taken only once, and yet changes the whole of life and fills it with memory which is wholly sweet! In all other earthly things[70] there is something of bitterness. In this holy joy of pure and sacred love there is no bitterness—no; not any. It leaves behind nothing of reproach or of repentance, of shame or of sorrow. It is altogether holy.

Now, when my boy had somewhat recovered from his first rapture, and I had assured him very earnestly that I was not, indeed, an angel, but a most sinful woman, daily offending in my inner thoughts (an assurance which he received, indeed, with an appearance of disbelief and scorn), I was able to consider his appearance, which was now very fine, though always, as I learned when I saw him among other gentlemen, with some soberness, as became one whose upbringing inclined him to plainness of dress as well as of speech and manner. He wore a long wig of brown hair, which might have been his own but for its length; his hat was laced and cocked, which gave him a gallant and martial appearance; his neckcloth was long and of fine lace; beside him in my russet gown I must have looked truly plain and rustic; but Robin was pleased not to think so, and love is a great magician to cheat the eyes.

He was home again; he told me he should travel no more (yet you shall hear how far he afterwards travelled against his will); his only desire now was to stay at home and live as his grandfather had lived, in his native village; he had nothing to pray for but the continuance of my love—of which, indeed, there was no doubt possible.

It was now close upon six o'clock, and I begged him to go away for the present, and if my father and Sir Christopher should agree, and if it should seem to his Honour a fit and proper thing that Robin should marry a girl so penniless as myself, why—then—we might meet again after breakfast, or after dinner; or, indeed, at any other time, and so discourse more upon the matter. So he left me, being very reluctant to go; and I, forgetting my garden and what I had come forth to do, returned to the house.

You must understand that all these things passed in the garden, divided from the lane by a thick hedge, and that passers-by—but there were none—could not, very well, have seen what was done, though they might have heard what was said. But if my father had looked out of his window he could have seen, and if my mother had come downstairs she also might have seen through the window, or through the open door. This I thought not upon, nor was there anything to hide—though one would not willingly suffer anyone, even one's own mother, to see and listen at such a moment. Yet mother has since told me that she saw Robin on his knees kissing my hands; but she withdrew, and would not look again.

When I stepped within the door she was at work with her wheel, and looked up with a smile upon her lips, but tears were lying in her eyes. Had I known what she had seen I should have been ashamed.

'Daughter,' she said softly, 'thy cheek is burning red. Hast thou, perchance, been too long in the sun?'

'No, mother, the sun is not too hot.'

'Daughter,' she went on, still smiling through her tears, 'thine eyes are bright and glowing. Hast thou a touch of fever by ill chance?'

'No, mother, I have no fever.'

'Child, thy lips are trembling and thy hands are shaking. My dear, my dear, what is it? Tell thy mother all.'

She held out her arms to me, and I threw myself at her feet, and buried my head in her lap as if I had been again a child.

'Mother! mother!' I cried, 'Robin hath come home again, and he says he loves me, and nothing will do but he must marry me.'

'My dear,' she said, kissing and fondling me, 'Robin hath always been a good lad, and I doubt not that he hath returned unspotted from the world; but, nay, do not let us be too sure. For, first, his Honour must consent, and then Madam; and thy father must be asked—and he would never, for any worldly honour—no, never—suffer thee to marry an ungodly man. As for thy lack of fortune, I know not if that will not also stand in the way; and as for family, thy father, though he was born in New England, cometh of a good stock, and I myself am a gentlewoman, and on both sides we bear an ancient coat-of-arms. And as for thyself, my dear, thou art—I thank God for it!—of a sweet temper and an obedient disposition. From the earliest thou hast never given thy mother any uneasiness, and I think thy heart hath been mercifully disposed towards goodness from thy childhood upwards. It is a special grace in this our long poverty and oppression; and it consoles me partly for the loss of my son Barnaby.' Here she was silent for a space, and her eyes filled and brimmed over. 'Daughter,' she said earnestly, 'thou art comely in the eyes of men; that have I known for long. It is partly for thy sweet looks that Sir Christopher loves thee; Mr. Boscorel plays music with thee partly because his eyes love to behold the beauty of woman. Nay, I mean no reproach, because it is the nature of men to love all things beautiful, whether it be the plumage of a bird or the shape of a woman's head. Yes; thou art beautiful, my dear. Beauty passes, but love remains. Thy husband will perchance never cease to think thee lovely if he still proves daily thy goodness and the loveliness of thy heart. My dear, thou hast long comforted thy mother; now shalt thou go, with the blessing of the Lord, to be the solace and the joy of thy husband.'

CHAPTER XII.

HUMPHREY.

Presently my father came in, the Bible in his hand. By his countenance it was plain that he had been already engaged in meditation, and that his mind was charged as with a message.

Alas! to think of the many great discourses that he pronounced (being as a dog who must be muzzled should he leave the farm-yard) to us women alone. If they were written down the world would lift up its hands with wonder, and ask if a prophet indeed had been vouchsafed to this unhappy country. The Roman Church will have that the time of Saints did not end with the last of the Apostles; that may be, and yet a Saint has no more power after death than remains in his written words and in the memory of his life. Shall we not, however, grant that there may still be Prophets, who see and apprehend the meaning of words and of things more fully than others even as spiritually minded as themselves? Now, I say, considering what was immediately to befall us, the passage which my father read and expounded that morning was in a manner truly prophetic. It was the vision of the Basket of Summer Fruit which was vouchsafed to the Prophet Amos. He read to us that terrible chapter—everybody knows it, though it hath but fourteen verses.

'I will turn your feasts into mourning and all your songs into lamentation.... I will send a famine in the land; not a famine of bread nor a thirst for water, but of hearing the words of the Lord.'

He then applied the chapter to these times, saying that the Scriptures and the prophecies apply not only to the Israel of the time when Amos or any other prophet lived, but to the people of God in all ages, yet so that sometimes one prophet seems to deliver the message that befits the time and sometimes another. All these things prophesied by Amos had come to pass in this country of Great Britain; so that there was, and had now been for twenty-five years, a grievous famine and a sore thirst for the words of the Lord. He continued to explain and to enlarge upon this topic for nearly an hour, when he concluded with a fervent prayer that the famine would pass away and the sealed springs be open again for the children of grace to drink and be refreshed.

This done, he took his breakfast in silence, as was his wont,[73] loving not to be disturbed by any earthly matters when his mind was full of his morning discourse. When he had eaten the bread and meat and taken the cup of cider, he arose and went back to his own room, and shut the door. We should have no more speech of him until dinner-time.

'I will speak with him, my dear,' said my mother. 'But not yet. Let us wait till we hear from Sir Christopher.'

'I would that my father had read us a passage of encouragement and promise on this morning of all mornings,' I said.

My mother turned over the leaves of the Bible. 'I will read you a verse of encouragement,' she said. 'It is the word of God as much as the Book of the Prophet Amos.' So she found and read for my comfort words which had a new meaning to me:—

'My beloved spake, and said unto me, Rise up, my love, my fair one, and come away. For, lo! the winter is past, the rain is over and gone; the flowers appear on the earth; the time of the singing of birds is come, and the voice of the turtle is heard in our land. The fig tree putteth forth her green figs, and the vines with the tender grape give a good smell. Arise, my love, my fair one, and come away.'

And again, these that follow:—

'Set me as a seal upon thine heart, as a seal upon thine arm: for love is strong as death; jealousy is cruel as the grave: the coals thereof are coals of fire, which hath a most vehement flame. Many waters cannot quench love, neither can the floods drown it. If a man would give all the substance of his house for love it would utterly be contemned.'

In these gracious, nay, these enraptured words, doth the Bible speak of love; and though I am not so ignorant as not to know that it is the love of the Church for Christ, yet I am persuaded by my own spiritual experience—whatever Doctors of Divinity may argue—that the earthly love of husband and wife may be spoken of in these very words as being the type of that other and higher love. And in this matter I know that my mother would also confirm my judgment.

It might have been between nine and ten that Humphrey came. Surely he was changed more than Robin: for the great white periwig which he wore (being now a physician) falling upon his shoulders did partly hide the deformity of his wry shape, and the black velvet coat did also become him mightily. As for his face, that was not changed at all. It had been grave and serious in youth; it was now more grave and more serious in manhood. He stood in the doorway, not seeing me—I was making a pudding for dinner, with my sleeves rolled up and my arms white with flour.

'Mistress Eykin,' he said, 'are old friends passed out of mind?'

'Why,' my mother left her wheel and gave him her hand, "tis Humphrey! I knew that we should see thee this morning, Humphrey. Is thy health good, my son, and is all well with thee?'

'All is well, madam, and my health is good. How is my master—thy husband?'

'He is always well, and—but thou knowest what manner of life he leads. Of late he hath been much disquieted; he is restless—his mind runs much upon the prophecies of war and pestilence. It is the news from London and the return of the Mass which keeps him uneasy. Go in and see him, Humphrey. He will willingly suffer thee to disturb him, though we must not go near him in his hours of study.'

'Presently; but where is my old playfellow—where is Alice?'

'She is behind you, Humphrey.'

He turned, and his pale face flushed when he saw me.

'Alice?' he cried. 'Is this truly Alice? Nay, she is changed indeed! I knew not—I could not expect—nay, how could one expect'——

'There is no change,' said my mother, sharply. 'Alice was a child, and is now a woman; that is all.'

'Humphrey expects,' I said, 'that we should all stop still while Time went on. You were to become a Bachelor of Medicine, sir, and a Fellow of All Souls' College, and to travel in Italy and France, and to come back in a velvet coat, and a long sword, and a periwig over your shoulders; and I was to be a little girl still.'

Humphrey shook his head.

'It is not only that,' he said; 'though I confess that one did not make due allowance for the flight of Time. It is that the sweet-faced child has become'——

'No, Humphrey,' I said, 'I want no compliments. Go now, sir, and speak with my father. Afterwards you shall tell me all that you have been doing.'

He obeyed, and opened my father's door.

'Humphrey!' My father sprang to his feet. 'Welcome, my pupil! Thou bringest good news? Nay; I have received thy letters: I read the good news in thy face—I see it in thine eyes. Welcome home!'

'Sir, I have, indeed, great news,' said Humphrey.

Then the door was closed.

He stayed there for half an hour and more; and we heard from within earnest talk—my father's voice sometimes uplifted, loud and angry, but Humphrey's always low, as if he did not wish us to overhear them. So, not to seem unto each other as if we were listening, mother and I talked of other things, such as the lightness of the pudding, and the quantity of suet which should be put into it, and the time it should boil in the pot, and other things, as women can whose hearts are full, yet they must needs be talking.

'Father hath much to say to Humphrey,' I said, after a time; 'he doth not use to like such interruption.'

'Humphrey's conversation is no interruption, my dear. They think the same thoughts and talk the same language. Your father may teach and admonish us, but he can only converse with a scholar such as himself. It is not the least evil of our oppression that he hath been cut off from the society of learned men, in which he used to take so much delight. If Humphrey remains here a little while you shall see your father lose the eager and anxious look which hath of late possessed him. He will talk to Humphrey, and will clear his mind. Then he will be contented again for a while, or, at least, resigned.'

Presently Humphrey came forth. His face was grave and serious. My father came out of the room after him.

'Let us talk more,' he said; 'let us resume our talk. Join me on the hillside, where none can hear us. It is, indeed, the Vision of the Basket of Summer Fruit that we read this morning.' His face was working with some inward excitement, and his eyes were full of a strange light as of a glad conqueror, or of one—forbid the thought!—who was taking a dire revenge. He strode down the garden and out into the lanes.

'Thus,' said my mother, 'will he walk out, and sometimes remain in the woods, walking, preaching to the winds, and swinging his arms the whole day long. Art thou a physician, and canst thou heal him, Humphrey?'

'If the cause be removed, the disease will be cured. Perhaps before long the cause will be removed.'

'The cause—oh! the cause—what is the cause but the tyranny of the Law? He who was ordered by Heaven itself to preach hath been, perforce, silent for five-and-twenty years. His very life hath been taken from him. And you talk of removing the cause!'

'Madam, if the Law suffer him once more to preach freely, would that satisfy him—and you?'

My mother shook her head. 'The Law,' she said, 'now we have a Papist on the throne is far more likely to lead my husband to the stake than to set him free.'

'That shall we shortly see,' said Humphrey.

My mother bent her head over her wheel as one who wishes to talk no more upon the subject. She loved not to speak concerning her husband to any except to me.

I went out into the garden with Humphrey. I was foolish. I laughed at nothing. I talked nonsense. Oh! I was so happy that if a pipe and tabor had been heard in the village I should have danced to the music, like poor Barnaby the night before he ran away. I regarded not the grave and serious face of my companion.

'You are merry, Alice,' said Humphrey.

'It is because you are come back again—you and Robin. Oh! the time has been long and dull—and now you have come back we shall all be happy again. Yes; my father will cease to fret and rage; he will talk Latin and Greek with you; Sir Christopher will[76] be happy only in looking upon you; Madam will have her son home again; and Mr. Boscorel will bring out all the old music for you. Humphrey, it is a happy day that brings you home again.'

'It may be a happy day also for me,' he said; 'but there is much to be done. When the business we have in hand is accomplished'——

'What business, Humphrey?' For he spoke so gravely that it startled me.

''Tis business of which thy father knows, child. Nay; let us not talk of it. I think and hope that it is as good as accomplished now before it is well taken in hand. It is not of that business that I would speak. Alice, thou art so beautiful and so tall'——

'Nay, Humphrey. I must not be flattered.'

'And I so crooked.'

'Humphrey, I will not hear this talk. You, so great a scholar, thus to speak of yourself!'

'Let me speak of myself, my dear. Hear me for a moment.' I declare that I had not the least thought of what he was going to say, my mind being wholly occupied with the idea of Robin.

'I am a physician, as you doubtless know. I am Medicinæ Doctor of Oxford, of Padua, Montpellier, and Leyden. I know all—I may fairly say, and without boasting—that may be learned by one of my age from schools of medicine and from books on the science and practice of healing. I believe, in short, that I am as good a physician as can be found within these seas. I am minded, as soon as tranquillity is restored, to set up as a physician in London, where I have already many friends, and am assured of some support. I think, humbly speaking, that reasonable success awaits me. Alice—you know that I have loved you all my life—will you marry me, crooked as I am? Oh! you cannot but know that I have loved you all my life. Oh! child,' he stretched forth his hands, and in his eyes there was a world of longing and of sadness which moved my heart. 'My dear, the crooked in body have no friends among men; they cannot join in their rough sports, nor drink with them, nor fight with them. They have no chance of happiness but in love, my dear. My dear, give me that chance. I love thee! Oh! my dear, give me that chance?'

Never had I seen Humphrey so moved before. I felt guilty and ashamed in the presence of this passion of which I was the most unworthy cause.

'Oh! Humphrey, stop—for Heaven's sake stop!—because I am but this very morning promised to Robin, who loves me, too—and I love Robin, Humphrey.' He sank back, pale and disordered, and I thought that he would swoon, but he recovered. 'Humphrey, never doubt that I love you, too. But oh! I love Robin, and Robin loves me.'

'Yes, dear—yes, child—yes, Alice,' he said in broken accents. 'I understand. Everything is for Robin—everything for Robin. Why, I might have guessed it! For Robin, the straight and comely[77] figure; for Robin, the strength; for Robin, the inheritance; for Robin, happy love. For me, a crooked body; for me, a feeble frame; for me, the loss of fortune; for me, contempt and poverty; for me, the loss of love—all for Robin—all for Robin!'

'Humphrey, surely thou wouldst not envy or be jealous of Robin!' Never had I seen him thus moved, or heard him thus speak.

He made no answer for a while. Then he said, slowly and painfully:—

'Alice, I am ashamed. Why should not Robin have all? Who am I that I should have anything? Forgive me, child. I have lived in a paradise which fools create for themselves. I have suffered myself to dream that what I ardently desired was possible and even probable. Forgive me. Let me be as before—your brother. Will you forgive me, dear?'

'Oh, Humphrey! there is nothing for me to forgive.'

'Nay, there is much for me to repent of. Forget it then, if there is nothing to forgive.'

'I have forgotten it already, Humphrey.'

'So'—he turned upon me his grave, sweet face (to think of it makes me yearn with tenderness and pity)—'so, farewell, fond dream! Do not think, my dear, that I envy Robin. 'Twas a sweet dream! Yet, I pray that Heaven in wrath may forget me if ever I suffer this passion of envy to hurt my cousin Robin or thyself!'

So saying, he burst from me with distraction in his face. Poor Humphrey! Alas! when I look back and consider this day, there is a doubt which haunts me. Always had I loved Robin: that is most true. But I had always loved Humphrey: that is most true. What if it had been Humphrey instead of Robin who had arisen in the early morning to find his sweetheart in the garden when the dew was yet upon the grass?

CHAPTER XIII.

ONE DAY.

In times of great sorrow the godly person ought to look forward to the never-ending joy and happiness that will follow this short life. Yet we still look backwards to the happy time that is past and can never come again. And then, how happy does it seem to have been in comparison with present affliction!

It pleased Heaven after many trials to restore my earthly happiness—at least, in its principal part, which is earthly love. Some losses—grievous and lamentable—there were which could not be restored. Yet for a long time I had no other comfort (apart from that hope which I trust was never suffered to leave me) than the recollection of one single day in its course, too short, from dewy morn till dusky eve. I began that day with the sweetest joy that a girl can ever experience—namely, the return of her lover and the happiness of learning that he loves her more than ever, with the knowledge that her heart hath gone forth from her and is wholly his. To such a girl the woods and fields become the very garden of Eden; the breath of the wind is as the voice of the Lord blessing another Eve; the very showers are the tears of gladness and gratitude; the birds sing hymns of praise; the leaves of the trees whisper words of love; the brook prattles of kisses; the flowers offer incense; the royal course of the sun in splendour, the glories of the sunrise and sunset, the twinkling stars of night, the shadows of the flying clouds, the pageant of the summer day—these are all prepared for that one happy girl and for her happy lover! Oh, Divine Gift of Love! which thus gives the whole world[79] with its fruits in season to each pair in turn! Nay, doth it not create them anew? What was Adam without Eve? And Eve was created for no other purpose than to be a companion to the man.

I say, then, that the day when Robin took me in his arms and kissed me—not as he had done when we parted and I was still a child, but with the fervent kiss of a lover—was the happiest day in all my life. I say that I have never forgotten that day, but, by recalling any point of it, I remember all: how he held my hand and how he made me confess that I loved him; how we kissed and parted, to meet again. As for poor Humphrey, I hardly gave him so much as a thought of pity. Then, how we wandered along the brook hand in hand!

'Never to part again, my dear,' said the fond lover. 'Here will we live, and here we will die. Let Benjamin become, if he please, Lord Chancellor, and Humphrey a great physician: they will have to live among men in towns, where every other man is a rogue. We shall live in this sweet country place, where the people may be rude but they are not knaves. Why, in that great city of London, where the merchants congregate upon the Exchange and look so full of dignity and wisdom, each man is thinking all the time that, if he fail to overreach his neighbour, that neighbour will overreach him. Who would live such a life when he can pass it in the fields with such a companion as my Alice?'

The pleasures of London had only increased his thirst for the country life. Surely, never was seen a swain more truly rustic in all his thoughts! The fine ladies at the playhouse, with their painted faces, made him, he told me, think of one who wore a russet frock in Somersetshire, and did not paint her sweet face—this was the way he talked. The plays they acted could never even be read, much less witnessed, by that dear girl—so full of wickedness they were. At the assemblies the ladies were jealous of each other, and put on scornful looks when one seemed preferred; at the taverns the men drank and bellowed songs and quarrelled; in the streets they fought and took the wall and swaggered; there was nothing but fighting among the baser sort, with horrid imprecations; at the coffee-houses the politicians argued and quarrelled. Nay, in the very churches the sermons were political arguments, and while the clergyman read his discourse the gallants ogled the ladies. All this and more he told me.

To hear my boy, one would think there was nothing in London but what was wicked and odious. No doubt it is a wicked place; where many men live together, those who are wicked easily find each other out, and are encouraged in their wickedness. Yet there must be many honest and God-fearing persons, otherwise the Judgment of Heaven would again fall upon that city as it did in the time of the Plague and in the Great Fire.

'My pretty Puritan,' said Robin, 'I am now come away from that place, and I hope never to see it again. Oh! native hills, I salute you! Oh! woods and meadows, I have returned, to wander[80] again in your delightful shade.' Then, which was unusual in my boy, and would have better become Mr. Boscorel or Humphrey, he began to repeat verses. I knew not that he had ever learned any:—

As I range these spacious fields, Feast on all that Nature yields; Everything inspires delight, Charms my smell, my taste, my sight; Every rural sound I hear Soothes my soul and tunes my ear.

I do not know where Robin found these verses, but as he repeated them, waving his arm around, I thought that Humphrey himself never made sweeter lines.

He then told me how Humphrey would certainly become the most learned physician of the time, and that he was already master of a polite and dignified manner which would procure him the patronage of the great and the confidence of all. It was pleasant to hear him praise his cousin without jealousy or envy. To be sure, he knew not then—though afterwards I told him—that Humphrey was his rival. Even had he known this, such was the candour of my Robin and the integrity of his soul that he would have praised him even more loudly.

One must not repeat more of the kind and lovely things that the dear boy said while we strolled together by the brook-side.

While thus abroad we walked—'twas in the forenoon, after Humphrey's visit—Sir Christopher, his grandfather, dressed in his best coat and his gold-laced hat, which he commonly kept for church, and accompanied by Madam, walked from the Manor House through the village till they came to our cottage. Then, with great ceremony, they entered, Sir Christopher bowing low and Madam dropping a deep courtesy to my mother, who sat humbly at her wheel.

'Madam,' said Sir Christopher, 'we would, with your permission, say a few words with the learned Dr. Eykin and yourself.'

My father, who had now returned and was in his room, came forth when he was called. His face had recovered something of its serenity, but his eyes were still troubled. Madam sat down, but Sir Christopher and my father stood.

'Sir,' said his Honour, 'I will proceed straight to the point. My grandson desires to marry your daughter Alice. Robin is a good lad—not a scholar if you will—for his religion, the root of the matter is in him; for the goodness of his heart I will answer; for his habit of life, he hath, so far as we can learn, acquired no vile vices of the city—he doth neither drink nor gamble, nor waste his health and strength in riotous living; and for his means they are my own. All that I have will be his. 'Tis no great estate, but 'twill serve him as it hath served me. Sir, the boy's mother and I have come to ask your daughter in marriage. We know her worth, and we are right well satisfied that our boy hath made so good and wise a choice.'

'They were marrying and giving in marriage when the Flood came; they will be marrying and giving in marriage in the Great Day of the Lord,' said my father.

'Yes, gossip; but that is no reason why they should not now be marrying and giving in marriage.'

'You ask my consent?' said my father. 'This surprises me. The child is too young: she is not yet of marriageable age'——

'Husband, she is nigh upon her twentieth birthday!'

'I thought she had been but twelve or thereabouts! My consent? Why, Sir Christopher, in the eyes of the world this is great condescension on your part to take a penniless girl. I looked, I suppose, to the marriage of my daughter some time—perhaps to a farmer—yet—yet, we are told that a virtuous woman hath a price far above rubies; and that it is she who buildeth up the house, and we are nowhere told that she must bring her husband a purse of gold. Sir Christopher, it would be the blackest ingratitude in us to deny you, even if this thing were (which I say not) against the mind of our daughter.'

'It is not—it is not,' said my mother.

'Wherefore, seeing that the young man is a good man as youths go, though in the matter of the Latin syntax he hath yet much to learn; and that his heart is disposed towards religion, I am right glad that he should take our girl to wife.'

'Bravely said!' cried Sir Christopher. 'Hands upon it, man! And we will have a merry wedding. But to-day I bid you both to come and feast with us. We will have holiday and rejoicing.'

'Yes,' said my father, 'we will feast; though to-morrow comes the Deluge.' I know now what he meant, but at that time we knew not, and it seemed to his Honour a poor way of rejoicing at the return of the boys and the betrothal of his daughter thus to be foretelling woes. 'The Vision of the Plumb-line is before mine eyes,' my father went on. 'Is the land able to bear all this? We talk of feasting and of marriages. Yet a few days, or perhaps already——But we will rejoice together, my old friend and benefactor, we will rejoice together.' With these strange words he turned and went back to his room, and after some tears with my mother, Madam went home and Sir Christopher with her. But in honour to the day he kept on his best coat.

Robin suffered me to go home, but only that I might put on my best frock (I had but two) and make my hair straight, which had been blown into curls, as was the way with my hair. And then, learning from my mother with the utmost satisfaction what had passed, he led me by the hand, as if I were already his bride, and so to the Manor House, where first Sir Christopher saluted me with great kindness, calling me his dear granddaughter, and saying that next to Robin's safe return he asked for nothing more than to see me Robin's wife. And Madam kissed me, with tears in her eyes, and said that she could desire nothing better for her son, and that she was sure I should do my best endeavours to make the boy happy. Then Humphrey, as quietly as if he had not also asked me to be his wife, kissed my hand, and wished me joy; and Mr. Boscorel also kissed me, and declared that Robin ought to be the happiest dog on earth. And so we sat down to our feast.

The conversation at dinner was graver than the occasion demanded. For though our travellers continually answered questions about the foreign lands and peoples they had seen, yet the subject returned always to the condition of the country, and to what would happen.

After dinner we sat in the garden, and the gentlemen began to talk of Right Divine and of Non-Resistance, and here it seemed to me as if Mr. Boscorel was looking on as from an eminence apart. For when he had once stated the texts and arguments upon which the High Church party do mostly rely, he retired and made no further objections, listening in silence while my father held forth upon the duty of rising against wicked princes. At last, however, being challenged to reply by Humphrey, Mr. Boscorel thus made answer:

'The doctrine that subjects may or may not rebel against their Sovereign is one which I regard with interest so long as it remains a question of logic and argument only. Unfortunately, the times are such that we may be called upon to make a practical application of it: in which case there may follow once more civil war, with hard knocks on both sides, and much loss of things temporal. Wherefore to my learned brother's arguments, which I admit to be plausible, I will, for the present, offer no reply, except to pray Heaven that the occasion may not arise of converting a disputed doctrine into a rule of conduct.'

Alas! even while he spoke the messenger was speeding swiftly towards us who was to call upon all present to take a side.

The question is now, I hope, decided for ever: but many men had first to die. It was not decided then, but three years later, when King William cut the knot, and, with the applause of the nation, pulled down his father-in-law, and mounted the throne himself with his gracious consort. We are agreed, at last, that kings, like judges, generals, and all great officers of State, are to hold their offices in good behaviour. If they enter into machinations against the liberty of the people and desert the national religion, they must descend, and let others take their place. But before that right could be established for the country, streams of blood must first flow.

While they talked, we—I mean Madam, my mother, and myself—sat and listened. But my mind was full of another subject, and I heard but little of what was said, noting chiefly the fiery ardour of my father and the careless grace of Mr. Boscorel.

Presently my father, who was never easy in the company of Mr. Boscorel—(so oil and water will not agree to fill a cup in friendship)—and, besides, being anxious to rejoin the society of his books, arose and went away, and with him my mother—he, in his ragged cassock, who was a learned scholar; she in her plain home-spun, who was a gentlewoman by birth. Often had I thought of our poverty with bitterness. But now it was with a softened heart that I saw them walk side by side across the lawns. For now I understood plainly—and for the first time—how love can strengthen and console. My mother was poor, but she was not therefore unhappy.

Mr. Boscorel also rose and went away with Humphrey. They went to talk of things more interesting to the Rector than the doctrine of Non-Resistance: of painting, namely, and statuary and medals. And when we presently walked from the Rectory gardens we heard a most gladsome scraping of fiddlestrings within, which showed that the worthy man was making the most of Humphrey's return.

When Sir Christopher had taken his pipe of tobacco he fell asleep. Robin and I walked in the garden and renewed our vows. Needs must that I should tell him all that I had done or thought since he went away. As if the simple thoughts of a country maid should be of interest to a man! Yet he seemed pleased to question and to listen, and presently broke into a rapture, swearing that he was in love with an angel. Young lovers, it is feared, may fall into grievous sin by permitting themselves these extravagances of speech and thought; yet it is hard to keep them sober, and besides (because every sin in man meeteth with its correspondent in woman), if the lover be extravagant, the maiden takes pleasure in his extravagance. To call a mortal, full of imperfections, an angel, is little short of blasphemy. Yet I heard it with, I confess, a secret pleasure. We know ourselves and the truth concerning ourselves; we do not deceive ourselves as to our imperfections; yet we are pleased that our lovers should so speak and think of us as if we were angels indeed.

Robin told me, presently ceasing his extravagances for a while, that he was certain something violent was on foot. To be sure, everybody expected so much. He said, moreover, that he believed Humphrey had certain knowledge of what was going to happen; that before they left the Low Countries Humphrey had been present at a meeting of the exiles in Rotterdam, where it was well known that Lord Argyle's expedition was resolved upon; that he had been much engaged in London after their return, and had paid many visits, the nature of which he kept secret; and that on the road there was not a town and scarcely a village where Humphrey had not someone to visit.

'My dear,' he said, 'Humphrey is slight as to stature and strength, but he carries a stout heart. There is no man more bitter against the King than he, and none more able if his counsels were listened to. Monmouth, I am certain, purposes to head an expedition into England like that of Lord Argyle in Scotland. The history of England hath many instances of such successful attempts. King Stephen, King Henry IV., King Henry VII., are all examples. If Monmouth lands, Humphrey will join him, I am sure. And I, my dear'——he paused.

'And you too, Robin? Oh! must you too go forth to fight? And yet, if the Duke doth head a rising all the world would follow. Oh! to drive away the Papist King and restore our liberty!'

'My dear, I will do what my grandfather approves. If it be my duty to go, he will send me forth.'

I had almost forgotten to say that Madam took me to her own chamber, where she opened a box and pulled out a gold chain, very fine. This she hung about my neck, and bade me sit down, and gave me some sound advice, reminding me that woman was the weaker vessel, and should look to her husband not only to love and cherish her, but also to prevent her from falling into certain grievous sins, as of temper, deceitfulness, vanity, and the like, to which the weaker nature is ever prone. Many other things she said, being a good and virtuous woman, but I pass them over.

After supper we went again into the garden, the weather being warm and fine. The sun went down, but the sky was full of light, though it was past nine o'clock and time for me to go home and to bed. Yet we lingered. The birds had gone to sleep; there was no whisper of the wind; the village was in silence. And Robin was whispering in my ear. I remember—I remember the very tones of his voice, which was low and sweet. I remember the words he said: 'Sweet love! Sweet love! How could I live so long without thee!' I remember my swelling heart and my glowing cheeks. Oh! Robin—Robin! Oh! poor heart! poor maid! The memory of this one day was nearly all thou hadst to feed upon for so long—so long a time!

CHAPTER XIV.

THE VISION OF THE BASKET.

Suddenly we heard footsteps, as of those who are running, and my father's voice speaking loud.

'Sing, O Daughter of Zion! Shout, O Israel! Be glad and rejoice with all the heart!'——

'Now, in the name of Heaven,' cried Sir Christopher, 'what meaneth this?'

'The Arm of the Lord! The Deliverance of Israel!'

He burst upon us, dragging a man with him by the arm. In the twilight I could only see, at first, that it was a broad, thick-set man. But my father's slender form looked taller as he waved his arms and cried aloud. Had he been clad in a sheepskin, he would have resembled one of those ancient Prophets whose words were always in his mouth.

'Good friend,' said Sir Christopher, 'what meaneth these cries? Whom have we here?'

Then the man with my father stepped forward and took off his hat. Why, I knew him at once; though it was ten years since I had seen him last! 'Twas my brother Barnaby—none other—come home again. He was now a great strong man—a stouter have I never seen, though he was somewhat under the middle height, broad in the shoulders, and thick of chest. Beside him Robin, though reasonable in breadth, showed like a slender sapling. But he had still the same good-natured face, though now much broader. It needed no more than the first look to know my brother Barnaby again.

'Barnaby,' I cried, 'Barnaby, hast thou forgotten me?' I caught one of his great hands—never, surely, were there bigger hands than Barnaby's! 'Hast thou forgotten me?'

'Why,' he said slowly—'twas ever a boy slow of speech and of understanding—'belike,'tis Sister.' He kissed my forehead. 'It is Sister,' he said, as if he were tasting a cup of ale and was pronouncing on its quality. 'How dost thou, Sister? Bravely, I hope. Thou art grown, Sister. I have seen my mother, and—and—she does bravely, too; though I left her crying. 'Tis their way, the happier they be.'

'Barnaby?' said Sir Christopher, 'is it thou, scapegrace? Where hast thou——But first tell us what has happened. Briefly, man.'

'In two words, Sir: the Duke of Monmouth landed the day[86] before yesterday at Lyme Regis with my Lord Grey and a company of a hundred—of whom I was one.'

The Duke had landed! Then what Robin expected had come to pass! And my brother Barnaby was with the insurgents! My heart beat fast.

'The Duke of Monmouth hath landed!' Sir Christopher repeated, and sat down again, as one who knows not what may be the meaning of the news.

'Ay, Sir, the Duke hath landed. We left Holland on the 24th of May, and we made the coast at Lyme at daybreak on Thursday the 11th. 'Tis now, I take it, Saturday. The Duke had with him on board ship Lord Grey, Mr. Andrew Fletcher of Saltoun, Mr. Heywood Dare of Taunton'——

'I know the man,' said Sir Christopher, 'for an impudent, loud-tongued fellow.'

'Perhaps he was, Sir,' said Barnaby, gravely. 'Perhaps he was, but now'——

'How "was"?'

'He was shot on Thursday evening by Mr. Fletcher for offering him violence with a cane, and is now dead.'

"Tis a bad beginning. Go on, Barnaby.'

'The Duke had also Mr. Ferguson, Colonel Venner, Mr. Chamberlain, and others whom I cannot remember. First we set Mr. Dare and Mr. Chamberlain ashore at Seatown, whence they were to carry intelligence of the rising to the Duke's friends. The Duke landed at seven o'clock with his company, in seven boats. First, he fell on his knees and prayed aloud. Then he drew his sword, and we all marched after to the market-place, where he raised his flag and caused the Declaration to be read. Here it is, your Honour.' He lugged out a copy of the Declaration, which Sir Christopher put aside, saying that he would read it in the morning.

'Then we tossed our hats and shouted "A Monmouth! A Monmouth!" Sixty stout young fellows 'listed on the spot. Then we divided our forces, and began to land the cannon—four pretty pieces as you could wish to see—and the arms, of which I doubt if we have enough, and the powder—two hundred and fifty barrels. The Duke lay on Thursday night at the George. Next day, before dawn, the country people began flocking in.'

'What gentlemen have come in?'

'I know not, Sir—my duty was most of the day on board. In the evening I received leave to ride home, and indeed, Sir Christopher, had orders to carry the Duke's Declaration to yourself. And now we shall be well rid of the King, the Pope, and the Devil!'

'Because,' said my father, solemnly—'because with lies ye have made the hearts of the righteous sad whom I have not made sad.'

'And what doest thou among this goodly company, friend Barnaby?'

'I am to be a Captain in one of the regiments,' said Barnaby, grinning with pride: 'though a sailor, yet can I fight with the best.[87] My Colonel is Mr. Holmes; and my Major, Mr. Parsons. On board the frigate I was master and navigated her.'

'There will be knocks, Barnaby; knocks, I doubt.'

'By your Honour's leave, I have been where knocks were flying for ten years, and I will take my share, remembering still the treatment of my father and the poverty of my mother.'

'It is rebellion, Barnaby!—rebellion!'

'Why, Sir, Oliver Cromwell was a rebel. And your Honour fought in the army of the Earl of Essex—and what was he but a rebel?'

I wondered to hear my brother speak with so much boldness, who ten years before had bowed low and pulled his hair in presence of his Honour. Yet Sir Christopher seemed to take this boldness in good part.

'Barnaby,' he said, 'thou art a stout and proper lad, and I doubt not thy courage—nay, I see it in thy face, which hath resolution in it and yet is modest; no ruffler or boaster art thou, friend Barnaby. Yet—yet—if rebellion fail—even rebellion in a just cause—then those who rise lose their lives in vain, and the cause is lost, until better times.' This he said as one who speaketh to himself. I saw him look upon his grandson. 'The King is—a Papist,' he said, 'that is most true. A Papist should not be suffered to rule this country. Yet to rise in rebellion! Have a care, lad! What if the time be not yet ripe? How know we who will join the Duke?'

'The people are flocking to his standard by thousands,' said Barnaby. 'When I rode away last night the Duke's secretaries were writing down their names as fast as they could be entered; they were landing the arms and already exercising the recruits. And such a spirit they show, Sir, it would do your heart good only once to witness!'

Now, as I looked at Barnaby, I became aware that he was not only changed in appearance, but that he was also very finely dressed—namely, in a scarlet coat and a sword with a silken sash, with laced ruffles, a gold-laced hat, a great wig, white breeches, and a flowered waistcoat. In the light of day, as I afterwards discovered, there were stains of wine visible upon the coat, and the ruffles were torn, and the waistcoat had marks upon it as of tar. One doth not, to be sure, expect in the sailing master of a frigate the same neatness as in a gallant of Saint James's. Yet, our runaway lad must have prospered.

'What doth the Duke intend?' Sir Christopher asked him.

'Indeed, Sir, I know not. 'Tis said by some that he will raise the West Country; and by some that he will march north into Cheshire, where he hath many friends; and by others that he will march upon London, and call upon all good Protestants to rise and join him. We look to have an army of twenty thousand within a week. As for the King, it is doubted whether he can raise a paltry five thousand to meet us. Courage, Dad'—he dared to call his[88] father, the Rev. Comfort Eykin, Doctor of Divinity, 'Dad!'—and he clapped him lustily upon the shoulder; 'thou shalt mount the pulpit yet, ay, of Westminster Abbey if it so please you!'

His father paid no heed to this conversation, being wrapt in his own thoughts.

'I know not,' said Sir Christopher, 'what to think. The news is sudden. And yet—and yet'——

'We waste time,' cried my father, stamping his foot. 'Oh! we waste the time talking. What helps it to talk? Every honest man must now be up and doing. Why, it is a plain duty laid upon us. The finger of Heaven is visible, I say, in this. Out of the very sins of Charles Stuart hath the instrument for the destruction of his race been forged. A plain duty, I say. As for me, I must preach and exhort. As for my son, who was dead and yet liveth'—he laid his hand upon Barnaby's shoulder—'time was when I prayed that he might become a godly minister of God's Word. Now I perceive clearly that the Lord hath ways of His own. My son shall fight and I shall preach. Perhaps he will rise and become another Cromwell!'——Barnaby grinned.

'Sir,' said my father, turning hotly upon his Honour, 'I perceive that thou art lukewarm. If the Cause be the Lord's, what matter for the chances? The issue is in the hands of the Lord. As for me and my household, we will serve the Lord. Yea, I freely offer myself, and my son, and my wife, and my daughter—even my tender daughter—to the Cause of the Lord. Young men and maidens, old men and children, the Voice of the Lord calleth!'

Nobody made reply; my father looked before him, as if he saw in the twilight of the summer night a vision of what was to follow. His face, as he gazed, changed. His eyes, which were fierce and fiery, softened. His lips smiled. Then he turned his face and looked upon each of us in turn—upon his son and upon his wife and upon me, upon Robin and upon Sir Christopher. 'It is, indeed,' he said, 'the Will of the Lord. Why, what though the end be violent death to me, and to all of us ruin and disaster? We do but share the afflictions foretold in the Vision of the Basket of Summer Fruit. What is death? What is the loss of earthly things compared with what shall follow to those who obey the Voice that calls? Children, let us up and be doing. As for me, I shall have a season of freedom before I die. For twenty-five years have I been muzzled or compelled to whisper and mutter in corners and hiding-places. I have been a dumb dog. I, whose heart was full and overflowing with the sweet and precious Word of God; I, to whom it is not life but death to sit in silence! Now I shall deliver my soul before I die. Sirs, the Lord hath given to every man a weapon or two with which to fight. To me he hath given an eye and a tongue for discerning and proclaiming the word of sacred doctrine. I have been muzzled—a dumb dog, I say—though sometimes I have been forced to climb among the hills and speak to the[89] bending tree-tops. Now I shall be free again, and I will speak, and all the ends of the earth shall hear.'

His eyes gleamed, he panted and gasped, and waved his arms.

'As for sister, Dad,' said Barnaby, 'she and mother may bide at home.'

'No; they shall go with me. I offer my wife, my son, my daughter, and myself to the Cause of the Lord.'

'A camp is but a rough place for a woman,' said Barnaby.

'She is offered; she is dedicated; she shall go with us.'

I know not what was in his mind, or why he wished that I should go with him, unless it was a desire to give everything that he had—to hold back nothing—to the Lord; therefore he would give his children as well as himself. As for me, my heart glowed to think that I was even worthy to join in such a Cause. What could a woman do? But that I should find out.

'Robin,' I whispered, "tis Religion calls. If I am to be among the followers of the Duke, thou wilt not remain behind?'

'Child,'—it was my mother who whispered to me; I had not seen her before—'Child, let us obey him. Perhaps it will be better for him if we are at his side. And there is Barnaby. But we must not be in their way. We shall find a place to sit aside and wait. Alas! that my son hath returned to us only to go fighting. We will go with them, daughter.'

'We should be better without women,' said Barnaby, grumbling; 'I would as lief have a woman on shipboard as in a camp. To be sure, if Dad has set his heart upon it—and then he will not stay long in camp, where the cursing of the men is already loud enough to scare a preacher out of his cassock. Dad, I say'——But my father was fallen again into a kind of rapture, and heard nothing.

'When doth the Duke begin his march?' he said suddenly.

'I know not. But we shall find him, never fear.'

'I must have speech with him at the earliest possible time. Hours are precious, and we waste them—we waste them.'

'Well, Sir, it is bedtime. To-morrow we can ride; unless, because it is the Sabbath, you would choose to wait till Monday. And as to the women, by your leave, it is madness to bring them to a camp.'

'Wait till Monday? Art thou mad, Barnaby? Art thou mad? Why, I have things to tell the Duke. Shall we waste eight precious hours? Up! let us ride all night. To-morrow is the Sabbath, and I will preach. Yea—I will preach. My soul longeth—yea, even it fainteth, for the Courts of the Lord. Quick! quick! let us mount and ride all night!'

At this moment Humphrey joined us.

'Lads,' said Sir Christopher, 'you are fresh from Holland. Knew you aught of this?'

'Sir,' said Humphrey, 'I confess that I have already told Dr. Eykin what to expect. I knew that the Duke was coming. Robin did not know, because I would not drag him into the conspiracy. I knew that the Duke was coming, and that without delay. I have myself had speech in Amsterdam with his Grace, who comes to restore the Protestant religion and to give freedom of worship to all good Protestant people. His friends have promises of support everywhere. Indeed, Sir, I think that the expedition is well planned, and is certain of support. Success is in the hands of the Lord; but we do not expect that there will be any serious opposition. With submission, Sir, I am under promise to join the Duke. I came over in advance to warn his friends, as I rode from London, of his approach. Thousands are waiting in readiness for him. But, Sir, of all this, I repeat,

Robin knew nothing. I have been for three months in the counsels of those who desire to drive forth the Popish King, but Robin have I kept in the dark.'

'Humphrey,' said Robin, reproachfully, 'am not I, also, a Protestant?'

CHAPTER XV.

A NIGHT AND MORNING.

When I read of men possessed by some Spirit—that is to say, compelled to go hither and thither where, but for the Spirit, they would not go, and to say things which they would not otherwise have said—I think of our midnight ride to Lyme, and of my father there, and of the three weeks' madness which followed. It was some Spirit—whether of good or evil, I cannot say, and I dare not so much as to question—which seized him. That he hurried away to join the Duke on the first news of his landing, without counting the cost or weighing the chances, is easy to be understood. Like Humphrey, he was led by his knowledge of the great numbers who hated the Catholic religion to believe that they, like himself, would rise with one accord. He also remembered the successful rebellion against the first Charles, and expected nothing less than a repetition of that success. This, I know, was what the exiles in Holland thought and believed. The Duke, they said, was the darling of the people; he was the Protestant champion: who would not press forward when he should draw the sword? But what other man—what man in his sober senses would have dragged his wife and daughter with him to the godless riot of a camp? Perhaps he wanted them to share his triumph, to listen while he moved the soldiers, as that ancient hermit Peter moved the people to the Holy Wars? But I know not. He said that I was to be, like Jephthah's daughter, consecrated to the Cause of the Lord; and what he meant by that I never understood.

He was so eager to start upon the journey that he would not wait a moment. The horses must be saddled; we must mount and away. Mark that they were Sir Christopher's horses which we borrowed; this also was noted afterwards for the ruin of that good old man, with other particulars: as that Monmouth's Declaration was found in the house (Barnaby brought it); one of Monmouth's Captains, Barnaby Eykin by name, had ridden from Lyme to Bradford in order to see him; he was a friend of the preacher Dr. Eykin; he was grandfather to one of the rebels and grand-uncle to another; with many other things. But these were enough.

'Surely, surely, friend,' said Sir Christopher, 'thou wilt not take wife and daughter? They cannot help the Cause; they have no place in a camp!'

'Young men and maidens: one with another. Quick! we waste the time.'

'And to ride all night? Consider, man—all night long!'

'What is a night? They will have all eternity for rest.'

'He hath set his heart upon it,' said my mother. 'Let us go—a night's weariness will not do much harm. Let us go, Sir Christopher, without further parley.'

'Go then, in the Name of God,' said the old man. 'Child, give me a kiss.' He took me in his arms and kissed me on the forehead. 'Thou art, then,' he said tenderly, 'devoted to the Protestant Cause. Why, thou art already promised to a Protestant since this morning: forget not that promise, child. Humphrey and Barnaby will protect thee—and'——

'Sir,' cried Robin quickly, 'by your leave, I alone have the right to go with her and to protect her.'

'Nay, Robin,' I said, 'stay here until Sir Christopher himself bids thee go. That will perhaps be very soon. Remember thy promise. We did not know, Robin, an hour ago, that the promise would be claimed so soon. Robin'—for he murmured—'I charge thee, remain at home until'——

'I promise thee, Sweetheart.' But he hung his head and looked ashamed.

Sir Christopher, holding my hand, stepped forth upon the grass and looked upwards into the clear sky, where in the transparent twilight we could see a few stars twinkling.

'This, friend Eykin—this, Humphrey,' he said, gravely, 'is a solemn night for all. No more fateful night hath ever fallen upon any of us; no! not that day when I joined Hampden's new regiment and followed with the army of Lord Essex. Granted that we have a righteous cause, we know not that our leader hath in him the root of the matter. To rise against the King is a most weighty matter—fatal if it fail, a dangerous precedent if it succeed. Civil war is, of all wars, the most grievous; to fight under a leader who doth not live after the Laws of God is, methinks, most dangerous. The Duke hath lit a torch which will spread flames everywhere'——

'It is the Voice of the Lord which calleth us!' my father interrupted. 'To-morrow I shall speak again to God's Elect.'

'Sir,' said Humphrey, very seriously, 'I pray you think not that this enterprise hath been rashly entered upon, nor that we depend upon the judgment of the Duke alone. It is, most unhappily, true that his life is sinful, and so is that of Lord Grey, who hath deserted his own lawful wife for her sister. But those who have pushed on the enterprise consider that the Duke is, at least, a true Protestant. They have, moreover, received solid assurances of support from every quarter. You have been kept in the dark from the beginning at my own earnest request, because, though I knew full well your opinion, I would not trouble your peace or endanger your person. Suffer us, then, to depart, and, for yourself, do nothing; and keep—oh! Sir, I entreat you—keep Robin at home until our success leaves no room for doubt.'

'Go, then, go,' said Sir Christopher; 'I have grievous misgivings that all is not well. But go, and Heaven bless the Cause!'

Robin kissed me, whispering that he would follow, and that before many days; and so we mounted and rode forth. In such hot haste did we depart that we took with us no change of raiment or any provision for the journey at all, save that Barnaby, who, as I afterwards found, never forgot the provisions, found time to get together a small parcel of bread and meat, and a flask of Canary, with which to refresh our spirits later on. We even rode away without any money.

My father rode one horse and my mother sat behind him: then I followed, Barnaby marching manfully beside me, and Humphrey rode last. The ways are rough, so that those who ride, even by daylight, go but slowly; and we, riding between high hedges, went much too slowly for my father, who, if he spoke at all, cried out impatiently, 'Quicker! Quicker! we lose the time.'

He sat bending over the horse's head, with rounded shoulders, his feet sticking out on either side, his long white hair and his ragged cassock floating in the wind. In his left hand he carried his Bible as a soldier carries his sword; on his head he wore the black silk cap in which he daily sat at work. He was praying and meditating; he was preparing the sermon which he would deliver in the morning.

Barnaby plodded on beside me: night or day made no difference to him. He slept when he could, and worked when he must. Sailors keep their watch day and night without any difference.

'It was Sir Christopher that I came after,' he told me presently. 'Mr. Dare—who hath since been killed by Mr. Fletcher—told the Duke that if Sir Christopher Challis would only come into camp, old as he is, the country gentlemen of his opinions would follow to a man, so respected is he. Well, he will not. But we have his grandnephew, Humphrey; and, if I mistake not, we shall have his grandson—if kisses mean anything. So Robin is thy Sweetheart, Sister: thou art a lucky girl. And we shall have Dad to preach to us. Well, I know not what will happen, but some will be knocked o' the head, and if Dad goes in the way of knocks——But, whatever[94] happens, he will get his tongue again—and so he will be happy.'

'As for preaching,' he went on, speaking with due pauses, because there was no hurry in these dark lanes, and he was never one of those whose words flow easily, 'if he thinks to preach daily, as they say was done in Cromwell's time, I doubt if he will find many to listen, for by the look of the fellows who are crowding into camp they will love the clinking of the can better than the division of the text. But if he cause his friends to join he will be welcomed: and for devoting his wife and daughter to the Cause, that, Sister, with submission, is rank nonsense, and the sooner you get out of the camp, if you must go there, the better. Women aboard ship are bad enough, but in camp they are the very devil.'

'Barnaby, speak not lightly of the Evil One.'

'Where shall we bestow you when the fighting comes? Well, it shall be in some safe place.'

'Oh, Barnaby! will there be fighting?'

'Good lack, child! what else will there be?'

'As the walls of Jericho fell down at the blast of the trumpet, so the King's armies will be dispersed at the approach of the Lord's soldiers.'

'That was a vast long time ago, Sister. There is now no such trumpet-work employed in war, and no priests on the march; but plenty of fighting to be done before anything is accomplished. But have no fear. The country is rising. They are sick at heart already of a Popish King. I say not that it will be easy work; but it can be done, and it will be done, before we all sit down again.'

'And what will happen when it is done?'

'Truly, I know not. When one King is sent a-packing they must needs put up another, I suppose. My father shall have the biggest church in the country to preach in; Humphrey shall be made physician to the new King—nothing less; you shall marry Robin, and he shall be made a Duke or a Lord at least; and I shall have command of the biggest ship in the King's navy, and go to fight the Spaniards, or to trade for negroes on the Guinea Coast.'

'But suppose the Duke should be defeated?'

'Well, Sister, if he is defeated it will go hard with all of us. Those who are caught will be stabbed with a Bridport dagger, as they say. Ask not such a question; as well ask a sailor what will happen to him if his ship is cast away. Some may escape in boats and some by swimming, and some are drowned, and some are cast upon savage shores. Every man must take his chance. Never again ask such a question. Nevertheless, I fear my father will get his neck as far in the noose as I myself. But remember, Sister Alice, do you and my mother keep snug. Let others carry on the rebellion, do you keep snug. For, d'ye see, a man takes his chance, and if there should happen (as there may) a defeat and the rout of these country lads, I could e'en scud by myself before the gale and[95] maybe get to a seaport and so aboard and away while the chase was hot. But for a woman! Keep snug, I say, therefore.'

The night, happily, was clear and fine. A slight breeze was blowing from the north-west, which made one shiver, yet it was not too cold. I heard the screech-owl once or twice, which caused me to tremble more than the cold. The road, when we left the highway, which is not often mended in these parts, became a narrow lane full of holes and deep ruts, or else a track across open country. But Barnaby knew the way.

It was about ten of the clock when we began our journey, and it was six in the morning when we finished it. I suppose there are few women who can boast of having taken so long a ride and in the night. Yet, strange to say, I felt no desire to sleep; nor was I wearied with the jogging of the horse, but was sustained by something of the spirit of my father. A wonderful thing it seemed to me that a simple country maid, such as myself, should help in putting down the Catholic King; women there have been who have played great parts in history—Jael, Deborah, Judith, and Esther, for example; but that I should be called (since then I have discovered that I was not called), this, indeed, seemed truly wonderful. Then I was going forth to witness the array of a gallant army about to fight for freedom and for religion, just as they were arrayed forty years before, when Sir Christopher was a young man and rode among them.

My brother, this stout Barnaby, was one of them; my father was one of them; Humphrey was one of them; and in a little while I was very sure (because Robin would feel no peace of mind if I was with the insurgents and he was still at home) my lover would be with them too. And I pictured to myself a holy and serious camp, filled with godly, sober soldiers, listening to sermons and reading the Bible, going forth to battle with hymns upon their lips; and withal so valiant that at their very first onset the battalions of the King would be shattered. Alas! anyone may guess the foolish thoughts of a girl who had no knowledge of the world, nor any experience. Yet all my life I had been taught that Resistance was at times a sacred duty, and that the Divine Right of the (so-called)

Lord's Anointed was a vain superstition. So far, therefore, was I better prepared than most women for the work in hand.

When we rode through Sherborne all the folk were a-bed and the streets were empty. From Sherborne our way lay through Yetminster and Evershott to Beaminster, where we watered and rested the horses, and took some of Barnaby's provisions. The country through which we rode was full of memories of the last great war. The castle of Sherborne was twice besieged; once by Lord Bedford, when the Marquis of Hertford held it for the King. That siege was raised; but it was afterwards taken by Fairfax, with its garrison of six hundred soldiers, and was then destroyed, so that it is now a heap of ruins; and as for Beaminster, the town hath never recovered from the great fire when Prince Maurice held[96] it, and it is still half in ruins, though the ivy hath grown over the blackened walls of the burned houses. The last great war, of which I had heard so much! And now, perhaps, we were about to begin another.

It was two o'clock in the morning when we dismounted at Beaminster. My mother sat down upon a bench and fell instantly asleep. My father walked up and down impatiently, as grudging every minute. Barnaby, for his part, made a leisurely and comfortable meal, eating his bread and meat—of which I had some—and drinking his Canary with relish, as if we were on a journey of pleasure and there was plenty of time for leisurely feeding. Presently he arose with a sigh (the food and wine being all gone), and said that, the horses being now rested, we might proceed. So he lifted my mother into her seat and we went on with the journey, the day now breaking.

The way, I say, was never tedious to me, for I was sustained by the novelty and the strangeness of the thing. Although I had a thousand things to ask Barnaby, it must be confessed that for one who had travelled so far he had marvellous little to tell. I daresay that the deck and cabins of a ship are much the same whether she be on the Spanish Main or in the Bristol Channel, and sailors, even in port, are never an observant race, except of weather and so forth. It was strange, however, only to look upon him and to mark how stout a man he was grown and how strong, and yet how he still spoke like the old Barnaby, so good-natured and so dull with his book, who was daily flogged for his Latin grammar, and bore no malice, but prepared himself to enjoy the present when the flogging was over, and not to anticipate the certain repetition of the flogging on the morrow. He spoke in the same slow way, as if speech were a thing too precious to be poured out quickly; and there was always sense in what he said (Barnaby was only stupid in the matter of syntax), though he gave me not such answers as I could have wished. However, he confessed, little by little, something of his history and adventures. When he ran away, it was, as we thought, to the port of Bristol, where he presently found a berth as cabin-boy on board a West India-man. In this truly enviable post— everybody on board has a cuff or a kick or a rope's-end for the boy—he continued for some time. 'But,' said Barnaby, 'you are not to think that the rope's-end was half so bad as my father's rod; nor the captain's oath so bad as my father's rebuke; nor the rough work and hard fare so bad as the Latin syntax.' Being so strong, and a hearty, willing lad to boot, he was quickly promoted to be an able seaman, when there were no more rope's-endings for him. Then, having an ambition above his station, and not liking his rude and ignorant companions of the fo'k'sle (which is the fore-part of a ship, where the common sailors sleep and eat), and being so fortunate as to win the good graces of the supercargo first and of the captain next, he applied his leisure time (when he had any leisure) to the method of taking observations, of calculating longitudes and latitudes, his knowledge of arithmetic having fortunately stuck in his mind longer than that of Latin. These things, I understand, are of the greatest use to a sailor and necessary to an officer. Armed with this knowledge, and the recommendation of his superiors, Barnaby was promoted from before the mast and became what they call a mate, and so rose by degrees until he was at last second captain. But by this time he had made many voyages to the West Indies, to New York and Baltimore, and to the West Coast of Africa in the service of his owners, and, I daresay, had procured much wealth for them, though but little for himself. And, being at Rotterdam upon his owners' business, he was easily persuaded—being always a stout Protestant, and desirous to strike a blow in revenge for the ejection of his father—to engage as sailing Master on board the frigate which brought over the Duke of Monmouth and his company, and then to join him on his landing. This was the sum of what he had to tell me. He had seen many strange people, wonderful things, and monsters of the deep: Indians, whom the cruelty and avarice of the Spaniards have well-nigh destroyed, the sugar plantations in the islands, negro slaves, negroes free in their own country, sharks and calamaries (of which I had read and heard)—he had seen all these things, and still remained (in his mind, I mean) as if he had seen nothing. So wonderfully made are some men that, whatever they see, they are in no way moved.

I say, then, that Barnaby answered my questions, as we rode along, briefly, and as if such matters troubled him not. When I asked him, for example, how the poor miserable slaves liked being captured and sold and put on board ship crowded together for so long a voyage, Barnaby replied that he did not know, his business being to buy them and carry them across the water, and if they rebelled on board ship to shoot them down or flog them; and when they got to Jamaica to sell them: where, if they would not work, they would be flogged until they came to a better mind. If a man was born a negro, what else, he asked, could he expect?

There was one question which I greatly desired to ask him, but dared not. It concerned the welfare of his soul. Presently, however, Barnaby answered that question, before I put it.

'Sister,' he said, 'my mother's constant affliction concerning me, before I ran away, was as to the salvation of my soul. And truly, that formerly seemed to me so difficult a thing to compass (like navigation to an unknown port over an unknown sea set everywhere with hidden rocks and liable to sudden gusts) that I could not understand how a plain man could ever succeed in it. Wherefore it comforted me mightily after I got to sea to learn on good authority that there is another way, which, compared with my father's, is light and easy. In short, Sister, though he knows it not, there is one religion for landsfolk and another for sailor-folk. A sailor (everybody knows) cannot get so much as a sail bent without cursing and swearing—this, which is desperately[98] wicked ashore, counts for nothing at all afloat: and so with many other things; and the long and the short of it is that if a sailor does his duty, fights his ship like a man, is true to his owners and faithful to his messmates, it matters not one straw whether he hath daily sworn great oaths, drunk himself (whenever he went ashore) as helpless as a log, and kissed a pretty girl whenever his good luck gave him the chance—which does, indeed, seldom come to most sailors'—he added this with a deep sigh—'I say, Sister, that for such a sailor, when his ship goes down with him, or when he gets a grapeshot through his vitals, or when he dies of fever, as happens often enough in the hot climates, there is no question as to the safety of his soul, but he goes straight to heaven. What he is ordered to do when he gets there,' said Barnaby, 'I cannot say; but it will be something, I doubt not, that a sailor will like to do. No catechism or Latin syntax. Wherefore, Sister, you can set my mother's heart—poor soul!—quite at rest on this important matter. You can tell her that you have conversed with me, and that I have that very same inward assurance of which my father speaks so much and at such length. The very same assurance it is—tell her that. And beg her to ask me no questions upon the matter.'

'Well, Barnaby; but art thou sure'——

'It is a heavenly comfort,' he replied, before I had time to finish, 'to have such an assurance. For why? A man that hath it doth never more trouble himself about what shall happen to him after he is dead. Therefore he goes about his duty with an easy mind; and so, Sister, no more upon this head, if you love me and desire peace of mind for my mother.'

So nothing more was said upon that subject then or afterwards. A sailor to be exempted by right of his calling from the religion of the landsman! 'Tis a strange and dangerous doctrine. But, if all sailors believe it, yet how can it be? This question, I confess, is too high for me. And as for my mother, I gave her Barnaby's message, begging her at the same time not to question him further. And she sighed, but obeyed.

Presently Barnaby asked me if we had any money.

I had none, and I knew that my mother could have but little. Of course, my father never had any. I doubt if he had possessed a single penny since his ejection.

'Well,' said Barnaby, 'I thought to give my money to mother. But I now perceive that if she has it she will give it to Dad; and, if he has it, he will give it all to the Duke for the Cause—wherefore, Sister, do you take it and keep it, not for me, but to be expended as seemeth you best.' He lugged out of his pocket a heavy bag. 'Here is all the money I have saved in ten years. Nay—I am not as some sailors, one that cannot keep a penny in purse, but must needs fling all away. Here are two hundred and fifty gold pieces. Take them, Alice. Hang the bag round thy neck, and never part with it, day or night. And say nothing[99] about the money either to mother or to Dad, for he will assuredly do with it as I have said. A time may come when thou wilt want it.'

Two hundred and fifty gold pieces! Was it possible that Barnaby could be so rich? I took the bag and hung it round my waist—not my neck—by the string which he had tied above the neck, and, as it was covered by my mantle, nobody ever suspected that I had this treasure. In the end, as you shall hear, it seemed to be useful.

It was now broad daylight, and the sun was up. As we drew near Bridport there stood a man in the road armed with a halbert.

'Whither go ye, good people?' he asked. 'What is your business?'

'Friend,' said Barnaby, flourishing his oaken staff, 'we ride upon our own business. Stand aside, or thou mayest henceforth have no more business to do upon this earth!'

'Ride on then—ride on,' he replied, standing aside with great meekness. This was one of the guards whom they posted everywhere upon the roads in order to stop the people who were flocking to the camp. In this way many were sent back, and many were arrested on their way to join Monmouth.

Now, as we drew near to Bridport, the time being about four o'clock, we heard the firing of guns and a great shouting.

'They have begun the fighting,' said Barnaby. 'I knew it would not be long a-coming.'

It was, in fact, the first engagement, when the Dorsetshire Militia were driven out of Bridport by the Duke's troops, and there would have been a signal victory at the very outset but for the cowardice of Lord Grey, who ran away with the Horse.

Well, it was a strange and a wonderful thing to think that close at hand were men killing each other on the Sabbath; yea, and some lying wounded on the roads; and that civil war had again begun.

'Let us push on,' said Humphrey, 'out of the way of these troops. They are but country lads all of them. If they retreat, they will run; and if they run they will be seized with a panic, and will run all the way back to Lyme, trampling on everything that is in the road.'

This was sound advice, which we followed, taking an upper track which brought us into the high road a mile or so nearer Charmouth.

I do not think there can be anywhere a finer road than that which runs from Charmouth to Lyme. It runneth over high hills, sometimes above the sea, which rolls far below, and sometimes above a great level inland plain, the name of which I have forgotten. The highest of the hills is called Golden Cap; the reason why was plainly shown this morning when the sky was clear and the sun was shining from the south-east full upon this tall pico. When we got into this road we found it full of young fellows, lusty and well-conditioned, all marching, running, walking, shouting, and singing[100] on their way to join Monmouth. Some were adorned with flowers, some wore the blue favour of the Duke, some had cockades in their hats, and some again were armed with musket or with sword; some carried pikes, some knives tied on to long poles, some had nothing but thick cudgels, which they brandished valiantly. At sight of these brave fellows my father lifted his head and waved his hand, crying 'A Monmouth! a Monmouth! Follow me, brave lads!' just as if he had been a captain encouraging his men to charge.

The church of Lyme standeth high upon the cliff which faces the sea; it is on the eastern side of the town, and before you get to the church, on the way from Charmouth, there is a broad field also on the edge of the cliff. It was this field that was the first camp of Monmouth's men. There were no tents for the men to lie in, but there were waggons filled, I suppose, with munitions of war; there were booths where things were sold, such as hot sausages fried over a charcoal fire, fried fish, lobsters and periwinkles, cold bacon and pork, bread, cheese, and such like, and barrels of beer and cider on wooden trestles. The men were haggling for the food and drink, and already one or two seemed fuddled. Some were exercising in the use of arms; some were dancing, and some singing. And no thought or respect paid at all to the Sabbath. Oh! was this the pious and godly camp which I had expected?

'Sister,' said Barnaby, 'this is a godly and religious place to which the wisdom of Dad hath brought thee. Perhaps he meaneth thee to lie in the open like the lads.'

'Where is the Duke?' asked my father, looking wrathfully at these revellers and Sabbath-breakers.

'The Duke lies at the George Inn,' said Barnaby. 'I will show the way.'

In the blue parlour of the George the Duke was at that time holding a council. There were different reports as to the Bridport affair. Already it was said that Lord Grey was unfit to lead the Horse, having been the first to run away; and some said that the Militia were driven out of the town in a panic, and some that they made a stand, and that our men had fled. I know not what was the truth, and now it matters little, except that the first action of our men brought them little honour. When the council was finished, the Duke sent word that he would receive Dr. Challis (that was Humphrey) and Dr. Comfort Eykin.

So they were introduced to the presence of his Grace, and first my father—as Humphrey told me—fell into a kind of ecstasy, praising God for the landing of the Duke, and foretelling such speedy victory as would lay the enemies of the country at his feet. He then drew forth a roll of paper in which he had set down, for the information of the Duke, the estimated number of the disaffected in every town of the south and west of England, with the names of such as could be trusted not only to risk their[101] own bodies and estates in the Cause, but would stir up and encourage their friends. There were so many on these lists that the Duke's eyes brightened as he read them.

'Sir,' he said, 'if these reports can be depended upon, we are indeed made men. What is your opinion, Dr. Challis?'

'My opinion, Sir, is that these are the names of friends and well-wishers; if they see your Grace well supported at the outset they will flock in; if not, many of them will stand aloof.'

'Will Sir Christopher join me?' asked the Duke.

'No, Sir; he is now seventy-five years of age.'

The Duke turned away. Presently he returned to the lists and asked many more questions.

'Sir,' said my father, at length, 'I have given you the names of all that I know who are well affected to the Protestant Cause; they are those who have remained faithful to the ejected Ministers. Many a time have I secretly preached to them. One thing is wanting: the assurance that your Grace will bestow upon us liberty of conscience and freedom of worship. Else will not one of them move hand or foot.'

'Why,' said the Duke, 'for what other purpose am I come? Assure them, good friend, assure them in my name; make the most solemn pledge that is in your power and in mine.'

'In that case, Sir,' said my father, 'I will at once write letters with my own hand to the brethren everywhere. There are many honest country lads who will carry the letters by ways where they are not likely to be arrested and searched. And now, Sir, I pray your leave to preach to these your soldiers. They are at present drinking, swearing, and breaking the Sabbath. The campaign which should be begun with prayer and humiliation for the sins of the country hath been begun with many deadly sins, with merriment, and with fooling. Suffer me, then, to preach to them.'

'Preach, by all means,' said the Duke. 'You shall have the parish church. I fear, Sir, that my business will not suffer me to have the edification of your sermon, but I hope that it will tend to the soberness and earnestness of my men. Forgive them, Sir, for their lightness of heart. They are for the most part young. Encourage them by promises rather than by rebuke. And so, Sir, for this occasion, farewell!'

In this way my father obtained the wish of his heart, and preached once more in a church before the people who were the young soldiers of Monmouth's army.

I did not hear that sermon, because I was asleep. It was in tones of thunder that my father preached to them. He spoke of the old war, and the brave deeds that their fathers had done under Cromwell; theirs was the victory. Now, as then, the victory should be theirs, if they carried the spirit of faithfulness into battle. He warned them of their sins, sparing none; and, in the end, he concluded with such a denunciation of the King as made[102] all who heard it, and had been taught to regard the King's Majesty as sacred, open their mouths and gape upon each other; for then, for the first time, they truly understood what it was that they were engaged to do.

While my father waited to see the Duke, Barnaby went about looking for a lodging. The town is small, and the houses were all filled, but he presently found a cottage (call it rather a hut) on the shore beside the Cobb, where, on promise of an extravagant payment, the fisherman's wife consented to give up her bed to my mother and myself. Before the bargain was concluded, I had laid myself down upon it and was sound asleep.

So I slept the whole day; though outside there was such a trampling on the beach, such a landing of stores and creaking of chains, as might have awakened the Seven Sleepers. But me nothing could awaken.

In the evening I woke up refreshed. My mother was already awake, but for weariness could not move out of her chair. The good woman of the cottage, a kindly soul, brought me rough food of some kind with a drink of water—the army had drunk up all the milk, eaten all the cheese, the butter, the eggs, and the pork, beef and mutton, in the place. And then Humphrey came and asked if I would go with him into the town to see the soldiers. So I went, and glad I was to see the sight. But Lord! to think that it was the Sabbath evening! For the main street of Lyme was full of men, swaggering with long swords at their sides and some with spurs—feathers in their hats, and pistols stuck in their belts—all were talking loud, as I am told is the custom in a camp of soldiers.

Outside the George there was a barrel on a stand, and vendors and drawers ran about with cans, fetching and carrying the liquor for which the men continually called. Then at the door of the George there appeared the Duke himself with his following of gentlemen. All rose and huzzaed while the Duke came down the steps and turned towards the camp outside the town.

I saw his face very well as he passed. Indeed, I saw him many times afterwards, but I declare that my heart sank when first I gazed upon him as he stood upon the steps of the George Inn. For on his face, plain to read, was the sadness of coming ruin. I say I knew from that moment what would be his end. Nay, I am no prophetess, nor am I a witch to know beforehand the counsels of the Almighty; yet the Lord hath permitted by certain signs the future to become apparent to those who know how to read them. In the Duke of Monmouth the signs were a restless and uneasy eye, an air of preoccupation, a trembling mouth and a hesitating manner. There was in him nothing of the confidence of one who knows that fortune is about to smile upon him. This, I say, was my first thought about the Duke, and the first thought is prophecy.

There sat beside the benches a secretary, or clerk, who took down the names of recruits. The Duke stopped and looked on. A young[103] man, in a sober suit of brown, in appearance different from the country lads, was giving in his name.

'Daniel Foe, your Grace,' said the clerk, looking up. 'He is from London.'

'From London,' the Duke repeated. 'I have many friends in London. I expect them shortly. Thou art a worthy lad and deservest encouragement.' So he passed on his way.

CHAPTER XVI.

ON THE MARCH.

At daybreak, next morning, the drums began to beat, and the trumpets began to blow, and, after breakfast, the newly-raised army marched out in such order as was possible. I have not to write a history of this rebellion, which hath already been done by able hands; I speak only of what I saw, and the things with which I was concerned.

First, then, it is true that the whole country was swiftly put into a ferment by the Duke's landing; and, had those who planned the expedition provided a proper supply of arms, the army would have quickly mustered 20,000 men, all resolute and capable of meeting any force that the King could have raised. Nay, it would have grown and swelled as it moved. But there were never enough arms from the outset. Everything at first promised well for the Duke. But there were not arms for the half of those who came in. The spirit of the Devon and Somerset Militia was lukewarm; they ran at Bridport, at Axminster, and at Chard; nay, some of them even deserted to join the Duke. There were thousands scattered about the country—those, namely, who still held to the doctrines of the persecuted ministers, and those who abhorred the Catholic religion—who wished well and would have joined—Humphrey knew well-wishers by the thousand whose names were on the lists in Holland—but how could they join when the army was so ill-found? And this was the principal reason, I have been assured, why the country gentlemen, with their following, did not come in at first—because there were no arms. How can soldiers fight when they have no arms? How could the Duke have been suffered to begin with so scanty a preparation of arms? Afterwards, when Monmouth proclaimed himself King, there were, perhaps, other reasons why the well-wishers held aloof. Some of them certainly, who were known to be friends of the Duke (among them our old friend Mr. Prideaux, of Ford Abbey), were arrested and thrown into prison, while many thousands who were flocking to the standard were either turned back upon the road or seized and thrown into prison.

As for the quality of the troops which formed the army, I know nothing, except that at Sedgemoor they continued to fight valiantly after their leaders had fled. They were raw troops—mere country lads—and their officers were, for the most part, simple tradesmen who had no knowledge of the art of war. Dare the younger was a goldsmith; Captain Perrot was a dyer; Captain Hucker, a maker of serge; and so on with all of them. It was unfortunate that Mr. Andrew Fletcher, of Saltoun, should have killed Mr. Dare the elder on the first day, because, as everybody agrees, the former was the most experienced soldier in the whole army.

The route proposed by the Duke was known to everybody. He intended to march through Taunton, Bridgwater, and Bristol to Gloucester, where he thought he would be joined by a new army raised by his friends in Cheshire. He also reckoned on receiving adherents everywhere on the road, and on easily defeating any force that the King should be able to send against him. How he fared in that notable scheme is common history.

Long before the army was ready to march, Humphrey came to advise with us. First of all, he endeavoured to have speech with my father, but in vain (henceforth my father seemed to have no thought of his wife and daughter). Humphrey, therefore, advised us to go home. 'As for your alleged dedication to the Cause,' he said, 'I think that he hath already forgotten it, seeing that it means nothing, and that your presence with us cannot help. Go home, then, Madam, and let Alice persuade Robin to stay at home in order to take care of you.'

'Nay,' said my mother; 'that may we not do. I must obey my husband, who commanded us to follow him. Whither he goeth thither also I will follow.'

Finding that she was resolute upon this point, Humphrey told us that the Duke would certainly march upon Taunton, where more than half of the town were his friends. He therefore advised that we should ride to that place—not following the army, but going across the country, most of which is a very wild and desolate part, where we should be in no danger except from gipsies and such wild people, robbers and rogues, truly, but now making the most of the disturbed state of the country, and running about the roads plundering and thieving. But he said he would himself provide us with a guide, one who knew the way, and a good stout fellow, armed with a cudgel, at least. To this my mother agreed, fearing to anger her husband if she should disturb him at his work.

Humphrey had little trouble in finding the guide for us. He was an honest lad from a place called Holford, in the Quantock Hills, who, finding that there were no arms for him, was going home again. Unhappily, when we got to Taunton, he was persuaded—partly by me, alas!—to remain. He joined Barnaby's company, and was either killed at Sedgemoor, or was one of those hanged at Weston Zoyland, or Bridgwater. For he was no more heard of.

This business settled, we went up to the churchyard in order to see the march of the army out of camp. And a brave show the gallant soldiers made.

First rode Colonel Wade with the vanguard. After them, with a due interval, rode the greater part of the Horse, already three hundred strong, under Lord Grey, of Wark. Among them was the company sent by Mr. Speke, of White Lackington, forty very stout fellows, well armed, and mounted on cart-horses. The main army was composed of four regiments. The first was the Blue Regiment, or the Duke's Own, whose Colonel was the aforesaid Wade. They formed the van, and were seven hundred strong. The others were the White, commanded by Colonel Foukes; the Green, by Colonel Holmes; and the Yellow, by Colonel Fox. All these regiments were fully armed, the men wearing favours or rosettes in their hats and on their arms of the colour from which their regiment was named.

The Duke himself, who rode a great white horse, was surrounded by a small bodyguard of gentlemen (afterwards they became a company of forty), richly dressed and well mounted. With him were carried the colours, embroidered with the words 'Pro Religione et Libertate.' This was the second time that I had seen the Duke, and again I felt at sight of his face the foreknowledge of coming woe. On such an occasion the chief should show a gallant mien and a face of cheerful hope. The Duke, however, looked gloomy, and hung his head.

Truly, it seemed to me as if no force could dare so much as to meet this great and invincible army. And certainly there could nowhere be gathered together a more stalwart set of soldiers, nearly all young men, and full of spirit. They shouted and sang as they marched. Presently there passed us my brother Barnaby, with his company of the Green Regiment. It was easy to perceive by the handling of his arms, and by his bearing, that he was accustomed to act with others, and already he had so begun to instruct his men that they set an example to the rest both in their orderliness of march and the carriage of their weapons.

After the main army they carried the ordnance—four small cannon—and the ammunition in waggons, with guards and horsemen. Lastly, there rode those who do not fight, yet belong to the army. These were the Chaplain to the army, Dr. Hooke, a grave clergyman of the Church of England; Mr. Ferguson, the Duke's private Chaplain, a fiery person, of whom many hard things have been said, which here concern us not; and my father, who thus rode openly with the other two, in order that the Nonconformists[107] might be encouraged by his presence, as an equal with the two chaplains. He was clad in a new cassock, obtained I know not whence. He sat upright in the saddle, a Bible in his hand, his long white locks lying on his shoulders like a perruque, but more venerable than any wig. His thin face was flushed with the joy of coming victory, and his eyes flashed fire. If all the men had shown such a spirit, the army would have overrun the whole country. The four surgeons—Dr. Temple, Dr. Gaylard, Dr. Oliver, and Humphrey—followed, all splendid in black velvet and great periwigs. Lastly marched the rear-guard; and after the army there followed such a motley crew as no one can conceive. There were gipsies, with their black tents and carts, ready to rob and plunder; there were tinkers who are nothing better than gipsies, and are even said to speak their language; there were men with casks on wheels filled with beer or cider; there were carts carrying bread, cakes, biscuits, and such things as one can buy in a booth or at a fair; there were women of bold and impudent looks, singing as they walked; there were, besides, whole troops of country lads, some of them mere boys, running and strutting along in hopes to receive arms and to take a place in the regiments.

Presently they were all gone, and Lyme was quit of them. What became in the end of all the rabble rout which followed the army I know not. One thing was certain: the godly disposition, the pious singing of psalms, and the devout exposition of the Word which I had looked for in the army were not anywhere apparent. Rather there was evident a tumultuous joy, as of schoolboys out for a holiday—certainly no schoolboys could have made more noise or showed greater happiness in their faces. Among them, however, there were some men of middle age, whose faces showed a different temper; but these were rare.

'Lord help them!' said our friendly fisherwoman, who stood with us. 'There will be hard knocks before those fine fellows go home again.'

'They fight on the Lord's side,' said my mother; 'therefore they may be killed, but they will not wholly perish.'

As for the hard knocks, they began without any delay, and on that very morning. For at Axminster they encountered the Somerset and Devon Militia, who thought to join their forces, but were speedily put to flight by the rebels—a victory which greatly encouraged them.

It hath been maliciously said, I have heard, that we followed the army—as if we were two sutler women—on foot, I suppose, tramping in the dust, singing ribald songs like those poor creatures whom we saw marching out of Lyme. You have heard how we agreed to follow Humphrey's advice. Well, we left Lyme very early the next morning (our fisherwoman having now become very friendly and loth to let us go) and rode out, our guide (poor lad! his death lies heavy on my soul, yet I meant the best: and, truly, he was on the side of the Lord) marching beside us armed with a stout bludgeon.[108] We kept the main road (which was very quiet at this early hour) as far as Axminster, where we left it; and, after crossing the river by a ford or wash, we engaged upon a track, or path, which led along the banks of a little stream for a mile or two—as far as the village of Chardstock. Here we made no halt; but, leaving it behind, we struck into a most wild and mountainous country full of old forests and great bare places. It is called the Forest of Neroche, and is said to shelter numbers of gipsies and vagabonds, and to have in it some of those wild people who live in the hills and woods of Somerset, and do no work except to gather the dry broom and tie it up and sell it, and so live hard and hungry lives, but know not any master. These are reported to be a harmless people, but the gipsies are dangerous because they are ready to rob and even murder. I thought of Barnaby's bag of gold tied about my waist, and trembled. However, we met with none of them on our journey, because just then they were all running after Monmouth's army. There was no path over the hills by the way we took; but our guide knew the country so well that he needed none, pointing out all the hills with a kind of pride as if they belonged to him, and telling us the name of every one; but these I have long since forgotten. The country, however, I can never forget, because it is so wild and beautiful. One place I remember. It is a very strange and wonderful place. The ground here is high, and at one place it rises to a kind of point or hill, falling away, on all sides but one, in steep sides, up which a man could climb with difficulty. Round the hill have been cut deep trenches, no doubt to fortify and strengthen the place, which is by nature a fortress. And on the side where the ground is level there are raised very high earth-works or walls with trenches beyond, most wonderful to consider. Within this double or triple circle of trenches and earthen walls there stands a farm-house, solitary among the hills. Here we found an ancient dame who told us that the place had been a castle of the Romans: yet it was not like unto the castle at Sherborne, which Oliver Cromwell slighted after he took the place, blowing it up with gunpowder: nor was it like the castle at Taunton which I afterwards saw, for there were no stone walls or towers, or any appearance of stone work. To be sure, Sherborne Castle was not built by the Romans. Then this old dame showed us bits of pots dug up within the walls, and rusty arrow heads and green copper things, which she said were buckles to fasten their clothes withal. She gave us a cup of cider while we rested and took here our dinner of cold bacon and bread which we had brought with us. After dinner our guide took us to the hill called the Beacon, and showed us the broad Vale of Taunton, spread out below us like unto a map, with its farm-houses, fields, orchards, and churches. 'And all for Monmouth,' he said. Surely there cannot be a richer, more fertile, or more lovely place in all England than the Vale of Taunton. When we had rested, and enjoyed this enchanting prospect, we remounted our nags and descended by a gradual incline[109] into the plain below. Humphrey had provided us with a letter commendatory. He, who knew the names of all who were well affected, assured us that the lady to whom the letter was addressed, Miss Susan Blake by name, was one of the most forward in the Protestant Cause. She was well known and much respected, and she kept a school for young gentlewomen, where many children of the Nonconformist gentry were educated. He instructed us to proceed directly to her house, and to ask her to procure for us a decent and safe lodging. He could not have given us a letter to any better person.

It was late in the afternoon when we rode into Taunton. The streets were full of people running about, talking now in groups and now by twos and threes; now shouting and now whispering; while we rode along the street, a man ran bawling—

'Great news! great news! Monmouth is upon us with twice ten thousand men!'

It seems that they had only that day learned of the defeat of the Militia by the rebels. A company of the Somerset Militia were in the town, under Colonel Luttrell, in order to keep down the people.

Taunton is, as everybody knows, a most rich, prosperous, and populous town. I had never before seen so many houses and so many people gathered together. Why, if the men of Taunton declared for the Duke, his cause, one felt sure, was already won. For there is nowhere, as I could not fail to know, a greater stronghold of Dissent than this town, except London, and none where the Nonconformists have more injuries to remember. Only two years before this their meeting-houses had been broken into, and their pulpits and pews brought out and burned, and they were forced, against their conscience, to worship in the parish church.

We easily found Miss Blake's house, and, giving our horses to the guide, we presented her with our letter. She was a young woman somewhat below the common stature, quick of speech, her face and eyes full of vivacity, and about thirty years of age. But when she had read the letter, and understood who we were, and whence we came, she first made a deep reverence to my mother and then she took my hands and kissed me.

'Madam,' she said, 'believe me, my poor house will be honoured indeed by the presence of the wife and the daughter of the godly Dr. Comfort Eykin. Pray, pray, go no further. I have a room that is at your disposal. Go thither, Madam, I beg, and rest after your journey. The wife of Dr. Comfort Eykin. 'Tis indeed an honour.' And so with the kindest words she led us upstairs, and gave us a room with a bed in it, and caused water for washing to be brought, and presently went out with me to buy certain things needful for us (who were indeed somewhat rustical in our dress), in order that we might present the appearance of gentlewomen—thanks to Barnaby's heavy purse, I could get them without troubling my mother's careful mind about the cost. She[110] then gave us supper, and told us all the news. The King, she said, was horribly afraid, and it was rumoured that the priests had all been sent away to France; the Taunton people were resolved to give the Duke a brave reception; all over the country, there was no doubt, men would rally by thousands; she was in a rapture of joy and gratitude. Supper over, she took us to her school-room, and here—oh! the pretty sight!—her school-girls were engaged in working and embroidering flags for the Duke's army.

'I know not,' she said, 'whether his Grace will condescend to receive them. But it is all we women can do.' Poor wretch! she afterwards suffered the full penalty for her zeal.

All that evening we heard the noise of men running about the town, with the clanking of weapons and the commands of officers; but we knew not what had happened.

Lo! in the morning the glad tidings that the Militia had left the town. Nor was that all: for at daybreak the people began to assemble, and, there being none to stay them, broke into the great church of St. Mary's and took possession of the arms that had been deposited for safety in the tower. They also opened the prison and set free a worthy Nonconformist divine, named Vincent. All the morning the mob ran about the streets, shouting, 'A Monmouth! A Monmouth!' the magistrates and Royalists not daring so much as to show their faces, and there was nothing talked of but the overthrow of the King and the triumph of the Protestant religion. Nay, there were fiery speakers in the market-place and before the west porch of the church, who mounted on tubs and exhorted the people. Grave merchants came forth and shook hands with each other; and godly ministers who had been in hiding walked forth boldly. It was truly a great day for Taunton.

The excitement grew greater when Captain Hucker, a well-known serge-maker of the town, rode in with a troop of Monmouth's Horse. Captain Hucker had been seized by Colonel Phillips on the charge of receiving a message from the Duke, but he escaped and joined the rebels, to his greater loss, as afterwards appeared. However, he now rode in to tell his fellow townsmen of his own wonderful and providential escape, and that the Duke would certainly arrive the next day, and he exhorted them to give him such a welcome as he had a right to expect at their hands. He also reminded them that they were the sons of the men who, forty years before, defended Taunton under Admiral Blake. There was a great shouting and tossing of caps after Captain Hucker's address, and no one could do too much for the horsemen with him, so that I fear these brave fellows were soon fain to lie down and sleep till the fumes of the strong ale should leave their brains.

All that day and half the night we sat in Miss Blake's school-room finishing the flags, in which I was permitted to join. There were twenty-seven flags in all presented to the army by the Taunton maids: twelve by Miss Blake, and fifteen by one Mrs. Musgrave, also a schoolmistress. And now, indeed, seeing that[111] the Militia at Axminster had fled almost at the mere aspect of one man, and that those of Taunton had also fled away secretly by night, and catching the zeal of our kind entertainer, and considering the courage and spirit of these good people, I began to feel confident again, and my heart, which had fallen very low at the sight of the Duke's hanging head and gloomy looks, rose again, and all dangers seemed to vanish. And so, in a mere fool's paradise, I continued happy indeed, until the fatal news of Sedgemoor fight awoke us all from our fond dreams.

CHAPTER XVII.

TAUNTON.

I never weary in thinking of the gaiety and happiness of those four days at Taunton among the rebels. There was no more doubt in any of our hearts: we were all confident of victory—and that easy and, perhaps, bloodless. As was the rejoicing at Taunton, so it would be in every town of the country. One only had to look out of window in order to feel assurance of that victory, so jolly, so happy, so confident looked every face.

'Why,' said Miss Blake, 'in future ages even we women, who have only worked the flags, will be envied for our share in the glorious deliverance. Great writers will speak of us as they speak of the Roman women.' Then all our eyes sparkled, and the needles flew faster and the flags grew nearer to completion.

If history should condescend to remember the poor Maids of Taunton at all, it will be, at best, with pity for the afflictions which afterwards fell upon them: none, certainly, will envy them; but we shall be forgotten. Why should we be remembered? Women, it is certain, have no business with affairs of State, and especially none with rebellions and civil wars. Our hearts and passions carry us away. The leaders in the Cause which we have joined appear to us to be more than human; we cannot restrain ourselves, we fall down and worship our leaders, especially in the cause of religion and liberty.

Now behold! On the very morning after we arrived at Taunton I was abroad in the streets with Miss Blake, looking at the town, which hath shops full of the most beautiful and precious things, and wondering at the great concourse of people (for the looms were all deserted, and the workmen were in the streets filled with a martial spirit), when I saw riding into the town no other than Robin himself. Oh! how my heart leapt up to see him! He was most gallantly dressed in a purple coat, with a crimson sash over his shoulders to carry his sword; he had pistols in his holsters, and wore great riding-boots, and with him rode a company of a dozen young men, mounted on good strong nags: why, they were men of our own village, and I knew them, every one. They were armed with muskets and pikes—I knew where those came from—and when they saw me the fellows all began to grin, and to square their shoulders so as to look more martial. But Robin leapt from his horse.

"Tis Alice!' he cried. 'Dear heart! Thou art then safe, so far? Madam, your servant.' Here he took off his hat to Miss Blake. 'Lads, ride on to the White Hart and call for what you want, and take care of the nags. This is a joyful meeting, Sweetheart.' Here he kissed me. 'The Duke, they say, draws thousands daily. I thought to find him in Taunton by this time. Why, we are as good as victorious already. Humphrey, I take it, is with his Grace. My dear, even had the Cause of Freedom failed to move me I had been dragged by the silken ropes of Love. Truly, I could not choose but come. There was the thought of these brave fellows marching to battle, and I all the time skulking at home, who had ever been so loud upon their side. And there was the thought of Humphrey, braving the dangers of the field, tender though he be, and I, strong and lusty, sitting by the fire, and sleeping on a feather bed; and always there was the thought of thee, my dear, among these rude soldiers—like Milton's lady among the rabble rout, because well I know that even Christian warriors (so-called) are not lambs; and, again, there was my grandfather, who could find no rest, but continually walked to and fro, with looks that at one time said, "Go, my son," and at others, "Nay, lest thou receive a hurt"; and the white face of my mother, which said as plain as eyes could speak: "He ought to go, he ought to go; and yet he may be killed."'

'Oh, Robin! Pray God there prove to be no more fighting.'

'Well, my dear, if I am not tedious to Madam here'——

'Oh, Sir!' said Miss Blake, 'it is a joy to hear this talk.' She told me afterwards that it was also a joy to look upon so gallant a gentleman, and such a pair of lovers. She, poor creature, had no sweetheart.

'Then on Monday,' Robin continued, 'the day before yesterday, I could refrain no longer, but laid the matter before my grandfather. Sweetheart! there is, I swear, no better man in all the world.'

'Of that I am well assured, Robin.'

'First, he said that if anything befell me he should go down in sorrow to his grave; yet that, as to his own end, an old man so near the grave should not be concerned about the manner of his end, so long as he should keep to honour and duty. Next, that in his own youth he had himself gone forth willingly to fight in the cause of Liberty, without counting the risk. Thirdly, that if my conscience did truly urge me to follow the Duke, I ought to obey that voice in the name of God. And this with tears in his eyes, and yet a lively and visible satisfaction that, as he himself had chosen, so his grandson would choose. "Sir," I said, "that voice of conscience speaks out very loudly and clearly. I cannot stifle it. Therefore, by your good leave, I will go." Then he bade me take the best horse in the stable, and gave me a purse of gold, and so I made ready.'

Miss Blake, at this point, said that she was reminded of David. It was, I suppose, because Robin was so goodly a lad to look upon; otherwise, David, though an exile, did never endeavour to pull King Saul from his throne.

'Then,' Robin continued, 'I went to my mother. She wept, because war hath many dangers and chances; but she would not say me "Nay." And in the evening when the men came home I went into the village and asked who would go with me. A dozen stout fellows—you know them all, Sweetheart—stepped forth at once; another dozen would have come, but their wives prevented them. And so, mounting them on good cart-horses, I bade farewell and rode away.'

'Sir,' said Miss Blake, 'you have chosen the better part. You will be rewarded by so splendid a victory that it will surprise all the world; and for the rest of your life—yes, and for generations afterwards—you will be ranked among the deliverers of your country. It is a great privilege, Sir, to take part in the noblest passage of English history. Oh!' she clasped her hands, 'I am sorry that I am not a man, only because I would strike a blow in this sacred Cause. But we are women, and we can but pray—and make flags. We cannot die for the Cause.'

The event proved that women can sometimes die for the Cause, because she herself, if any woman ever did, died for her Cause.

Then Robin left us in order to take steps about his men and himself. Captain Hucker received them in the name of the Duke. They joined the cavalry, and Robin was told that he should be made a Captain. This done, he rode out with the rest to meet the Duke.

Now, when his approach was known, everybody who had a horse rode forth to meet him, so that there followed him, when he entered the town, not counting his army, so great a company that they almost made another army.

As soon as it was reported that the Duke was within a mile (they had that day marched sixteen miles, from Ilminster) the church bells were set a-ringing; children came out with baskets of flowers in readiness to strew them at his feet as he should pass—there were roses and lilies and all kinds of summer flowers, so that his horse had a most delicate carpet to walk upon; the common people crowded the sides of the streets; the windows were filled with ladies, who waved their handkerchiefs and called aloud on Heaven to bless the good Duke, the brave Duke, the sweet and lovely Duke. If there were any malcontents in the town they kept snug; it would have cost them dear even to have been seen in the streets that day. The Duke showed on this occasion a face full of hope and happiness; indeed, if he had not shown a cheerful countenance on such a day, he would have been something less, or something greater, than human. I mean that he would have been either insensible and blockish not to be moved by such a welcome, or else he would have been a prophet, as foreseeing what would follow. He rode bareheaded, carrying his hat in his hand; he was[115] dressed in a shining corslet with a blue silk scarf and a purple coat; his long brown hair hung in curls upon his shoulders; his sweet lips were parted with a gracious smile; his beautiful brown eyes—never had any Prince more lovely eyes—looked pleased and benignant; truly there was never made any man more comely than the Duke of Monmouth. The face of his father, and that of his uncle, King James, were dark and gloomy, but the Duke's face was naturally bright and cheerful; King Charles's long nose in him was softened and reduced to the proportions of manly beauty; in short, there was no feature that in his father was harsh and unpleasing but was in him sweet and beautiful. If I had thought him comely and like a King's son when four years before he made his Progress, I thought him now ten times as gracious and as beautiful. He was thinner in the face, which gave his appearance the greater dignity; he had ever the most gracious smile and the most charming eyes; and at such a moment as this who could believe the things which they said about his wife and Lady Wentworth? No—they were inventions of his enemies; they must be base lies—so noble a Presence could not conceal a guilty heart; he must be as good and virtuous as he was brave and lovely. Thus we talked, sitting in the window, and thus we cheered our souls. Even now, to think how great and good he looked on that day, it is difficult to believe that he was in some matters so vile. I am not of those who expect one kind of moral conduct from one man and a different kind from another; there is but one set of commandments for rich and poor, for prince and peasant. But the pity of it—oh! the pity of it, with such a prince!

Never, in short, did one see such a tumult of joy; it is impossible to speak otherwise: the people had lost their wits with excess of joy. Nor did they show their welcome in shouting only, for all doors were thrown wide open, and supplies and necessaries of all kinds were sent to the soldiers in the camp outside the town, so that the country lads declared they had never fared more sumptuously. There now rode after the Duke several Nonconformist ministers, beside my father. Thus there was the pious Mr. Larke, of Lyme: he was an aged Baptist preacher, who thought it no shame to his profession to gird on a sword and to command a troop of Horse; and others there were, whose names I forget, who had come forth to join the deliverer.

Lord Grey rode on one side of him, and Colonel Speke on the other; Dr. Hooke, the Chaplain, and my father rode behind. My heart swelled with joy to hear how the people, when they had shouted themselves hoarse, cried out for my father, because his presence showed that they would have once more that liberty of worship for want of which they had so long languished. The Duke's own Chaplain, Mr. Ferguson, had got a naked sword in his hand, and was marching on foot, crying out, in a most vainglorious manner, 'I am Ferguson, the famous Ferguson, that Ferguson for whose head so many hundred pounds were offered. I am that man! I am that man!' He wore a great gown and a silken cassock, which consorted ill with the sword in his hand, and in the evening he preached in the great church, while my father preached in the old meeting-house to a much larger congregation, and, I venture to think, with a much more edifying discourse.

The army marched through the town in much the same order as it had marched out of Lyme, and it seemed not much bigger, but the men marched more orderly, and there was less laughing and shouting. But the streets were so thronged that the men could hardly make their way.

In the market-place the Duke halted, while his Declaration was read aloud. One thing I could not approve. They dragged forth three of the Justices—High Churchmen and standing stoutly for King James—and forced them to listen, bareheaded, to the Declaration: a thing which came near afterwards to their destruction. Yet they looked sour and unwilling, as anyone would have testified. The Declaration was a long document, and the reading of it took half an hour at least; but the people cheered all the time.

After this, they read a Proclamation, warning the soldiers against taking aught without payment. But Robin laughed, saying that this was the way with armies, where the General was always on the side of virtue, yet the soldiers were always yielding to temptation in the matter of sheep and poultry; that human nature must not be too much tempted, and that camp rations are sometimes scanty. But it was a noble Proclamation, and I cannot but believe that the robberies afterwards complained of were committed by the tattered crew who followed the camp, rather than by the brave fellows themselves.

The Duke lay at Captain Hucker's house, over against the Three Cups Inn. This was a great honour for Mr. Hucker, a plain serge-maker, and there were many who were envious, thinking that the Duke should not have gone to the house of so humble a person. It was also said that for his services Mr. Hucker boasted that he should expect nothing less than a coronet and the title of Peer, once the business was safely dispatched. A Peer to be made out of a Master Serge-maker! But we must charitably refuse to believe all that is reported, and, indeed (I say it with sorrow of that most unfortunate lady, Miss Blake), much idle tattle concerning neighbours was carried on in her house, and I was told that it was the same in every house of Taunton, so that the women spent all their time in talking of their neighbours' affairs, and what might be going on in the houses of their friends. This is a kind of talk which my father would never permit, as testifying to idle curiosity and leading to undue importance concerning things which are fleeting and trivial.

However, the Duke was bestowed in Captain Hucker's best bed—of that there was no doubt; and the bells rang and bonfires blazed, and the people sang and shouted in the streets.

CHAPTER XVIII.

THE MAIDS OF TAUNTON.

The next day was made remarkable in our eyes by an event which, though doubtless of less importance than the enlistment of a dozen recruits, seemed to us a very great thing indeed—namely, the presentation to the Duke of the colours embroidered for him by Susan Blake's school-girls. I was myself permitted to walk with the girls on this occasion, as if I had been one of them, though a stranger to the place, and but newly arrived—such was the kindness of Susan Blake and her respect for the name of the learned and pious Dr. Comfort Eykin.

At nine of the clock the girls who were to carry the flags began to gather in the school-room. There were twenty-seven in all; but twelve only were the pupils of Miss Blake. The others were the pupils of Mrs. Musgrave, another school-mistress in the town. I remember not the names of all the girls, but some of them I can still write down. One was Katharine Bovet, daughter of Colonel Bovet: she it was who walked first and named to the Duke those who followed; there was also Mary Blake, cousin of Susan, who was afterwards thrown into prison with her cousin, but presently was pardoned. Miss Hucker, daughter of Captain Hucker, the Master-Serge-maker who entertained the Duke, was another; there were three daughters of Captain Herring; two daughters of Mr. Thomas Baker, one of Monmouth's Privy Councillors; there was Mary Meade, the girl who carried the famous Golden Flag; and others whom I have forgotten. When we were assembled, being dressed all in white, and each maid wearing the Monmouth colours, we took our flags and sallied forth. In the street there was almost as great a crowd to look on as the day before, when the Duke rode in; and, certainly, it was a very pretty sight to see. First marched a man playing on the crowd very briskly; after him, one who beat a tabor, and one who played a fife; so that we had music on our march. When the music stopped, we lifted our voices and sang a Psalm all together; that done the crowder began again.

As for the procession, no one surely had ever seen the like of it! After the music walked six-and-twenty maids, the youngest eight and the eldest not more than twelve. They marched two by two, very orderly, all dressed in white with blue favours, and every girl carrying in her hands a flag of silk embroidered by herself, assisted by Miss Blake or some other older person, with devices appropriate to the nature of the enterprise in hand. For one flag had upon it, truly figured in scarlet silk, an open Bible, because it was for liberty to read and expound that book that the men were going forth to fight. Upon another was embroidered a great cross; upon a third were the arms of the Duke; a fourth bore upon it, to show the zeal of the people, the arms of the town of Taunton; and a fifth had both a Bible and a drawn sword; and so forth, every one with a legend embroidered upon it plain for all to read. The flags were affixed to stout white staves, and as the maids walked apart from each other and at a due distance, the flags all flying in the wind made a pretty sight indeed; so that some of the women who looked on shed tears. Among the flags was one which I needs must mention, because, unless the device was communicated by some person deep in the Duke's counsels, it most strangely jumped with the event of the following day. Mary Meade, poor child! carried it. We called it the Golden Flag, because it had a crown worked in gold thread upon it and the letters 'J. R.' A fringe of lace was sewn round it, so that it was the richest flag of all. What could the

Crown with the letters 'J. R.' mean, but that James, Duke of Monmouth, would shortly assume the Crown of these three kingdoms?

Last of all walked Miss Susan Blake, and I by her side. She bore in one hand a Bible bound in red leather, stamped with gold, and in the other a naked sword.

The Duke came forth to meet us, standing bareheaded before the porch. There were standing beside and behind him, the Lord Grey, his two Chaplains, Dr. Hooke and Mr. Ferguson, my father, Mr. Larke, the Baptist minister of Lyme Regis (he wore a corslet and carried a sword), and the Colonels of his regiments. His bodyguard were drawn up across the street, looking brave and splendid in their new favours. The varlets waited beyond with the horses for the Duke's party. Who, to look upon the martial array, the bravery of the Guard, the gallant bearing of all, the confidence in their looks, and the presence, which should surely bring a blessing, of the ministers of religion, would think that all this pomp and promise could be shattered at a single blow?

As each girl advanced in her turn, she knelt on one knee and offered her flag, bowing her head (we had practised this ceremony several times at the school until we were all quite perfect in our parts). Then the Duke stepped forward and raised her, tenderly kissing her. Then she stood aside holding her flag still in her hands.

My turn—because I had no flag—came last but one, Miss Susan Blake being the last. Now—I hope it was not folly, or a vainglorious desire to be distinguished by any particular notice of his Grace—I could not refrain from hanging the ring, which the Duke had given me at Ilchester five years ago, outside my dress by a blue ribbon. Miss Blake, to whom I had told the story of the ring, advised me to do so, partly to show my loyalty to the Duke, and partly because it was a pretty thing and one which some women would much desire to possess.

Miss Katharine Bovet informed the Duke that I was the daughter of the learned preacher, Dr. Comfort Eykin. When I knelt he raised me. Then, as he was about to salute me, his eyes fell upon the ring, and he looked first at me and then at the ring.

'Madam,' he said, 'this ring I ought to know. If I mistake not, there are the initials of "J. S." upon it.'

'Sir,' I replied, 'the ring was your own. Your Grace was so good as to bestow it upon me in your progress through the town of Ilchester five years ago.'

'Gad so!' he said, laughing; 'I remember now. 'Twas a sweet and lovely child whom I kissed—and now thou art a sweet and lovely maiden. Art thou truly the daughter of Dr. Comfort Eykin?'—he looked behind him; but my father neither heard nor attended, being wrapped in thought. "Tis strange: his daughter! 'Tis indeed wonderful that such a child should'——Here he stopped. 'Fair Rose of Somerset I called thee then. Fair Rose of Somerset I call thee again. Why, if I could place thee at the head of my army all England would certainly follow, as if Helen of Troy or Queen Venus herself did lead.' So he kissed me on the cheek with much warmth—more, indeed, than was necessary to show a gracious and friendly goodwill; and suffered me to step aside. 'Dr. Eykin's daughter!' he repeated, with a kind of wonder. 'How could Dr. Eykin have such a daughter!'

When I told Robin of this gracious salutation, he first turned very red and then he laughed. Then he said that everybody knew the Duke, but he must not attempt any Court freedoms in the Protestant camp; and if he were to try——Then he broke off short, changed colour again, and then he kissed me, saying that, of course, the Duke meant nothing but kindliness, but that, for his own part, he desired not his sweetheart to be kissed by anybody but himself. So I suppose my boy was jealous. But the folly of being jealous of so great a Prince, who could not possibly have the least regard for a simple country maiden, and who had known the great and beautiful Court ladies! It made me laugh to think that Robin could be so foolish as to be jealous of the Duke.

Then it was Miss Susan Blake's turn. She stepped forward very briskly, and knelt down, and placed the Bible in the Duke's left hand and the sword in his right.

'Sir,' she said (speaking the words we had made up and she had learned), 'it is in the name of the women of Taunton—nay, of the women of all England—that I give you the Book of the Word of God, the most precious treasure vouchsafed to man, so that all may learn that you are come for no other purpose than to maintain the right of the English people to search the Scriptures for themselves. I give you also, Sir, a sword with which to defend those rights. In addition, Sir, the women can only give your Grace the offering of their continual prayers in behalf of the Cause, and for the safety and prosperity of your Highness and your army.'

'Madam,' said the Duke, much moved by this spectacle of devotion, 'I am come, believe me, for no other purpose than to defend the truths contained in this book, and to seal my defence with my blood, if that need be.'

Then the Duke mounted, and we marched behind him in single file, each girl led by a soldier, till we came to the camp, when our flags were taken from us, and we returned home and took off our white dresses. I confess that I laid mine down with a sigh. White becomes every maiden, and my only wear till then had been of russet brown. And all that day we acted over again—in our talk and in our thoughts—our beautiful procession, and we repeated the condescending words of the Duke, and admired the graciousness of his kisses, and praised each other for our admirable behaviour, and listened, with pleasure unspeakable while Susan Blake prophesied that we should become immortal by the ceremony of that day.

CHAPTER XIX.

KING MONMOUTH AND HIS CAMP.

Next day, the town being thronged with people, and the young men pressing in from all quarters to enrol themselves (over four thousand joined the colours at Taunton alone), another Proclamation was read—that, namely, by which the Duke claimed the throne. Many opinions have been given as to this step. For the Duke's enemies maintain—first, that his mother was never married to King Charles the Second (indeed, there is no doubt that the King always denied the marriage); next, that an illegitimate son could never be permitted to sit upon the ancient throne of this realm; and, thirdly, that in usurping the Crown the Duke broke faith with his friends, to whom he had solemnly given his word that he would not put forward any such pretensions. Nay, some have gone so far as to allege that he was not the son of Charles at all, but of some other whom they even name; and they have pointed to his face as showing no resemblance at all to that swarthy and gloomy-looking King. On the other hand, the Duke's friends say that there were in his hands clear proofs of the marriage; that the promise given to his friends was conditional, and one which could be set aside by circumstances; that the country gentry, to whom a Republic was most distasteful, were afraid that he designed to re-establish that form of government; and, further, that his friends were all fully aware, from the beginning, of his intentions.

On these points I know nothing; but, when a thing has been done, it is idle to spend time in arguing that it was well or ill done. James, Duke of Monmouth, was now James, King of Great Britain and Ireland; and if we were all rebels before, who had risen in the name of religion and liberty, I suppose we were all ten times as much rebels now, when we had, in addition, set up another King, and declared King James to be an usurper, and no more than the Duke of York. Nay, that there might be wanting no single circumstance of aggravation, it was in this Proclamation declared that the Duke of York had caused his brother, the late King, to be secretly poisoned. I know not what foundation exists for this accusation; but I have been told that it gave offence unto many, and that it was an ill-advised thing to say.

The Proclamation was read aloud at the Market Cross by Mr. Tyley, of Taunton, on the Saturday morning, before a great concourse of people. It ended with the words, 'We, therefore, the noblemen, gentlemen, and Commons at present assembled, in the names of ourselves and of all the loyal and Protestant noblemen, gentlemen, and Commons of England, in pursuance of our duty and allegiance, and for the delivering of the Kingdom from Popery, tyranny, and oppression, do recognise, publish, and proclaim the said high and mighty Prince James, Duke of Monmouth, as lawful and rightful Sovereign and King, by the name of James II., by the grace of God, King of England, Scotland, France, and Ireland, Defender of the Faith. God save the King!'

After this the Duke was always saluted as King, prayed for as King, and styled 'His Majesty.' He also touched some (as only the King can do) for the king's-evil, and, it is said, wrought many miracles of healing—a thing which, being noised abroad, should have strengthened the faith of the people in him. But the malignity of our enemies caused these cases of healing to be denied, or else explained as fables and inventions of the Duke's friends.

Among the accessions of this day was one which I cannot forbear to mention. It was that of an old soldier who had been one of Cromwell's captains, Colonel Basset by name. He rode in—being a man advanced in years, yet still strong and hale—at the head of a considerable company raised by himself. 'Twas hoped that his example would be followed by the adhesion of many more of Cromwell's men, but the event proved otherwise. Perhaps, being old Republicans, they were deterred by the Proclamation of Monmouth as King. Perhaps they had grown slothful with age, and were now unwilling to face once more the dangers and fatigues of a campaign. Another recruit was the once-famous Colonel Perrot, who had been engaged with Colonel Blood in the robbery of the Crown Jewels—though the addition of a robber to our army was not a matter of pride. He came, it was afterwards said, because he was desperate, his fortunes broken, and with no other hope than to follow the fortunes of the Duke.

It became known in the course of the day that the army was to march on the Sunday. Therefore, everybody on Saturday evening repaired to the camp: some to bid farewell and Godspeed to their friends, and others to witness the humours of a camp. I was fortunate in having Robin for a companion and protector—the place being rough and the behaviour and language of the men coarse even beyond what one expects at a country fair. The recruits still kept pouring in from all parts; but, as I have already said, many were disheartened when they found that there were no arms, and went home again. They were not all riotous and disorderly. Some of the men, those, namely, who were older and more sober-minded, we found gathered together in groups, earnestly engaged in conversation.

'They are considering the Proclamation,' said Robin. 'Truly, we did not expect that our Duke would so soon become King. They say he is illegitimate. What then? Let him mount the throne by right of arms, as Oliver Cromwell could have done had he pleased—who asks whether Oliver was illegitimate or no? The country will not have another Commonwealth—and it will no longer endure a Catholic King. Let us have King Monmouth, then: who is there better?'

In all the camp there was none who spoke with greater cheerfulness and confidence than Robin. Yet he did not disguise from himself that there might be warm work.

'The King's troops,' he said, 'are closing in all round us. That is certain. Yet, even if they all join we are still more numerous and in much better heart; of that I am assured. At Wellington, the Duke of Albemarle commands the Devonshire Militia; Lord Churchill is at Chard with the Somerset Regiment; Lord Bath is reported to be marching upon us with the Cornishmen; the Duke of Beaufort hath the Gloucester Militia at Bristol; Lord Pembroke is at Chippenham with the Wiltshire Trainbands; Lord Feversham is on the march with the King's standing army. What then? are these men Protestants or are they Papists? Answer me that, Sweetheart.'

Alas! had they been true Protestants there would have been such an answer as would have driven King James across the water three years sooner.

The camp was now like a fair, only much finer and bigger than any fair I have ever seen. That of Lyme Regis could not be compared with it. There were booths where they sold gingerbread, cakes, ale, and cider; Monmouth favours for the recruits to sew upon their hats or sleeves; shoes and stockings were sold in some, and even chap-books were displayed. There was a puppet show with Patient Grizzle; and a stand where a monkey danced. Men and women carried about in baskets last year's withered apples, with Kentish cobs and walnuts; there were booths where they fried sausages and roasted pork all day long; tumblers and clowns were performing in others; painted and dressed-up girls danced in others; there was a bull-baiting; a man was making a fiery oration on the Duke's Proclamation: but I saw no one preaching a sermon. There were here and there companies of country lads exercising with pike and halbert; and others, more advanced, with the loading and firing of their muskets. There were tables at which sat men with cards and dice, gambling: shouting when they won and cursing when they lost; others, of more thrifty mind, sat on the ground practising their trade of tailor or cobbler—thus losing no money, though they did go soldiering; some polished weapons and sharpened swords, pikes, and scythes; nowhere did we find any reading the Bible, or singing of hymns, or listening to sermons. Save for a few groups of sober men of whom I have spoken, the love of amusement carried all away; and the officers of the army, who might have turned them back to sober thought, were not visible. Everywhere noise; everywhere beating of drums, playing of pipes, singing of songs, bowling and laughing. Among the men there ran about a number of saucy gipsy girls, their brown faces showing under red kerchiefs, their black eyes twinkling (truly they are pretty creatures to look upon when they are young; but they have no religion, and say of themselves that they have no souls). These girls talked with each other in their own language, which none out of their own nation—except the tinker-folk, who are said to be their cousins—understand. But English they talk very well, and they are so clever that, it is said, they will talk to a Somersetshire man in good broad Somerset, and to a man of Norfolk in his own speech, though he of Norfolk would not understand him of Somerset.

'They are the vultures,' said Robin, 'who follow for prey. Before the battle these women cajole the soldiers out of their money, and after the battle their men rob and even murder the wounded and plunder the dead.'

Then one of them ran and stood before us.

'Let me tell thy fortune, handsome gentleman? Let me tell thine, fair lady? A sixpence or a groat to cross my palm, Captain, and you shall know all that is to happen.'

Robin laughed, but gave her sixpence.

'Look me in the face, fair lady'—she spoke good, plain English, this black-eyed wench, though but a moment before she had been talking broad Somerset to a young recruit—'look me in the face; yes. All is not smooth. He loves you; but there will be separation and trouble. One comes between, a big man with a red face; he parts you. There is a wedding, I see your ladyship plain. Why, you are crying at it, you cry all the time; but I do not see this gentleman. Then there is another wedding—yes, another—and I see you at both. You will be twice married. Yet, be of good heart, fair lady.'

She turned away and ran after another couple, no doubt with much the same tale.

'How should there be a wedding,' I asked, 'if I am there and you not there, Robin—and I to be crying? And how could I—oh! Robin—how could I be married twice?'

'Nay, Sweetheart, she could not tell what wedding it was. She only uttered the gibberish of her trade; I am sorry that I wasted a sixpence upon her.'

'Robin, is it magic that they practise—these gipsies? Do they traffic with the Devil? We ought not to suffer witches to live amongst us.'

'Most are of opinion that they have no other magic than the art of guessing, which they learn to do very quickly, putting things together, from their appearance; so that if brother and sister walk out together they are taken to be lovers, and promised a happy marriage and many children.'

That may be so, and perhaps the fortune told by this gipsy was only guess-work. But I cannot believe it; for the event proved that she had in reality possessed an exact knowledge of what was about to happen.

Some of the gipsy women—but these were the older women, who had lost their good looks, though not their impudence—were singing songs, and those, as Robin told me, songs not fit to be sung; and one old crone, sitting before her tent beside a roaring wood fire over which hung a great saucepan, sold charms against shot and steel. The lads bought these greedily, giving sixpence apiece for them; so that the old witch must have made a sackful of money. They came and looked on shyly. Then one would say to the other, 'What thinkest, lad? Is there aught in it?' And the other would say, 'Truly, I know not; but she is a proper witch, and I'll buy one. We may have to fight. Best make sure of a whole skin.' And so he bought one, and then all bought. The husbands of the gipsy women were engaged, meantime, we understood, in robbing the farm-yards in the neighbourhood, the blame being afterwards laid upon our honest soldiers.

Then there was a ballad-monger singing a song about a man and a broom, and selling it (to those who would buy) printed on a long slip of paper. The first lines were—

There was an old man and he lived in a wood, And his trade it was making a broom,

but I heard no more, because Robin hurried me away. Then there were some who had drunk too much cider or beer, and were now reeling about with stupid faces and glassy eyes; there were some who were lying speechless or asleep upon the grass; and some were cooking supper over fires after the manner of the gipsies.

'I have seen enough, Robin,' I said. 'Alas for sacred Religion if these are her defenders!'

"Tis always so,' said Robin, 'in time of war. We must encourage our men to keep up their hearts. Should we be constantly reminding them that to-morrow half of them may be lying dead on the battle-field? Then they would mope and hang their heads, and would presently desert.'

'One need not preach of death, but one should preach of godliness and of sober joy. Look but at those gipsy wenches and those lads rolling about drunk. Are these things decent? If they escape the dangers of war, will it make them happy to look back upon the memory of this camp? Is it fit preparation to meet their Maker?'

'In times of peace, sweet Saint, these lads remember easily that in the midst of life we are in death, and they govern themselves accordingly. In times of war, every man hopes for his own part to escape with a whole skin, though his neighbour fall. That is why we are all so blithe and jolly. Let us now go home—before the night falls and the mirth becomes riotous and unseemly.'

We passed a large booth, whence there issued sounds of singing.[126] It was a roofless inclosure of canvas. Some ale-house man of Taunton had set it up. Robin drew aside the canvas door.

'Look in,' he said. 'See the brave defenders of Religion keeping up their hearts.'

It was furnished with benches and rough tables: at one end were casks. The benches were crowded with soldiers, every man with a pot before him, and the varlets were running backwards and forwards with cans of ale and cider. Most of the men were smoking pipes of tobacco, and they were singing a song which seemed to have no end. One bawled the lines, and when it came to the 'Let the hautboys play!' and the 'Huzza!' they all roared out together:—

Now, now, the Duke's health, And let the hautboys play, While the troops on their march shall roar Huzza! huzza! huzza!
Now, now, the Duke's health, And let the hautboys play, While the drums and the trumpets sound from the shore Huzza! huzza! huzza!

They sang this verse several times over. Then another began—

Now, now, Lord Grey's health, And let the hautboys play, While the troops on their march shall roar Huzza! huzza! huzza!
Now, now, Lord Grey's health, And let the hautboys play, While the drums and the trumpets sound from the shore Huzza! huzza! huzza!

Next a third voice took it up—

Now, now, the Colonel's health, And let the hautboys play,

and then a fourth and a fifth, and the last verse was bawled as lustily and with so much joy that one would have thought the mere singing would have gotten them the victory. Men are so made, I suppose, that they cannot work together without singing and music to keep up their hearts. Sailors sing when they weigh anchor; men who unlade ships sing as they carry out the bales; even Cromwell's Ironsides could not march in silence, but sang Psalms as they marched.

The sun was set and the twilight falling when we left the camp; and there was no abatement of the roaring and singing, but rather an increase.

'They will go on,' said Robin, 'until the drink or their money gives out; then they will lie down and sleep. You have now seen our camp, Sweetheart. It is not, truth to say, as decorous as a conventicle, nor is the talk so godly as in Sir Christopher's hall. For rough fellows there must be rough play; in a month these lads will be veterans; the singing will have grown stale to them; the black-eyed gipsy-women will have no more power to charm away their money; they will understand the meaning of war; the camp will be sober if it is not religious.'

So we walked homewards, I, for my part, saddened to think in what a spirit of riot these young men, whom I had pictured so full of godly zeal, were preparing to meet the chance of immediate death and judgment.

'Sweet,' said Robin, 'I read thy thoughts in thy troubled eyes. Pray for us. Some will fight none the worse for knowing that there are good women who pray for them.'

We were now back in the town; the streets were still full of people, and no one seemed to think of bed. Presently we passed the Castle Inn; the windows were open, and we could see a great company of gentlemen sitting round a table on which were candles lit and bowls full of strong drink; nearly every man had his pipe at his lips and his glass before him, and one of them was singing to the accompaniment of a guitar. Their faces were red and swollen, as if they had taken too much. At one end of the table sat Humphrey. What? could Humphrey, too, be a reveller with the rest? His face, which was gloomy, and his eyes, which were sad, showed that he was not.

'The officers have supped together,' said Robin. 'It may be long before we get such good quarters again. A cup of hipsy and a song in good fellowship, thou wilt not grudge so much?'

'Nay,' I said, "tis all of a piece. Like man, like master. Officers and men alike—all drinking and singing. Is there not one good man in all the army?'

As I spoke one finished a song at which all laughed, except Humphrey, and drummed the table with their fists and shouted.

Then one who seemed to be the president of the table turned to Humphrey.

'Doctor,' he said, 'thou wilt not drink, thou dost not laugh, and thou hast not sung. Thou must be tried by court-martial, and the sentence of the court is a brimming glass of punch or a song.'

'Then, gentlemen,' said Humphrey, smiling, 'I will give you a song. But blame me not if you mislike it: I made the song in praise of the sweetest woman in the world.' He took the guitar and struck the strings. When he began to sing, my cheeks flamed and my breath came and went, for I knew the song; he had given it to me four years agone. Who was the sweetest woman in the world? Oh! he made this song for me!—he made this song for me, and none but me! But these rude revellers would not know that—and I never guessed that the song was for me. How could I think that he would write these extravagances for me? But poets cannot mean what they say—

As rides the moon in azure skies, The twinkling stars beside; As when in splendour she doth rise, Their lesser lights they hide. So beside Celia, when her face we see, All unregarded other maidens be.[128]
As Helen in the town of Troy Shone fair beyond all thought, That to behold her was a joy By death too poorly bought. So when fair Celia deigns the lawn to grace, All life, all joy, dwells in her lovely face.

As the sweet river floweth by Green banks and alders tall, It stayeth not for prayer or sigh, Nor answereth if we call. So Celia heeds not though Love cry and weep; She heavenward wendeth while we earthward creep.

The marbled Saint, so cold and pure, Minds naught of earthly ways; Nor can man's gauds entice or lure That fixéd heavenly gaze. So Celia, though thou Queen and Empress art, To heaven, to heaven alone, belongs thy heart.

Now, while Humphrey sang this song, a hush fell upon the revellers; they had expected nothing but a common drinking-song. After the bawling and the noise and the ribaldry 'twas like a breath of fresh air after the closeness of a prison; or like a drink of pure water to one half-dead with thirst.

'Robin,' I said, 'there is one good man in the camp.' I say that while Humphrey sang this song—which, to be sure, was neither a drinking-song, nor a party song, nor a song of wickedness and folly—the company looked at each other in silence, and neither laughed nor offered to interrupt. Nay, there were signs of grace in some of their faces, which became grave and thoughtful. When Humphrey finished it he laid down the guitar and rose up with a bow, saying, 'I have sung my song, gentlemen all—and so, good-night!' and walked out of the room.

'Robin,' I said again, 'thank God there is one good man in the camp! I had forgotten Humphrey.'

'Yes,' Robin replied; 'Humphrey is a good man, if ever there was one. But he is glum. Something oppresses him. His eyes are troubled, and he hangs his head; or, if he laughs at all, it is as if he would rather cry. Yet all the way home from Holland he was joyful, save when his head was held over the side of the ship. He sang and laughed; he spoke of great things about to happen. I have never known him more happy. And now his face is gloomy, and he sighs when he thinks no one watcheth him. Perhaps, like thee, Sweet, he cannot abide the noise and riot of the camp. He would fain see every man Bible in hand. To-day he spent two hours with the Duke before the Council, and was with thy father afterwards. 'Tis certain that the Duke hath great confidence in him. Why is he so gloomy? He bitterly reproached me for leaving Sir Christopher, as if he alone had a conscience to obey or honour to remember!'

Humphrey came forth at this moment and stood for a moment on the steps. Then he heaved a great sigh and walked away slowly with hanging head, not seeing us.

'What is the matter with him?' said Robin. 'Perhaps they flout him for being a physician. These fellows have no respect for learning or for anyone who is not a country gentleman. Well, perhaps when we are on the march he will again pick up his spirits. They are going to sing again. Shall we go, Child?'

But the president called a name which made me stop a little longer.

'Barnaby!' he cried; 'jolly Captain Barnaby! Now that Doctor Graveairs hath left us we will begin the night. Barnaby, my hero, thy song. Pill up, gentlemen! The night is young, and to-morrow we march. Captain Barnaby, tip us a sea-song. Silence, gentlemen, for the Captain's song.'

It was my brother that they called upon—no other. He got up from his place at the summons and rose to his feet. Heavens! what a broad man he seemed compared with those who sat beside him! His face was red and his cheeks swollen because of the strong drink he had taken. In his hand he held a full glass of it. Robin called it hipsy—and it is a mixture of wine, brandy, and water with lemon juice and sugar—very heady and strong.

Said not Barnaby that there was one religion for a landsman and another for a sailor? I thought of that as he stood looking round him. If it were so, it would be truly a happy circumstance for most sailors; but I know not on what assurance this belief can be argued. Then Barnaby waved his hand.

'Yoho! my lads!' he shouted. 'The ship's in port and the crew has gone ashore!'

Then he began to sing in a deep voice which made the glasses ring—

Shut the door—lock the door— Out of window fling the key. Hasten; bring me more, bring me more: Fill it up. Fill it up for me. The daylight which you think, The daylight which you think, The daylight which you think, 'Tis but the candle's flicker: The morning star will never wink, The morning star will never wink, Till there cometh stint of liquor. For 'tis tipple, tipple, tipple all around the world, my lads, And the sun in drink is nightly lapped and curled, my lads, And to-night let us drink, and to-morrow we'll to sea; For 'tis tipple, tipple, tipple—yes, 'tis tipple, tipple, tipple— Makes the world and us to jee.

'Take me home, Robin,' I said, 'I have seen and heard enough. Alas! we have need of all the prayers that we can utter from the depths of our heart, and more!'

CHAPTER XX.

BENJAMIN'S WARNING.

Since I have so much to tell, before long, of Benjamin's evil conduct, it must in justice be recorded of him that at this juncture he endeavoured, knowing more of the world than we of Somerset, to warn and dissuade his cousins from taking part in any attempt which should be made in the West. And this he did by means of a letter written to his father. I know not how far the letter might have succeeded, but, unfortunately, it arrived two or three days too late—when our boys had already joined the insurgents.

'Honoured Sir,' he wrote, 'I write this epistle, being much concerned in spirit lest my grandfather, whose opinions are well known, not only in his own county, but also at the Court, should be drawn into, or become cognisant of, some attempt to raise the West Country against their lawful King. It will not be news to you that the Earl of Argyle hath landed in Scotland, where he will meet with such a reception which will doubtless cause him to repent of his rashness. It is also currently reported, and everywhere believed, that the Duke of Monmouth intends immediately to embark and cross the sea, with the design of raising the country in rebellion. The Dissenters, who have been going about with sour looks for five-and-twenty years, venture now to smile and look pleased in anticipation of another civil war. This may follow, but its termination, I think, will not be what they expect.

'I have also heard that my cousin Humphrey, Dr. Eykin's favourite pupil, who hath never concealed his opinions, hath lately returned from Holland (where the exiles are gathered), and passed through London accompanied by Robin. I have further learned that while in London he visited (but alone, without Robin's knowledge) many of those who are known to be friends of the Duke and red-hot Protestants. Wherefore, I greatly fear that he hath been in correspondence with the exiles, and is cognisant of their designs, and may even be their messenger to announce the intentions of his Protestant champion. Certain I am that should any chance occur of striking a blow for freedom of worship, my cousin, though he is weak and of slender frame, will join the attempt. He will also endeavour to draw after him everyone in his power. Therefore, my dear father, use all your influence to withstand him, and, if he must for his own part plunge into ruin, persuade my grandfather and my cousin Robin to stay quiet at home.

'I hear it on the best authority that the temper of the country, and especially in your part of it, hath been carefully studied by the Government, and is perfectly well known. Those who would risk life and lands for the Duke of Monmouth are few indeed. He may, perhaps, draw a rabble after him, but no more. The fat tradesmen, who most long for the conventicle, will not fight, though they may pray for him. The country gentlemen may be Protestants, but they are mostly for Church and King. It is quite true that his Majesty is a Roman Catholic, nor hath he ever concealed or denied his religion, being one who scorns deception. It is also true that his profession of faith is a stumbling-block to many who find it hard to reconcile their teaching of Non-Resistance and Divine Right with the introduction of the Mass and the Romish Priest. But the country had not yet forgotten the sour rule of the Independent; and, rather than suffer him to return, the people will endure a vast deal of Royal Prerogative.

'It is absolutely certain—assure my grandfather on this point, whatever he may learn from Humphrey—that the better sort will never join Monmouth, whether he comes as another Cromwell to restore the Commonwealth, or whether he aspires to the Crown and dares to maintain—a thing which King Charles did always stoutly deny—that his mother was married. Is it credible that the ancient throne of these Kingdoms should be usurped by the base-born son of Lucy Waters?

'I had last night the honour of drinking a bottle of wine with that great lawyer, Sir George Jeffreys. The conversation turned upon this subject. We were assured by the Judge that the affections of the people are wholly with the King; that the liberty of worship which he demands for himself he will also willingly extend to the country, so that the last pretence of reason for disaffection shall be removed. Why should the people run after Monmouth, when, if he were successful, he could give no more than the King is ready to give? I was also privately warned by Sir George that my grandfather's name is unfavourably noted, and his actions and speeches will be watched. Therefore, Sir, I humbly beg that you will represent to him and to my cousins, and to Dr. Eykin himself, first the hopelessness of any such enterprise and the certainty of[132] defeat; and next the punishment which will fall upon the rebels and upon those who lend them any countenance. Men of such a temper as Dr. Comfort Eykin will, doubtless, go to the scaffold willingly with their mouths full of the texts which they apply to themselves on all occasions. For such I have no pity, yet for the sake of his wife and daughter I would willingly, if I could, save him from the fate which will be his if Monmouth lands in the West. And as for my grandfather, 'tis terrible to think of his white hairs blown by the breeze while the hangman adjusts the knot; and I should shudder to see the blackened limbs of Robin stuck upon poles for all the world to see.

'It is my present intention, if my affairs permit, to follow my fortunes on the Western Circuit in the autumn, when I shall endeavour to ride from Taunton or Exeter to Bradford Orcas. My practice grows apace. Daily I am heard in the Courts. The Judges already know me and listen to me. The juries begin to feel the weight of my arguments. The attorneys besiege my chambers. For a junior I am in great demand. It is my prayer that you, Sir, may live to see your son Chancellor and a Peer of the realm. Less than Lord Chancellor will not content me. As for marriage, that might hinder my rise; I shall not marry yet. There is in your parish, Sir, one who knows my mind upon this matter. I shall be pleased to think that you will assure her—you know very well whom I mean—that my mind is unaltered, and that my way is now plain before me. So, I remain, with dutiful respect, your obedient son,

B. B.'

This letter arrived, I say, after the departure of Robin with his company of village lads.

When Mr. Boscorel had read it slowly and twice over, so as to lose no point of the contents, he sat and pondered awhile. Then he arose, and with troubled face he sought Sir Christopher, to whom he read it through. Then he waited for Sir Christopher to speak.

'The boy writes,' said his Honour, after a while, 'according to his lights. He repeats the things he hears said by his boon companions. Nay, more, he believes them. Why, it is easy for them to swear loyalty and to declare in their cups where the affections of the people are placed.'

'Sir Christopher, what is done cannot be undone. The boys are gone—alas!—but you still remain. Take heed for a space what you say as well as what you do.'

'How should they know the temper of the country?' Sir Christopher went on, regardless. 'What doth the foul-mouthed profligate Sir George Jeffreys know concerning sober and godly people? These are not noisy Templars; they are not profligates of the Court; they are not haunters of tavern and pot-house; they are not those who frequent the play-house. Judge Jeffreys knows none such. They are lovers of the Word of God; they wish to worship after their fashion; they hate the Pope and all his works. Let us hear what these men say upon the matter.'

'Nay,' said Mr. Boscorel; 'I care not greatly what they say. But would to God the boys were safe returned.'

'Benjamin means well,' Sir Christopher went on. 'I take this warning kindly; he means well. It pleases me that in the midst of the work and the feasting, which he loves, he thinks upon us. Tell him, son-in-law, that I thank him for his letter. It shows that he hath preserved a good heart.'

'As for his good heart'—Mr. Boscorel stroked his nose with his forefinger—'so long as Benjamin gets what he wants—which is Benjamin's mess, and five times the mess of any other—there is no doubt of his good heart.'

'Worse things than these,' said Sir Christopher, 'were said of us when the civil wars began. The King's troops would ride us down; the country would not join us; those of us who were not shot or cut down in the field would be afterwards hanged, drawn, and quartered. Yet we drove the King from his throne.'

'And then another King came back again. So we go up, and so we go down. But about this expedition and about these boys my mind misgives me.'

'Son-in-law,' Sir Christopher said solemnly, 'I am now old, and the eyes of my mind are dim, so that I no longer discern the signs of the times, or follow the current of the stream; moreover, we hear but little news, so that I cannot even see any of those signs. Yet to men in old age, before they pass away to the rest provided by the Lord, there cometh sometimes a vision by which they are enabled to see clearly when younger men are still groping their way in a kind of twilight. Monmouth hath landed; my boys are with him; they are rebels; should the rising fail, their lives are forfeit; and that of my dear friend Dr. Comfort Eykin's—yea, and my life as well belike, because I have been a consenting party. Ruin and death will in that event fall upon all of us. Whether it will so happen I know not, nor do I weigh the chance of that event against the voice of conscience, duty, and honour. My boys have obeyed that voice; they have gone forth to conquer or to die. My vision doth not tell me what will happen to them. But it shows me the priest flying from the country, the King flying from the throne, and that fair angel, whom we call Freedom of Conscience, returning to bless the land. To know that the laws of God will triumph—ought not that to reconcile a man, already seventy-five years of age, to death, even a death upon the gallows? What matter for this earthly body so that it be spent until the end in the service of the Lord?'

CHAPTER XXI.

WE WAIT FOR THE END.

I have said that my father from the beginning unto the end of this business was as one beside himself, being in an ecstasy or rapture of mind insomuch that he heeded nothing. The letters he sent out to his friends, the Nonconformists, either brought no answer or else they heaped loads of trouble, being intercepted and read, upon those to whom they were addressed. But he was not moved. The defection of his friends and of the gentry caused him no uneasiness. Nay, he even closed his eyes and ears to the drinking, the profane oaths, and the riotous living in the camp. Others there were, like-minded with himself, who saw the hand of the Lord in this enterprise, and thought that it would succeed by a miracle. The desertions of the men, which afterwards followed, and the defection of those who should have joined—these things were but the weeding of the host, which should be still further weeded—as in a well-known chapter in the Book of Judges—until none but the righteous should be left behind. These things he preached daily, and with mighty fervour, to all who would listen; but these were few in number.

As regards his wife and daughter he took no thought for them at all, being wholly enwrapped in his work; he did not so much as ask if we had money—to be sure, for five-and-twenty years he had never asked that question—or if we were safely bestowed; or if we were well. Never have I seen any man so careless of all earthly affections when he considered the work of the Lord. But when the time came for the army to march, what were we to do? Where should we be bestowed?

'As to following the army,' said Robin, 'that is absurd. We know not whither we may march or what the course of events may order. You cannot go home without an armed escort, for the country is up; the clubmen are out everywhere to protect their cattle and horses, a rough and rude folk they would be to meet; and the gipsies are robbing and plundering. Can you stay here until we come back, or until the country hath settled down again?'

Miss Blake generously promised that we should stay with her as long as we chose, adding many kind things about myself, out of friendship and a good heart; and so it was resolved that we should remain in Taunton, where no harm could befall us, while my father still accompanied the army to exhort the soldiers.

'I will take care of him,' said Barnaby. 'He shall not preach of a morning till he hath taken breakfast, nor shall he go to bed until he hath had his supper. So long as the provisions last out he shall have his ration. After that I cannot say. Maybe we shall all go on short commons, as hath happened to me already; and, truth to tell, I love it not. All these things belong to the voyage, and are part of our luck. Farewell, therefore, mother. Heart up!—all will go well! Kiss me, Sis; we shall all come back again. Never fear. King Monmouth shall be crowned in Westminster. Dad shall be Archbishop of Canterbury, and I shall be Captain of a King's ship. All our fortunes shall be made, and you, Sis, shall have a great estate, and shall marry whom you please—Robin or another. As for the gentry who have not come forward, hang 'em, we'll divide their estates between us and so change places, and they will be so astonished at not being shot for cowardice that they will rejoice and be glad to clean our boots. Thus shall we all be happy.'

So they marched away, Monmouth being now at the head of an army seven thousand strong, and all in such spirits that you would have thought nothing could withstand them. And when I consider, and remember how that army marched away, with the cheers of the men and the laughter and jokes of the young recruits, the tears run down my cheeks for thinking how their joy was turned to mourning, and life was exchanged for death. The last I saw of Robin was that he was turning in his saddle to wave his hand, his face full of confidence and joy. The only gloomy face in the whole army that morning was the face of Humphrey. Afterwards I learned that almost from the beginning he foresaw certain disaster. In the first place, none of those on whom the exiles of Holland had relied came into camp. These were the backbone of the Protestant party—the sturdy blood that had been freely shed against Charles I. This was a bitter disappointment. Next, he saw in the army nothing but a rabble of country lads, with such officers as Captain Hucker, the Serge-maker, instead of the country gentlemen, with their troops, as had been expected; and from the beginning he distrusted the leaders—even the Duke himself. So he hung his head and laughed not with the rest. But his doubts he kept locked up in his own heart. Robin knew none of them.

It was a pretty sight to see the Taunton maids walking out for a mile and more with their lovers who had joined Monmouth. They walked hand-in-hand with the men; they wore the Monmouth favours; they had no more doubt or fear of the event than their sweethearts. Those who visit Taunton now may see these women (now grown old) creeping about the streets lonely and sorrowful, mindful still of that Sunday morning when they saw their lovers for the last time.

When I consider the history of this expedition I am amazed that it did not succeed. It was, surely, by a special judgment of God that the victory was withheld from Monmouth and reserved for William. I say not (presumptuously) that the judgment was pronounced against the Duke on account of his sinful life, but I think it was the will of Heaven that the country should endure for three years the presence of a Prince who was continually seeking to advance the Catholic religion. The people were not yet ripe, perhaps, for that universal disgust which caused them without bloodshed (in this island at least) to pull down King James from his throne. When, I say, I consider the temper and the courage of that great army which left Taunton, greater than any which the King could bring against it; when I consider the multitudes who flocked to the standard at Bridgwater, I am lost in wonder at the event.

From Sunday, the 21st, when the army marched out of Taunton, till the news came of their rout on Sedgemoor, we heard nothing certain about them. On Tuesday the Duke of Albemarle, hearing that the army had gone, occupied Taunton with the Militia, and there were some who expected severities on account of the welcome given to the Duke and the recruits whom he obtained here. But there were no acts of revenge that I heard of—and, indeed, he did not stay long in the town. As for us, we remained under the shelter of Miss Blake's roof, and daily expected news of some great and signal victory. But none came, save one letter. Every day we looked for this news, and every day we planned and laid down the victorious march for our army.

'They will first occupy Bristol,' said Miss Blake. 'That is certain, because there are many stout Protestants in Bristol, and the place is important. Once master of that great city, our King will get possession of ships, and so will have a fleet. There are, no doubt, plenty of arms in the town, with which he will be able to equip an army ten times greater than that which he now has. Then with—say, thirty thousand men—he will march on London. The Militia will, of course, lay down their arms or desert at the approach of this great and resolute army. The King's regiments will prove, I expect, to be Protestants, every man. Oxford will open her gates, London will send out her train-bands to welcome the Deliverer, and so our King will enter in triumph and be crowned at Westminster Abbey, one King James succeeding another. Then there shall be restored to this distracted country'—being a schoolmistress, Miss Blake could use language worthy of the dignity of history—'the blessings of religious freedom; and the pure Word of God, stripped of superstitious additions made by man, shall be preached through the length and breadth of the land.'

'What shall be done,' I asked, 'with the Bishops?'

'They shall be suffered to remain,' she said, speaking with a voice of authority, 'for those congregations which desire a prelacy, but stripped of their titles and of their vast revenues. We will not persecute, but we will never suffer one Church to lord it over another. Oh! when will the news come? Where is the army now?'

The letter of which I have spoken was from Robin.

'Sweetheart,' he said, 'all goes well so far. At Bridgwater we have received a welcome only second to that of Taunton. The Mayor and Aldermen proclaimed our King at the High Cross, and the people have sent to the camp great store of provisions and arms of all kinds. We are now six regiments of foot with a thousand cavalry, besides the King's own body-guard. We have many good friends at Bridgwater, especially one, Mr. Roger Hoar, who is a rich merchant of the place, and is very zealous in the Cause. Your father preached on Sunday evening from the text (Deuteronomy vii. 5), "Ye shall destroy their altars, and break down their images, and cut down their groves, and burn their graven images with fire." It was a most moving discourse, which fired the hearts of all who heard it.

'They say that our chief is downhearted because the nobility and gentry have not come in. They only wait for the first victory, after which they will come in by hundreds. But some of our men look forward to depriving them of their estates, and dividing them among themselves; and already the Colonels and Majors are beginning to reckon up the great rewards which await them. As for me, there is but one reward for which I pray—namely, to return unto Bradford Orcas and to the arms of my sweet saint. Lord Churchill is reported to be at Chard; there has been a brush in the Forest of Neroche between the scouts, and it is said that all the roads are guarded so that recruits shall be arrested or at least driven back. Perhaps this is the reason why the gentry sit down. Barnaby says that so far there have been provisions enough and to spare; and he hopes the present plenty may continue. No ship's crew can fight, he says, on half rations. Our march will be on Bristol. I hope and believe that when we have gotten that great town our end is sure. Humphrey continueth glum.'

Many women there were who passed that time in prayer, continually offering up supplications on behalf of husband, brother, lover or son. But at Taunton the Vicar, one Walter Harte, a zealous High Churchman, came forth from hiding, and, with the magistrates, said prayers daily for King James II.

To tell what follows is to renew a time of agony unspeakable. Yet must it be told. Farewell, happy days of hope and confidence! Farewell, the sweet exchange of dreams! Farewell to our lovely hero, the gracious Duke! All the troubles that man's mind can conceive were permitted to be rained upon our heads—defeat, wounds, death, prison—nay, for me such a thing as no one could have expected or even feared—such a fate as never entered the mind of man to invent.

When the Duke marched out of Bridgwater, across Sedgemoorto Glastonbury, the weather, which had been hot and fine, became cold and rainy, which made the men uncomfortable. At Glastonbury they camped in the ruins of the old abbey. Thence they went to Shepton Mallet, the spirits of the men still being high. From Shepton Mallet they marched to a place called Pensford, only five miles from Bristol. Here they heard that the bridge over the Avon at Keynsham was broken down. This being presently repaired, the army marched across. They were then within easy reach of Bristol.

And now began the disasters of the enterprise. Up to this time everything had prospered. Had the Duke boldly attacked Bristol—I speak not of my own wisdom, having none in such matters, but from others' wisdom—he would have encountered no more than twenty companies or thereabouts of Militia, and a regiment of two hundred and fifty horse. Moreover, Bristol was full of Dissenters, who wanted nothing but encouragement to join the Protestant champion. Not only the Duke's friends, but also his enemies, agree in declaring that it wanted nothing but courage to take that great, rich, and populous city, where he would have found everything that he wanted—men and money, arms and ammunition. I cannot but think that for his sins, or for the sins of the nation, a judicial blindness was caused to fall upon the Duke, so that he chose, of two ways open to him, that which led to his destruction. In short, he turned away from Bristol, and drew up his forces against Bath. When he summoned that city to surrender, they shot his herald, and scoffed at him. Then, instead of taking the town, the Duke retired to Philip's Norton, where, 'tis said, he expected some great reinforcements. But none came; and he now grew greatly dejected, showing his dejection in his face, which could conceal nothing. Yet he fought an action with his half-brother, the Duke of Grafton, in which he was victorious, a thing which ought to have helped him. In this action Lieutenant Blake, Miss Blake's cousin, was killed. From Philip's Norton the army marched to Frome, and here such was the general despondency that two thousand men—a third of the whole army—deserted in the night and returned to their own homes. I think, also, it was at Frome that they learned the news of Lord Argyle's discomfiture.

Then a council was held, at which it was proposed that the army should be disbanded and ordered to return, seeing that the King had proclaimed a pardon to all who would peacefully lay down their arms and return home; and that the Duke, with Lord Grey, and those who would be certainly exempted from that pardon, should make the best of their way out of the country.

Alas! here was a way open to the safety of all those poor men; but again was the Duke permitted to choose the other way—that, namely, which led to the destruction of his army and himself. Yet they say that he himself recommended the safer course. He must have known that he wanted arms and ammunition; that his men[139] were deserting; and that no more recruits came in. Colonel Venner, one of his principal men, was at this juncture sent away to Holland in order to get assistance in arms and money. And the King's proclamation of pardon was carefully kept from the knowledge of the soldiers.

On July the 4th the army returned to Bridgwater, and now Dr. Hooke, chaplain to the army, and some of the officers were sent away secretly in order to raise an insurrection in London and elsewhere; the only hope being that risings in various parts would call away some of the King's forces from the West. Some of the Taunton men in the army rode from Bridgwater to see their friends. But we women (who, for the most part, remained at home) learned no news save that as yet there had been no signal victory: we did not hear of the large desertions nor of the Duke's despondency. Therefore, we continued in our fool's paradise and looked every day for some great and crowning mercy. Those who are on the side of the Lord are always expecting some special interference; whereas, they ought to be satisfied with being on the right side, whether victory or defeat be intended for them. In this enterprise I doubt not that those godly men (there were, I dare say, some godly men) who fell in battle, or were afterwards executed, received their reward, and that a far, far greater reward than their conduct deserved—for who can measure the short agony of death beside the everlasting life of glory and joy unspeakable?

The last day of this fatal expedition was Sunday, the fifth day of July: so that it took no more than three weeks in all between its first beginning and its failure. Only three weeks! But how much longer was it before the punishment and the expiation were concluded? Nay, are they even yet concluded when thousands of innocent women and children still go in poverty and mourning for the loss of those who should have worked for them?

In the morning my father preached to the soldiers on the text (Joshua xxii. 22), 'The Lord God of gods, the Lord God of gods, He knoweth, and Israel he shall know; if it be in rebellion, or if in transgression against the Lord, save us not this day.'

And now the time was come when the last battle was to be fought.

The Earl of Feversham, who had been at Somerton, marched this day across Sedgemoor and encamped at Weston Zoyland, which is but five or six miles from Bridgwater.

Now it chanced that one William Sparke, of Chedzoy, hearing of this advance, climbed the church tower, and, by aid of a spying-glass, such as sailors use at sea, he discerned clearly the approach of the army and its halt at Weston. Being a well-wisher to the Duke, he sent one of his men, Richard Godfrey by name, with orders to spy into and learn the position and numbers of the Earl's army, and to carry his information straightway to Bridgwater. This duty the fellow promised, and most faithfully performed.

The Duke had already learned the approach of Lord Feversham, and, being now wellnigh desperate with his continued losses, and seeing his army gradually wasting away, with no fresh recruits, he had resolved upon not waiting to be attacked, but on a retreat northwards, hoping to get across the bridge at Keynsham, and so march into Shropshire and Cheshire, where still he hoped to raise another army. But (says he who hath helped me with this brief account of the expedition) the retreat, which would have been harassed by Lord Feversham's horse, would have turned into flight; the men would have deserted in all directions; and when the remains of the army arrived at Keynsham Bridge they would certainly have found it occupied by the Duke of Beaufort.

The carriages were already loaded in readiness for this march; it was to begin at nightfall; when the arrival of the man Godfrey, and the news that he brought, caused the Duke to change everything. For he now perceived that such a chance was offered him as had never before occurred since his landing: viz., a night surprise, and, if he were fortunate, the rout of the King's best troops.

It is said that had the Duke shown the same boldness in the matter of Bristol that he showed in this night attack, he would have gained that city first and his own cause next. Nor did it appear at all a desperate attempt. For, though Lord Feversham had 2,500 men with him, horse and foot, with sixteen field-pieces, the Duke had nearly 3,000 foot (counting those armed with pikes and scythes) and 600 horse with four field-pieces, and though the King's troops included many companies of Grenadiers, with a battalion of that famous regiment the Coldstream Guards, and some hundred horse of the King's regiment and dragoons, the Duke had with him at least 2,000 men well armed and resolute, as the event showed. Besides this, he had the advantage of the surprise and confusion of a night attack. And in addition, the camp was not entrenched, the troopers had all gone to bed, the foot-soldiers were drinking cider, and the officers were reported to be all drunk.

Therefore, it was resolved that the intended flight into Shropshire should be abandoned, and that the whole matter should be brought to an issue that very night.

Had the attack succeeded, all might yet have gone well with the Duke. His enemies boasted that his raw country lads would be routed at the first charge of regular soldiers; if he proved the contrary, those who had deserted him would have returned; those who held aloof would join. It was not the Cause which found men lukewarm; it was the doubt—and nothing but the doubt—whether the Duke's enterprise would be supported. And I never heard that any found aught but commendation of the boldness and spirit which brought us to the battle of Sedgemoor.

All that day we spent in quiet meditation, in prayer, in the reading of the Bible, and in godly discourses, and herein I must commend the modesty as well as the piety of Miss Susan Blake, in that she invited my mother, as her elder and the wife of an eminent minister, to conduct the religious exercises, though as the hostess she might have demanded that privilege. We stirred not abroad at all that day. The meeting-houses, which had been opened when the Duke marched in, were now closed again.

In the evening, while we sat together discoursing upon the special mercies vouchsafed to the people of the Lord, a strange thing happened. Nay, I do not say that news may not have reached Taunton already of the Duke's intentions, and of the position of the King's forces. But this seems incredible, since it was not known—except to the council by whom it was decided—till late in the afternoon, and it was not to be thought that these would hurry to spread the news abroad, and so ruin the whole affair. The window being open, then, we could hear the voices of those who talked in the street below. Now, there passed two men, and they were talking as they went. Said one—and these were the words we heard—

'I tell thee that the Duke will have no more to do than to lock the stable doors, and so seize the troopers in their beds.'

We all started and listened. The voice below repeated—

'I say, Sir, and I have it first hand, that he hath but to lock the stable doors and so seize all the troopers in their beds.'

Then they passed on their way.

Said my mother: 'My husband hath told me that not only may the conscience be awakened by a word which seemeth chance, but the future may be revealed by words which were perhaps meant in another sense. What we have heard this evening may be a foretelling of victory. My children, let us pray, and so to bed.'

CHAPTER XXII.

THE DAY AFTER THE FIGHT.

It was five o'clock when I awoke next morning. Though the hour was so early, I heard a great trampling and running about the streets, and, looking out of window, I saw a concourse of the townspeople gathered together, listening to one who spoke to them. But in the middle of his speech they broke away from him and ran to another speaker, and so distractedly, and with such gestures, that they were clearly much moved by some news, the nature of which I could not guess. For in some faces there was visible the outward show of triumph and joy, and on others there lay plainly visible the look of amazement or stupefaction; and in the street I saw some women weeping and crying. What had happened? Oh! what had happened? Then, while I was still dressing, there burst into the room Susan Blake, herself but half dressed, her hair flying all abroad, the comb in her hand.

'Rejoice!' she cried. 'Oh! rejoice, and give thanks unto the Lord! What did we hear last night? That the Duke had but to shut the stable doors and seize the troopers in their beds. Look out of window. See the people running and listening eagerly. Oh! 'tis the crowning mercy that we have looked for: the Lord hath blown and His enemies are scattered. Remember the strange words we heard last night. What said the unknown man?—nay, he said it twice: "The Duke had but to lock the stable doors." Nay, and yesterday I saw, and last night I heard, the screech-owl thrice—which was meant for the ruin of our enemies. Oh! Alice, Alice, this is a joyful day!'

'But look,' I said, 'they have a downcast look; they run about as if distracted, and some are wringing their hands——'

"Tis with excess of joy,' she replied, looking out of the window with me, though her hair was flying in the wind. 'They are so surprised and so rejoiced that they cannot speak or move.'

'But there are women weeping and wailing; why do they weep?'

'It is for those who are killed. Needs must in every great victory that some are killed—poor brave fellows!—and some are wounded. Nay, my dear, thou hast three at least at the camp, who are dear to thee; and God knows I have many. Let us pray that we do not have to weep like those poor women.'

She was so earnest in her looks and words, and I myself so willing to believe, that I doubted no longer.

'Listen! oh! listen!' she cried; 'never, never before have bells rung a music so joyful to my heart.'

For now the bells of the great tower of St. Mary's began to ring. Clash, clash, clash, all together, as if they were cracking their throats with joy, and at the sound of the bells those men in the street, who seemed to me stupefied as by a heavy blow, put up their hands to their ears and fled as if they could not bear the noise, and the women who wept wrung their hands, and shrieked aloud in anguish, as if the joy of the chimes mocked the sorrow of their hearts.

'Poor creatures!' said Susan. 'From my heart I pity them. But the victory is ours, and now it only remains to offer up our humble prayers and praises to the Throne of all mercy.'

So we knelt and thanked God.

'O Lord! we thank and bless Thee! O Lord! we thank and bless Thee!' cried Susan, the tears of joy and gratitude running down her cheeks.

Outside, the noise of hurrying feet and voices increased, and more women shrieked, and still the joy-bells clashed and clanged.

'O Lord! we thank Thee! O Lord! we bless Thee!' Susan repeated on her knees, her voice broken with her joy and triumph. 'Twas all that she could say.

I declare that at that moment I had no more doubt of the victory than I had of the sunshine. There could be no doubt. The joy-bells were ringing: how should we know that the Rev. Mr. Harte, the Vicar, caused them to be rung, and not our friends? There could be no manner of doubt. The people running to and fro in the street had heard the news, and were rushing to tell each other and to hear more—the women who wept were mothers or wives of the slain. Again, we had encouraged each other with assurances of our success, so that we were already fully prepared to believe that it had come. Had we not seen a splendid army, seven thousand strong, march out of Taunton town, led by the bravest man and most accomplished soldier in the English nation? Was not the army on the Lord's side? Were we not in a Protestant country? Were not the very regiments of the King Protestants? Why go on? And yet—oh! sad to think!—even while we knelt and prayed, the army was scattered like a cloud of summer gnats by a shower and a breeze, and hundreds lay dead upon the field, and a thousand men were prisoners; and many were already hanging in gemmaces upon the gibbets, where they remained till King William's coming suffered them to be taken down; and the rest were flying in every direction hoping to escape.

'O Lord! we thank Thee! O Lord! we bless Thee!'

While thus we prayed we heard the door below burst open, and a trampling of a man's boots; and Susan, hastily rolling up her hair, ran downstairs, followed by mother and myself.

There stood Barnaby. Thank God! one of our lads was safe out of the fight. His face and hands were black with powder; his red coat, which had been so fine, was now smirched with mud and stained with I know not what—marks of weather, of dust, and of gunpowder; the right-hand side was torn away; he had no hat upon his head, and a bloody clout was tied about his forehead.

'Barnaby!' I cried.

'Captain Barnaby!' cried Susan, clasping her hands.

'My son!' cried mother. 'Oh! thou art wounded! Quick, Alice, child—a basin of water, quick!'

'Nay—'tis but a scratch,' he said; 'and there is no time for nursing.'

'When—where—how?' we all cried together, 'was the victory won? Is the enemy cut to pieces? Is the war finished?'

'Victory?' he repeated, in his slow way—'what victory? Give me a drink of cider, and if there is a morsel of victual in the house——'

I hurried to bring him both cold meat and bread and a cup full of cider. He began to eat and drink.

'Why,' he said, talking between his mouthfuls, 'if the worst comes 'tis better to face it with a——Your health, Madam': he finished the cider. 'Another cup, Sister, if you love me: I have neither eaten nor drunk since yesterday at seven o'clock, or thereabouts.' He said no more until he had cleared the dish of the gammon and left nothing but the bone. This he dropped into his pocket. 'When the provisions are out,' he said wisely, 'there is good gnawing in the shankbone of a ham.' Then he drank up the rest of the cider and looked around. 'Victory? Did someone speak of victory?'

'Yes—where was it? Tell us quick!'

'Well, there was in some sort a victory. But the King had it.'

'What mean you, Barnaby? The King had it?—what King?'

'Not King Monmouth. That King is riding away to find some port and get some ship, I take it, which will carry him back to Holland.'

'Barnaby, what is it? Oh! what is it? Tell us all.'

'All there is to tell, Sister, is that our army is clean cut to pieces, and that those who are not killed or prisoners are making off with what speed they may. As for me, I should have thrown away my coat and picked up some old duds and got off to Bristol and so aboard ship and away, but for Dad.'

'Barnaby,' cried my mother, 'what hath happened to him? Where is he?'

'I said, mother,' he replied very slowly, and looking in her face strangely, 'that I would look after him, didn't I? Well, when we marched out of Bridgwater at nightfall nothing would serve but he must go too. I think he compared himself with Moses who stood afar off and held up his arms. Never was there any man more eager to get at the enemy than Dad. If he had not been a minister, what a soldier he would have made!'

'Go on—quick, Barnaby.'

'I can go, Sister, no quicker than I can. That is quite sure.'

'Where is he, my son?' asked my mother.

Barnaby jerked his thumb over his left shoulder.

'He is over there, and he is safe enough for the present. Well, after the battle was over, and it was no use going on any longer, Monmouth and Lord Grey having already run away——'

'Run away? Run away?'

'Run away, Sister. Aboard ship the Captain stands by the crew to the last, and, if they strike, he is prisoner with them. Ashore, the General runs away and leaves his men to find out when they will give over fighting. We fought until there was no more ammunition, and then we ran with the rest. Now, I had not gone far before I saw lying on the moor at my very feet the poor old Dad.'

'Oh!'

'He was quite pale, and I thought he was dead. So I was about to leave him when he opened his eyes. "What cheer, Dad?" He said nothing; so I felt his pulse and found him breathing. "But what cheer, Dad?" I asked him again. "Get up if thou canst, and come with me." He looked as if he understood me not, and he shut his eyes again. Now, when you run away, the best thing is to run as fast and to run as far as you can. Yet I could not run with Dad lying in the road half dead. So while I tried to think what to do, because the murdering Dragoons were cutting us down in all directions, there came galloping past a pony harnessed to a kind of go-cart, where, I suppose, there had been a barrel or two of cider for the soldiers. The creature was mad with the noise of the guns, and I had much ado to catch him and hold the reins while I lifted Dad into the cart. When I had done that, I ran by the side of the horse and drove him off the road across the moor, which was rough going, but for dear life one must endure much, to North Marton, where I struck the road to Taunton, and brought him safe, so far.'

'Take me to him, Barnaby,' said my mother. 'Take me to him.'

'Why, mother,' he said kindly, 'I know not if 'tis wise. For, look you—if they catch us, me they will hang or shoot, though Dad they may let go, for he is sped already—and for a tender heart like thine 'twould be a piteous sight to see thy son hanging from a branch with a tight rope round his neck and thy husband dead on a hand-cart.'

'Barnaby, take me to him!—take me to him!'

'Oh! Is it true? Is it true? Oh! Captain Barnaby, is it really true? Then, why are the bells a-ringing?'

Clash! Clash! Clash! The bells rang out louder and louder. One would have thought the whole town was rejoicing. Yet there were a thousand lads in the army belonging to Taunton town alone, and I know not how many ever came home again.

'They are ringing,' said Barnaby, 'because King Monmouth's army is scattered and the rebellion is all over. Well: we have had our chance and we are undone. Now must we sing small again. Madam,' he said earnestly, addressing Susan, 'if I remember right, they were your hands that carried the naked sword and the Bible?'

'Sir, they were my hands. I am proud of that day.'

'And they were your scholars who worked the flags and gave them to the Duke that day when you walked in a procession?'

'They were my scholars,' she said proudly.

'Then, Madam, seeing that we have, if all reports be true, a damned unforgiving kind of King, my advice to you is to follow my example and run. Hoist all sail, Madam, and fly to some port—any port. Fly false colours. When hanging, flogging, branding, and the like amusements set in, I think they will remember the Maids of Taunton. That is my advice, Madam.'

'Sir,' said Susan bravely, though her cheek grew pale when he spoke of floggings and brandings, 'I thank you. Whither should I fly? Needs must I stay here and bear whatever affliction the Lord may lay upon me. And, since our Protestant hero is defeated, methinks it matters little what becomes of any of us.'

'Why,' Barnaby shook his head, 'King Monmouth is defeated, that is most true; but we who survive have got ourselves to look after. Sister, get a basket and put into it provisions.'

'What will you have, Barnaby?'

'Everything that you can find. Cold bacon for choice, and bread, and a bottle of drink if you have any, and—all you can lay hands upon. With your good leave, Madam.'

'Oh! Sir, take all—take all. I would to God that everything I have in the world could be used for the succour of these my friends!' And with that she began to weep and to cry.

I filled a great basket with all that there was in the house, and he took it upon his arm. And then we went away with many tears and fond farewells from this kind soul who had done so much for the Cause, and was now about to pay so heavy a penalty for her zeal.

Outside in the street the people recognised Barnaby for one of Monmouth's Captains, and pressed round him and asked him a thousand questions, but he answered shortly.

'We were drubbed, I tell you. King Monmouth hath run away. We have all run away. How should I know how many are killed? Every man who doth not wish to be hanged had best run away and hide. The game is up—friend, we are sped. What more can I say? How do I know, in the Devil's name, whose fault it was? How can I tell, Madam, if your son is safe? If he is safe, make him creep into a hiding-place'—and so on to a hundred who crowded after him and questioned him as to the nature and meaning of the defeat. Seeing that no more news could be got from him, the people left off following us, and we got out of the town on the east side, where the road leads to Ilminster; but it is a bad road and little frequented.

Here Barnaby looked about him carefully to make sure that no one was observing us, and then, finding that no one was within sight, he turned to the right down a grassy lane between hedges.

"Tis this way that I brought him,' he said. 'Poor old Dad! he can now move neither hand nor foot; and his legs will no more be any use to him. Yet he seemed in no pain, though the jolting of the cart must have shaken him more than a bit.'

The lane led into a field, and that field into another and a smaller one, with a plantation of larches on two sides and a brook shaded with alders on a third side. In one corner was a linney, with a thatched roof supported on wooden pillars in front and closed in at back and sides. It was such a meadow as is used for the pasture of cattle and the keeping of a bull.

At the entrance of this meadow Barnaby stopped and looked about him with approbation.

'Here,' he said slowly, 'is a hiding-place fit for King Monmouth himself. A road unfrequented; the rustics all gone off to the wars—though now, I doubt not, having had their bellyfull of fighting. I suppose there were once cattle in the meadow, but they are either driven away by the clubmen for safety, or they have been stolen by the gipsies. No troopers will this day come prying along this road, or if they do search the wood, which is unlikely, they will not look in the linney; here can we be snug until we make up our minds what course is best.'

'Barnaby,' I said, 'take us to my father without more speech.'

'I have laid him,' he went on, 'upon the bare ground in the linney; but it is soft and dry lying, and the air is warm, though last night it rained and was cold. He looks happy, mother, and I doubt if he hath any feeling left in his limbs. Once I saw a man[148] shot in the backbone and never move afterwards, but he lived for a bit. Here he is.'

Alas! lying motionless on his back, his head bare, his white hair lying over his face, his eyes closed, his cheek white, and no sign of life in him except that his breast gently heaved, was my father. Then certain words which he had uttered came back to my memory. 'What matters the end,' were the words he said, 'if I have freedom of speech for a single day?'

He had enjoyed that freedom for three weeks.

My mother threw herself on her knees beside him and raised his head.

'Ah! my heart,' she cried, 'my dear heart, my husband, have they killed thee? Speak, my dear—speak if thou canst! Art thou in pain? Can we do aught to relieve thee? Oh! is this the end of all?'

But my father made no reply. He opened his eyes, but they did not move: he looked straight before him, but he saw nothing.

And this, until the end, was the burden of all. He spoke no word to show that he knew anyone, or that he was in pain, or that he desired anything. He neither ate nor drank, yet for many weeks longer he continued to live.

CHAPTER XXIII.

IN HIDING.

Thus we began our miserable flight. Thus, in silence, we sat in the shade of the linney all the morning. Outside, the blackbird warbled in the wood and the lark sang in the sky. But we sat in silence, not daring so much as to ask each other if those things were real or if we were dreaming a dreadful dream. Still and motionless lay my father's body, as if the body of a dead man. He felt no pain—of that I am assured; it makes me sick even to think that he might have suffered pain from his wound; he had no sense at all of what was going on. Yet once or twice, during the long trance or paralysis into which he had fallen, he opened his lips as if to speak. And he breathed gently—so that he was not dead. Barnaby, for his part, threw himself upon his face, and, laying his head upon his arm, fell asleep instantly. The place was very quiet; at the end of the meadow was a brook, and there was a wood upon the other side; we could hear the prattling of the water over the pebbles; outside the linney, a great elm-tree stretched out its branches; presently I saw a squirrel sitting upon one and peering curiously at us, not at all afraid, so still and motionless we were. I remember that I envied the squirrel. He took no thought even for his daily bread. He went not forth to fight. And the hedge-sparrows, no more afraid than if the linney was empty, hopped into the place and began picking about among the straw. And so the hours slowly passed away, and by degrees I began to understand a little better what had happened to us, for at the first shock one could not perceive the extent of the disaster, and we were as in a dream when we followed Barnaby out of the town. The great and splendid army was destroyed; that gallant hero, the Duke, was in flight; those of the soldiers who were not killed or taken prisoners were running hither and thither trying to escape; my father was wounded, stricken to death, as it seemed, and deprived of power to move, to feel, or to think. While I considered this, I remembered again how he had turned his eyes from gazing into the sky, and asked me what it mattered even if the end would be death to him and ruin unto all of us. And I do firmly believe that at that moment he had an actual vision of the end, and really saw before his eyes the very things that were to come to pass, and that he knew all along what the end would be. Yet[150] he had delivered his soul—why, then he had obtained his prayer—and by daily exhortation had doubtless done much to keep up the spirit of those in the army who were sober and godly men. Did he also, like Sir Christopher, have another vision which should console and encourage him? Did he see the time to follow when a greater than the Duke should come and bring with him the deliverance of the country? There are certain gracious words with which that vision closes (the last which he did expound to us), the vision, I mean, of the Basket of Summer Fruit. Did those words ring in his mind and comfort him even in the prospect of his own end? Then my thoughts, which were swift and yet beyond my control, left him and considered the case of Barnaby. He had been a Captain in the Green Regiment; he would be hanged, for certain, if he were caught. My sweetheart, my Robin, had also been a Captain in the Duke's army. All the Duke's officers would be hanged if they were caught. But perhaps Robin was already dead—dead on the battlefield—his face white, his hands stiff, blood upon him somewhere, and a cruel wound upon his dear body! Oh, Robin! Yet I shed no tears. Humphrey, who had been one of the Duke's chyrurgeons, he would also be surely hanged if he were caught. Why—since all would be hanged—why not hang mother and me as well, and so an end!

About noon Barnaby began to stir; then he grunted and went to sleep again: presently he moved once more, then he rolled over on his broad back and went to sleep again. It was not until the sun was quite low that he awoke, sitting up suddenly, and looking about him with quick suspicion, as one who hath been sleeping in the country of an enemy, or where wild beasts are found.

Then he sprang to his feet and shook himself like a dog.

'Sister,' he said, 'thou shouldst have awakened me earlier. I have slept all the day. Well, we are safe, so far.' Here he looked cautiously out of the linney towards the wood and the road. 'So far, I say, we are safe. I take it we had best not wait until to-morrow, but budge to-night. For not only will the troopers scour the country, but they will offer rewards; and the gipsies—ay, and even the country-folk—will hasten to give information out of their greedy hearts. We must budge this very night.'

'Whither shall we go, Barnaby?'

He went on as if he had not heard my question.

'We shall certainly be safe here for to-night; but for to-morrow I doubt. Best not run the chance. For to-day their hands are full: they will be hanging the prisoners. Some they will hang first and try afterwards, some they will try first and hang afterwards. What odds if they are to be hanged in the end? The cider orchards never had such fruit as they will show this autumn, if the King prove revengeful—as, to judge by his sour face, he will be.'

Here he cursed the King, his sour face, his works and ways, his past, his present, and his future, in round language, which I hope his wounded father did not hear.

'We must lie snug for a month or two somewhere, until the unlucky Monmouth men will be suffered to return home in peace. Ay! 'twill be a month and more, I take it, before the country will be left quiet. A month and more—and Dad not able to crawl!'

'Where shall we lie snug, Barnaby?'

'That, Sister, is what I am trying to find out. How to lie snug with a couple of women and a wounded man who cannot move? 'Twas madness of the poor old Dad to bring thee to the camp, Child. For now we cannot—any of us—part company, and if we stay together 'twill maybe bring our necks to the halter.'

'Leave us, Barnaby,' I said. 'Oh! leave us to do what we can for the poor sufferer, and save thyself.'

'Ta, ta, ta, Sister—knowest not what thou sayest. Let me consider. There may be some way of safety. As for provisions, now: we have the basket full—enough for two days say—what the plague did Dad, the poor old man, want with women when fighting was on hand? When the fighting is done, I grant you, women, with the tobacco and punch, are much in place. Those are pretty songs, now, that I used to sing about women and drink.'

'Barnaby, is this a time to be talking of such things as drink and singing?'

'All times are good. Nevertheless, all company is not fitting. Wherefore, Sis, I say no more.'

'Barnaby, knowest thou aught of Robin? Or of Humphrey?'

'I know nothing. They may be dead; they may be wounded and prisoners; much I fear, knowing the spirit of the lads, that both are killed. Nay, I saw Humphrey before the fight, and he spoke to me——'

'What did Humphrey say?'

'I asked why he hung his head and looked so glum, seeing that we were at last going forth to meet the King's army. This I said because I knew Humphrey to be a lad of mettle, though his arm is thin and his body is crooked. "I go heavy, Barnaby," he said, speaking low lest others should hear, "because I see plainly that, unless some signal success come to us, this our business will end badly." Then he began to talk about the thousands who were to have been raised all over the country; how he himself had brought to the Duke promises of support gathered all the way from London to Bradford Orcas, and how his friends in Holland even promised both men and arms; but none of these promises had been kept; how Dad had brought promises of support from all the Nonconformists of the West, but hardly any, save at Taunton, had come forward; and how the army was melting away, and no more recruits coming in. And then he said that he had been the means of bringing so many to the Duke that if they died their deaths would lie upon his conscience. And he spoke lovingly of Robin and of thee, Sister. And so we parted, and I saw him no more. As for what he said, I minded it not a straw. Many a croaker turns out in the long run to be brave in the fight. Doubtless he is dead; and Robin, too. Both are dead. I take it, Sis, thou hast lost thy sweetheart. Cry a little, my dear,' he added kindly; "twill ease the pain at thy heart. 'Tis natural for a woman to cry.'

'I cannot cry, Barnaby: I wish I could. The tears rise to my eyes, but my throat is dry.'

'Try a prayer or two, Sister. 'Twas wont to comfort the heart of my mother when she was in trouble.'

'A prayer? Brother, I have done nothing but pray since this unfortunate rebellion began. A prayer? Oh, I cannot pray! If I were to pray now it would be as if my words were echoed back from a wall of solid rock. We were praying all yesterday; we made the Sabbath into a day of prayer without ceasing; and this morning, when you opened the door, we were praising and thanking God for the mercy of the great victory bestowed upon us. And at that time the poor brave men——'

'They were brave enough to the end,' said Barnaby.

'The poor brave men lying cold and dead upon the field (among them, maybe, Robin!), and the prisoners huddled together somewhere, and men hanging already upon the gibbets. We were praising God—and my father lying on the ground stricken to death, and thou a fugitive, and all of us ruined! Prayer? How could I pray from such a pit of woe?'

'Child'—my mother lifted her pale face—'in the darkest hour pray without ceasing. Even if there happen a darker hour than this, in everything, by prayer and supplication with thanksgiving, let your requests be made known—with thanksgiving, my daughter.'

Alas! I could not obey the apostolic order. 'Twas too much for me. So we fell into silence. When the sun had quite gone down Barnaby went forth cautiously. Presently he came back.

'There is no one on the road,' he said. 'We may now go on our way. The air of Taunton is dangerous to us. It breeds swift and fatal diseases. I have now resolved what to do. I will lift my father upon the cart again and put in the pony. Four or five miles sou'-west or thereabouts is Black Down, which is a No-Man's-Land. Thither will we go and hide in the combs, where no one ever comes, except the gipsies.'

'How shall we live Barnaby?'

'That,' he said, 'we shall find out when we come to look about us. There is provision for two days. The nights are warm. We shall find cover or make it with branches. There is water in the brooks and dry wood to burn. There we may, perhaps, be safe. When the country is quiet, we will make our way across the hills to Bradford Orcas, where no one will molest you, and I can go off to Bristol or Lyme, or wherever there are ships to be found. When sailors are shipwrecked, they do not begin by asking what they shall do on dry land: they ask only to feel the stones beneath their feet. We must think of nothing now but of a place of safety.'

'Barnaby, are the open hills a proper place for a wounded man?'

'Why, Child, for a choice between the hills and what else may happen if we stay here, give me the hills, even for a wounded man. But, indeed'—he whispered, so that my mother should not hear him—'he will die. Death is written on his face. I know not how long he will live. But he must die. Never did any man recover from such evil plight.'

He harnessed the pony to the cart, which was little more than a couple of planks laid side by side, and laid father upon them, just as he had brought him from Taunton. My mother made a kind of pillow for him, with grass tied up in her kerchief, and so we hoped that he would not feel the jogging of the cart.

'The stream,' said Barnaby, 'comes down from the hills. Let us follow its course upwards.'

It was a broad stream with a shallow bed, for the most part flat and pebbly, and on either side of the stream lay a strip of soft turf, broad enough for the cart to run upon. So that, as long as that lasted, we had very easy going, my mother and I walking one on each side, so as to steady the pillow and keep the poor head upon it from pain. But whether we went easy, or whether we went rough, that head made no sign of feeling aught, and lay, just as in the linney, as if dead.

I cannot tell how long we went on beside that stream. 'Twas in a wild, uncultivated country; the ground ascended; the stream became narrower and swifter; presently the friendly strip of turf failed altogether, and then we had trouble to keep the cart from upsetting. I went to the pony's head, and Barnaby, going behind the cart, lifted it over the rough places, and sometimes carried his end of it. The night was chilly; my feet were wet with splashing in the brook, and I was growing faint with hunger, when Barnaby called a halt.

'We are now,' he said, 'at the head of the stream. In half an hour, or thereabouts, it will be break of day. Let us rest. Mother, you must eat something. Come, sister, 'tis late for supper, and full early for breakfast. Take some meat and bread and half a cup of cider.'

It is all I remember of that night.

CHAPTER XXI

THE CAMP IN THE COMB.

Our camping-place, when I awoke in the morning, I found to be near the head of a most beautiful comb or valley among the Black Down Hills. I knew it not at the time, but it was not far from that old Roman stronghold which we had passed on our way to Taunton, called Castle Ratch. The hills on the Somerset side are of a gentle or gradual slope, and the valley was not deep, but yet, where we lay, so grown over with trees as to afford a complete shelter and hiding-place, while at our feet the brook took its rise in a green quagmire and began to make its way downwards among ferns and bushes, and through a wild, uncultivated country, beyond which the farms and fields began. The birds were singing, the sun was already high, and the air was warm, though there was a fresh breeze blowing. The warmth and sweetness filled my soul when I awoke, and I sat up with joy, until suddenly I remembered why we were here, and who were here with me. Then my heart sank like a lump of lead in water. I looked around. My father lay just as he had been lying all the day before, motionless, white of cheek, and as one dead, save for the slight motion of his chest and the twitching of his nostril. As I looked at him in the clear morning light, it was borne in upon me very strongly that he was indeed dead, inasmuch as his soul seemed to have fled. He saw nothing, he felt nothing. If the flies crawled over his eyelids he made no sign of disturbance; yet he breathed, and from time to time he murmured—but as one that dreameth. Beside him lay my mother sleeping, worn out by the fatigues of the night. Barnaby had spread his coat to cover her so that she should not take cold, and he had piled a little heap of dead leaves to make her a pillow. He was lying at her feet, head on arm, sleeping heavily. What should be done, I wondered, when next he woke?

First I went down the comb a little way till the stream was deep enough, and there I bathed my feet, which were swollen and bruised by the long walk up the comb. Though it was in the midst of so much misery there was a pleasure of dabbling my feet in the cool water and afterwards of walking about barefoot in the grass. I disturbed an adder which was sleeping on a flat stone in the sun, and it lifted its venomous head and hissed, but did not spring upon me. Then I washed my face and hands and made my hair as smooth as without a comb it was possible. When I had done this I remembered that perhaps my father might be thirsty or at least able to drink, though he seemed no more to feel hunger or thirst. So I filled the tin pannikin—it was Barnaby's—with water and tried to pour a little into his mouth. He seemed to swallow it, and I gave him a little more until he would swallow no more. Observe that he took no other nourishment than a little water, wine, or milk, or a few drops of broth until the end. So I covered his face with a handkerchief to keep off the flies, and left him. Then I looked into the basket. All that there was in it would not be more than enough for Barnaby's breakfast, unless his appetite should fail him by reason of fear; though, in truth, he had no fear being captured, or of anything else. There was in it a piece of bacon, a large loaf of bread, a lump of cheese, a bottle of cider; nothing more. When these provisions were gone, what next? Could we venture into the nearest village and buy food, or to the first farm-house? Then we might fall straight into the jaws of the enemy, who were probably running over the whole country in search of the fugitives. Could we buy without money? Could we beg without arousing suspicions? If the people were well-inclined to the Protestant cause we might trust them. But how could we tell that? So in my mind I turned over everything except the one thing which might have proved our salvation, and that you shall hear directly. Also, which was a very strange thing, I quite forgot that I had upon me, tied by a string round my waist and well concealed, Barnaby's bag of gold—two hundred and fifty pieces. Thus there was money enough and to spare. I discovered, next, that our pony had run away in the night. The cart was there, but no pony to drag it. Well, it was not much; but it seemed an additional burden to bear. I ventured a little way up the valley, following a sheep-track which mounted higher and higher. I saw no sign anywhere of man's presence; that, I take it, is marked in woods by circles of burnt cinders, by trees felled, by bundles of broom or fern tied up, or by shepherds' huts. Here there was nothing at all; you would have said that the place had never been[156] visited by man. Presently I came to a place where the woods ceased, the last of the trees being much stunted and blown over from the west; and then the top of the hill began, not a sharp pico or point, but a great open plain, flat, or swelling out here and there with many of the little hillocks which people say are ancient tombs. And no trees at all, but only bare turf, so that one could see a great way off. But there was no sign of man anywhere: no smoke in the comb at my feet; no shepherd on the hill. At this juncture of our fortunes any stranger might be an enemy; therefore I returned, but so far well pleased.

Barnaby was now awake, and was inspecting the basket of provisions.

'Sister,' he said, 'we must go upon half rations for breakfast; but I hope, unless my skill fails, to bring you something better for supper. The bread you shall have, and mother. The bacon may keep till to-morrow. The cider you had better keep against such times as you feel worn out and want a cordial, though a glass of Nantz were better, if Nantz grew in the woods.' He looked around as if to see whether a miracle would not provide him with a flask of strong drink, but, seeing none, shook his head.

'As for me,' he went on, 'I am a sailor, and I understand how to forage. Therefore, yesterday, foreseeing that the provisions might give out, I dropped the shank of the ham into my pocket. Now you shall see.'

He produced this delicate morsel, and, sitting down, began to gnaw and to bite into the bone with his strong teeth, exactly like a dog. This he continued, with every sign of satisfaction, for a quarter of an hour or so, when he desisted, and replaced the bone in his pocket.

'We throw away the bones,' he said. 'The dogs gnaw them and devour them. Think you that it is for their amusement? Not so; but for the juices and the nourishment that are in and around the bone; for the marrow and for the meat that still will stick in odd corners.' He went down to the stream with the pannikin and drank a cup or two of water to finish what they called a horse's meal—namely, the food first and the water afterwards.

'And now,' he added, 'I have breakfasted. It is true that I am still hungry, but I have eaten enough to carry me on for a while. Many a poor lad cast away on a desert shore would find a shank of a ham a meal fit for a king; aye, and a meal or two after that. I shall make a dinner presently off this bone; and I shall still keep it against a time when there may be no provision left.'

Then he looked about him, shading his eyes with his hand. 'Let us consider,' he said. 'The troopers, I take it, are riding along the roads. Whether they will ride over these hills, I know not; but I think they will not, because their horses cannot well get up these combs. Certainly, if they do, it will not be by the way we came. We are here, therefore, hidden away snug. Why should we budge? Nowhere is there a more deserted part of the country than Black Down, on whose side we are. And I do not think, further, that we should find anywhere a safer place to hide ourselves in than this comb, where, I dare to say, no one comes, unless it be the gipsies or the broom-squires, all the year round. And now they are all laden with the spoil of the army—for, after a battle, this gentry swoop down upon the field like the great birds which I have seen abroad upon the carcases of drowned beasts, and plunder the dead. Next they must go into town in order to sell their booty; then they will be fain to drink about till all is spent; so they will leave us undisturbed. Therefore, we will stay here, Sister. First, I will go and try the old tricks by which I did often in the old time improve the fare at home. Next, I will devise some way of making a more comfortable resting-place. Thank the Lord for fine weather, so far.'

He was gone a couple of hours. During that time my mother awoke. Her mind was broken by the suddenness of this trouble, and she cared no more to speak, sitting still by the side of her husband, and watching for any change in him. But I persuaded her to take a little bread and a cup of cider.

When Barnaby came back, he brought with him a blackbird, a thrush, and two wood-pigeons. He had not forgotten the tricks of his boyhood, when he would often bring home a rabbit, a hare, or a basket of trout. So that my chief terror, that we might be forced to abandon our hiding-place through sheer hunger, was removed. But Barnaby was full of all kinds of devices.

He then set to work with his great knife, cutting down a quantity of green branches, which he laid out side by side, with their leaves on, and then bound them together, cleverly interlacing the smaller shoots and branches with each other, so that he made a long kind of hurdle, about six feet high. This, which by reason of the leaves was almost impervious to the wind, he disposed round the trunks of three young trees growing near each other. Thus he made a small three-cornered inclosure. Again, he cut other and thicker branches, and laid them over and across this hurdle, and cut turf which he placed upon the branches, so that here was now a hut with a roof and walls complete. Said I not that Barnaby was full of devices?

'There,' he said, when all was ready, 'is a house for you. It will have to rain hard and long before the water begins to drop through the branches which make the roof and the slabs of turf. Well, 'tis a shelter. Not so comfortable as the old cottage, perhaps, but nearly as commodious. If it is not a palace, it will serve us to keep off the sun by day and the dew by night.'

Next he gathered a great quantity of dry fern, dead leaves, and heather, and these he disposed within the hut, so that they made a thick and warm carpet or covering. Nay, at night they even formed a covering for the feet and prevented one from feeling cold. When all was done, he lifted my father gently and laid him with great tenderness upon this carpet within the rude shelter.

'This shall be a warmer night for thee than the last, Dad,' he said. 'There shall be no jolting of thy poor bones. What, mother? We can live here till the cold weather comes. The wind will perhaps blow a bit through the leaves to-night, but not much, and to-morrow I will see to that. Be easy in your mind about the provisions'—Alas! my poor mother was thinking of anything in the world except the provisions—'There are rabbits and birds in plenty; we can catch them and eat them; bread we must do without when what we have is gone, and as for strong drink and tobacco'—he sighed heavily—'they will come again when better times are served out.'

In these labours I helped as much as I was able, and particularly in twisting the branches together. And thus the whole day passed, not tediously, and without any alarms, the labour being cheered by the hopefulness of Barnaby's honest face. No one, to look at that face, could believe that he was flying for his life, and would be hanged if he was caught. After sunset we lit a fire, but a small one only, and well hidden by the woods, so that its light might not be seen from below. Then Barnaby dexterously plucked and trussed the birds and roasted them in the embers, so that had my heart been at rest I should have had a most delicious supper. And I confess that I did begin to pluck up a little courage, and to hope that we might yet escape, and that Robin might be living. After supper my mother prayed, and I could join with more of resignation and something of faith. Alas! in times of trial how easily doth the Christian fall from faith! The day before, prayer seemed to me a mockery; it was as if all prayer were addressed to a deaf God, or to one who will not hear; for our prayers had all been for safety and victory, and we were suddenly answered with disaster and defeat.

After supper, Barnaby sat beside the embers and began to talk in a low voice.

"Twill be a sorrowful barley-mow song this year,' he said; 'a dozen brave lads from Bradford alone will be dead.'

'Not all dead, Barnaby! Oh! not all!'

'I know not. Some are prisoners, some are dead, some are running away.' Then he began to sing in a low voice,

'Here's a health to the barley-mow—

I remember, Sister, when I would run a mile to hear that song, though my father flogged me for it in the morning. 'Tis the best song ever written.' He went on singing in a kind of whisper—

'We'll drink it out of the nipperkin, boys—

Robin—poor Robin! he is dead!—was a famous hand at singing it; but Humphrey found the words too rustical. Humphrey—who is now dead, too!—was ever for fine words, like Mr. Boscorel.

'We'll drink it out of the jolly brown bowl—

'I think I see him now—poor Robin! Well; he is no more. He used to laugh in all our faces while he sang it:—

'We'll drink it out o' the river, my boys. Here's a health to the barley-mow! The river, the well, the pipe, the hogshead, the half- Hogshead, the anker, the half-anker, the gallon, the Pottle, the quart, the pint, the half-pint, the quarter- Pint, the nipperkin, the jolly brown bowl, my boys, Here's a health to the barley-mow!'

He trolled out the song in a melodious whisper. Oh! Barnaby, how didst thou love good companionship with singing and drinking!

"Twill be lonely for thee, Sister, at Bradford when thou dost return; Sir Christopher, I take it, will not long hold up his head, and Madam will pine away for the loss of Robin, and mother looks as if she would follow after, so white and wan is she. If she would speak or complain or cry it would comfort her, poor soul! 'Twas a sad day for her when she married the poor old Dad. Poverty and hard work, and now a cruel end—poor mother!'

'Barnaby, you tear my heart!'

'Nay, Child, 'tis better to talk than to keep silence. Better have your heart torn than be choked with your pain. Thou art like unto a man who hath a wounded leg, and if he doth not consent to have it cut off, though the anguish be sharp, he will presently bleed to death. Say to thyself therefore, plain and clear, "Robin is dead; I have lost my sweetheart."'

'No—no—Barnaby—I cannot say those cruel words! Oh! I cannot say them; I cannot feel that Robin is truly dead!'

'Put the case that he is living. Then he is either a prisoner or he is in hiding. If a prisoner, he is as good as dead; because the Duke's officers and the gentlemen who joined him, they will never forgive—that is quite certain. If I were a prisoner I should feel my neck already tightened. If he is not a prisoner, where is he to hide?—whither betake himself? I can get sailors' duds and go abroad before the mast; and ten to one nobody will find me out, because, d'ye see, I can talk the sailors' language, and I know their manners and customs. But Robin—what is Robin to do, if he is alive? And this, I say, is doubtful. Best say to thyself, "I have lost my sweetheart." So wilt thou all the sooner recover thy cheerfulness.'

'Barnaby, you know not what you say! Alas! if my Robin is dead—if my boy is truly dead—then I ask for nothing more than swift death—speedy death—to join him and be with him!'

'If he escape he will make for Bradford Orcas and hide in the Corton woods. That is quite certain. They always make for home. I would that we were in that friendly place, so that you could go live in the cottage and bring provisions, with tobacco and drink, to us unsuspected and unseen. When we have rested here a while we will push across the hills and try to get there by night; but it is a weary way to drag that wounded man. However'—he broke off and said earnestly—'make up thy mind, Child, to the worst. 'Tis as if a shipwrecked man should hope that enough of the ship would float to carry him home withal. Make up thy mind. We are all ruined and lost—all—all—all. Thy father is dying—thy lover is dead—thou art thyself in great danger by reason of that affair at Taunton. Everything being gone, turn round therefore and make thyself as comfortable as possible. What will happen we know not. Therefore count every day of safety for gain, and every meal for a respite.'

He was silent for a while, leaving me to think over what he had said. Here, indeed, was a philosopher. Things being all lost, and our affairs in a desperate condition, we were to turn round and make ourselves as comfortable as we could! This, I suppose, is what sailors are wont to do; certainly they are a folk more exposed to misfortune than others, and therefore, perhaps, more ready to make the best of whatever happens.

'Barnaby,' I said presently, 'how can I turn round and make myself comfortable?'

'The evening is still,' he said, without replying. 'See, there is a bat, and there another. If it were not for the trouble in there'—he pointed to the hut—'I should be easy in my mind and contented. I could willingly live here a twelvemonth. Why, compared with the lot of the poor devils who must now be in prison, what is ours? They get the foul and stinking clink, with bad food, in the midst of wounded men whose hurts are putrefying, with jail fever, and with the whipping-post or the gallows to come. We breathe sweet air, we find sufficient food—to-morrow, if I know any of the signs, thou shalt taste a roasted hedgehog, dish fit for a king! I found at the bottom of the comb a pot left by some gipsies: thou shalt have boiled sorrel and mushrooms to thy supper. If we stay here long enough there will be nuts and blackberries and whortleberries. Pity, a thousand pities, there is not a drop of drink! I dream of punch and hipsy. Think upon what remains, even if thou canst not bear to think of what is lost. Hast ever seen a tall ship founder in the waves? They close over her as she sinks, and, in an instant, it is as if that tall ship with all her crew had never been in existence at all. The army of Monmouth is scattered and ruined. Well; it is, with us, amidst these woods, just as if there had been no army. It has been a dream perhaps. Who can tell? Sometimes all the past seems to have been a dream. It is all a dream—past and future. There is no past and there is no future; all is a dream. But the present we have. Let us be content therewith.'

He spoke slowly and with measured accents as one enchanted. Sometimes Barnaby was but a rough and rude sailor. At other times, as these, he betrayed signs of his early education and spoke as one who thought.

'It is ten years and more since last I breathed the air of the hills. I knew not that I loved so much the woods and valleys and the streams. Some day, if I survive this adventure, I will build me a hut and live here alone in the woods. Why, if I were alone I should have an easy heart. If I were driven out of one place I could find another. I am in no hurry to get down among men and towns. Let us all stay here and be happy. But there is Dad—who lives not, yet is not dead. Sister, be thankful for thy safety in the woods, and think not too much upon the dead.'

We lived in this manner, the weather being for the most part fine and warm, but with showers now and then, for a fortnight or thereabouts, no one coming up the comb and there being still no sign of man's presence in the hills. Our daily fare consisted of the wild birds snared by Barnaby, such creatures as rabbits, hedgehogs, and the like, which he caught by ingenious ways, and trout from the brook which he caught with a twisted pin or by tickling them with his hand. There were also mushrooms and edible leaves, such as the nettle, wild sorrel, and the like of which he knew. These we boiled and ate. He also plucked the half-ripe blackberries and boiled them to make a sour drink, and one which, like the cider loved by our people, would grip his throat because he could not endure plain cold water. And he made out of the bones of the birds a kind of thin broth for my father, of which he daily swallowed a teaspoonful or so. So that we fared well, if not sumptuously. The bread, to be sure, which Barnaby left for mother and me, was coming to the last crust, and I know not how we should have got more without venturing into the nearest village.

Now, as I talked every night with my brother, I found out what a brave and simple soul it was—always cheerful and hopeful, talking always as if we were the most fortunate people in the world, instead of the most miserable, and yet by keeping the truth before me, preventing me from getting into another Fool's Paradise as to our safety and Robin's escape, such as that into which I had fallen after the army marched out of Taunton. I understand now, that he was always thinking how to smooth and soften things for us, so that we might not go distracted with anxiety and grief; finding work for me, talking about other things—in short, the most thoughtful and affectionate brother in all the world. As for my mother, he could do nothing to move her. She still sat beside her wounded husband, watching all day long for any sign of consciousness or change.

Seeing that Barnaby was so good and gentle a creature, I could not understand how it was that in the old days he used to get a flogging most days for some offence or other, so that I had grown up to believe him a very wicked boy indeed. I put this question to him one night.

He put it aside for a while, replying in his own fashion.

'I remember Dad,' he said, 'before thou canst, Sister. He was always thin and tall, and he always stooped as he walked. But his hair, which now is white, was brown, and fell in curls which he could not straighten. He was always mighty grave; no one, I am[162] sure, ever saw him laugh; I have never seen him so much as smile, except sometimes when he dandled thee upon his knee, and thou wouldst amuse him with innocent prattle. All his life he hath spent in finding out the way to Heaven. He did find the way—I suppose he hath truly discovered it—and a mighty thorny and difficult way it is, so that I know not how any can succeed in reaching port by such navigation. The devil of it is that he believes there is no other way; and he seemed never so happy as when he had found another trap or pitfall to catch the unwary, and send them straight to hell.

'For my part,' Barnaby went on slowly, 'I could never love such a life. Let others, if they will, find out rough and craggy ways that lead to heaven. For my part, I am content to jog along the plain and smooth high road with the rest of mankind, though it brings us in the end to a lower place, inhabited by the baser sort. Well, I dare say I shall find mates there, and we will certainly make ourselves as comfortable as the place allows. Let my father, therefore, find out what awaits him in the other world; let me take what comes in this. Some of it is sweet and some is bitter; some of it makes us laugh and sing and dance; and some makes us curse and swear and bellow out, as when one is lashed to the hatches and the cat falls on his naked back. Sometimes, Sister, I think the naked negroes of the Guiney Coast the happiest people in the world. Do they trouble their heads about the way to heaven? Not they. What comes they take, and they ask no more. Has it made Dad the happier to find out how few are those who will sit beside him when he hath his harp and crown? Not so. He would have been happier if he had been a jolly ploughboy whistling to his team, or a jolly sailor singing over his pannikin of drink of a Saturday night. He tried to make me follow in his footsteps; he flogged me daily in the hope of making me take, like himself, to the trade of proving out of the Holy Bible that most people are surely damned. The more he flogged, the less I yearned after that trade;

till at last I resolved that, come what would, I would never thump a pulpit like him in conventicle or church. Then, if you will believe me, Sister, I grew tired of flogging, which, when it comes every day, wearies a boy at fourteen or fifteen more than you would think. Now, one day, while I was dancing to the pipe and tabor with some of the village girls, as bad luck would have it, Dad came by. "Child of Satan!" he roared, seizing me by the ear, which I verily thought he would have pulled off. Then to the girls, "Your laughter shall be turned into mourning," and so lugged me home and sent me supperless to bed, with the promise of such a flogging in the morning as should make all previous floggings seem mere fleabites or joyous ticklings in comparison. This decided me. So in the dead of night I crept softly down the stairs, cut myself a great hunch of bread and cheese, and ran away and went to sea.'

'Barnaby, was it well done—to run away?'

'Well, Sister, 'tis done; and if it was ill done, 'tis by this time, no doubt, forgotten. Now, remember, I blame not my father. Before all things he would save my soul alive. That was why he flogged me. He knew but one way, and along that way he would drive me. So he flogged me the harder. I blame him not. Yet had I remained he would doubtless be flogging me still. Now, remember again, that ever since I understood anything I have always been enraged to think upon the monstrous oppression which silenced him and brought us all to poverty, and made my mother, a gentlewoman born, work her fingers to the bone, and caused me to choose between being a beggarly scholar, driven to teach brats and endure flouts and poverty, or to put on an apron and learn a trade. Wherefore when I found that Monmouth was going to hoist his flag, I came with him in order to strike a blow, and I hoped a good blow, too, at the oppressors.'

'You have struck that blow, Barnaby, and where are we?'

He laughed.

'We are in hiding. Some of the King's troopers did I make to bite the dust. They may hang me for it, if they will. They will not bring those troopers back to life. Well—— Sister, I am sleepy. Good night!'

We might have continued this kind of life I know not how much longer. Certainly, till the cold nights came. The weather continued fine and warm; the hut kept off dews at night; we lay warm among the heather and the ferns; Barnaby found a sufficiency of food; my father grew no worse, to outward seeming; and we seemed in safety.

Then an ill chance and my own foolishness marred all.

One day, in the afternoon, Barnaby being away looking after his snares and gins, I heard, lower down the comb, voices as of boys talking. This affrighted me terribly. The voices seemed to be drawing nearer. Now if the children came up as high as our encampment, they could not fail to see the signs of habitation. There was the hut among the trees and the iron pot standing among the grey embers of last night's fire. The cart stood on one side. We could not possibly remain hidden. If they should come up so far and find us, they would certainly carry the report of us down to the village.

I considered, therefore, what to do, and then ran quickly down the comb, keeping among the trees so as not to be seen.

After a little I discovered, a little way off, a couple of boys about nine years of age. They were common village boys, rosy faced and wholesome: they carried a basket, and they were slowly making their way up the stream, stopping now to throw a stone at a squirrel, and now to dam the running water, and now to find a nut or filbert ripe enough to be eaten. By the basket which they carried I knew that they were come in search of whortleberries, for which purpose they would have to get quite to the end of the comb and the top of the hill.

Therefore, I stepped out of the wood and asked them whence they came and whither they were going.

They told me in plain Somersetshire (the language which I love, and would willingly have written this book in it, but for the unfortunate people who cannot understand it) that they were sent by their parents to get whortleberries, and that they came from the little village of Corfe, two miles down the valley. This was all they had to say, and they stared at me as shyly as if they had never before encountered a stranger. I clearly perceive now that I ought to have engaged them in conversation and drawn them gently down the valley in the direction of their village until we reached the first appearance of a road, when I could have bidden them farewell or sent them up the hill by another comb. But I was so anxious that they should not come up any higher that I committed a great mistake, and warned them against going on.

'Boys,' I said, 'beware! If you go higher up the comb you will certainly meet wild men, who always rob and beat boys;' here they trembled, though they had not a penny in the world. 'Ay, boys! and sometimes have been known to murder them. Turn back—turn back—and come no farther.'

The boys were very much frightened, partly at the apparition of a stranger where they expected to find no one, and partly at the news of wild and murderous men in a place where they had never met with anyone at all, unless it might have been a gipsy camp. After gazing at me stupidly for a little while they turned and ran away, as fast as their legs could carry them, down the comb.

I watched them running, and when they were out of sight I went back again, still disquieted, because they might return.

When I told Barnaby in the evening, he, too, was uneasy. For, he said, the boys would spread abroad the report that there were people in the valley. What people could there be but fugitives?

'Sister,' he said, 'to-morrow morning must we change our quarters. On the other side of the hills looking south, or to the east in Neroche Forest, we may make another camp, and be still more secluded. For to-night I think we are in safety.'

What happened was exactly as Barnaby thought. For the lads ran home and told everybody that up in the comb there were wild men who robbed and murdered people: that a lady had come out of the wood and warned them to go no farther, lest they should be robbed and murdered. They were certain it was a lady, and not a country-woman; nor was it a witch; nor a fairy or elf, of whom there are many on Black Down. No; it was a lady.

This strange circumstance set the villagers a-talking; they talked about it at the inn, whither they nightly repaired.

In ordinary times they might have talked about it to their heart's content, and no harm done; but in these times talk was dangerous. In every little village there are one or two whose wits are sharper than the rest, and, therefore, they do instigate whatever mischief is done in that village. At Corfe, the cobbler it was[165] who did the mischief. For he sat thinking while the others talked, and he presently began to understand that there was more in this than his fellows imagined. He knew the hills; there were no wild men upon them who would rob and murder two simple village boys. Gipsies there were, and broom-squires sometimes, and hedge-tearers: but murderers of boys—none. And who was this gentlewoman? Then he guessed the whole truth: there were people lying hidden in the comb; if people hidden, they were Monmouth's rebels. A reward would be given for their capture. Fired with this thought he grasped his cudgel and walked off to the village of Orchard Portman, where, as he had heard, there was lying a company of Grenadiers sent out to scour the country. He laid his information, and received the promise of reward. He got that reward, in short; but nothing prospered with him afterwards. His neighbours, who were all for Monmouth, learned what he had done, and shunned him. He grew moody; he fell into poverty, who had been a thriving tradesman; and he died in a ditch. The judgments of the Lord are sometimes swift and sometimes slow, yet they are always sure. Who can forget the dreadful end of Tom Boilman, as he was called, the only wretch who could be found to cut up the limbs of the hanged men and dip them in the cauldrons of pitch? For he was struck dead by lightning—an awful instance of the wrath of God!

Early next morning, about five of the clock, I sat before the hut in the shade. Barnaby was up and had gone to look at his snares. Suddenly I heard steps below, and the sound as of weapons clashing against each other. Then a man came into sight—a fellow he was with a leathern apron, who stood gazing about him. There was no time for me to hide, because he immediately saw me and shouted to them behind to come on quickly. Then a dozen soldiers, all armed, ran out of the wood and made for the hut.

'Gentlemen,' I cried, running to meet them, 'whom seek you?'

'Who are you?' asked one, who seemed to be a Sergeant over them. 'Why are you in hiding?'

Then a thought struck me. I know not if I was wise or foolish.

'Sir,' I replied, 'my father, it is true, was with the Duke of Monmouth. But he was wounded, and now lies dead in this hut. You will suffer us to bury our dead in peace.'

'Dead is he? That will we soon see.'

So saying, he entered the hut and looked at the prostrate form. He lifted one hand and let it drop. It fell like the hand of one who is recently dead. He bent over the body and laid his hand upon the forehead. It was cold as death. The lips were pale as wax, and the cheeks were white. He opened an eye: there was no expression of light in it.

'Humph!' he said; 'he seems dead. How did he come here?'

'My mother and I drove him here for safety in yonder cart. The pony hath run away.'

'That may be so; that may be so. He is dressed in a cassock: what is his name?'

'He was Dr. Comfort Eykin, an ejected minister and preacher in the Duke's army.'

'A prize, if he had been alive!' Then a sudden suspicion seized him. He had in his hand a drawn sword. He pointed it at the breast of the dead man. 'If he be truly dead,' he said, 'another wound will do him no harm. Wherefore'—he made as if he would drive the sword through my father's breast, and my mother shrieked and threw herself across the body.

'So!' he said, with a horrid grin, 'I find that he is not dead, but only wounded. My lads, here is one of Monmouth's preachers; but he is sore wounded.'

'Oh!' I cried, 'for the love of God suffer him to die in peace!'

'Ay, ay, he shall die in peace, I promise you so much. Meanwhile, Madam, we will take better care of him in Ilminster Jail than you can do here. The air is raw upon these hills.' The fellow had a glib tongue and a mocking manner. 'You have none of the comforts which a wounded man requires. They are all to be found in Ilminster prison, whither we shall carry him. There will he have nothing to think about, with everything found for him. Madam, your father will be well bestowed with us.'

At that moment I heard the footsteps of Barnaby crunching among the brushwood.

'Fly! Barnaby, fly!' I shrieked. 'The enemy is upon us!'

He did not fly. He came running. He rushed upon the soldiers, and hurled this man one way and that man another, swinging his long arms like a pair of cudgels. Had he had a cudgel I believe he would have sent them all flying. But he had nothing except his arms and his fists; and in a minute or two the soldiers had surrounded him, each with a bayonet pointed, and such a look in every man's eye as meant murder had Barnaby moved.

'Surrender!' said the Sergeant.

Barnaby looked around leisurely.

'Well,' he said, 'I suppose I must. As for my name, it is Barnaby Eykin; and, for my rank, I was Captain in the Green Regiment of the Duke's valiant army.'

'Stop!' said the Sergeant, drawing a paper from his pocket. '"Captain Eykin,"' he began to read, '"has been a sailor. Rolls in his walk; height, about five foot five; very broad in the shoulders; long in the arms; of great strength."'

'That is so,' said Barnaby, complacently.

'"Legs short and figure stumpy."'

'What?' cried Barnaby, 'stumpy?'

'"Legs short and figure stumpy,"' repeated the Sergeant reading.

'That is so set down is it? Then,' said Barnaby, looking down at his limbs, ''twas a pity that, with such legs as these, I did not deny my name. Call these short, brother?'

CHAPTER XXV.

ILMINSTER CLINK.

How can I tell—oh! how can I sit down to tell in cold blood the story of all that followed? Some parts of it for very pity I must pass over. All that has been told or written of the Bloody Assize is most true, and yet not half that happened can be told. There are things, I mean, which the historian cannot, for the sake of pity, decency, and consideration for living people, relate, even if he hath seen them. You who read the printed page may learn how in one place so many were hanged; in another place so many; how some were hung in gemmaces, so that at every cross-road there was a frightful gibbet with a dead man on it; how some died of small-pox in the crowded prisons, and some of fever; and how Judge Jeffreys rode from town to town, followed by gangs of miserable prisoners driven after him to stand their trial in towns where they would be known; how the wretched sufferers were drawn and quartered, and their limbs seethed in pitch, and stuck up over the whole country; how the women and boys of tender years were flogged through market-towns—you, I say, who read these things on the cold page presently (even if you be a stickler for the Right Divine and hold rebellion as a mortal sin) feel your blood to boil with righteous wrath. The hand of the Lord was afterwards heavy upon those who ordered these things; nay, at the very time (this is a most remarkable Judgment, and one little known) when this inhuman Judge was thundering at his victims—so that some went mad and even dropped down dead with fear—he was himself, as Humphrey hath assured me, suffering the most horrible pain from a dire disease; so that the terrors of his voice and of his fiery eyes were partly due to the agony of his disease, and he was enduring all through that Assize, in his own body, pangs greater than any that he ordered! As for his miserable end, and the fate that overtook his master, that we know; and candid souls cannot but confess that here were truly Judgments of God, visible for all to see and acknowledge. But no pen can truly depict what the eye saw and the ear heard during that terrible time. And, think you, if it was a terrible and a wretched time for those who had no relations among the rebels, and only looked on and saw these bloody executions and heard the lamentations of the poor women who lost their lovers or their husbands, what must it have been for me, and those like me, whose friends and all whom they loved—yea, all, all!—were overwhelmed in one common ruin, and expected nothing but death?

Our own misery I cannot truly set forth. Sometimes the memory of it comes back to me, and it is as if long afterwards one should feel again the sharpness of the surgeon's knife. Oh! since I must write down what happened, let me be brief. And you who read it, if you find the words cold where you would have looked for fire; if you find no tears where there should have been weeping and wailing, remember that in the mere writing have been shed again (but these you cannot see) the tears which belonged to that time, and in the writing have been renewed (but these you cannot hear) the sobbings and wailings and terrors of that dreadful autumn.

The soldiers belonged to a company of Grenadiers of Trelawny's Regiment, stationed at Ilminster, whither they carried the prisoners. First they handcuffed Barnaby, but, on his giving his parole not to escape, they let him go free; and he proved useful in the handling of the cart on which my unhappy father lay. And, though the soldiers' talk was ribald, their jests unseemly, and their cursing and swearing seemed verily to invite the wrath of God, yet they proved honest fellows in the main. They offered no rudeness to us, nor did they object to our going with the prisoners; nay, they even gave us bread and meat and cider from their own provisions when they halted for dinner at noon. Barnaby walked sometimes with the soldiers, and sometimes with us; with them he talked freely, and as if he were their comrade and not their prisoner: with us he put in a word of encouragement or consolation, such as 'Mother, we shall find a way out of this coil yet;' or 'Sister, we shall cheat Tom Hangman. Look not so gloomy upon it;' or, again, he reminded us that many a shipwrecked sailor gets safe ashore, and that where there are so many they cannot hang all. 'Would the King,' he asked, 'hang up the whole county of Somerset?' But he had already told me too much. In his heart I knew he had small hope of escape; yet he preserved his cheerfulness, and walked towards his prison (to outward seeming) as insensible of fear, and with as unconcerned a countenance as if he were going to a banquet or a wedding. This cheerfulness of his was due to a happy confidence in the ordering of things rather than to insensibility. A sailor sees men die in many ways, yet himself remains alive. This gives him something of the disposition of the Oriental, who accepts his fate with outward unconcern, whatever it may be. Perhaps (I know not) there may have been in his mind that religious Assurance of which he had told me. Did Barnaby at this period, when death was very near unto him, really believe that there was one religion for landsmen and another for sailors—one way to heaven for ministers, another for seamen? Indeed, I cannot tell; yet how otherwise account for his courage and cheerfulness at all times—even in the very presence of death?

'Brother,' he asked the Sergeant, 'we have been lying hid for a fortnight, and have heard no news. Tell me, how go the hangings?'

'Why, Captain,' the fellow replied with a grin, 'in this respect there is little for the rebels to complain of. They ought to be satisfied, so far, with the attentions paid to them. Lord Feversham hanged twenty odd to begin with. Captain Adlan and three others are trussed up in chains for their greater honour; and, in order to put the rest in good heart, one of them ran a race with a horse, being promised his life if he should win. When he had beaten the horse, his Lordship, who was ever a merry man, ordered him to be hanged just to laugh at him. And hanged he was.'

'Ay,' said Barnaby, 'thus do the Indians in America torture their prisoners first and kill them afterwards.'

'There are two hundred prisoners laying in Weston Zoyland church,' the Sergeant went on; 'they would have been hanged, too, but the Bishop interfered. Now they are waiting to be tried. Lord! what signifies trial, except to give them longer rope?'

'Ay, ay; and how go things in Bridgwater and Taunton?'

'From Weston to Bridgwater there is a line of gibbets already; in Taunton, twenty, I believe, have swung—twenty, at least. The drums beat, the fifes played, and the trumpets sounded, and Colonel Kirke drank to the health of every man (such was his condescension!) before he was turned off. 'Twould have done your heart good, Captain, only to see the brave show.'

'Ay, ay,' said Barnaby, unmoved; 'very like, very like. Perhaps I shall have the opportunity of playing first part in another brave show if all goes well. Hath the Duke escaped?'

'We heard yesterday that he is taken somewhere near the New Forest. So that he will before long lay his lovely head upon the block. Captain, your friends have brought their pigs to a pretty market.'

'They have, Brother; they have,' replied Barnaby, still with unmoved countenance. 'Yet many a man hath recovered from worse straits than these.'

I listened with sinking heart. Much I longed to ask if the Sergeant knew aught of Robin; but I refrained, lest merely to name him might put the soldiers on the look-out for him, should he, happily, be in hiding.

Next the Sergeant told us (which terrified me greatly) that there was no part of the country where they were not scouring for fugitives; that they were greatly assisted by the clergy, who, he said, were red-hot for King James; that the men were found hiding, as we had hidden, in linneys, in hedges, in barns, in woods; that they were captured by treachery—by information laid, and even, most cruel thing of all, by watching and following the men's sweethearts who were found taking food to them. He said also that, at the present rate, they would have to enlarge their prisons to admit ten times their number, for they were haling into them not only the men who had followed Monmouth, but also those who had helped him with money, arms, or men. The Sergeant was a brutal fellow, yet there was about him something of good nature, and even of compassion for the men he had captured. But he seemed to take delight in speaking of the sufferings of the unfortunate prisoners. The soldiers, he told us, were greatly enraged towards the rebels—not, I suppose, on account of their rebellion, because three years later they themselves showed how skin-deep was their loyalty, but because the rustics, whom they thought contemptible, had surprised and nearly beaten them. And this roused in them the spirit of revenge.

'Captain,' said the Sergeant, "tis pity that so lusty a gentleman as thou shouldst die. Hast thou no friends at Court? No? Nor any who would speak for thee? 'Tis pity. Yet a man can die but once. With such a thick neck as thine, bespeak, if so much grace be accorded thee, a long rope and a high gallows. Else, when it comes to the quartering'—he stopped and shook his head—'but there—I wish you well out of it, Captain.'

In the evening, just before sunset, we arrived at Ilminster, after a sad and weary march of ten miles, at least; but we could not leave the prisoners until we knew how and where they were bestowed; and during all this time my mother, who commonly walked not abroad from one Sabbath to the next, was possessed with such a spirit that she seemed to feel no weariness. When we rode all night in order to join the Duke she complained not; when we rode painfully across the hills to Taunton she murmured not; nor when we carried our wounded man up the rough and steep comb; no, nor on this day, when she walked beside her husband's head, careful lest the motion of the cart should cause him pain. But he felt nothing, poor soul! He would feel nothing any more.

Ilminster is a goodly town, rich and prosperous with its spinners and weavers. This evening, however, there was no one in the streets except the troopers, who swaggered up and down or sat drinking at the tavern door. There is a broad open place before the market, which stands upon great stone pillars. Outside the market is the Clink, whither the soldiers were taking their prisoners. The troopers paid not the least heed to our mournful little procession—a wounded man; a prisoner in scarlet and lace, but the cloth tattered and stained and the lace torn. They were only two more men on their way to death. What doth a soldier care for the sight of a man about to die?

'Mother,' said Barnaby when we drew near the prison gates, 'come not within. I will do all that I can for him. Go now and find a decent lodging, and, Sister, hark ye, the lads in our army were rough, but they were as lambs compared with these swaggering troopers. Keep snug, therefore, and venture not far abroad.'

I whispered in his ear that I had his bag of money safe, so that he could have whatever he wanted if that could be bought. Then the prison gates were closed, and we stood without.

It would have been hard indeed if the wife and daughter of Dr. Comfort Eykin could not find a lodging among godly people, of whom there are always many in every town of Somerset. We presently obtained a room in the house of one Martha Prior, widow of the learned and pious Joshua Prior, whilom preacher and ejected minister. Her case was as hard as our own. This poor woman had two sons only, and both had gone to join the Duke; one already risen to be a Master Serge-maker and one a Draper of the town. Of her sons she could hear no news at all: whether they were alive or dead. If they were already dead, or if they should be hanged, she would have no means of support, and so must starve or eat the bread of charity. (I learned afterwards that she never did hear anything of them, so that it is certain that they must have been killed on the battle-field or cut down by the dragoons in trying to escape. But the poor soul survived not long their loss.)

The church of Ilminster stands upon a rising ground; on the north of the church is the grammar school, and on the other three sides are houses of the better sort, of which Mrs. Prior had one. The place, which surrounds the churchyard, and hath no inn or ale-house in it, is quiet and retired. The soldiers came not thither, except once or twice, with orders to search the houses (and with a private resolution to drink everything that they might lay their hands upon), so that, for two poor women in our miserable circumstances, we could not have a more quiet lodging.

Despite our troubles, I slept so well that night that it was past seven in the morning when I awoke. The needs of the body do sometimes overcome the cares of the spirit. For a whole fortnight had we been making our beds on the heather, and, therefore, without taking off our clothes; and that day we had walked ten miles, at least, with the soldiers, so that I slept without moving or waking all the night. In the morning, I dressed quickly and hurried to the jail, not knowing whether I might be admitted or should be allowed speech of Barnaby. Outside the gate, however, I found a crowd of people going into the prison and coming out of it. Some of them, women like ourselves, were weeping—they were those whose brothers or lovers, husbands or sons, were in those gloomy walls. Others there were who brought, for such of the prisoners as had money to buy them, eggs, butter, white bread, chickens, fruit, and all kinds of provisions; some brought wine, cider, and ale; some, tobacco. The warders who stood at the gates made no opposition to those who would enter. I pressed in with a beating heart, prepared for a scene of the most dreadful repentance and gloomy forebodings. What I saw was quite otherwise.

The gates of the prison opened upon a courtyard, not very big, where the people were selling their wares, and some of the prisoners were walking about, and some were chaffering with the women who had the baskets. On the right-hand side of the yard was the Clink itself; on the left hand were houses for the warders or officers of the prison. In general, a single warder, constable, or head-borough is enough for a town such as Ilminster, to keep the peace of the prison, which is for the most part empty, save when they enforce some new Act against Nonconformists and fill it with them or with Quakers. Now, however, so great was the press that, instead of two, there were a dozen guards, and, while a stout cudgel had always been weapon enough, now every man went armed with pike and cutlass to keep order and prevent escapes. Six of them occupied the gate-house; other six were within, in a sort of guard-house, where they slept on the left hand of the court.

The ground floor of the Clink we found to be a large room, at least forty feet each side in bigness. On one side of it was a great fireplace, where, though it was the month of July, there was burning a great fire of Welsh coal, partly for cooking purposes, because all that the prisoners ate was cooked at this fire; and partly because a great fire kept continually burning sweetens the air, and wards off jail fever. On another side was a long table and several benches. Thick wooden pillars supported the joists of the rooms above; the windows were heavily barred, but the shutters had been taken down, and there was no glass in them. In spite of fire and open windows, the place was stifling, and smelt most horrible. Never have I breathed so foul an air. There lived in this room about eighty prisoners (later on the numbers were doubled); some were smoking tobacco and drinking cider or ale; some were frying pieces of meat or smoked herrings over the fire; and the tobacco, the ale, the wine, the cooking, and the people themselves—nearly all country lads, unwashed, who had slept since Sedgemoor, at least, in the same clothes without once changing—made so foul an air that jail fever, putrid throats, and small-pox (all of which afterwards broke out) should have been expected sooner.

They were all talking, laughing, and even singing, so that, in addition to the noisome stench of the place, there was such a din as one may hear at Sherborne Fair of an evening. I expected, as I have said, a gloomy silence with the rattling of chains, the groans of those who looked for death, and, perhaps, a godly repentance visible upon every countenance. Yet they were all laughing, except a few who sat retired and who were wounded. I say that they were all laughing. They had nothing to expect but death, or at the best to be horribly flogged, to be transported, to be fined, branded, and ruined. Yet they laughed! What means this hardness and indifference in men? Could they not think of the women they had left at home? I warrant that none of them were laughing.

Among them—a pipe of tobacco in his lips and a mug of strong ale before him on the table, his hat flung backwards—sat Barnaby, his face showing, apparently, complete satisfaction with his lot.

When he saw us at the door, he rose and came to meet us.

'Welcome,' he said. 'This is one of the places where King Monmouth's men are to receive the honour due to them. Courage, gentle hearts. Be not cast down. Everywhere the prisons are full, and more are brought in every day. Our very numbers are our safety. They cannot hang us all. And hark!' here he whispered, 'Sister, we now know that Colonel Kirke hath been selling pardons at ten pounds, twenty pounds, and thirty pounds apiece. Wherefore we are well assured that somehow or other we shall be able to buy our release. There are plenty besides Colonel Kirke who will sell a prisoner his freedom.'

'Where is your father?' asked my mother.

'He is bestowed above, where it is quieter, except for the groaning of the wounded. Go up-stairs, and you will find him. And there is a surprise for you, besides. You will find with him one you little expect to see.'

'Oh! Barnaby, is there new misery for me? Is Robin a prisoner?'

'Robin is not here, Sis; and as for misery, why, that is as you take it. To be sure the man above is in prison, but no harm will happen to him. Why should it? He did not go out with Monmouth's men. But go up-stairs—go up-stairs, and see for yourselves.'

CHAPTER XXVI.

SIR CHRISTOPHER.

I know not whom I expected to find in consequence of Barnaby's words, as we went up the dark and dirty stairs which led to the upper room. Robin was not a prisoner. Why—then—but I knew not what I thought, all being strange and dreadful.

At the top of the stairs we found ourselves in a room of the same size as the lower chamber, but not so high, and darker, being a gloomy place indeed, insomuch that it was not for some minutes that one could plainly discern things. It was lighted by a low, long window, set very close with thick bars, the shutters thrown open so that all the light and air possible to be admitted might come in. It had a great fireplace, but there was no fire burning, and the air of the room struck raw, though outside it was a warm and sunny day. The roof was supported, as in the room below, by means of thick square pillars, studded with great nails set close together, for what purpose I know not. Every part of the woodwork in the room was in the same way stuck full of nails. On the floor lay half a score mattresses, the property of those who could afford to pay the warders an exorbitant fee for the luxury. At Ilminster, as I am told, at Newgate, the chief prison of the country, the same custom obtains of exacting heavy fees from the poor wretches clapped into ward. It is, I suppose, no sin to rob the criminal, the debtor, the traitor, or the rebel. For those who had nothing to pay there were only a few bundles of straw, and on these were lying half a dozen wretches, whose white faces and glazed eyes showed that they would indeed cheat Tom the Hangman, though not in the way that Barnaby hoped. These were wounded either in the Sedgemoor fight or in their attempt to escape.

My father lay on a pallet bed. His face showed not the least change; his eyes were closed, and you would have thought him dead; and beside him, also on a pallet, sat, to my astonishment, none other than Sir Christopher himself.

He rose and came to meet us, smiling sadly.

'Madam,' he said, taking my mother's hand, 'we meet in a doleful place, and we are, indeed, in wretched plight. I cannot bid you welcome; I cannot say that I am glad to see you. There is nothing that I can say of comfort or of hope, except, which you know already, that we are always in the hands of the Lord.'

'Sir Christopher,' said my mother, 'it was kind and neighbourly in you to come. But you were always his best friend. Look at his poor white face!' she only thought upon her husband. 'You would think him dead! More than a fortnight he hath lain thus—motionless. I think he feels no pain. Husband, if thou canst hear me, make some sign—if it be but to open one eye! No!' she cried. 'Day after day have I thus entreated him and he makes no answer! He neither sees nor hears! Yet he doth not die; wherefore I think that he may yet recover speech and sit up again, and presently, perhaps, walk about, and address himself again unto his studies.'

She waited not for any answer, but knelt down beside him and poured some drops of milk into the mouth of the sick man. Sir Christopher looked at her mournfully and shook his head.

Then he turned to me, and kissed me without saying a word.

'Oh! Sir,' I cried, 'how could you know that my father would be brought unto this place? With what goodness of heart have you come to our help!'

'Nay, child,' he replied gravely, 'I came because I had no choice but to come. Like your father and your brother, Alice, I am a prisoner.'

'You, Sir? You a prisoner? Why, you were not with the Duke.'

'That is most true. And yet a prisoner. Why, after the news of Sedgemoor fight I looked for nothing else. They tried to arrest Mr. Speke, but he has fled; they have locked up Mr. Prideaux, of Ford Abbey; Mr. Trenchard has retired across the seas. Why should they pass me over? Nay, there were abundant proofs of my zeal for the Duke. My grandson and my grandnephew had joined the rebels. Your father and brother rode over to Lyme on my horses; with my grandson rode off a dozen lads of the village. What more could they want? Moreover, I am an old soldier of Lord Essex's army; and, to finish, they found in the window-seat a copy of Monmouth's Declaration—which, indeed, I had forgotten, or I might have destroyed it.'

'Alas! alas!' I cried, wringing my hands. 'Your Honour, too, a prisoner!'

Since the Sergeant spoke to Barnaby about the interest of friends, I had been thinking that Sir Christopher, whose power and interest, I fondly thought, must be equal to those of any Lord in the land, would interpose to save us all. And he was now a prisoner himself, involved in the common ruin! One who stands upon a bridge and sees with terror the last support carried away by the raging flood feels such despair as fell upon my soul.

'Oh, Sir!' I cried again. 'It is Line upon Line—Woe upon Woe!'

He took my hand in his, and held it tenderly.

'My child,' he said, 'to an old man of seventy-five what doth it matter whether he die in his bed or whether he die upon a[176] scaffold? Through the pains of death, as through a gate, we enter upon our rest.'

'It is dreadful!' I cried again. 'I cannot endure it!'

'The shame and ignominy of this death,' he said, 'I shall, I trust, regard lightly. We have struck a blow for Freedom and for Faith. Well; we have been suffered to fail. The time hath not yet come. Yet, in the end, others shall carry on the Cause, and Religion shall prevail. Shall we murmur who have been God's instruments?'

'Alas! alas!' I cried again.

'To me, sweet child, it is not terrible to contemplate my end. But it is sad to think of thee, and of thy grave and bitter loss. Hast thou heard news of Robin and of Humphrey?'

'Oh, Sir!—are they also in prison—are they here?'

'No; but I have news of them. I have a letter brought to me but yesterday. Read it, my child, read it.'

He pulled the letter out of his pocket and gave it to me. Then I read aloud, and thus it ran:—

'Honoured Sir and Grandfather,

'I am writing this letter from the prison of Exeter, where, with Humphrey and about two hundred or more of our poor fellows, I am laid by the heels, and shall so continue until we shall all be tried.

'It is rumoured that Lord Jeffreys will come down to try us, and we are assured by report that the King shows himself revengeful, and is determined that there shall be no mercy shown. After Sedgemoor fight they hanged, as you will have heard, many of the prisoners at Weston Zoyland, at Bridgwater, and at Taunton, without trial. If the King continue in this disposition it is very certain that, though the common sort may be forgiven, the gentlemen and those who were officers in the rebel army will certainly not escape. Therefore I have no hope but to conclude my life upon the gallows—a thing which, I confess, I had never looked to do. But I hope to meet my fate with courage and resignation.

'Humphrey is with me, and it is some comfort (though I know not why) that we shall stand or fall together; for if I was a Captain in the army he was a Chyrurgeon. That he was also a secret agent of the exiles, and that he stirred up the Duke's friends on his way from London to Sherborne, that they know not, or it would certainly go hard with him. What do I say? Since they will hang him, things cannot very well go harder.

'When the fight was over, and the Duke and Lord Grey fled, there was nothing left but to escape as best we might. I hope that some of the Bradford lads will make their way home in safety: they stood their ground and fought valiantly. Nay, if we had been able to arm all who volunteered and would have enlisted, and if our men had all shown such a spirit as your valiant lads of Bradford Orcas, then, I say, the enemy must have been cut to pieces.

'When we had no choice left but to run, I took the road to Bridgwater, intending to ride back to that place, where, perhaps, our forces might be rallied. But this proved hopeless. There I found, however, Humphrey, and we resolved that the safest plan would be to ride by way of Taunton and Exeter, leaving behind us the great body of the King's army, and so escape to London if possible, where we should certainly find hiding-places in plenty, until the pursuit should be at an end. Our plan was to travel along byways and bridle-paths, and that by night only, hiding by day in barns, linneys, and the like. We had money for the charges of our journey. Humphrey would travel as a physician returning to London from the West as soon as we had gotten out of the insurgents' country; I was to be his servant. Thus we arranged the matter in our minds, and already I thought that we were safe, and in hiding somewhere in London, or across the seas in the Low Countries again.

'Well, to make short my story, we got no further than Exeter, where we were betrayed by a rascal countryman who recognised us, caused us to be arrested, and swore to us. Thereupon we were clapped into jail, where we now lie.

'Hon'd Sir: Humphrey, I am sorry to write, is much cast down, not because he dreads death, which he doth not, any more than to lie upon his bed; but because he hath, he says, drawn so many to their ruin. He numbers me among those—though, indeed, it was none of his doing, but by my own free will, that I entered upon this business, which, contrary to reasonable expectation, hath turned out so ill. Wherefore, dear Sir, since there is no one in the world whose opinion and counsel Humphrey so greatly considers as your own, I pray you, of your goodness, send him some words of consolation and cheer.'

'That will I, right readily,' said Sir Christopher. 'At least the poor lad cannot accuse himself of dragging me into the Clink.'

'I hear,' continued Robin's letter, 'that my mother hath gone with Mr. Boscorel to London, to learn if aught can be done for us. If she do not return before we are finished, bid her think kindly of Humphrey and not to lay these things to his charge. As for my dear girl, my Alice, I hear nothing of her. Miss Blake, who led the Maids when they gave the flags to the Duke, is, I hear, clapped into prison. Alice is not spoken of. I am greatly perturbed in spirit concerning her, and I would gladly, if that might be compassed, have speech with her before I die. I fear she will grieve and weep; but not more than I myself at leaving her, poor maid! I hear, also, nothing concerning her father, who was red-hot for the Cause, and therefore, I fear, will not be passed over or forgotten. Nor do I hear aught of Barnaby, who, I hope, hath escaped on shipboard, as he said that he should do if things went ajar. Where are they all? The roads are covered with rough men, and it is not fit for such as Alice and her mother to be travelling. I hope that they have returned in safety to Bradford Orcas, and that my old master, Dr. Eykin, hath forgotten his zeal[178] for the Protestant Duke, and is already seated again among his books. If that is so, tell Alice, Honoured Sir, that there is no hour of the day or night but I think of her continually; that the chief pang of my approaching fate is the thought that I shall leave her in sorrow, and that I cannot say or do anything to stay her sorrow. Comfort her I cannot, save with words which will come better from the saintly lips of her father. I again pray thee to assure her of my faithful love. Tell her that the recollection of her sweet face and steadfast eyes fills me with so great a longing that I would fain die at once so as to bring nearer the moment when we shall be able to sit together in heaven. My life hath been glorified, if I may say so in humility, by her presence in my heart, which drove away all common and unclean things. Of such strength is earthly love. Nay, I could not, I now perceive, be happy even with the joys of heaven if she were not by my side. Where is she, my heart, my love? Pray God, she is in safety.

'And now, Sir, I have no more to say: The prison is a hot and reeking place; at night it is hard to bear the foulness and the stench of it. Humphrey says that we may shortly expect some jail fever or small-pox to break out among us, in which case the work of the Judges may be lightened. The good people of this ancient city are in no way afraid of the King's vindictiveness, but send in of their bounty quantity of provisions—fruit, eggs, fresh meat, salted meat, ale, and cider—every day for the poor prisoners, which shows which way their opinions do lean, even although the clergy are against us.

Honoured Sir, I am sure and certain that the miscarriage of our enterprise was caused by the conduct of those who had us in hand. In a year or two there shall be seen (but not by us) another uprising; under another leader with another end.

'So no more. I send to thee, dear and Honoured Sir, my bounden duty and my grateful thanks for all that I owe to your tender care and affection. Pray my mother, for me, to mourn no more for me than is becoming to one of her piety and virtue.

'Alas! it is thinking upon her, and upon my poor lost Alice, that my heart is wellnigh torn in pieces. But (tell Humphrey) through no fault—no—through no fault of his.

'From thy dutiful and obedient grandson,—

'R. C.'

I read this all through. Then I folded up the letter and returned it to Sir Christopher. As he took it the tears came into his dear and venerable eyes and rolled down his cheeks.

'My dear—my dear,' he said, 'it is hard to bear. Everyone who is dear to thee will go; there is an end of all; unless some way, of which we know nothing, be opened unto us.'

'Why,' I said, 'if we were all dead and buried, and our souls together in heaven'——

'Patience, my dear,' said the old man.

'Oh! must they all die—all? My heart will burst! Oh! Sir, will not one suffice for all? Will they not take me and hang me, and let the rest go free?'

'Child,' he took my hand between his own, 'God knows that if one life would suffice for all, it should be mine. Nay, I would willingly die ten times over to save thy Robin for thee. He is not dead yet, however. Nor is he sentenced. There are so many involved that we may hope for a large measure of mercy. Nay, more. His mother hath gone to London, as he says in his letter, with my son-in-law, Philip Boscorel, to see if aught can be done, even to the selling of my whole estate, to procure the enlargement of the boys. I know not if anything can be done, but be assured Philip Boscorel will leave no stone unturned.'

'Oh! can money buy a pardon? I have two hundred gold pieces. They are Barnaby's'——

'Then, my dear, they must be used to buy pardon for Barnaby and thy father—though I doubt whether any pardon need be bought for one who is brought so low.'

Beside the bed my mother sat crouched, watching his white face as she had done all day long in our hiding-place. I think she heeded nothing that went on around her, being wrapped in her hopes and prayers for the wounded man.

Then Sir Christopher kissed me gently on the forehead.

'They say the King is unforgiving, my dear. Expect not, therefore, anything. Say to thyself, every morning, that all must die. To know the worst brings with it something of consolation. Robin must die; Humphrey must die; your brother Barnaby must die; your father—but he is wellnigh dead already—and I myself, all must die upon the scaffold if we escape this noisome jail. In thinking of this, remember who will be left. My dear, if thou art as a widow and yet a maiden, I charge thee solemnly that thou forget thine own private griefs and minister to those who will have none but thee to help them. Live not for thyself, but to console and solace those who, like thyself bereaved, will need thy tender cares.'

CHAPTER XXVII.

BEFORE THE ASSIZE.

Then we sat down and waited. 'Twas all that we could do. Day after day we went to the prison, where my mother sat by my father, whose condition never changed in the least, being always that of one who slept, or, if his eyes were open, was unconscious, and though he might utter a few rambling words, had no command of his mind or of his speech. Wherefore we hoped that he suffered nothing. "Twas a musket ball had struck,' the surgeon said, 'in his backbone between the shoulders, whereby his powers of motion and of thought were suspended.' I know not whether anyone attempted to remove the ball, or whether it was lodged there at all, because I am ignorant of such matters; and to me, whether he had been struck in the back or no, it was to my mind sure and certain that the Lord had granted my father's earnest prayer that he should again be permitted to deliver openly the message that was upon his soul; nay, had given him three weeks of continual and faithful preaching, the fruits of which, could we perceive them, should be abundant. That prayer granted, the Lord, I thought, was calling him to rest. Therefore, I looked for no improvement.

One other letter came from Robin, inclosing one for me, with which (because I could not leave my mother at such a time) I was forced to stay my soul, as the lover in the Canticle stayeth his soul with apples. I have that letter still; it hath been with me always; it lay hanging from my neck in the little leathern bag in which I carried the Duke's ring; I read it again and again until I knew it by heart; yet still I read it again, because even to look at my lover's writing had in it something of comfort even when things were at their worst, and Egyptian darkness lay upon my soul. But this letter I cannot endure to copy out or suffer others to read it, because it was written for mine own eye in such a time of trouble. 'Oh! my love!' he said. 'Oh, my tender heart!' and then a hundred prayers for my happiness, and tears for my tears, and hopes for the future (which would be not the earthly life but the future reserved by merciful Heaven for those who have been called and chosen). As for the sharp and painful passage by which we must travel from this world to the next, Robin bade me take no thought of that at all, but to think of him either as my lover walking with me as of old beside the stream at home, or as a spirit waiting for me to join him in the heavenly choir. And so ending with as many farewells (the letter being written when he expected the Judges to arrive and the Assize to begin) as showed his tender love for me. No—I cannot write down this letter for the eyes of all to read. There are things which must be kept hidden in our own hearts; and, without doubt, every woman to whom good fortune hath given a lover such as Robin, with a heart as fond and a pen as ready (though he could never, like Humphrey, write sweet verses), hath received an epistle or two like unto mine for its love and tenderness, but (I hope) without the sadness of impending death.

It was four weeks after we were brought to Ilminster that the news came to us of the coming trials. There were five Judges—but the world knows but of one, namely, George Lord Jeffreys, Chief Justice of England—and now, indeed, we began to understand the true misery of our situation. For everyone knew the character of the Judge, who, though a young man still, was already the terror alike of prisoners, witnesses, and juries. It promised to be a black and bloody Assize indeed, since this man was to be the Judge.

The aspect of the prison by this time was changed. The songs and merriment, the horseplay and loud laughter by which the men had at first endeavoured to keep up their hearts were gone. The country lads pined and languished in confinement; their cheeks grew pale and their eyes heavy. Then, the prison was so crowded that there was barely room for all to lie at night, and the yard was too small for all to walk therein by day. In the morning, though they opened all the shutters, the air was so foul that in going into it from the open one felt sick and giddy, and was sometimes fain to run out and drink cold water. Oh! the terrible place for an old man such as Sir Christopher! Yet he endured without murmuring the foulness and the hardness, comforting the sick, still reproving blasphemies, and setting an example of cheerfulness. The wounded men all died, I believe; which, as the event proved, was lucky for them. It would have saved the rest much suffering if they had all died as well. And to think that this was only one of many prisons thus crowded with poor captives! At Wells, Philip's Norton, Shepton Mallet, Bath, Bridgwater, Taunton, Ilchester, Somerton, Langport, Bristol and Exeter, there was a like assemblage of poor wretches thus awaiting their trials.

I said that there was now little singing. There was, however, drinking enough, and more than enough. They drank to drown their sorrows, and to forget the horrid place in which they lay and the future which awaited them. When they were drunk they would bellow some of their old songs; but the brawling of a drunkard will not communicate to his companions the same joy as the music of a merry heart.

While we were expecting to hear that the Judge had arrived at Salisbury, the fever broke out in the prison of Ilminster. At Wells they were afflicted with the small-pox, but at Ilminster it was jail fever which fell upon the poor prisoners. Everybody hath heard of this terrible disorder, which is communicated by those who have it to those who go among them—namely, to the warders and turnkeys, and even to the judges and the juries. On the first day after it broke out—which was with an extraordinary virulence—four poor men died and were buried the next morning. After this, no day passed but there were funerals at the churchyard, and the mounds of their graves—the graves of these poor countrymen who thought to fight the battles of the Lord—stood side by side in a long row, growing continually longer. We—that is, good Mrs. Prior and myself—sat at the window and watched the funerals, praying for the safety of those we loved.

So great was the fear of infection in the town that no one was henceforth allowed within the prison, nor were the warders allowed to come out of it. This was a sad order for me, because my mother chose to remain within the prison, finding a garret at the house of the Chief Constable, and I could no longer visit that good old man, Sir Christopher, whose only pleasure left had been to converse with me daily, and, as I now understand, by the refreshment the society of youth brings to age, to lighten the tedium of his imprisonment.

Henceforth, therefore, I went to the prison door every morning and sent in my basket of provisions, but was not suffered to enter; and though I could have speech with my mother or with Barnaby, they were on one side the bars and I on the other.

It was at this time that I made the acquaintance of Mr. George Penne. This creature—a villain, as I afterwards discovered, of the deepest dye—was to external appearance a grave and sober merchant. He was dressed in brown cloth and laced shirt, and carried a gold-headed stick in his hand. He came to Ilminster about the end of August or the beginning of September, and began to inquire particularly into the names and the circumstances of the prisoners, pretending (such was his craftiness) a great tenderness for their welfare. He did the same thing, we heard afterwards, wherever the Monmouth prisoners were confined. At Ilminster, the fever being in the jail, he did not venture within, but stood outside and asked of any who seemed to know, who were the prisoners within, and what were their circumstances.

He accosted me one morning when I was standing at the wicket waiting for my basket to be taken in.

'Madam,' he said, 'you are doubtless a friend of some poor prisoner. Your father or your brother may unhappily be lying within?'

Now I was grown somewhat cautious by this time. Wherefore, fearing some kind of snare or trap, I replied gravely, that such, indeed, might be the case.

'Then, Madam,' he said, speaking in a soft voice and looking full of compassion, 'if that be so, suffer me, I pray you, to wish him a happy deliverance; and this, indeed, from the bottom of my heart.'

'Sir,' I said, moved by the earnestness of his manner, 'I know not who you may be, but I thank you. Such a wish, I hope, will not procure you the reward of a prison. Sir, I wish you a good day.'

So he bowed and left me, and passed on.

But next day I found him in the same place. And his eyes were more filled with compassion than before and his voice was softer.

'I cannot sleep, Madam,' he said, 'for thinking of these poor prisoners; I hear that among them is none other than Sir Christopher Challis, a gentleman of great esteem and well stricken in years. And there is also the pious and learned—but most unfortunate—Dr. Comfort Eykin, who rode with the army and preached daily, and is now, I hear, grievously wounded and bedridden.'

'Sir,' I said, 'Dr. Comfort Eykin is my father. It is most true that he is a prisoner, and that he is wounded.'

He heaved a deep sigh and wiped a tear from his eyes.

'It is now certain,' he said, 'that Lord Jeffreys will come down to conduct the trials. Nay, it is reported that he has already arrived at Salisbury, breathing fire and revenge, and that he hath with him four other Judges and a troop of horse. What they will do with so many prisoners I know not. I fear that it will go hard with all; but, as happens in such cases, those who have money, and know how to spend it, may speedily get their liberty.'

'How are they to spend it?'

'Why, Madam, it is not indeed to be looked for that you should know. But when the time comes for the trial, should I, as will very likely happen, be in the way, send for me, and whatever the sentence I warrant we shall find a way to 'scape it—even if it be a sentence of death. Send for me—my name is George Penne, and I am a well-known merchant of Bristol.'

It was then that Barnaby came to the other side of the wicket. We could talk, but could not touch each other.

'All is well, Sis,' he said: 'Dad is neither better nor worse, and Sir Christopher is hearty, though the prison is like the 'tween decks of a ship with Yellow Jack aboard—just as sweet and pleasant for the air and just as merry for the crew.'

'Barnaby,' I said, 'the Judges are now at Salisbury.'

'Ay, ay; I thought they would have been there before. We shall be tried, they tell me, at Wells, which it is thought will be taken after other towns. So there is still a tidy length of rope. Sis, this continual smoking of tobacco to keep off infection doth keep a body dry. Cider will serve, but let it be a runlet, at least.'

'He called you "Sister," Madam,' said Mr. Penne curiously. 'Have you brother as well as father in this place?'

'Alas! Sir, I have not only my father, my mother, and my brother in this place, but my father-in-law (as I hoped soon to call him); and in Exeter Jail is my lover and his cousin. Oh! Sir, if you mean honestly'——

'Madam'—he laid his hand upon his breast—'I assure you I am all honesty. I have no other thought, I swear to you, than to save, if possible, the lives of these poor men.'

He walked with me to my lodging, and I there told him not only concerning our own people, but also all that I knew of the prisoners in this jail—they were for the most part poor and humble men. He made notes in a book, which caused me some misgivings; but he assured me again and again that all he desired was to save their lives. And I now understand that he spoke the truth indeed, but not the whole truth.

'Your brother, for instance,' he said. 'Oh! Madam, 'twere a thousand pities that so brave a young man, so stout withal, should be hanged, drawn, and quartered. And your lover at Exeter, doubtless a tall and proper youth; and the other whom you have named, Dr. Humphrey Challis, and your grandfather (as I hope he will be) Sir Christopher; and your own father—why, Madam,' he grew quite warm upon it, 'if you will but furnish some honest merchant—I say not myself, because I know not yet if you would trust me—but some honest merchant with the necessary moneys, I will engage that they shall all be saved from hanging. To be sure, these are all captains and officers, and to get their absolute pardon will be a great matter—perhaps above your means. Yet, Sir Christopher hath a good estate, I am told.'

This George Penne was, it is true, a Bristol merchant, engaged in the West India trade; that is to say, he bought sugar and tobacco, and had shares in ships which sailed to and from Bristol and the West Indies, and sometimes made voyages to the Guinea Coast for negroes. But, in common with many Bristol merchants, he had another trade, and a very profitable trade it is, namely, what is called kidnapping: that is, buying or otherwise securing criminals who have been pardoned or reprieved on condition of going to the Plantations. They sell these wretches for a term of years to the planters, and make a great profit by the transaction. And, foreseeing that there would presently be a rare abundance of such prisoners, the honest Mr. George Penne was going from prison to prison finding out what persons of substance there were who would willingly pay for their sentence to be thus mitigated. In the event, though things were not ordered exactly as he could have wished, this worthy man (his true worth you shall presently hear) made a pretty penny, as the saying is, out of the prisoners. What he made out of us, and by what lies, you shall learn; but, by ill-fortune for him, he gat not the fingering of the great sums which he hoped of us.

And now the news—from Winchester first, and from Dorchester afterwards—filled the hearts of all with a dismay which it is beyond all power of words to tell. For if an ancient lady of good repute (though the widow of a regicide), such a woman as Lady Lisle, seventy years of age, could be condemned to be burned—and was, in fact, beheaded—for no greater offence than harbouring two rebels, herself ignorant of who they were or whence they came, what could any hope who had actually borne arms? And, again, at Dorchester, thirty who pleaded not guilty were found guilty and condemned to be hanged, and nearly three hundred who pleaded guilty were sentenced to be hanged at the same time. It was not an idle threat intended to terrify the rest, because thirteen of the number were executed on the following Monday, and eighty afterwards. Among those who were first hanged were many whom we knew. The aged and pious Mr. Sampson Larke, the Baptist Minister of Lyme, for instance, was one; Colonel Holmes (whom the King had actually pardoned) was another; and young Mr. Hewling—whose case was like that of Robin. This terrible news caused great despondency and choking in the prison, where also the fever daily carried off one or two.

Oh! my poor heart fell, and I almost lost the power of prayer, when I heard that from Dorchester the Judge was riding in great state, driving his prisoners before him to Exeter, where there were two hundred waiting their trial. And among them Robin—Alas! alas!—my Robin.

CHAPTER XXVIII.

BENJAMIN.

I t was the evening of September the Sixteenth, about nine of the clock. I was sitting alone in my lodging. Downstairs I heard the voice of the poor widow, Mrs. Prior, who had received us. She was praying aloud with some godly friends for the safety of her sons. These young men, as I have said, were never more heard of, and were therefore already, doubtless, past praying for. I, who ought to have been praying with them, held Robin's last letter in my hands. I knew it by heart; but I must still be reading it again and again; thinking it was his voice which was indeed speaking to me, trying to feel his presence near me, to hear his breath, to see his very eyes. In the night, waking or sleeping, I still would hear him calling to me aloud. 'My heart! my life! my love!' he would cry. I heard him, I say, quite plainly. By special mercy and grace this power was accorded to me; because I have no doubt that in his mind, while lying in his noisome prison, he did turn his thoughts, yea, and the yearnings of his fond heart, to the maid he loved. But now the merciless Judge who had sentenced three hundred men to one common doom—three hundred men!—was such a sentence ever known?—had left Dorchester, and was already, perhaps, at Exeter. Oh!—perhaps Robin had by this time stood his trial: what place was left for prayer? For if the poor, ignorant clowns were condemned to death, how much more the gentlemen, the officers of Monmouth's army! Perhaps he was already executed—my lover, my boy, my Robin!—taken out and hanged, and now a cold and senseless corpse! Then the wailings and prayers of the poor woman below, added to the distraction of these thoughts, made me feel as if I was indeed losing my senses. At this time, it was blow upon blow—line upon line. The sky was black—the heavens were deaf. Is there—can there be—a more miserable thing than to feel that the very heavens are deaf? The mercy of the Lord—His kindly hearkening to our cries and prayers—these we believe as we look for the light of day and the warmth of the sun. Nay, this belief is the very breath of our life; so that there is none but the most hardened and abandoned sinner who doth not still feel that he hath in the Lord a Father as well as a Judge. To lose that belief—'twere better to be a lump of senseless clay. The greatest misery of the lost soul, even greater than his continual[187] torment of fire, and his never-ending thirst, and the gnawing of remorse, must be to feel that the heavens are deaf to his prayers—deaf for ever and for ever!

At this time, my prayers were all for safety. 'Safety, good Lord! give them safety! Save them from the executioner? Give them safety?' Thus, as Barnaby said, the shipwrecked mariner clinging to the mast asks not for a green, pleasant, and fertile shore, but for land—only for land. I sat there, musing sadly, the Bible on the table and a lighted candle. I read not in the Bible, but listened to the wailing of the poor soul below, and looked at the churchyard without, the moonlight falling upon the fresh mounds which covered the graves of the poor dead prisoners. Suddenly I heard a voice—a loud and harsh voice—and footsteps. I knew both footsteps and voice, and I sprang to my feet trembling, because I was certain that some new disaster had befallen us.

Then the steps mounted the stairs; the door was opened, and Benjamin—none other than Benjamin—appeared. What did he here? He was so big, with so red a face, that his presence seemed to fill the room. And with him—what did this mean?—came Madam herself, who I thought to have been at Exeter. Alas! her eyes were red with weeping; her cheeks were thin and wasted with sorrow; her lips were trembling.

'Alice!' she cried, holding out her hands. 'Child, these terrible things are done, and yet we live! Alas! we live! Are our hearts made of stone that we still live? As for me, I cannot die, though I lose all—all—all!'

'Dear Madam, what hath happened? More misery! More disaster! Oh! tell me! tell me!'

'Oh! my dear, they have been tried—they have been tried, and they are condemned to die—both Robin—my son Robin—and with him Humphrey, who dragged him into the business and alone ought to suffer for both. But there is now no justice in the land. No—no more justice can be had. Else Humphrey should have suffered for all.'

There was something strange in her eyes—she did not look like a mother robbed of her children; she gazed upon me as if there was something else upon her mind. As if the condemnation of her son was not enough.

'Robin will be hanged,' she went on. 'He hath been the only comfort of my life since my husband was taken from me, when he was left an infant in my arms. Robin will be hanged like any common gipsy caught stealing a sheep. He will be hanged, and drawn and quartered, and those goodly limbs of his will be stuck upon poles for all to see!'

Truly I looked for nothing less. Barnaby bade me look for nothing less than this; but at the news I fell into a swoon. So one who knoweth beforehand that he is to feel the surgeon's knife, and thinks to endure the agony without a cry, is fain to shriek and scream when the moment comes.

When I recovered I was sitting at the open window, Madam applying a wet cloth to my forehead.

'Have no fear,' Benjamin was saying. 'She will do what you command her, so only that he may go free.'

'Is there no way but that?' she asked.

'None!' And then he swore a great oath.

My eyes being opened and my sense returned, I perceived that Mrs. Prior was also in the room. And I wondered (in such moments the mind finds relief in trifles) that Benjamin's face should have grown so red and his cheeks so fat.

'Thou hast been in a swoon, my dear,' said Madam. 'But 'tis past.' 'Why is Benjamin here?' I asked.

He looked at Madam, who cast down her eyes, I knew not why.

'Benjamin is now our only friend,' she replied without looking up. 'It is out of his kindness—yes—his kindness of heart that he hath come.'

'I do not understand. If Robin is to die what kindness can he show?'

'Tell her, Benjamin,' said Madam, 'tell her of the trials at Exeter.'

'His Lordship came to Exeter,' Benjamin began, 'on the evening of September the Thirteenth, escorted by many country gentlemen and a troop of horse. I had the honour of riding with him. The trials began the day before yesterday, the Fourteenth.'

'Pray, good Sir,' asked the poor woman who had lost her sons, 'did you observe my boys among the prisoners?'

'How the devil should I know your boys?' he replied, turning upon her roughly, so that she asked no more questions. 'If they were rebels they deserve hanging'—here she shrieked aloud, and fled the room. 'The trials began with two fellows who pleaded "Not guilty," but were quickly proved to have been in arms, and were condemned to death, one of them being sent out to instant execution. The rest who were brought up that day—among whom were Robin and Humphrey—pleaded "Guilty," being partly terrified and partly persuaded that it was their only chance of escape. So they, too, were condemned—two hundred and forty in all—every man Jack of them, to be hanged, drawn, and quartered, and their limbs to be afterwards stuck on poles for the greater terror of evildoers'—he said these words with such a fire in his eyes, and in such a dreadful threatening voice, as made me tremble. 'Then they were all taken back to jail, where they will lie until the day of execution, and the Lord have mercy upon their souls!'

The terrible Judge Jeffreys himself could not look more terrible than Benjamin when he uttered the prayer with which a sentence to death is concluded.

'Benjamin, were you in the court to see and hear the condemnation of your own cousins?'

'I was. I sat in the body of the court, in the place reserved for Counsel.'

'Could you say nothing that would help them?'

'Nothing. Not a word from anyone could help them. Consider—one of them was an officer, and one a surgeon in the army. The ignorant rustics whom they led may some of them escape, but the officers can look for no mercy.'

'Madam,' I cried, 'I must see Robin before he dies; though, God knows, there are those here who want my services daily. Yet I must see Robin. He will not die easy unless he can see me and kiss me once.'

Madam made no reply.

'For a week,' said Benjamin, 'they are safe. I do not think they will be executed for a week at least. But it is not wise to reckon on a reprieve even for an hour: the Judge may at any time order their execution.'

'I will go to-morrow.'

'That will be seen,' said Benjamin.

'My dear,' said Madam, 'my nephew Benjamin is a friend of the Judge, Lord Jeffreys.'

'Say rather a follower and admirer of that great, learned, and religious man. One who is yet but a member of the Outer Bar must not assume the style and title of friend to a man whose next step must be the Woolsack.'

'Heavens! He called the inhuman wretch who had sentenced an innocent old woman of seventy to be burned alive, and five hundred persons to be hanged, and one knows not how many to be inhumanly flogged—great and religious!'

'If interest can save any,' Madam said softly, 'Benjamin can command that interest, and he is on the side of mercy, especially where his cousins are concerned.'

I now observed that Madam, who had not formerly been wont to regard her nephew with much affection, behaved towards him with the greatest respect and submission.

'Madam,' he replied, 'you know the goodness of my heart. What man can do shall be done by me, not only for Robin, but for the others who are involved with him in common ruin. But there are conditions with which I have taken pains to acquaint you.'

Madam sighed heavily, and looked as if she would speak, but refrained; and I saw the tears rolling down her cheeks.

'What conditions, Benjamin?' I asked him. 'Conditions for trying to save your own cousins and your own grandfather! Conditions? Why, you should be moving heaven and earth for them instead of making conditions.'

'It needs not so much exertion,' he replied with an unbecoming grin. 'First, Alice, I must own, Child, that the two years or thereabouts since I saw thee last have added greatly to thy charms; at which I rejoice.'

'Oh! what have my charms to do with the business?'

'Much; as thou wilt presently discover. But let me remind you both that there threaten—nay, there are actually overhanging —disasters, the like of which never happen save in time of civil war and of rebellion. My grandfather is in prison, and will be tried on a charge of sending men and horses to join Monmouth. Nay, the Duke's Proclamation was found in his house; he will be certainly condemned and his estates confiscated. So there will be an end of as old a family as lives in Somerset. Then there is thy father, Child, who was Preacher to the army, and did make mischief in stirring up the fanatical zeal of many. Think you that he can escape? Then there is thy brother Barnaby, who was such a fool as to meddle in what concerned him not, and now will hang therefor. What can we expect? Are men to go unpunished who thus rebel against the Lord's anointed? Is treason—rank treason—the setting up of a Pretender Prince (who is now lying headless in his coffin) as the rightful heir, to be forgiven? We must not look for it. Alas! Madam, had I been with you instead of that conceited, fanatical, crookback Humphrey, whom I did ever detest, none of these things should have happened.'

'Humphrey,' I said, 'has more worth in one finger than you in all your great body, Benjamin.'

'My dear, my dear, do not anger Benjamin. Oh, do not anger our only friend!'

'She may say what she pleases. My time will come. Listen then. They must all be hanged unless I can succeed in getting them pardoned.'

'Nay—but—forgive my rudeness, Benjamin; they are your own cousins—it is your own grandfather. What need of conditions? Oh! what does this mean? Are you a man of flesh and blood?'

'My conditions, Child'—why did he laugh?—'will assure you that such is truly the nature of my composition.'

'If money is wanted'—I thought of my bag of gold and of Mr. Penne's hints—'how much will suffice?'

'I know not. If it comes to buying them off, more thousands than could be raised on the Bradford Orcas estates. Put money out of mind.'

'Then, Benjamin, save them if thou canst.'

'His Lordship knows that I have near relations concerned in the Rebellion. Yet, he assured me if his own brothers were among the prisoners he would hang them all.'

'Nay, then, Benjamin; I say no more. Tell me what are these conditions, and, if we can grant or contrive them, we will comply.' I had no thought of what was meant by his conditions, nor did I even guess until the morning, when Madam told me. 'Oh! Madam, is there anything in the world—anything that we would not do to save them?'

Madam looked at me with so much pity in her eyes that I wondered. It was pity for me and not for her son that I read in that look. Why did she pity me?

I understood not.

'My dear,' she said, 'there are times when women are called upon to make sacrifices which they never thought to make, which seem impossible to be even asked——'

'Oh! there are no sacrifices which we would not gladly make. What can Benjamin require that we should not gladly do for him? Nay, he is Robin's cousin, and your nephew, and Sir Christopher's grandson. He will, if need be, join us in making these sacrifices.'

'I will,' said Benjamin—again, why did he laugh?—'I will join you in making one sacrifice at least, with a willing heart.'

'I will tell her to-morrow,' said Madam. 'No, I cannot tell her to-night. Let us first rest. Go, Sir; leave us to our sorrow. It may be that we may yet think the sacrifice too great even for the lives and the safety of those we love. Go, Sir, for to-night, and return to-morrow.'

'Surely, Child,' said Madam presently, when he was gone, and we were alone, 'we are the most unhappy women in the world.'

'Nay,' I replied. 'There have been other women before us who have been ruined and widowed by civil wars and rebellions. If it be any comfort to think that others have suffered like ourselves, then we may comfort ourselves. But the thought brings no consolation to me.'

'Hagar,' said Madam, 'was a miserable woman because she was cast out by the man she loved, even the father of her son; but she saved her son. Rachel was unhappy until the Lord gave her a son. Jephthah's daughter was unhappy—my dear, there is no case except hers which may be compared with ours—and Jephthah's daughter was happy in one circumstance: that she was permitted to die. Ah! happy girl, she died! That was all her sacrifice—to die for the sake of her father! But what is ours?'

So she spoke in riddles or dark sayings, of which I understood nothing. Nevertheless, before lying down, I did solemnly and, in her presence and hearing, aloud, upon my knees, offer unto Almighty God myself—my very life—if so that Robin could be saved. And then, with lighter heart than I had known for long, I lay down and slept.

At midnight, or thereabouts, Madam woke me up.

'Child,' she said, 'I cannot sleep. Tell me truly: is there nothing that thou wouldest refuse for Robin's sake?'

'Nothing, verily! Ah, Madam, can you doubt it?'

'Even if it were a sacrifice of which he would not approve?'

'Believe me, Madam, there is nothing that I would not do for Robin's safety.'

'Child, if we were living in the days of persecution wouldest thou hear the Mass and adopt the Catholic religion to save thy lover's life?'

'Oh, Madam, the Lord will never try us above our strength!'

'Sleep, my child, sleep; and pray that, as thy temptation, so may be thy strength!'

CHAPTER XXIX.

ON WHAT CONDITIONS?

In the morning I awoke with a lighter heart than I had known for a long time. Benjamin was going to release our prisoners! I should go to meet Robin at the gate of his prison. All would be well, except that my father would never recover. We should return to the village and everything would go on as before. Oh! poor fond wretch! how was I deluded! and, oh! miserable day that ended with such shame and sadness, yet began with so much hope.

Madam was already dressed. She was sitting at the window looking into the churchyard. She had been crying. Alas! how many women in Somersetshire were then weeping all day long!

'Madam,' I said, 'we now have hope. We must not weep and lament any more. Oh! to have at last a little hope—when we have lived so long in despair—it makes one breathe again. Benjamin will save our prisoners for us. Oh! after all, it is Benjamin who will help us. We did not use to love Benjamin, because he was rude and masterful and wanted everything for himself and would never give up anything. Yet, you see, he had, after all, a good heart.' Madam groaned. 'And he cannot forget, though he followeth not his grandfather's opinions, that he is his Honour's grandson—the son of his only daughter—and your nephew, and first cousin to Robin, and second cousin once removed to Humphrey and Barnaby; playfellows of old. Why, these are ties which bind him as if with ropes! He needs must bestir himself to save their lives. And since he says that he can save them, of course he must have bestirred himself to some purpose. Weep no more, dear Madam; your son will be restored to us! We shall be happy again—thanks to Benjamin!'

'Child,' she replied, 'my heart is broken! It is broken, I say! Oh, to be lying dead and at peace in yonder churchyard! Never before did I think that it must be a happy thing to be dead and at rest, and to feel nothing and to know nothing!'

'But, Madam, the dead are not in their graves. There lie only the bodies. Their souls are above.'

'Then they still think and remember. Oh! can a time ever come when things can be forgotten? Will the dead ever cease to reproach themselves?'

She wrung her hands in an ecstasy of grief, though I knew not what should move her so. Indeed, she was commonly a woman of sober and contained disposition, entirely governed both in her temper and her words. What was in her mind that she should accuse herself? Then, while I was dressing, she went on talking, being still full of this strong passion.

'I shall have my boy back again,' she said. 'Yes; he will come back to me. And what will he say to me when I tell him all? Yet I *must* have him back. Oh! to think of the hangman tying the rope about his neck'—she shuddered and trembled—'and afterwards the cruel knife'—she clasped her hands and could not say the words—'I see the comely limbs of my boy. Oh! the thought tears my heart—it tears me through and through. I cannot think of anything else day or night. And yet in the prison he is so patient and so cheerful. I marvel that men can be so patient with this dreadful death before them.' She broke out again into another passion of sobbing and crying. Then she became calmer, and tried to speak of things less dreadful.

'When first I visited my boy in prison,' she said, 'Humphrey came humbly to ask my pardon. Poor lad! I have had hard thoughts of him. It is certain that he was in the plot from the beginning. Yet had he not gone so far, should we have sat down when the rising began? But he doth still accuse himself of rashness and calls himself the cause of all our misfortunes. He fell upon his knees, in the sight of all, to ask forgiveness, saying that it was he and none other who had brought ruin upon us all. Then Robin begged me to raise him up and comfort him, which I did, putting aside my hard thoughts and telling him that, being such stubborn Protestants, our lads could not choose but join the Duke, whether he advised it or whether he did not. Nay, I told him that Robin would have dragged him willy nilly. And so I kissed him, and Robin took him by the hand and solemnly assured him that his grandfather had no such thought in his mind.'

'Nay,' I said, 'my father and Barnaby would certainly have joined the Duke, Humphrey or not. Never were any men more eager for rebellion.'

'I have been to London,' she went on. "Tis a long journey and I effected nothing; for the mind of the King, I was assured, is harder than the nether millstone. My brother-in-law, Philip Boscorel, went with me, and I left him there. But I have no hope that he will be able to help us, his old friends being much scattered and many of them dead, and some hostile to the Court and in ill-favour. So I returned, seeing that, if I could not save my son I could be with him until he died. The day before yesterday he was tried—if you call that a trial when hundreds together plead guilty and are all alike sentenced to death.'

'Have you seen him since the trial?'

'I went to the prison as soon as they were brought back from Court. Some of the people—for they were all condemned to death—every one—were crying and lamenting. And there were many women among them—their wives or their mothers—and these were shrieking and wringing their hands; so that it was a terrible spectacle. But some of the men called for drink, and began to carouse, so that they might drown the thought of impending death. My dear, I never thought to look upon a scene so full of horror. As for our own boys, Robin was patient and even cheerful; and Humphrey, leading us to the most quiet spot in that dreadful place, exhorted us to lose no time in weeping or vain laments, but to cheer and console our hearts with the thought that death—even violent death—is but a brief pang and life is but a short passage, and that heaven awaits us beyond. Humphrey should have been a godly minister, such is the natural piety and goodness of his heart. So he spoke of the happy meeting in that place of blessedness where earthly love would be purged of its grossness, and our souls shall be so glorified that we shall each admire the beauty and the excellence of the other. Then Robin talked of thee, my dear, and sent thee a loving message bidding thee grieve for him, but not without hope—and that a sure and certain hope—of meeting again. There are other things he bade me tell thee; but now I cannot!—oh, I must not!'

'Nay, Madam; but if they are words that he wished me to hear'——

'Why, they were of his constant love—and—no, I cannot tell them!'

'Well,' I said, 'fret not thy poor heart with thinking any more of the prison; for Benjamin will surely save him, and then we shall love Benjamin all our lives.'

'He will, perhaps, save him. And yet'——she turned her head—'Oh, how can I tell *her*—we shall shed many more tears. How can I tell *her*? How can I tell *her*?'

So she broke off again, but presently recovered and went on talking. In time of great trouble the mind wanders backwards and forwards, and though one talks still, it is disjointedly. So she went back to the prison.

'The boys have been well, though the prison is full and the air is foul. Yet there hath been as yet no fever, for which they are[195] thankful. They had no money, the soldiers who took them prisoners having robbed them of their money, and indeed stripped them as well to their shirts, telling them that shirts were good enough to be hanged in. Yet the people of Exeter have treated the prisoners with great humanity, bringing them daily food and drink, so that there has been nothing lacking. The time, however, doth hang upon hands in a place where there is nothing to do all day but to think of the past and to dread the future. One poor prisoner I was told had gone distracted with the terror of this thought. Child, every day that I visited my son, while he talked with me, always cheerful and smiling, my mind turned continually to the scaffold and the gibbet.' Then she returned to the old subject from which she could in no way escape. 'I saw the hangman, I saw my son hanging to the shameful tree—oh! my son! my son!—till I could bear it no longer, and would hurry away from the prison and walk about the town over the fields—yea, all night long—to escape the dreadful thought. Oh! to be blessed with such a son and to have him torn from my arms for such a death! If he had been killed upon the field of battle 'twould have been easier to bear. But now he dies daily—he dies a thousand deaths in my mind. My child!'—she turned again to the churchyard—'the rooks are cawing in their nests; the sparrows and the robins hop among the graves; the dead hear nothing; all their troubles are over, all their sins are forgiven.'

I comforted her as well as I could. Indeed, I understood not at all what she meant, thinking that perhaps all her trouble had caused her to be in that frame of mind when a woman doth not know whether to laugh or to cry. And then, taking my basket, I sallied forth to provide the day's provisions for my prisoners.

'Barnaby,' I said, when he came to the wicket, 'I have good news for thee.'

'What good news? That I am to be flogged once a year in every market-town in Somersetshire, as will happen to young Tutchin?'

'No, no—not that kind of news, but freedom, Brother, hope for freedom.'

He laughed. 'Who is to give us freedom?'

'Benjamin hath found a way for the enlargement of all.'

'Ben Boscorel? What! will he stir finger for the sake of anybody? Then, Sis, if I remember Ben aright, there will be something for himself. But if it is upon Ben that we are to rely we are truly well sped. On Ben, quotha!'

'My Brother, he told me so himself.'

"Ware hawks, Sister. If Ben is a tone end of the rope and the hangman at the other, I think I know who will be stronger. Well, Child, believe Ben if thou wilt. Thy father looks strange this morning. He opened his eyes and seemed to know me. I wonder if there is a change. 'Tis wonderful how he lasts. There are six men sickened since yesterday of the fever. Three of them brought[196] in last week are already dead. As for the singing that we used to hear, it is all over, and if the men get drunk they are dumb drunk. Sir Christopher looks but poorly this morning. I hope he will not take the fever. He staggered when he arose, which is a bad sign.'

'Tell mother, Barnaby, what Benjamin hath undertaken to do.'

'Nay, that shall I not, because, look you, I believe it not. There is some trick or lie at the bottom, unless Ben hath repented and changed his disposition, which used to be two parts wolf, one part bear, and the rest fox. If there were anything left it was serpent. Well, Sister, I am no grumbler, but I expect this job to be over in a fortnight or so, when they say the Wells Assizes will be held. Then we shall all be swinging, and I only hope that we may carry with us into the Court such a breath of jail fever as shall lay the Judge himself upon his back and end his days. In the next world he will meet the men whom he has sentenced, and it will fare worse for him in their hands than with fifty thousand devils.'

So he took a drink of the beer, and departed within the prison. And for many months I saw him no more.

On my way home I met Benjamin.

'Hath Madam told you yet of my conditions?' he asked eagerly.

'Not yet; she will doubtless tell me presently. Oh! what matter for the conditions? It can only be something good for us, contrived by your kind heart, Ben. I have told Barnaby, who will not believe in our good fortune.'

'It is, indeed, something very good for you, Alice, as you will find. Come with me and walk in the meadows beyond the reach of this doleful place, where the air reeks with jail fever, and all day long they are reading the Funeral Service.'

So he led me out upon the sloping sides of a hill, where we walked a while upon the grass very pleasantly, my mind being now at rest.

'You have heard of nothing,' he said, 'of late, but of the Rebellion and its consequences. Let us talk about London.'

So he discoursed concerning his own profession and his prospects, which, he said, were better than those of any other young lawyer, in his own opinion. 'For my practice,' he said, 'I already have one which gives me an income far beyond my wants, which are simple. Give me plain fare, and for the evening a bottle or two of good wine, with tobacco, and friends who love a cheerful glass. I ask no more. My course lies clear before me: I shall become a King's Counsel, I shall be made a Judge; presently, I shall become Lord Chancellor. What did I tell thee, Child, long ago? Well, that time has now arrived.'

Still I was so foolish, being so happy, that I could not understand what he meant.

'I am sure, Benjamin,' I said, 'that we at home shall ever rejoice and be proud of your success. Nobody will be more happy to hear of it than Robin and I.'

Here he turned very red and muttered something.

'You find your happiness in courts and clubs and London,' I went on; 'as for Robin and myself, we shall find ours in the peaceful place which we have always decided to have.'

'What the Devil!' he cried, 'she will not tell you the conditions? She came with me for no other purpose. I have borne with her company all the way from Exeter for this only. Go back to her, and ask what it is! Go back, I say, and make her tell! What! am I to take all this trouble for nothing?'

His face became purple with sudden rage; his eyes grew swiftly fierce, and he roared and bawled at me. Why, what had I said?

'Benjamin,' I cried, 'what is the matter? How have I angered you?'

'Go back!' he roared again. 'Tell her that if I presently come and find thee still in ignorance 'twill be the worse for all! Tell her that *I* say it. 'Twill else be worse for all!'

CHAPTER XXX.

A SLIGHT THING AT THE BEST.

So I left Benjamin much frightened, and marvelling, both at his violent passion, and at the message which he sent to Madam.

She was waiting for me at the lodging.

'Madam,' I said, 'I have seen Benjamin. He is very angry. He bade me go home and ask you concerning his conditions. We must not anger our best friend, dear Madam.'

She rose from her chair and began to walk about, wringing her hands as if torn by some violent emotion.

'Oh! my child,' she cried; 'Alice, come to my arms—if it is for the last time—my daughter. More than ever mine, though I must never call thee daughter.'

She held me in her arms, kissing me tenderly. 'My dear, we agreed that no sacrifice could be too great for the safety of our boy. Yes, we agreed to that. Let us kiss each other before we do a thing after which we can never kiss each other again. No, never again.'

'Why not again, Madam?'

'Oh,' she pushed me from her, 'it is now eight of the clock, he will be here at ten! I promised I would tell thee before he came! And all is in readiness.'

'For what, Madam?'

Why, even then I guessed not her meaning, though I might have done so; but I never thought that so great a wickedness was possible!

'No sacrifice should be too great for us!' she cried, clasping her head with her hands and looking wildly about. 'None too great! Not even the sacrifice of my own son's love—no; not that! Why, let us think of the sacrifices men make for their country, for their religion. Abraham was ready to offer his son, Isaac; Jephthah sacrificed his daughter; King Mesha slew his eldest son for a burnt offering. Thousands of men die every year in battle for their country. What have we to offer? If we give ourselves, it is but a slight thing that we offer at the best.'

'Surely, Madam,' I cried, 'you know that we would willingly die for the sake of Robin?'

'Yes, Child; to die—to die were nothing. It is to live—we must live—for Robin.'

'I understand not, Madam.'

'Listen then—for the time presses, and if he arrives and finds that I have not broken the thing to thee, he will perhaps ride back to Exeter in a rage. When I left my son after the trial, being very wretched and without hope, I found Benjamin waiting for me at the prison gates. He walked with me to my lodging, and on the way he talked of what was in my mind. First, he said, that for the better sort there was little hope, seeing that the King was revengeful and the Judge most wrathful, and in a mood which allowed of no mercy. Therefore, it would be best to dismiss all hopes of pardon or of safety either to these two or to the prisoners of Ilminster. Now, when he had said this a great many times, we being now arrived at my lodging, he told me that there was in my case a way out of the trouble—and one way only: that if we consented to follow that way, which, he said, would do no manner of harm to either of us or to our prisoners, he would undertake and faithfully engage to secure the safety of all our prisoners. I prayed him to point out this way, and, after much entreaty, he consented.'

'What is the way?' I asked, having not the least suspicion. And yet the look in her eyes should have told me what was coming.

'Is it true, Child, that long ago you were betrothed to Benjamin?'

'No, Madam, that is most untrue.'

'He says that when you were quite a little child he informed you of his intention to marry you, and none but you.'

'Why, that is true, indeed.' And now I began to understand the way that was proposed; and my heart sank within me. 'That is true. But to tell a child such a thing is not a betrothal.'

'He says that only three or four years ago he renewed that assurance.'

'So he did, but I gave him no manner of encouragement.'

'He says that he promised to return and marry you when he had arrived at some practice, and that he engaged to become Lord Chancellor and make you a Peeress of the Realm.'

'All that he said, and more. Yet did I never give him the least encouragement, but quite the contrary, for always have I feared and disliked Benjamin. Never at any time was it possible for me to think of him in that way. That he knows, and cannot pretend otherwise. Madam, doth Benjamin wish evil to Robin because I am betrothed to him?'

'He also says, in his rude way—Benjamin was always a rude and coarse boy—that he had warned you, long ago, that if anyone else came in his way he would break the head of that man.'

'Yes: I remember, now, that he threatened some violence.'

'My dear'—Madam took my hand—'his time of revenge is come. He says that he has the life of the man whom you love in his own hands; and he will, he swears, break his head for him, and so keep the promise made to you by tying the rope round his neck. My dear, Benjamin has always been stubborn and obstinate from his birth. Stubborn and obstinate was he as a boy; stubborn and obstinate is he now. He cares for nobody in the world except himself; he has no heart; he has no tenderness; he has no scruples; if he wants a thing, he will trample on all the world to get it, and break all the laws of God. I know what manner of life he leads. He is the friend and companion of the dreadful Judge who goeth about like a raging lion. Every night do they drink together until they are speechless and cannot stand. Their delight it is to drink, and smoke tobacco, with unseemly jests and ribald songs which would disgrace the playhouse or the country fair. Oh! 'tis the life of a hog that he delights in! Yet, for all that, he is, like his noble friend, full of ambition. Nothing will do but he must rise in the world. Therefore, he works hard at his profession—and'——

'Madam—the condition!—what is the condition? For Heaven's sake tell me quickly! Is it—is it!—oh! no—no—no! Anything but that!'

'My child—my daughter'—she laid her hand upon my head. 'It is that condition—that, and none other. Oh! my dear, it is laid upon thee to save us!—it is to be thy work alone—and by such a sacrifice as, I think, no woman ever yet had to make! Nay, perhaps it is better not to make it, after all. Let all die together, and let us live out our allotted lives in sorrow. I thought of it all night, and it seemed better so—better even that thou wert lying in thy grave. His condition! Oh! he must be a devil thus to barter for the lives of his grandfather and his cousins—no human being, surely, would do such a thing: the condition, my dear, is that thou must marry him—now: this very morning—and this once done, he will at once take such steps—I know not what they may be, but I take it that his friend the Judge will grant him the favour—such steps, I say, as will release unto us all our prisoners.'

At first I made no answer.

'If not,' she added after a while, 'they shall all be surely hanged.'

I remained silent. It is not easy at such a moment to collect one's thoughts and understand what things mean. I asked her presently if there was no other way.

'None,' she said: 'there was no other way.'

'What shall I do? What shall I do?' I asked. 'God, it seems, hath granted my daily prayer; but how? Oh! what shall I do?'

'Think of what thou hast in thy power.'

'But to marry him—to marry Benjamin—oh! to marry him! How should I live? How should I look the world in the face?'

'My dear, there are many other unhappy wives. There are other husbands brutal and selfish; there are other men as wicked as my nephew. Thou wilt swear in church to love, honour, and obey him. Thy love is already hate; thy honour is contempt; thy obedience will be the obedience of a slave. Yet death cometh at length, even to a slave and to the harsh task-master.'

'Oh! Madam, miserable indeed is the lot of those whose only friend is death.'

She was silent, leaving me to think of this terrible condition.

'What would Robin say? What would Humphrey say? Nay, what would his Honour himself say?'

'Why, Child,' she replied, with a kind of laugh, 'it needs not a wizard to tell what they would say. For one and all, they would rather go to the gallows than buy their lives at such a price. Thy brother Barnaby would mount the ladder with a cheerful heart rather than sell his sister to buy his life. That we know already. Nay, we know more. For Robin will never forgive his mother who suffered thee to do such a thing. So shall I lose what I value more than life—the love of my only son. Yet would I buy his life at such a price. My dear, if you lose your lover I lose my son. Yet, we will save him whether he will or no.' She took my hands and pressed them in her own. 'My dear, it will be worse for me than for you. You will have a husband, it is true, whom you will loathe; yet you will not see him, perhaps, for half the day at least; and, perhaps, he will leave thee to thyself for the other half. But for me, I shall have to endure the loss of my son's affections all my life, because I am very sure and certain that he can never forgive me. Think, my dear! Shall they all die?—all!—think of father and brother, and of your mother!—or will you willingly endure a life of misery with this man for husband in order that they may live?'

'Oh, Madam,' I said, 'as for the misery—any other kind of misery I would willingly endure; but it is marriage—marriage! Yet who am I that I should choose my sacrifice? Oh, if good works were of any avail, then would the way to heaven be opened wide for me by such an act and such a life! Oh, what will Robin say of me? What will he think of me? Will he curse me and loathe me for being able to do this thing? Should I do it? Is it right? Doth God command it? Yet to save their dear lives—only to set them free—to send that good old man back to his home—to suffer my father to die in peace!—I must do it—I must do it! Yet Robin could never forgive me. Oh! he told me that betrothal was a sacrament. I have sworn to be his. Yet, to save his life, I cannot hesitate. If it is wrong, I pray that Robin will forgive me. Tell him—oh, tell him that it is I who am to die instead of him. Perhaps the Lord will suffer me to die quickly. Tell him that I loved him, and only him; that I would rather have died; that for his life alone I would not have done this thing, because he would not have suffered it. But it is for all—it is for all! Oh! he must forgive me! Some day you will send me a message of forgiveness from him. But I must go away and live in London, far from all of you; never to see him or any one of you again—not even my own mother. It is too shameful a thing to do. And you will tell his Honour, who hath always loved me and would willingly have called me his granddaughter. It was not that I loved not Robin—God knoweth that; but for all—for him and Robin and all—to save his grey hairs from the gallows, and to send him back to his home. Oh! tell him that'——

'My dear—my dear,' she replied, but could say no more.

Then for a while we sat in silence, with beating hearts.

'I am to purchase the lives of five honest men,' I said presently, 'by my own dishonour. I know very well that it is by my dishonour and my sin that their lives are to be bought. It doth not save me from dishonour that I am first to stand in the church and be married according to the Prayer Book. Nay, does it not make the sin greater and the dishonour more certain that I shall first swear what I cannot ever perform—to love and honour that man?'

'Yes, girl—yes!' said Madam. 'But the sin is mine more than yours. Oh! let me bear the sin upon myself.'

'You cannot, it is my sin and my dishonour; nay, it is a most dreadful wicked thing that I am to do. It is all the sins in one: I do not honour my parents in thus dishonouring myself; I kill myself—the woman that my Robin loved; I steal the outward form which belonged to Robin and give it to another; I live in a kind of adultery. It is truly a terrible sin in the sight of Heaven. Yet I will do it!—I must do it! I love him so that I cannot let him die; rather let me be overwhelmed with shame and reproach if only he can live!'

'Said I not, my dear, that we two could never kiss each other again? When two men have conspired together to commit a crime they consort no more together, it is said, but go apart and loathe each other. So it is now with us.'

So I promised to do this thing. The temptation was beyond my strength. Yet had I possessed more faith I should have refused. And then great, indeed, would have been my reward. Alas! how was I punished for my want of faith! Well, it was to save my lover. Love makes us strong for evil as well as strong for good.

And all the time, to think that we never inquired or proved his promises! To think that we never thought of doubting or of asking how he, a young barrister, should be able to save the lives of four active rebels, and one who had been zealous in the cause! That two women should have been so simple is now astonishing.

When the clock struck ten I saw Benjamin walking across the churchyard. It was part of the brutal nature of the man that he should walk upon the graves, even those newly-made and not covered up with turf. He swung his great burly form, and looked up at the window with a grin which made Madam tremble and shrink back. But for me, I was not moved by the sight of him, for now I was strong in resolution. Suppose one who hath made up her mind to go to the stake for her religion, as would doubtless have happened unto many had King James been allowed to continue in his course, do you think that such a woman would begin[203] to tremble at the sight of her executioner? Not so. She would arise and go forth to meet him, with pale face, perhaps (because the agony is sharp), but with a steady eye. Benjamin opened the door, and stood looking from one to the other.

'Well,' he said to Madam, roughly, 'you have by this time told her the condition?'

'I have told her—alas! I have told her, and already I repent me that I have told her.'

'Doth she consent?'

'She does. It shall be as you desire.'

'Ha!' Benjamin drew a long breath. 'Said I not, Sweetheart'—he turned to me—'that I would break the head of any who came between us? What? Have I not broken the head of my cousin when I take away his girl? Very well, then. And that to good purpose. Very well, then. It remains to carry out the condition.'

'The condition,' I said, 'I understand to be this. If I become your wife, Benjamin, you knowing full well that I love another man and am already promised to him'——

'Ta—ta—ta!' he said. 'That you are promised to another man matters not one straw. That you love another man I care nothing. What! I promise, Sweetheart, that I will soon make thee forget that other man. And as for loving any other man after marrying me, that, d'ye see, my pretty, will be impossible. Oh! thou shalt be the fondest wife in the Three Kingdoms.'

'Nay: if such a thing cannot move your heart, I say no more. If I marry you, then all our prisoners will be enlarged?'

'I swear'—he used a great round oath, very horrid from the lips of a Christian man—'I swear that, if you marry me, the three—Robin, Humphrey, and Barnaby—shall all save their lives. And as for Sir Christopher and thy father, they also shall be enlarged. Can I say aught in addition?'

I suspected no deceit. I understood, and so did Madam, that this promise meant the full and free forgiveness of all. Yet there was something of mockery in his eyes, which should have made us suspicious. But I, for one, was young and ignorant, and Madam was country-bred and truthful.

'Benjamin,' I cried, falling on my knees before him, 'think what it is you ask! Think what a wicked thing you would have me do!—to break my vows, who am promised to your cousin! And would you leave your grandfather to perish all for a whim about a silly girl? Benjamin, you are playing with us. You cannot—you could not sell the lives—the very lives of your grandfather and your cousins for such a price as this! The play has gone far enough, Benjamin. Tell us that it is over, and that you never meant to be taken seriously, and we will forgive you the anguish you have caused us.'

'Get up,' he said, 'get up, I say, and stop this folly.' He then began to curse and to swear. 'Playing, is it? You shall quickly discover that it is no play, but serious enough to please you all,[204] Puritans though you be. Playing! Get up, I say, and have done.'

'Then,' I said, 'there is not in the whole world a more inhuman monster than yourself.'

'Oh! my dear—my dear, do not anger him!' cried Madam.

'All is fair in love, my pretty,' said Benjamin with a grin. 'Before marriage call me what you please—inhuman monster—anything that you please. After marriage my wife will have to sing a different tune.'

'Oh! Benjamin, treat her kindly,' Madam cried.

'I mean not otherwise. Kindness is my nature, I am too kind for my own interests. Obedience I expect, and good temper and a civil tongue, with such respect as is due to one who intends to be Lord Chancellor. Come, Child, no more hard words. Thou shalt be the happiest woman, I say, in the world. What? Monmouth's rebellion was only contrived to make thy happiness. Instead of a dull country house thou shalt have a house in London; instead of the meadows, thou shalt have the parks; instead of skylarks, the singers at the playhouse; in due course thou shalt be My Lady'——

'Oh! stop—stop; I must marry you since you make me, but the partner in your ambitions will I never be.'

'My dear,' Madam whispered, 'speak him fair. Be humble to him. Remember he holds in his hands the lives of all.'

'Yes,' Benjamin overheard her. 'The lives of all. The man who dares to take my girl from me—mine—deserves to die. Yet so clement, so forgiving, so generous am I, that I am ready to pardon him. He shall actually save his life. If, therefore, it is true that (before marriage) you love that man and are promised to him, come to church with me, out of your great love to him, in order to save his life; but if you love him not, then you can love me, and, therefore, can come to please yourself, willy nilly. What! am I to be thwarted in such a trifle? Willy nilly, I say, I will marry thee. Come—we waste the time.'

He seized my wrist as if he would have dragged me towards the door.

'Benjamin,' cried Madam, 'be merciful! she is but a girl, and she loves my poor boy—be merciful! Oh! it is not yet too late.' She snatched me from his grasp and stood between us, her arms outstretched. 'It is not too late; they may die and we will go in sorrow, but not in shame. They may die. Go! murderer of thy kith and kin! Go, send thy grandfather to die upon the scaffold; but, at least, leave us in peace.'

'No, Madam,' I said. 'With your permission, if there be no other way, I will save their lives.'

'Well, then,' Benjamin said sulkily, 'there must be an end of this talk and no further delay; else, by the Lord! I know not what may happen. Will Tom Boilman delay to prepare his cauldron of hot pitch? If we wait much longer, Robin's arms and legs will be seething in that broth! Doth the Judge delay with his warrant? Already he signs it—already they are putting up the gibbet on which he will hang! Come, I say.'

Benjamin was sure of his prey, I suppose, because we found the clergyman waiting for us in the church, ready with surplice and book. The clerk was standing beside him, also with his book, open at the Service for Marriage. While they read the Service Madam threw herself prostrate on the Communion steps, her head in her hands, as one who suffers the last extremities of remorse and despair for sin too grievous to be ever forgiven. Let us hope that sometimes we may judge ourselves more harshly than Heaven itself doth judge us.

The clerk gave me away, and was the only witness of the marriage besides that poor distracted mother.

'Twas a strange wedding. There had been no banns put up; the bride was pale and trembling; the bridegroom was gloomy; the only other person present wept upon her knees while the parson read through his ordered prayer and psalm and exhortation; there was no sign of rejoicing.

'So,' said Benjamin, when all was over, 'now thou art my wife. They shall not be hanged therefor. Come, wife, we will this day ride to Exeter, where thou shalt thyself bear the joyful news of thy marriage and their safety to my cousins. They will own that I am a loving and a careful cousin.'

He led me, thus talking, out of church. Now, as we left the churchyard, there passed through the gates—oh, baleful omen!—four men carrying between them a bier. Upon it was the body of another poor prisoner, dead of jail fever. I think that even the hard heart of Benjamin—now my husband!—oh! merciful Heavens! he was my husband!—quailed, and was touched with fear at meeting this most sure and certain sign of coming woe, for he muttered something in his teeth, and cursed the bearers aloud for not choosing another time.

My husband, then—I must needs call him my husband—told me, brutally, that I must ride with him to Exeter, where I should myself bear the joyful news of their safety to his cousins. I did not take that journey, nor did I bear the news, nor did I ever after that moment set eyes upon him again, nor did I ever speak to him again. His wife I remained, I suppose, because I was joined to him in church. But I never saw him after that morning. And the reason why you shall now hear.

At the door of our lodging, which was, you know, hard by the church, stood Mr. Boscorel himself.

'What means this?' he asked, with looks troubled and confused. 'What doth it mean, Benjamin? What hath happened, in the name of God?'

'Sir,' said Benjamin, 'you know my character. You will acknowledge that I am not one of those who are easily turned from[206] their purpose. Truly, the occasion is not favourable for a wedding, but yet I present to you my newly-married wife.'

'*Thy* wife! Child, *he* thy husband? Why, thou art betrothed to Robin! Hath the world gone crazy? Do I hear aright? Is this—this—this—a time to be marrying? Hast thou not heard? Hast thou not heard, I say?'

'Brother-in-law,' said Madam, 'it is to save the lives of all that this is done.'

'"To save the lives of all?"' Mr. Boscorel repeated. 'Why—why—hath not Benjamin, then, told what hath happened, and what hath been done?'

'No, Sir, I have not,' said his son. 'I had other fish to fry.'

'Not told them? Is it possible?'

'Benjamin hath promised to save all their lives if this child would marry him. To save their lives hath Alice consented, and I with her. He will save them through his great friendship with Judge Jeffreys.'

'Benjamin to save their lives? Sirrah'—he turned to his son with great wrath in his face—'what villainy is this? Thou hast promised to save their lives? What villainy, I say, is this? Sister-in-law, did he not tell you what hath been done?'

'He has told us nothing. Oh! is there new misery?'

'Child'—Mr. Boscorel spoke with the tears running down his cheeks—'thou art betrayed—alas! most cruelly and foully betrayed. My son—would to God that I had died before I should say so—is a villain! For, first, the lives of these young men are already saved, and he hath known it for a week and more. Learn, then, that with the help of certain friends I have used such interests at Court that for these three I have received the promise of safety. Yet they will not be pardoned. They are given, among other prisoners, to the courtiers and the ladies-in-waiting. One Mr. Jerome Nipho hath received and entered on his list the names of Robin and Humphrey Challis and Barnaby Eykin; they will be sold by him, and transported to Jamaica or elsewhere for a term of years.'

'They were already saved!' cried Madam. 'He knew, then, when they were tried and sentenced, that their lives were already spared. Oh, child! poor child! Oh, Alice! Oh, my daughter! what misery have we brought upon thee!'

Benjamin said nothing. On his face lay a scowl of obstinacy. As for me, I was clinging to Madam's arm. This man was my husband—and Robin was already saved—and by lies and villainy he had cheated us!

'They were already saved,' Mr. Boscorel continued. 'Benjamin knew it—I sent him a letter that he might tell his cousins. My son—alas!—I say again, my only son—my only son—my son is a villain!'

'No one shall take my girl,' said Benjamin sullenly. 'What? All is fair in love.'

'He has not told you, either, what hath happened in the prison? Thou hadst speech, I hear, with Barnaby, early this morning, Child. The other prisoners'—he lowered his voice and folded his hands, as in prayer—'they have since been enlarged.'

'How?' Madam asked. 'Is Sir Christopher free?'

'He hath received his freedom—from One who never fails to set poor prisoners free. My father-in-law fell dead in the courtyard at nine o'clock this morning—weep not for him. But, Child, there is much more; about that same time thy father breathed his last. He, too, is dead; he, too, hath his freedom, Benjamin knew of this as well, Alice, my child'—the kindly tears of compassion rolled down his face. 'I have loved thee always, my dear; and it is my son who hath wrought this wickedness—my own son—my only son'——he shook his cane in Benjamin's face. 'Oh, villain!' he cried; 'oh, villain!'

Benjamin made no reply; but his face was black and his eyes obstinate.

'There is yet more—oh! there is more. Alas! my child, there is more. Thou hast lost thy mother as well. For at the sight of her husband's death, his poor, patient wife could no longer bear the trouble, but she, too, fell dead—of a broken heart; yea, she fell dead upon his dead body—the Lord showed her this great and crowning mercy—so that they all died together. This, too, Benjamin knew. Oh! villain! villain!'

Benjamin heard unmoved, except that his scowl grew blacker.

'Go,' his father continued, 'I load thee not, my son, with a father's curse. Thy wickedness is so great that thy punishment will be exemplary. The judgments of God descend upon the most hardened. Get thee gone out of my sight. Let me never more behold thee until thou hast felt the intolerable pangs of remorse. Get thee hence I say! begone!'

'I go not,' said Benjamin, 'without my loving wife. I budge not, I say, without my tender and loving wife. Come, my dear.'

He advanced with outstretched hands, but I broke away and fled shrieking. As I ran, Mr. Boscorel stood before his son and barred the way, raising his right hand.

'Back, boy! Back!' he said, solemnly. 'Back, I say! Before thou reachest thy most unhappy wife, first shalt thou pass over thy father's body!'

CHAPTER XXXI.

THE VISION OF CONSOLATION.

I ran so fast, being then young and strong, that Benjamin, I am sure, could not have overtaken me had he tried, because he was already gross of body and short of breath in consequence of his tippling. I have since heard that he did not follow me, nor did he dare to push aside his father. But he laughed and said, 'Let her run; let her run. I warrant I shall find her and bring her back;' thinking, I suppose, that I had run from him as a girl in play runs from her companions. I ran also so long, fear lending me strength, that the sun was getting even into the afternoon before I ventured to stop. I looked round from time to time, but saw no one following me. I do not remember by what road, track, or path I went: pasture fields and plantations I remember; twice I crossed a stream on stepping-stones; once I saw before me a village with a church tower; but this I avoided for fear of the people. When I ventured to stop, I was in a truly wild and desolate country—our county of Somerset hath in it many such wild places, given over to forests, fern, and heather. Presently I remembered the place, though one forest is much like another, and I knew that I had been in this part before, on that day when we rode from Lyme to Taunton, and again on the day when we walked prisoners with the soldiers to Ilminster. I was on the Black Down Hills again.

When, therefore, I understood where I was, I began to recover a little from the first horror which had driven me to fly like one possessed of an evil spirit; and, seeing that no one was in pursuit, I began to collect my senses and to ask myself whither I was going, and what I should do. I was then near that ancient inclosure called Castle Ratch, from whose walls one looks down upon the broad vale of Taunton Dean. In the distance, I thought I could discern the great tower of St. Mary's Church: but perhaps that was only my imagination. I sat down, therefore, upon the turf under these ancient walls, and set myself to consider my condition, which was indeed forlorn.

First, I had no friends or protectors left in the whole world, because after what I had done I could never look upon Robin or even Humphrey again; nor could I importune Madam, because she would not anger her son (I represented him in my mind as most unforgiving); nor could I seek the help of Mr. Boscorel, because that might help his son to find me out, and everybody knows that a husband may command the obedience of his wife. And Sir Christopher was dead, and my father was dead, and my mother was dead, and I could not even weep beside their coffins or follow their bodies to the grave. A woman without friends in this world is like unto a traveller in a sandy desert without a bottle of water.

Yet was I so far better than some of these poor friendless creatures, because I had, concealed upon me, a bag containing all the money which Barnaby had given me—two hundred and fifty gold pieces—save a little which we had expended at Taunton and Ilminster. This is a great sum, and by its help I could, I thought with satisfaction, live for a long time, perhaps all my life, if I could find some safe retreat among godly people.

No friends? Why, there was Susan Blake of Taunton—she who walked with the Maids when they gave Monmouth the Bible, the sword, and the flags. I resolved that I would go to her and tell her all that had happened. Out of her kindness she would take me in and help me to find some safe hiding-place and perhaps some honest way of living, so as to save his money against Barnaby's return from the Plantations.

Then I thought I would find out the valley where we had lived for a fortnight, and rest for one night in the hut, and in the early morning before daybreak walk down the comb and so into Taunton while as yet the town was still sleeping. And this I did. It was very easy to find the head of the comb and the source of the stream, where we had made our encampment. Close by, beneath the trees, was Barnaby's hut: no one had been there to disturb or destroy it; but the leaves upon the boughs which formed its sides were now dead. Within it the fern and the heath which had formed my bed were still dry. Outside, the pot hung over the black embers of our last fire; and, to my great joy, in the basket which had contained our provisions I found a large crust of bread. It was, to be sure, dry and hard; but I dipped it in the running water of the stream and made my supper with it. For dessert I had blackberries, which were by this time ripe, and are nowhere bigger or sweeter than on Black Down. There were also filberts and nuts, now ripe, of which I gathered a quantity, so that I had breakfast provided for me, as well as supper.

When I had done this, I was so tired and my head was so giddy with the terror of the day, that I lay down upon the fern in the hut and there fell fast asleep and so continued until far into the night.

Now, in my sleep a strange thing happened unto me. For my own part, I account it nothing less than a Vision granted unto me by mercy and special grace of Heaven. Those who read of it may call it what they please. It was in this wise. There appeared before my sleeping eyes (but they seemed wide open), as it were, a broad and open champaign; presently there came running across the plain in great terror, shrieking and holding her hands aloft, a girl, whose face at first I could not see. She ran in this haste and terrible anguish of fear because there followed after her a troop of dogs, barking and yelping. Behind the dogs rode on horseback one whose face I saw not any more than that of the girl. He cursed and swore (I knew the voice, but could not tell, being in a dream, to whom it belonged), and cracked a horrid whip and encouraged the dogs, lashing the laggards. In his eyes (though his face was in some kind of shadow) there was such a look as I remembered in Benjamin's when he put the ring upon my finger—a look of resolute and hungry wickedness, which made me tremble and shake.

Now, as I looked, the dogs still gained upon her who ran, and yelped as if in a few moments they would spring upon her and tear her flesh from her bones. Then suddenly, between her who ran and those who pursued, there arose an awful form. He was clad in white, and in his hand he bore a sword, and he turned upon that hunter a face filled with wrath. Lightnings shot from his eyes and a cloud of thunder lay upon his brow. At the sight of that face the dogs stopped in their running, cowered, and fell dead. And at the dreadful aspect of that face the hunter's horse fell headlong, and his rider, falling also with a shriek of terror, broke his neck, and so lay prostrate and dead. Then this dreadful minister of God's wrath turned from him to the flying figure, and lo! his face was now transformed; his eyes became soft and full of love; he smiled graciously; a crown of glory was upon his head; white robes flowed downward to his feet; his fiery sword was a palm branch: he was the Angel of Consolation. 'Have no more fear,' he said, 'though the waves of the sea rise up against thee and the winds threaten to drown thee in the deep. Among the ungodly and the violent thou shalt be safe; in all times of peril the Lord will uphold thee; earthly joy shall be thine. Be steadfast unto the end.'

And then I looked again, those blessed words ringing in my ears; and behold! I saw then, which I had not seen before, that the flying figure was none other than myself; that he who cruelly hunted after with the dogs and the whip was none other than myhusband; and that the Angel of Wrath, who became the Angel of Consolation, was none other than my father himself! But he was glorified! Oh! the face was his face— that, anyone could see; but it was changed into something—I know not what—so far brighter and sweeter than the earthly face, that I marvelled! Then the Vision disappeared, and I awoke.

So bright and clear had it been that I seemed to see it still, though I was sitting up with my eyes open, and it was night. Then it slowly vanished. Henceforth, however, I was assured of two things: first, that no harm would happen unto me, but that I should be protected from the malice of my enemies, whatever they might design (indeed, I had but one enemy—to wit, the man who had that morning sworn to love and cherish me); and next, that I had seen with mortal eyes what, indeed, hath been vouchsafed to few, the actual spiritual body—the glorified body, like to the earthly, but changed—with which the souls of the Elect are clothed.

So I arose now without the least fear. It was night; but in the East there showed the first grey of the dawn, and the birds were already beginning to twitter as if they were dreaming of the day. The wind was fresh, and I was lightly clad, but the splendour of the Vision made me forget the cold. Oh! I had received a voice from heaven! How could I henceforth fear anything? Nay, there was no room even for grief, though those terrible things had fallen upon me, and I was now alone and friendless, and the world is full of ungodly men.

It must have been about half-past four in the morning. It grew light quickly, so that not only the trees became visible, but the black depths between them changed into glades and underwood, and I could see my way down the comb beside the stream. Then, without waiting for the sun to rise (which he presently did in great warmth and splendour), I started, hoping to get into Taunton before the people were up and the streets became crowded. But I did not know the distance, which must have been seven miles at least, because it was nearly eight o'clock when I reached the town, having followed the course of the stream through three villages, which I have since learned must have been those of Pitminster, Trull, and Wilton.

It was market day, and the streets were full of country people—some of them farmers with bags of corn in their hands, going to the corn-market, and some with carts full of fresh fruit and other things. Their faces were heavy and sad, and they talked in whispers as if they were afraid. They had, indeed, good cause for fear; for the prison held over five hundred unfortunate men waiting for their trial, and the terrible Judge was already on his way with his carts filled with more prisoners rumbling after him. Already Colonel Kirke had caused I know not how many to be hanged, and the reports of what had been done at Dorchester and Exeter sufficiently prepared the minds of the wretched prisoners at Taunton for what was about to be done there. Among them was the unfortunate Captain Hucker, the Serge-Maker, who had looked for a Peerage, and was now to receive a halter. There was also among them that poor man, Mr. Simon Hamlyn, who was hanged only for riding into Taunton in order to dissuade his son from joining Monmouth. This the Mayor of Taunton pointed out to the bloodthirsty Judge; but in vain. The whole five hundred prisoners were, in the end, sentenced to death; and one hundred and forty-five actually suffered, to the great indignation of those who looked on, even of the King's party. Nay, at one of the executions, when nineteen were hanged at the same time, and a great fire was made so that the sufferers might actually see before their death the fire that was to burn their bowels, the very soldiers wept, saying that it was so sad a thing they scarce knew how to bear it. Three years later, the hard heart of the King met with its proper punishment.

The soldiers were among the crowd, some leaning against bulkheads, some drinking at the ale-houses, some haggling for the fruit; some were also exercising upon Castle Green. They looked good-natured, and showed in their faces none of the cruelty and rage which belonged to their officers. But what a doleful change from the time when Monmouth's soldiers filled the town, and all hearts were full of joy, and every face shone with happiness! What a change, indeed!

As I passed among the crowd, one caught me by the arm. It was a little old woman, her face all wrinkled and puckered. She was sitting on a stool beside a great basketful of apples and plums, and a short pipe of tobacco within her lips.

'Mistress,' she whispered, taking the pipe from her mouth. 'Thou wert with the Maids the day of the Flags: I remember thy pretty face. What dost thou here abroad among the people? The air of Taunton town is unwholesome! There may be others who will remember thee as well as I. Take an old woman's advice, and get thee gone. How fares it with thy father, the worthy Dr. Eykin?'

'Alas!' I said, 'he died in Ilminster Jail.'

"Tis pity. But he was old and pious: he hath gone to glory. Whither will those poor lads in the Clink go when they are hanged? Get thee gone, get thee gone! The air is already foul with dead men's bodies: they tell strange stories of what hath been done by women for the safety of their brothers. Get thee gone, pretty maid, lest something worse than prison happen to thee. And Judge Jeffreys is coming hither like the Devil, having much wrath.'

I could not tell her that nothing would happen to me, because I was protected by a Heavenly Guard.

'I was in the town forty years agone,' the old woman went on, 'when Blake defended it, and we were well-nigh starved. But never have I seen such things as have been done here since the Duke was routed. Get thee gone!—haste away, as from the mouth of Hell!—get thee gone, poor child!'

So I left her, and went on my way, hanging my head, in hopes that no one else would recognise me. Fortunately, no one did, though I saw many faces which I had seen in the town before. They were then tossing their caps and shouting for Monmouth, but were now gloomily whispering, as if every man feared that his own turn would come next. Over the great gateway of the Castle was stuck up a high row of heads, arms, and legs of rebels blackened with pitch—a horrid sight. Unto this end had come those brave fellows who went forth to dethrone the King. No one noticed or accosted me, and I arrived safely at Susan's house. The door seemed shut, but when I pushed I found that it was open—the lock having been broken from its fastening. Barnaby did that, I remembered. I went in shutting it, after me. No doubt Susan was with her children in the schoolroom. Strange that she should not repair her lock, and that at a time when the town was full of soldiers, who always carry with them their riotous and lawless followers. 'Twas unlike her orderly housekeeping.

There was no one in the back parlour, where Susan commonly took her meals and conducted the morning and evening prayers. The dishes were on the table, as if of last night's supper or yesterday's dinner. This was, also, unlike a tidy housewife. I opened the door of the front parlour. Though it was already past the hour for school, there were no children in the room; the lesson-books and copying-books and slates lay about the floor. What did this untidy litter mean? Then I went up-stairs and into the bedrooms, of which there were three—namely, two on the floor above, and one a garret. No one was in them, and the beds had not been made. There remained only the kitchen. No one was there. The house was quite empty; I observed also that the garden, which was wont to be kept with the greatest neatness, now looked neglected; the ripe plums were dropping from the branches trained upon the wall; the apples lay upon the grass; the flower-beds were cumbered with weeds; grass grew in the walks; the lawn, which had been so neat and trim, was covered with long grass.

What had happened? Where was Susan? Then I seemed to hear her voice above thanking God for the victory, as she had done when Barnaby burst in upon us; and methought I heard her singing a hymn with the children, as she had done while we all sat embroidering the Flags. Oh! the pretty Flags! And oh! the pretty sight of the innocents in white and blue carrying those Flags! The house was filled with the sounds of bygone happiness. Had I stayed another moment I am certain that I should have seen the ghosts of those who filled the rooms in the happy days when the army was in the town. But I did not stay. Not knowing what to do or whither to fly, I ran quickly out of the house, thinking only to get away from the mournful silence of the empty and deserted rooms. Then, as I stepped into the street, I met, face to face, none other than Mr. George Penne, the kind-hearted gentleman who had compassionated the prisoners at Ilminster.

CHAPTER XXXII.

THE MAN OF SAMARIA.

Tis no other than the Fair Maid of Ilminster!' said Mr. Penne, with surprise. 'Madam, with submission, is it safe—is it prudent—for one who walked with the Maids of Taunton on a certain memorable day, to venture openly into the streets of this city at such a time? Judge Jeffreys doth approach to hold his Court. Thy friends are in prison or in hiding. The Maids are scattered all.'

'I sought shelter,' I said, 'at the house of Susan Blake, the schoolmistress.'

'How? You have not heard, then? Miss Susan Blake is dead.'

'She is dead?'

'She died in Dorchester Jail, whither she was sent, being specially exempted from any pardon. 'Twas fever carried her off. She is dead! Alas! the waste of good lives! She might have bought her freedom after a while, and then—but—well, 'tis useless to lament these mishaps.'

'Alas! alas!' I cried, wringing my hands. 'Then am I in evil plight indeed! All, all are dead!—all my friends are dead!'

'Madam,' he replied very kindly, 'not all your friends, if I may say so. I have, I assure you, a most compassionate heart. I bleed for the sufferings of others; I cannot rest until I have brought relief. This is my way. Oh! I take not credit to myself therefor. It is that I am so constituted; I am not proud or uplifted on this account. Only tell me your case, entrust your safety to me. You may do so safely if you reflect for one moment, because—see—one word from me and you would be taken to prison by yon worthy clergyman, who is none other than the Rev. Mr. Walter Harte, the Vicar of Taunton. No one is more active against the rebels, and he would rejoice in committing thee on the charge of having been among the Maids. A word from me would, I say, cause you to be hauled to jail; but, observe, I do not speak that word—God forbid that I should speak that word!'

'Oh, Sir!' I said, 'this goodness overwhelms me.'

'Then, Madam, for greater privacy, let us go back into the house and converse there.'

So we went back into the empty house and sat in the back parlour.

'As for the nature of your trouble, Madam,' he began, 'I hope you have no dear brothers or cousins among those poor fellows in Taunton Jail.'

'No, Sir; my only brother is at Ilminster, and my cousins are far away in New England.'

'That is well. One who, like myself, is of a compassionate disposition, cannot but bewail the grievous waste in jail fever, smallpox, scarlet fever, or putrid throat (to say nothing of the hangings), which now daily happens in the prison. What doth it avail to hang and quarter a man, when he might be usefully set to work upon his Majesty's Plantations? It is a most sinful and foolish waste, I say'—he spoke with great sincerity and warmth—'and a robbing of the pockets of honest merchants.'

'Indeed, Sir,' I said, 'your words prove the goodness of your heart.'

'Let my deeds rather than my words prove that. How fare the prisoners with whom you are most concerned?'

'Alas! Sir Christopher is dead! and my father hath also died of his wound.'

'So?—indeed? More waste! They are dead. More waste! But one was old: had Sir Christopher been sent to the Plantations, his value would have been but small, though, indeed, a ransom—but he is dead; and your father, being wounded—but they are dead, and so no more need be said. There are, however, others, if I remember aright?'

'There is my brother in Ilminster Prison, and——'

'Yes; the two young gentlemen—Challis is their name—in Exeter. I have seen them and conversed with them. Strong young men, especially one of them. 'Tis sad, indeed, to think that they may be cut off in the very bloom of their age when they would command so high a price in Jamaica or Barbadoes. I ventured to beg before their trial that they would immediately begin to use whatever interest they might be able to command in order to get their sentence (which was certain) commuted. Many will be suffered to go abroad—why not these young gentlemen? But they have no interest, they assured me; and therefore I fear that they will die. 'Tis most sad. They cannot hang all—that is quite true; but then these young gentlemen were officers in the army, and therefore an example will be made of them if they have no interest at Court.'

'Well, Sir,' I told him, pleased to find him of such a kindly and thoughtful disposition, 'you will be glad to hear that they are already pardoned, and have been presented by the King to a gentleman at Court.'

'Aha! Sayest thou so?' His eyes glittered, and he rubbed his hands. 'This is, indeed, joyful news. One of them, Mr. Robin Challis, is a goodly lad, like to whom there are few sent out[216] to the Plantations. He will certainly fetch a good price. The other, Mr. Humphrey, who is somewhat crooked, will go for less. Who hath obtained the gift of these young gentlemen?'

'It is a person named Mr. Nipho.'

'Mr. Jerome Nipho. I know him well. He is a good Catholic—I mean a Papist—and is much about the Court. He is lucky in having had many prisoners given to him. And now, Madam, I hope you will command my services.'

'In what way, Sir?'

'In this way. I am, as I have told you'—here he wagged his head and winked both his eyes, and laughed pleasantly—'one of those foolish busybodies who love to be still doing good to their fellow-creatures. To do good is my whole delight. Unfortunately, the opportunities are rare of conferring exemplary benefit upon my fellow-men. But here the way seems clear.'

He rubbed his hands and laughed again, repeating that the way was clear before him, so that I believed myself fortunate in falling in with so virtuous a person.

'Oh, Sir,' I cried, 'would that the whole world would so live and so act!'

'Truly, if it did, we should have the prisons cleared. There should be no more throwing away of good lives in hanging; no more waste of stout fellows and lusty wenches by fever and small-pox. All should go to the Plantations—all. Now, Madam, to our business, which is the advantage of these young gentlemen. Know, therefore, that Mr. Jerome Nipho, with all those who have received presents of prisoners, straightway sells them to persons who engage to transport them across the seas to his Majesty's Plantations in Jamaica, Virginia, or elsewhere. There they are bound to work for a certain term of years. Call it not work, however,' he added quickly; 'say rather that they are invited every day to exercise themselves in the cotton and the sugar fields. The climate is delightful; the sky is seldom clouded; there are never any frosts or snows; it is always summer; the fruits are delicious; they have a kind of spirit distilled from the sugar canes which is said to be finer and more wholesome than the best Nantz; the food is palatable and plentiful, though plain. The masters or employers (call them rather friends) are gentlemen of the highest humanity, and the society is composed of sober merchants, wealthy planters, and gentlemen, like your brother, who have had the misfortune to differ in opinions from the Government.'

'Why, Sir,' I said, 'I have always understood that the transported prisoners are treated with the greatest inhumanity: forced to work in heat such as we never experience, driven with the lash, and half-starved, so that none ever come back.'

He shook his head gently. 'See now,' he said, 'how prejudices arise. Who could have thought that the Plantations should be thus regarded? 'Tis true that there are estates cultivated by convicts of another kind—I mean robbers, highwaymen, petty thieves, and the like. Bristol doth every year send away a shipload at least of such. Nay, 'tis reported that rather than hang murderers and the like the Bristol merchants buy them of the magistrates; but this is out of the kindness of their hearts. Madam,' he thrust his hand into his bosom and looked me in the face, 'I myself am sometimes engaged in that trade. I myself buy these unhappy prisoners and send them to estates where I know they will be treated with the greatest kindness. Do I look like a dishonest man, Madam? As for my name it is George Penne, and I am known to every man of credit in Bristol. Do I talk like one who would make money out of his neighbours' sufferings? Nay, if that is so, let us part at once and say no more. Madam, your humble servant—no harm is done: your humble servant, madam.' He put his hat under his arm, and made as if he would go; but I begged him to remain, and to advise me further in the matter.

Then I asked him if transported persons ever came home again.

'Surely,' he replied, 'some of them come home laden with gold. Some, possessed of places both of honour and of profit, who return to visit their friends, and then go back to the new country. It is a very Eldorado, or land of gold, to those who are willing to work;

and for those who have money and choose to buy exemption from work, it is only an agreeable residence in cheerful society for a certain term of years. Have you, by chance, Madam, any friends who can influence Mr. Jerome Nipho?'

'No, Sir, I have none.'

'Then will I myself communicate with that gentleman. Understand, Madam, that I shall have to pay him so much a head for every prisoner; that I shall be engaged to place every man on board ship; that the prisoners will then be taken across the seas and again sold. But in the case of those who have money, a ransom can be procured, by means of which they will not have to work.'

So far he had spoken in the belief that I was at Taunton on my brother's business, or that of my friends. I told him, therefore, that certain events had occurred which would prevent me from seeing the prisoners at Exeter. And because I could not forbear from weeping while I spoke, he very earnestly begged me to inform him fully in every particular as to my history, adding that his benevolence was not confined to the unhappy case of prisoners, but that it was ready to be extended in any other direction that happy chance might offer.

Therefore, being, as you have seen, so friendless and so ignorant, and so fearful of falling into my husband's hands, and at the same time so grateful to this good man for his kindly offers (indeed, I took him for an instrument provided by Heaven for the safety promised in my vision of the night), that I told him everything exactly, concealing nothing. Nay, I even told him of the bag of gold which I had tied round my waist—a thing which I had hitherto concealed, because the money was not mine, but Barnaby's. But I told it to Mr. Penne.

While I related my history he interrupted me by frequent ejaculations, showing his abhorrence of the wickedness with which Benjamin compassed his design, and when I finished, he held up his hands in amazement.

'Good God!' he cried; 'that such a wretch should live! That he should be allowed still to cumber the earth! What punishment were fitting for this devil in the shape of a man? Madam, your case is, indeed, one that would move the heart of Nero himself. What is to be done?'

'Nay, that I know not. For if I go back to our village he will find me there; and if I find out some hiding-place he will seek me out and find me; I shall never know rest or peace again. For of one thing am I resolved—I will die—yea, I will indeed die—before I will become his wife more than I am at present.'

'I cannot but commend that resolution, Madam. But, to be plain with you, there is no place in the world more unsafe for you than Taunton at this time. Therefore, if you please, I will ride with you to Bristol without delay.'

'Sir, I cannot ask this sacrifice of your business.'

'My business lies at Bristol. I can do no more here until Judge Jeffreys hath got through his hangings, of which, I fear, there may be many, and so more sinful waste of good convicts. Let us, therefore, hasten away as quickly as may be; as for what shall be done afterwards, that we will consider on the way.'

Did ever a woman in misfortune meet with so good a man? The Samaritan himself was not of better heart.

Well, to be brief, half an hour afterwards we mounted and rode to Bristol, by way of Bridgwater (this town was even more melancholy than Taunton), taking three days; the weather being now wet and rainy, so that the ways were bad. Now, as we rode along—Mr. Penne and I—side by side, and his servant behind, armed with a blunderbuss, our conversation was grave, turning chiefly on the imprudence of the people in following Monmouth, when they should have waited for the gentry to lead the way. I found my companion (whom I held to be my benefactor) sober in manners and in conversation; no drunkard; no user of profane oaths; and towards me, a woman whom he had (so to say) in his own power, he behaved always with the greatest ceremony and politeness. So that I hoped to have found in this good man a true protector.

When we reached Bristol he told me that, for my better safety, he would lodge me apart from his own house; and so took me to a house in Broad Street, near St. John's Gate, where there was a most respectable old lady of grave aspect, though red in the cheeks.

'I have brought you, Madam,' he said, 'to the house of a lady whose virtue and piety are well known.'

'Sir,' said the old lady, 'this house is well known for the piety of those who use it. And everybody knows that you are all goodness.'

'No,' said Mr. Penne; 'no man is good. We can but try our[219] best. In this house, however, Madam, you will be safe. I beg and implore you not at present to stir abroad, for reasons which you very well know. This good woman has three or four daughters in the house, who are sometimes, I believe, merry——'

'Sir,' said the old lady, 'children will be foolish.'

'True, true,' he replied laughing. 'Take care, then, that they molest not Madam.'

'No, Sir; they shall not.'

'Then, Madam, for the moment I leave you. Rest and be easy in your mind. I have, I think, contrived a plan which will answer your case perfectly.'

In the evening he returned and sent me word, very ceremoniously, that he desired the favour of a conversation with me. As if there could be anything in the world that I desired more!

'Madam,' he said, 'I have considered carefully your case, and I can find but one advice to give.'

'What is it, Sir?'

'We might,' he went on, 'find a lodging for you in some quiet Welsh town across the Channel. At Chepstow, for instance, or at Newport, you might find a home for a while. But, the country being greatly inflamed with dissensions, there would everywhere be the danger of some fanatical busybody inquiring into your history—whence you came, why you left your friends—and so forth. And, again, in every town there are women (saving your presence, Madam), whose tongues tittle-tattle all day long. Short work they make of a stranger. So that I see not much safety in a small town. Then, again, you might find a farm-house where they would receive you; but your case is not that you wish to be hidden for a time, as one implicated in the Monmouth business. Not so; you desire to be hidden all your life, or for the whole life of the man who, if he finds you, may compel you to live with him, and to live for—how long? Sixty years, perhaps, in a dull and dirty farm-house, among rude boors, would be intolerable to a person of your manners and accomplishments.'

'Then, Sir, in the name of Heaven'—for I began to be wearied with this lengthy setting up of plans only to pull them down again—'what shall I do?'

'You might go to London. At first I thought that London offered the best hope of safe retreat. There are parts of London where the gentlemen of the robe are never seen, and where you might be safe. Thus, about the eastern parts of the city there are never any lawyers at all. There you might be safe. But yet—it would be a perpetual risk. Your face, Madam, if I may say so, is one which will not be quickly forgotten when it hath once been seen—you would be persecuted by would-be lovers; you would go in continual terror, knowing that one you fear was living only a mile away from you. You would have to make up some story, to maintain which would be troublesome; and presently the time would come when you would have no more money. What, then, would you do?'

'Pray, Sir, if you can, tell me what you think I should do, since there are so many things that I cannot do.'

'Madam, I am going to submit to you a plan which seems to me at once the safest and the best. You have, you tell me, cousins in the town of Boston, which is in New England.'

'Yes, I have heard my father speak of his cousins.'

'I have myself visited that place, and have heard mention of certain Eykins as gentlemen of substance and reputation. I propose, Madam, that you should go to these cousins, and seek a home among them.'

'Leave England? You would have me leave this country and go across the ocean to America?'

'That is my advice. Nay, Madam'—he assumed a most serious manner—'do not reject this advice suddenly; sleep upon it. You are not going among strangers, but among your own people, by whom the name of your pious and learned father is doubtless held in great honour. You are going from a life (at best) of danger and continual care to a place where you will be certainly free from persecution. Madam, sleep upon it.'

CHAPTER XXXIII.

ON BOARD THE JOLLY THATCHER.

I lay awake all night thinking of this plan. The more I thought upon it, the more I was pleased with it. To fly from the country was to escape the pursuit of my husband, who would never give over looking for me because he was so obstinate and masterful. I should also escape the reproaches of my lover, Robin, and break myself altogether from a passion which was now (through my own rashness) become sinful. I might also break myself from the loathing and hatred which I now felt towards my wicked husband, and might even, in time and after much prayer, arrive at forgiving him. At that time—yea, and for long afterwards—I did often surprise myself in such a fit of passion as, I verily believe, would have made me a murderess had opportunity or the Evil One sent that man my way. Yea, not once or twice, but many times have I thus become a murderess in thought and wish and intention—I confess this sin with shame, though I have long since repented of it. To have been so near unto it—nay, to have already committed it in my imagination, covers me with shame. And now when I sometimes (my Lord, the master of my affections, doth allow it) visit the Prison of Ilchester and find therein some poor wretch who hath yielded to temptation and sudden wrath (which is the possession by the Devil), and so hath committed what I only imagined, my heart goes forth to that poor creature, and I cannot rest until I have prayed with her and softened her heart, and left her to go contrite to the shameful tree. Nay, since, as you shall hear, I have been made to pass part of my life among the most wicked and profligate of my sex, I am filled with the thought that the best of us are not much better than the worst, and that the worst of us are in some things as good as the best; so that there is no room for pride and self-sufficiency, but much for humiliation and distrust of one's own heart.

Well, if I would consent to fly from the country; across the seas, I should find kith and kin who would shelter me. There should I learn to think about other things—poor wretch, as if I could ever forget the village—and Robin! Oh! that I should have to try—even to try—to forget Robin! I was to learn that though the skies be changed the heart remains the same.

How I fled—and whither—you shall now hear.

Mr. George Penne came to see me next morning, sleek and smiling and courteous.

'Madam,' he said, 'may I know your decision, if you have yet arrived at one?'

'Sir, it is already made. I have slept upon it; I have prayed upon it; I will go.'

'That is well. It is also most opportune, because a ship sails this very day. It is most opportune I say—even Providential. She will drop down the Channel with the coming tide. You will want a few things for the voyage.'

'It will be winter when we arrive, and the winters in that country are cold; I must buy some thicker clothing. Will there be any gentlewoman on board?'

'Surely'—he smiled—'surely. There will be, I am told, more than one gentlewoman on board that ship. There will be, in fact, a large and a cheerful company. Of that you may be assured. Well, since that is settled, a great load of care is removed, because I have heard that your husband rode into Taunton with Judge Jeffreys; that he learned from someone—I know not from whom—of your presence in the town, and of your departure with me.'

'It must have been the market-woman.'

'Doubtless the market-woman'—I have often asked myself whether this was a falsehood or not—'and he is even now speeding towards Bristol hoping to find you. Pray Heaven that he hath not learned with whom you fled!'

'Oh!' I cried. 'Let us go on board the ship at once! Let us hasten!'

'Nay; there is no hurry for a few hours. But stay withindoors. Everything that is wanted for the voyage shall be put on board for you. As for your meals, you will eat with'—here he paused for a moment—'with the rest of the company under the care of the Captain. For your berth, it will be as comfortable as can be provided. Next, as to the money. You have, I understand, two hundred pounds and more?'

I took the bag from my waist and rolled out the contents. There were in all two hundred and forty-five pounds and a few shillings. The rest had been expended at Ilminster.

He counted it carefully, and then replaced the money in the bag.

'The Eykins of Boston, in New England,' he said, 'are people of great credit and substance. There will be no necessity for you to take with you this money should you wish it to be expended to the advantage of your brother and your friends.'

'Take it all, kind Sir. Take it all, if so be it will help them in their need.'

'Nay, that will not do, either,' he replied, smiling, his hand still upon the bag. 'For, first, the Captain of your ship must be paid for his passage; next, you must not go among strangers (though your own kith and kin) with no money at all in purse. Therefore, I will set aside (by your good leave) fifty pounds for your private purse. So: fifty pounds. A letter to my correspondent at Boston, which I will write, will cause him to pay you this money on your landing. This is a safer method than to carry the money in a bag or purse, which may be stolen. But if the letter be lost, another can be written. We merchants, indeed, commonly send three such letters of advice in case of shipwreck and loss of the bags. This done, and the expenses of the voyage provided, there remains a large sum, which, judiciously spent, will, I think, insure for your friends from the outset the treatment reserved for prisoners of distinction who can afford to pay—namely, on their arrival they will be bought (as it is termed) by worthy merchants, who (having been previously paid by me) will suffer them to live where they please, without exacting of them the least service or work. Their relatives at home will forward them the means of subsistence, and so their exile will be softened for them. If you consent thereto, Madam, I will engage that they shall be so received, with the help of this money.'

If I consented, indeed! With what joy did I give my consent to such laying out of my poor Barnaby's money! Everything now seemed turning to the best, thanks to my new and benevolent friend.

At his desire, therefore, I wrote a letter to Barnaby recommending him to trust himself, and to advise Robin and Humphrey to trust themselves, entirely to the good offices of this excellent man. I informed him that I was about to cross the seas to our cousins in New England, in order to escape the clutches of the villain who had betrayed me. And then I told him how his money had been bestowed, and bade him seek me when he should be released from the Plantations (wherever they might send him) at the town of Boston among his cousins. The letter Mr. Penne faithfully promised to deliver. (Nota bene—the letter was never given to Barnaby.)

At the same time he wrote a letter for me to give to his correspondent at Boston, telling me that on reading that letter his friend would instantly pay me the sum of fifty pounds.

Thus was the business concluded, and I could not find words, I told him, to express the gratitude which I felt for so much goodness towards one who was a stranger to him. I begged him to suffer me to repay at least the charges to which he had been put at the inns and the stabling since he took me into his own care and protection. But he would take nothing. 'Money,' he said, 'as payment for such services as he had been enabled to render would be abhorrent to his nature. Should good deeds be bought? Was it seemly that a merchant of credit should sell an act of common Christian charity?'

'What!' he asked, 'are we to see a poor creature in danger of being imprisoned if she is recognised—and of being carried off against her will by a husband whom she loathes, if he finds her—are we to see such a woman and not be instantly fired by every generous emotion of compassion and indignation to help that woman at the mere cost of a few days' service and a few guineas spent?'

I was greatly moved—even to tears—at these words, and at all this generosity, and I told him that I could not sufficiently thank him for all he had done, and that he should have my prayers always.

'I hope I may, Madam,' he said, smiling strangely. 'When the ship hath sailed you will remember, perhaps, the fate of Susan Blake, and, whatever may be your present discomfort on board a rolling ship, say to yourself that this is better than to die in a noisome prison. You will also understand that you have fallen into the hands of a respectable merchant, who is much more lenient than Judge Jeffreys, and will not consent to the wasting of good commercial stuff in jails and on gibbets.'

'Nay, Sir,' I said, 'what doth all this mean?'

'Nothing, Madam; nothing. I was only anxious that you should say to yourself, "Thus and thus have I been saved from a jail."' Such was Mr. Penne's humanity!

'Understand it! Oh! dear Sir, I repeat that my words are not strong enough to express my gratitude.'

'Now, Madam, no doubt your gratitude runs high. Whether to-morrow——'

'Can I ever forget? To-morrow? To-morrow? Surely, Sir——'

'Well, Madam, we will wait until to-morrow. Meantime, lie snug and still all day, and in the afternoon I will come for you. Two hundred and forty-five pounds—'tis not a great sum, but a good day's work—a good day's work, added to the satisfaction of helping a most unfortunate young gentlewoman—most unfortunate.'

What did the good man mean by still talking of the morrow?

At half-past twelve the good woman of the house brought me a plate of meat and some bread.

'So,' she said—her face was red, and I think she had been drinking—'he hath determined to put you on board with the rest, I hear.'

'Hush! If you have heard, say nothing.'

'He thinks he can buy my silence. Come, Madam; though, indeed, some would rather take their chance with Judge Jeffreys—they say he is a man who can be moved by the face of a woman—than with—well, as for my silence, there——It is usual, Madam, to compliment the landlady, and though, I confess, you are not of the kind which do commonly frequent this house, yet one may expect'——

'Alas! my good woman, I have nothing. Mr. Penne has taken all my money.'

'What! you had money? And you gave it to Mr. Penne? You gave it to him? Nay, indeed—why, in the place where thou art going'——

She was silent, for suddenly we heard Mr. Penne's step outside; and he opened the door.

'Come,' he said roughly; 'the Captain says that he will weigh anchor in an hour: the tide serves—come.'

I hastened to put on my hat and mantle.

'Farewell,' I said, taking the old woman's hand. 'I have nothing to give thee but my prayers. Mr. Penne, who is all goodness, will reward thee for thy kindness to me.'

'He all goodness?' asked the old woman. 'He? Why, if there is upon the face of the whole earth'——

'Come, Child!' Mr. Penne seized my hand and dragged me away.

'The woman,' he said, 'hath been drinking. It is a bad habit she hath contracted of late. I must see into it, and speak seriously to her: but a good nature at heart. Come, we must hasten. You will be under the special care of the Captain. I have provided a box full of warm clothing and other comforts. I think there is nothing omitted that may be of use. Come.'

He hurried me along the narrow streets until we came to a quay, where there were a great number of ships, such as I had never before seen. On one of them the sailors were running about clearing away things, coiling ropes, tossing sacks and casks aboard, with such a 'Yo-hoing!' and noise as I never in my life heard before.

"Tis our ship,' said Mr. Penne. Then he led me along a narrow bridge, formed by a single plank, to the deck of the ship. There stood a gentleman of a very fierce and resolute aspect, armed with a sword, hanging from a scarlet sash, and a pair of pistols in his belt. 'Captain,' said Mr. Penne, 'are all aboard?'

'Ay; we have all our cargo. And a pretty crew they are! Is this the last of them? Send her for'ard.'

'Madam,' said Mr. Penne, 'suffer me to lead you to a place where, until the ship sails and the officers have time to take you to your cabin, you can rest and be out of the way. It is a rough assemblage, but at sailing one has no choice.'

Gathered in the forepart of what they call the waist there was[226] a company of about a hundred people. Some were young, some old; some were men, some women; some seemed mere children. All alike showed in their faces the extreme of misery, apprehension, and dismay.

'Who are these?' I asked.

'They will tell you themselves presently. Madam, farewell.' With that Mr. Penne left me standing among this crowd of wretches, and, without waiting for my last words of gratitude, hurried away immediately.

I saw him running across the plank to the quay. Then the boatswain blew a shrill whistle; the plank was shoved over; some ropes were cast loose, and the ship began slowly to move down the river with the tide, now beginning to run out, and a wind from the north-east.

I looked about me. What were all these people? Why were they going to New England? Then, as the deck was now clearer, and the sailors, I suppose, at their stations, I ventured to walk towards the afterpart of the ship with the intention to ask the Captain for my cabin. As I did so, a man stood before me armed with a great cane, which he brandished, threatening, with a horrid oath, to lay it across my back if I ventured any further aft.

'Prisoners, for'ard!' he cried. 'Back you go, or—by the Lord'——

'Prisoner?' I said. 'I am no prisoner. I am a passenger.'

'Passenger? Why, as for that, you are all passengers.'

'All? Who are these, then?'

He informed me with plainness of speech who and what they were—convicts taken from the prisons, branded in the hand, and sentenced to transportation.

'But I am a passenger,' I repeated. 'Mr. Penne hath paid for my passage to New England. He hath paid the Captain'——

'The ship is bound for Barbadoes, not New England. 'Tis my duty not to stir from this spot; but here's the Mate—tell him.'

This was a young man, armed, like the Captain, with pistols and sword.

'Sir,' I said, 'I am a passenger brought on board by Mr. Penne, by whom my passage hath been paid to New England.'

'By Mr. George Penne, you say?'

'The same. He hath engaged a cabin for me, and hath purchased clothes—and'——

'Is it possible,' said the Mate, 'that you do not know where you are, and whither you are going?'

'I am going, under the special care of the Captain, to the city of Boston, in New England, to my cousin, Mr. Eykin, a gentleman of credit and substance of that town.'

He gazed at me with wonder.

'I will speak to the Captain,' he said, and left me standing there.

Presently he returned. 'Come with me,' he said.

'You are Alice Eykin?' said the Captain, who had with him a paper from which he read.

'That is my name.'

'On a certain day in July, your father being a preacher in the army of the Duke of Monmouth, you walked with a procession of girls bearing flags which you presented to that rebel?'

'It is true, Sir.'

'You have been given by the King to some great Lord or other, I know not whom, and by him sold to the man Penne, who hath put you on board this ship, the "Jolly Thatcher," Port of London, to be conveyed, with a hundred prisoners, all rogues and thieves, to the Island of Barbadoes, where you will presently be sold as a servant for ten years; after which period, if you choose, you will be at liberty to return to England.'

Then, indeed, the Captain before me seemed to reel about, and I fell fainting at his feet.

CHAPTER XXXIV.

THE GOOD SAMARITAN.

This was indeed the truth: I had parted with my money on the word of a villain; I put myself into his power by telling him the whole of my sad story; and, on the promise of sending me by ship to my cousins in New England, he had entered my name as a rebel sold to himself (afterwards I learned that he made it appear as if I was one of the hundred given to Mr. Jerome Nipho, all of whom he afterwards bought and sent to the Plantations), and he had then shipped me on board a vessel on the point of sailing with as vile a company of rogues, vagabonds, thieves, and drabs as were ever raked together out of the streets and the prisons.

When I came to my senses the Captain gave me a glass of cordial, and made me sit down on a gun-carriage while he asked me many questions. I answered him all truthfully, concealing only the reason of my flight and of my visit to Taunton, where, I told him truly, I hoped to see my unhappy friend Miss Susan Blake, of whose imprisonment and death I knew nothing.

'Madam,' said the Captain, stroking his chin, 'your case is indeed a hard one. Yet your name is entered on my list, and I must deliver your body at St. Michael's Port, Barbadoes, or account for its absence. This must I do: I have no other choice. As for your being sold to Mr. George Penne by Mr. Jerome Nipho, this may very well be without your knowing even that you had been given to that gentleman by the King. They say that the Maids of Taunton have all been given away, mostly to the Queen's Maids of Honour, and must either be redeemed at a great price or be sold as you have been. On the other hand, there may be villainy, and in this case it might be dangerous for you to move in the matter lest you be apprehended and sent to jail as a rebel, and so a worse fate happen unto you.'

He then went on to tell me that this pretended merchant, this Mr. George Penne, was the most notorious kidnapper in the whole of Bristol; that he was always raking the prisons of rogues and sending them abroad for sale on the Plantations; that at this time he was looking to make a great profit, because there were so many prisoners that all could not be hanged, but most must be either flogged and sent about their business, or else sold to him and his like for servitude. 'As for any money paid for your passage,' he[229] went on, 'I assure you, Madam, upon my honour, that nothing at all has been paid by him; nor has he provided you with any change of clothes or provisions of any kind for the voyage; nor hath he asked or bargained for any better treatment of you on board than is given to the rogues below; and that, Madam,' he added, 'is food of the coarsest, and planks, for sleep, of the hardest. The letter which you have shown me is a mere trick. I do not think there is any such person in Boston. It is true, however, that there is a family of your name in Boston, and that they are substantial merchants. I make no doubt that as he hath treated you, so he will treat your friends; and that all the money which he has taken from you will remain in his own pocket.'

'Then,' I cried, 'what am I to do? Where look for help?'

"Tis the damnedest villain!' cried the Captain, swearing after the profane way of sailors. 'When next I put in at the Port of Bristol, if the Monmouth scare be over, I will take care that all the world shall know what he hath done. But, indeed, he will not care. The respectable merchants have nothing to say with him—he is now an open Catholic, who was formerly concealed in that religion. Therefore, he thinks his fortune is at the flood. But what is to be done, Madam?'

'Indeed, Sir, I know not.'

He considered a while. His face was rough and coloured like a ripe plum with the wind and the sun; but he looked honest, and he did not, like Mr. Penne, pretend to shed tears over my misfortunes.

'Those who join rebellions,' he said, but not unkindly, 'generally find themselves out in their reckoning in the end. What the deuce have gentlewomen to do with the pulling down of Kings! I warrant, now, you thought you were doing a grand thing, and so you must needs go walking with those pretty fools, the Maids of Taunton! Well; 'tis past praying for. George Penne is such a villain that keelhauling is too good for him. Flogged through the fleet at Spithead he should be. Madam, I am not one who favours rebels; yet you cannot sleep and mess with the scum down yonder. 'Twould be worse than inhuman—their talk and their manners would kill you. There is a cabin aft which you can have. The furniture is mean, but it will be your own while you are aboard. You shall mess at my table if you will so honour me. You shall have the liberty of the quarter-deck. I will also find for you, if I can, among the women aboard, one somewhat less villainous than the rest, who shall be your grumeta, as the Spaniards say—your servant, that is—to keep your cabin clean and do your bidding. When we make Barbadoes there is no help for it, but you must go ashore with the rest and take your chance.'

This was truly generous of the Captain, and I thanked him with all my heart. He proved as good as his word, for though he was a hard man, who duly maintained discipline, flogging his prisoners with rigour, he treated me during the whole voyage with kindness[230] and pity, never forgetting daily to curse the name of George Penne and drink to his confusion.

The voyage lasted six weeks. At first we had rough weather with heavy seas and rolling waves. Happily, I was not made sick by the motion of the ship, and could always stand upon the deck and look at the waves (a spectacle, to my mind, the grandest in the whole world). But, I fear, there was much suffering among the poor wretches—my fellow-prisoners. They were huddled and crowded together below the deck; they were all sea-sick; there was no doctor to relieve their sufferings, nor were there any medicines for those who were ill. Fever presently broke out among them, so that we buried nine in the first fortnight of our voyage. After this, the weather growing warm and the sea moderating, the sick mended rapidly, and soon all were well again.

I used to stand upon the quarter-deck and look at them gathered in the waist below. Never had I seen such a company. They came, I heard, principally from London, which is the rendezvous or headquarters of all the rogues in the country. They were all in rags—had any one among them possessed a decent coat it would have been snatched from his back the very first day; they were dirty from the beginning; many of them had cuts and wounds on their heads gotten in their fights and quarrels, and these were bound about with old clouts; their faces were not fresh-coloured and rosy, like the faces of our honest country lads, but pale and sometimes covered with red blotches, caused by their evil lives and their hard drinking; on their foreheads was clearly set the seal of Satan. Never did I behold wickedness so manifestly stamped upon the human countenance. They were like monkeys for their knavish and thievish tricks. They stole everything that they could lay hands upon: pieces of rope, the sailors' knives when they could get them, even the marlinspikes if they were left about. When they were caught and flogged they would make the ship terrible with their shrieks, being cowards as prodigious as they were thieves. They lay about all day ragged and dirty on deck, in the place assigned to them, stupidly sleeping or else silent and dumpish, except for some of the young fellows who gambled with cards—I know not for what stakes—and quarrelled over the game and fought. It was an amusement among the sailors to make these lads fight on the forecastle, promising a pannikin of rum to the victor. For this miserable prize they would fight with the greatest fury and desperation, even biting one another in their rage, while the sailors clapped their hands and encouraged them. Pity it is that the common sort do still delight themselves with sport so brutal. On shore these fellows would be rejoicing in cock-fights and bull-baitings: on board they baited the prisoners.

There were among the prisoners twenty or thirty women, the sweepings of the Bristol streets. They, too, would fight as readily as the men, until the Captain forbade it under penalty of a flogging. These women were to the full as wicked as the men; nay, their language was worse, insomuch that the very sailors would stand aghast to hear the blasphemies they uttered, and would even remonstrate with them, saying, 'Nan,' or 'Poll'—they were all Polls and Nans—''tis enough to cause the ship to be struck with lightning! Give over, now! Wilt sink the ship's company with your foul tongue?' But the promise of a flogging kept them from fighting. Men, I think, will brave anything for a moment's gratification; but not even the most hardened woman will willingly risk the pain of the whip.

The Captain told me that of these convicts, of whom every year whole shiploads are taken to Virginia, to Jamaica, and to Barbadoes, not one in a hundred ever returns. 'For,' he said, 'the work exacted from them is so severe, with so much exposure to a burning sun, and the fare is so hard, that they fall into fevers and calentures. And, besides the dangers from the heat and the bad food, there is a drink called rum, or arrack, which is distilled from the juice of the sugar-cane, and another drink called "mobbie," distilled from potatoes, which inflames their blood, and causes many to die before their time. Moreover, the laws are harsh, and there is too much flogging and branding and hanging. So that some fall into despair and, in that condition of mind, die under the first illness which seizes on them.'

'Captain,' I said, 'you forget that I am also to become one of these poor wretches.'

The Captain swore lustily that, on his return, he would seek out the villain Penne and break his neck for him. Then he assured me that the difference between myself and the common herd would be immediately recognised; that a rebel is not a thief, and must not be so treated; and that I had nothing to fear—nay, that he himself would say what he could in my favour. But he entreated me with the utmost vehemence to send home an account of where I was, and what I was enduring, to such of my friends as might have either money to relieve me from servitude or interest to procure a pardon. Alas! I had no friends. Mr. Boscorel, I knew full well, would move heaven and earth to help me. But he could not do that without his son finding out where I was; and this thought so moved me that I implored the Captain to tell no one who I was, or what was my history; and, for greater persuasion, I revealed to him those parts of my history which I had hitherto concealed, namely, my marriage and the reason of that rash step and my flight.

'Madam,' he said, 'I would that I had the power of revenging these foul wrongs. For them, I swear, I would kidnap both Mr. George Penne and Mr. Benjamin Boscorel; and, look you, I would make them mess with the scum and the sweepings whom we carry for'ard; and I would sell them to the most inhuman of the planters, by whom they would be daily beaten and cuffed and flogged; or, better still, would cause them to be sold at Havana to the Spaniards, where they would be employed, as are the English[232] prisoners commonly by that cruel people, namely, in fetching water under negro overseers. I leave you to imagine how long they would live, and what terrible treatment they would receive.'

So it was certain that I was going to a place where I must look for very little mercy, unless I could buy it; and where the white servant was regarded as worth so many years of work; not so much as a negro, because he doth sooner sink under the hardships of his lot, while the negro continues frolick and lusty, and marries and has children, even though he has to toil all day in the sun, and is flogged continually to make him work with the greater heart.

Among the women on board was a young woman, not more than eighteen or thereabout, who was called Deb. She had no other name. Her birthplace she knew not; but she had run about the country with some tinkers, whose language she said is called 'Shelta' by those people. This she could still talk. They sold her in Bristol; after which her history is one which, I learn, is common in towns. When the Captain bade her come to the cabin, and ordered her to obey me in whatsoever I commanded, she looked stupidly at him, shrinking from him if he moved, as if she was accustomed (which was indeed the case) to be beaten at every word. I made her first clean herself and wash her clothes. This done, she slept in my cabin, and, as the Captain promised, became my servant. At first she was not only afraid of ill-treatment, but she would wilfully lie; she purloined things and hid them; she told me so many tales of her past life, all of them different, that I could believe none. Yet when she presently found out that I was not going to beat her, and that the Captain did never offer to cuff or kick her (which the poor wretch expected), she left off telling falsehoods and became as handy, obliging, and useful a creature as one could desire. She was a great, strapping girl, black-eyed and with black hair, as strong as any man, and a good-looking creature as well, to those who like great women.

This Deb, when, I say, she ceased to be afraid of me, began to tell me her true history, which was, I suppose, only remarkable because she seemed not to know that it was shameful and wicked. She lived, as the people among whom she had been brought u lived, without the least sense or knowledge of God; indeed, no heathen savage could be more without religion than the tinkers and gipsies on the road. They have no knowledge at all; they are born; they live; they die; they are buried in a hedgeside, and are forgotten. It was surprising to me to find that any woman could grow up in a Christian country so ignorant and so uncared for. In the end, as you shall hear, she showed every mark of penitence and fell into a godly and pious life.

My Captain continued in the same kindness towards me throughout the voyage—suffering me to mess at his table, where the provisions were plain but wholesome, and encouraging me to talk to him, seeming to take pleasure in my simple conversation. In the mornings when, with a fair wind and full sail, the ship ploughed through the water, while the sun was hot overhead, he would make me a seat with a pillow in the shade, and would then entreat me to tell him about the rebellion and our flight to Black Down. Or he would encourage me in serious talk (though his own conversation with his sailors was over-much garnished with profane oaths), listening with grave face. And sometimes he would ask me questions about the village of Bradford Orcas, my mother and her wheel, Sir Christopher and the Rector, showing a wonderful interest in everything that I told him. It was strange to see how this man, hard as he was with the prisoners (whom it was necessary to terrify, otherwise they might mutiny), could be so gentle towards me, a stranger, and a costly one too, because he was at the expense of maintaining me for the whole voyage, and the whole time being of good manners, never rude or rough, or offering the least freedom or familiarity—a thing which a woman in my defenceless position naturally fears. He could not have shown more respect unto a Queen. The Lord will surely reward him therefor.

One evening at sunset, when we had been at sea six weeks, he came to me as I was sitting on the quarter-deck and pointed to what seemed a cloud in the west. 'Tis the island of Barbadoes,' he said. 'To-morrow, if this wind keeps fair, we shall make the Port of St. Michael's, which some call the Bridge, and then, Madam, alas!'—he fetched a deep sigh—'I must put you ashore and part with the sweetest companion that ever sailed across the ocean.'

He said no more, but left me as if he had other things to say but stifled them. Presently the sun went down and darkness fell upon the waters; the wind also fell and the sea was smooth, so that there was a great silence. 'To-morrow,' I thought, 'we shall reach the port, and I shall be landed with these wretches and sent, perhaps, to toil in the fields.' But yet my soul was upheld by the vision which had been granted to me upon the Black Down Hills, and I feared nothing. This I can say without boasting, because I had such weighty reasons for the faith that was in me.

The Captain presently came back to me.

'Madam,' he said, 'suffer me to open my mind to you.'

'Sir,' I told him, 'there is nothing which I could refuse you, saving my honour.'

'I must confess,' he said, 'I have been torn in twain for love of you, Madam, ever since you did me the honour to mess at my table. Nay, hear me out. And I have been minded a thousand times to assure you first that your marriage is no marriage, and that you have not indeed any husband at all; next, that since you can never go back to your old sweetheart, 'tis better to find another who would protect and cherish you; and thirdly, that I am ready—ay! and longing—now to become your husband and protector, and to love you with all my heart and soul.'

'Sir,' I said, 'I thank you for telling me this, which indeed I did not suspect. But I am (alas! as you know) already married—even though my marriage be no true one—and can never forget the[234] love which I still must bear to my old sweetheart. Wherefore, I may not listen to any talk of love.'

'If,' he replied, 'you were a woman after the common pattern you would right gladly cast aside the chains of this marriage ceremony. But, Madam, you are a saint. Therefore, I refrained.' He sighed. 'I confess that I have been dragged as by chains to lay myself at your feet. Well; that must not be.' He sighed again. 'Yet I would save you, Madam, from the dangers of this place. The merchants and planters do, for the most part, though gentlemen of good birth, lead debauched and ungodly lives, and I fear that, though they may spare you the hardships of the field, they may offer you other and worse indignities.'

I answered in the words of David: 'The Lord hath delivered me out of the paw of the lion, and out of the paw of the bear: He will deliver me out of the hand of the Philistines.'

'Nay; but there is a way; you need not land at all. It is but a scratch of the pen, and I will enter your name among those who died upon the voyage. There will be no more inquiry, any more than after the other names, and then I can carry you back with me to the Port of London, whither I am bound after taking in my cargo.'

For a space I was sorely tempted. Then I reflected. It would be, I remembered, by consenting to the Captain's treachery towards his employers, nothing less, that I could escape this lot.

'No, Sir,' I said, 'I thank you from my heart for all your kindness and for your forbearance; but we may not consent together unto this sin. Again, I thank you, but I must suffer what is laid upon me.'

He knelt at my feet and kissed my hands, saying nothing more, and presently I went to my cabin, and so ended my first voyage across the great Atlantic Ocean. In the morning when I awoke, we were beating off Carlisle Bay, and I felt like unto one of those Christian martyrs, of whom I have read, whom they were about to lead forth and cast unto the lions.

CHAPTER XXXV.

THE WHITE SLAVE.

When we dropped anchor in the port or road of Carlisle Bay we were boarded by a number of gentlemen, who welcomed the Captain, asked him the news, and drank with him. I meantime kept in my cabin, knowing that I must shortly come forth; and presently I heard the boatswain's pipe, and the order to all the prisoners to come on deck. Then one knocked softly at my door. It was the Captain.

'Madam,' he said, with a troubled voice, 'it is not too late. Suffer me, I pray you, to enter your name as one of those who died on the voyage. It is no great deception: the villain Penne will alone be hurt by it; and I swear to take you home, and to place you until better times with honest and Godfearing people in London.'

'Oh! Sir!' I replied, 'tempt me not, I pray you. Let me go forth and take my place among the rest.'

He entreated me again, but, finding that he could not prevail, he suffered me to come out. Yet, such was his kindness to the last that he would not place me with the rest, but caused his men to give me a chair on the quarter-deck. Then I saw that we were all to be sold. The prisoners were drawn up standing in lines one behind the other, the men on one side and the women on the other. The hardships of the voyage had brought them so low that, what with their rags and dirt, and their dull scowls and savage faces, and their thin, pale cheeks, they presented a forbidding appearance indeed.

Three or four gentlemen (they were, I found, planters of the island) were examining them, ordering them to lift up their arms, stretch out their legs, open their mouths, and, in short, treating them like so many cattle: at which the women laughed with ribald words, but the men looked as if they would willingly, if they dared, take revenge.

'Faugh!' cried one of the planters. 'Here is a goodly collection indeed! The island is like to become the dust-heap of Great Britain, where all the rubbish may be shot. Captain, how long before these bags of bones will drop to pieces? Well, sweet ladies and fair gentlemen'—he made a mock bow to the prisoners—'you are welcome. After the voyage, a little exercise will do you good. You will find the air of the fields wholesome; and the gentlewomen, I assure you, will discover that the drivers and overseers will willingly oblige any who want to dance with a skipping-rope.'

There were now twenty or thirty gentlemen, all of them merchants and planters, on board, and a man stepped forward with a book and pencil in hand, who was, I perceived, the salesman.

'Gentlemen,' he said, 'this parcel of servants' (he called them a parcel, as if they were a bale of dry goods) 'is consigned to my care by Mr. George Penne, of Bristol, their owner. They are partly from that city and partly from London, though shipped at the port of Bristol. A tedious voyage, following after a long imprisonment in Newgate and Bridewell, hath, it is true, somewhat reduced them. But there are among them, as you will find on examination, many lusty fellows and stout wenches, and I doubt not that what you buy to-day will hereafter prove good bargains. They are to be sold without reserve, and to the highest bidder. Robert Bull'—he read the first name on the list—'Robert Bull, shoplifter. Stand forth, Robert Bull.'

There arose from the deck where he had been lying a poor wretch who looked as if he could hardly stand, wasted with fever and privation, his eyes hollow (yet they looked full of wicked cunning). The planters shook their heads.

'Come, gentlemen,' said the salesman, 'we must not judge by appearances. He is at present, no doubt, weak, but not so weak as he looks. I warrant a smart cut or two of the whip would show another man. Who bids for Robert Bull?'

He was sold after a little parley for the sum of five pounds. Then the speaker called another, naming his offence as a qualification. No pillory could be more shameful. Yet the men looked dogged and the women laughed.

The sale lasted for three or four hours, the prisoners being knocked down, as they say, for various sums, the greatest price being given for those women who were young and strong. The reason, I have been told, is that the women make better servants, endure the heat more patiently, do not commonly drink the strong spirit which destroys the men, and, though they are not so strong, do more work.

Last of all, the man called my name. 'Alice Eykin, Rebel. Stand forth, Alice Eykin, Rebel.'

'Do not go down among them,' said the Captain. 'Let them see at once that yours is no common case. Stand here.'

He led me to the top of the ladder or steps which they call the companion—leading from the waist to the quarter-deck.

'Madam,' he said, 'it will be best to throw back your hood.'

This I did, and so stood before them all bareheaded.

Oh! ye who are women of gentle nurture, think of such a thing as this: to stand exposed to the curious gaze of rough and ribald men; to be bought and sold like a horse or an ox at the fair! At first my eyes swam and I saw nothing, and should have fallen but that the Captain placed his hand upon my arm, and so I was steadied. Then my sight cleared, and I could look down upon the faces of the men below. There was no place whither I could fly and hide. It would be more shameful still (because it might make them laugh) to burst into tears. Why, I thought, why had I not accepted the Captain's offer and suffered my name to be entered as one of those who had died on the voyage and been buried in the sea?

Down in the waist the gentlemen gazed and gasped, in astonishment. It was no new thing for the planters to buy political prisoners. Oliver Cromwell sent over a shipload of Irishmen first, and another shipload of those engaged in the rising of Penruddock and Grove (among them were gentlemen, divines, and officers, of whom a few yet survived on the island). But as yet no gentlewoman at all had been sent out for political reasons.

Wherefore, I suppose, they looked so amazed, and gazed first at me and then at one another and then gasped for breath.

'Alice Eykin, gentlemen,' said the salesman, who had a tongue which, as they say, ran upon wheels, 'is a young gentlewoman, the daughter, I am informed, of the Rev. Comfort Eykin, Doctor of Divinity, deceased, formerly Rector of Bradford Orcas, in the county of Somerset, and sometime Fellow of his college at Oxford, a very learned Divine. She hath had the misfortune to have taken part in the Monmouth Rebellion, and was one of those Maids of Taunton who gave the Duke his flags, as you have heard by the latest advices. Therefore, she is sent abroad for a term of ten years. Gentlemen, there can be no doubt that her relations will not endure that this young lady—as beautiful as she is unfortunate, and as tender as she is beautiful—should be exposed to the same hard treatment as the rogues and thieves whom you have just had put up for sale. They will, I am privately assured'—I heard this statement with amazement—'gladly purchase her freedom, after which, unless she is permitted to return, the society of our Colony will rejoice in the residence among them of one so lovely and so accomplished. Meantime, she must be sold like the rest.'

'Did Monmouth make war with women for his followers?' asked a gentleman of graver aspect than most. 'I, for one, will have no part or share in such traffic. Are English gentlewomen, because their friends are rebels, to be sent into the fields with the negroes?'

'Your wife would be jealous,' said another, and then they all laughed.

I understood not until afterwards that the buying and selling of such a person as I appeared to be is a kind of gambling. That is to say, the buyer hopes to get his profit, not by any work that his servant should do, but by the ransom that his friends at home should offer. And so they began to bid, with jokes rude and unseemly, and much laughter, while I stood before them still bareheaded.

'Ten pounds,' one began; 'Twelve,' cried another; 'Fifteen,' said a third; and so on, the price continually rising, and the salesman with honeyed tongue continually declaring that my friends (as he very well knew) would consent to give any ransom—any—so only that I was set free from servitude: until, for sixty pounds, no one offering a higher price, I was sold to one whose appearance I liked the least of any. He was a gross, fat man, with puffed cheeks and short neck, who had bought already about twenty of the servants.

'Be easy,' he said, to one who asked him how he looked to get his money back. 'It is not for twice sixty pounds that I will consent to let her go. What is twice sixty pounds for a lovely piece like this?'

Then the Captain, who had stood beside me, saying nothing, interfered.

'Madam,' he said, 'you can put up your hood again. And harkee, Sir,' he spoke to the planter, 'remember that this is a pious and virtuous gentlewoman, and'—here he swore a round oath—'if I hear when I make this port again that you have offered her the least freedom—you shall answer to me for it. Gentlemen all,' he went on, 'I verily believe that you will shortly have the greatest windfall that hath ever happened to you, compared with which the Salisbury Rising was but a flea-bite. For the trials of the Monmouth rebels were already begun when I left the port of Bristol, and, though the Judges are sentencing all alike to death, they cannot hang them all—therefore his Majesty's Plantations, and Barbadoes in particular, will not only have whole cargoes of stout and able-bodied servants, compared with whom these poor rogues are like so many worthless weeds; but there will also be many gentlemen, and perhaps gentlewomen—like Madam here—whose freedom will be bought of you. So that I earnestly advise and entreat you not to treat them cruelly, but with gentleness and forbearance, whereby you will be the gainers in the end, and will make their friends the readier to find the price of ransom. Moreover, you must remember that though gentlemen may be flogged at whipping-posts, and beat over the head with canes, as is your[239] habit with servants both black and white, when the time of their deliverance arrives they will be no longer slaves but gentlemen again, and able once more to stand upon the point of honour and to run you through the body, as you will richly deserve, for your barbarity. And in the same way any gentlewomen who may be sent here have brothers and cousins who will be ready to perform the same act of kindness on their behalf. Remember that very carefully, gentlemen, if you please.'

The Captain spoke to all the gentlemen present, but in the last words he addressed himself particularly unto my new master. It was a warning likely to be very serviceable, the planters being one and all notoriously addicted to beating and whipping their servants. And I have no doubt that these words did a great deal towards assuring for the unfortunate gentlemen who presently arrived such consideration and good treatment as they would not otherwise have received.

The island of Barbadoes, as many people know, is one of the Caribby Islands. It is, as to size, a small place, not more than twenty miles in length by fifteen in breadth, but in population it is a very considerable place indeed, for it is said to have as many people in it as the City of Bristol. It is completely settled, and of the former inhabitants not one is left. They were the people called Indians or Caribs, and how they perished I know not. The island had four ports, of which the principal is that of St. Michael or the Bridge, or Bridgetown, in Carlisle Bay. The heat by day is very great, and there is no winter, but summer all the year round. There is, however, a cool breeze from the sea which moderates the heat. A great number of vessels call here every year (there is said to be one every day, but this I cannot believe). They bring to the island all kinds of European manufactures, and take away with them cargoes of Muscovada sugar, cotton, ginger, and logwood. The island hath its shores covered with plantations, being (the people say) already more thickly cultivated than any part of England, with fewer waste places, commons, and the like. The fruits which grow here are plentiful and delicious—such as the pineapple, the pappau, the guava, the bonannow, and the like—but they are not for the servants and the slaves. The fertility of the country is truly astonishing; and the air, though full of moisture, whereby knives and tools of all kinds quickly rust and spoil, is considered more healthy than that of any other West Indian island. But, for the poor creatures who have to toil in the hot sun, the air is full of fatigue and thirst; it is laden with fevers, calentures, and sunstrokes. Death is always in their midst; and after death, whatever awaits them cannot, I think, be much worse than their condition on the island.

After the sale was finished, the Captain bade me farewell, with tears in his eyes, and we were taken into boats and conveyed ashore, I, for my part, sitting beside my purchaser, who addressed no word at all to me. I was, however, pleased to find that among[240] the people whom he had bought was the girl Deb, who had been my maid (if a woman who is a convict may have a maid who is a sister-convict). When we landed, we walked from the quay or landing-place to a great building like a barn, which is called a barracoon, in which are lodged the negro slaves and servants before they go to their masters. But at this time it was empty. Hither came presently a certain important person in a great wig and a black coat, followed by two negro beadles, each carrying a long cane or stick. After commanding silence, this officer read to us in a loud voice those laws of the colony which concern servants, and especially those who, like ourselves, are transported for various offences. I forget what these laws were; but they seemed to be of a cruel and vindictive nature, and all ended with flogging and extension of the term of service. I remember, for instance—because the thought of escape from a place in the middle of the ocean seemed to me mad—that, by the law, if any one should be caught endeavouring to run away, he should be first flogged and then made to serve three years after his term was expired; and that no ship was allowed to trade with the island, or to put in for water, unless the captain had given security with two inhabitants of the island in the sum of 2,000*l.* sterling not to carry off any servant without the owner's consent.

When these laws had been read, the officer proceeded, further, to inform us that those who were thus sent out were sent to work as a punishment; that the work would be hard, not light; and that those who shirked their work, or were negligent in their work, would be reminded of their duties in the manner common to Plantations; that if they tried to run away they would most certainly be caught, because the island was but small; and that when they were caught, not only would their term of years be increased, but that they would most certainly receive a dreadful number of lashes. He added, further, that as nothing would be gained by malingering, sulking, or laziness, so, on the other hand, our lot might be lightened by cheerfulness, honesty, and zeal. A more surly, ill-conditioned crew I think he must have never before harangued. They listened, and on most faces I read the determination to do no more work than was forced from them. This is, I have learned, how the plantation servants do commonly begin; but the most stubborn spirit is not proof against the lash and starvation. Therefore, before many days they are as active and as zealous as can be desired, and the white men, even in the fields, will do double the work that can be got out of the black.

Then this officer went away followed by his beadles, who cast eyes of regret upon us, as if longing to stay and exercise their wands of office upon the prisoners' backs. This done, we were ordered to march out. My master's horse was waiting for him, led by a negro; and two of his overseers, also mounted and carrying whips in their hands, waited his commands. He spoke with them a few minutes, and then rode away.

They brought a long cart with a kind of tilt to it, drawn by two asses (here they call them assinegoes), and invited me courteously to get into it. It was loaded with cases and boxes, and a negro walked beside the beasts. Then we set out upon our march. First walked the twenty servants—men and women—newly bought by the master; after them, or at their side, rode the overseers, roughly calling on the laggards to quicken their pace, and cracking their whips horribly. Then came the cart in which I sat. The sun was high in the heavens, for it was not more than three of the clock; the road was white and covered with dust; and the distance was about six or seven miles, and we went slowly, so that it was already nigh unto sunset when we arrived at the master's estate.

Thus was I, a gentlewoman born, sold in the Island of Barbadoes for a slave. Sixty pounds the price I fetched. Oh! even now, when it is all passed long since, I remember still with shame how I stood upon the quarter-deck, my hood thrown back, while all those men gazed upon me, and passed their ribald jests, and cried out the money they would give for me!

CHAPTER XXXVI.

THE FIRST DAY OF SERVITUDE.

Thus began my captivity. Thus I began to sit beside the waters of Babylon, more wretched than the daughters of Zion, because they wept together, while I wept alone. I looked for no release or escape until the Lord should mercifully please to call me away by opening the Gate of Death. For even if I were released—if by living out the ten years of servitude I could claim my freedom, of what use would it be to me? Whither could I fly? where hide myself? Yet you shall hear, if you will read, how a way, terrible at first and full of peril, was unexpectedly opened, and in what strange manner was wrought my deliverance.

We arrived at our new master's estate—which was, as I have said, about seven miles from the port—towards sundown. We were marched (rather, driven) to a kind of village, consisting of a double row of huts or cottages, forming a broad street, in the middle of which there were planted a large number of the fruit-trees named here bonannows (they are a kind of plantain). The green fruit was hanging in clusters, as yet unripe; but the leaves, which are also the branches, being for the most part blown into long shreds, or rags, by the wind, had an untidy appearance. The cottages looked more like pigsties for size and shape; they were built of sticks, withs, and plantain-leaves both for sides and for roof. Chimneys had they none, nor windows; some of them had no door, but an opening only. Thus are housed the servants and slaves of a plantation. The furniture within is such as the occupants contrive. Sometimes there is a hammock or a pallet with grass mats and rugs; there are some simple platters and basins. In each hut there are two, three, or four occupants.

Here let me in brief make an end of describing the buildings on this estate, which were, I suppose, like those of every other. If you were to draw a great square, in which to lay down or figure the buildings, you would have in one corner the street or village of the people; next to the village lies the great pond which serves for drinking-water as well as for washing. The negroes are fond of swimming and bathing in it, and they say that the water is not fouled thereby, which I cannot understand. In the opposite corner you must place the Ingenio, or house where the sugar-canes are brought to[243] be crushed and ground, and the sugar is made. There are all kinds of machines, with great wheels, small wheels, cogs, gutters for running the juice, and contrivances which I cannot remember. Some of the Ingenios are worked by a windmill, others by horses and assinegoes. There is in every one a still where they make that fiery spirit which they call "kill-devil." Near the Ingenio are the stables, where there are horses, oxen, assinegoes, and the curious beast spoken of in Holy Writ called the camel. It hath been brought here from Africa, and is much used for carrying the sugar. The open space around the Ingenio is generally covered and strewed with trash, which is the crushed stalk of the cane. It always gives forth a sour smell (as if fermenting), which I cannot think to be wholesome. In the fourth corner is the planter's house. Considering that these people sometimes grow so rich that they come home and buy great estates, it is wonderful that they should consent to live in houses so mean and paltry. They are of wood, with roofs so low that one can hardly stand upright in them; and the people are so afraid of the cool wind which blows from the east that they have neither doors nor windows on that side; but will have them all towards the west, whence cometh the chief heat of the sun—namely, the afternoon heat. Their furniture is rude, and they have neither tapestry, nor wainscoted walls, nor any kind of ornament. Yet they live always in the greatest luxury, eating and drinking of the best. Some of the houses—my master's among them—have an open verandah (as they call it: in Somersetshire we should call it a linney) running round three sides of the house, with coarse canvas curtains which can be let down so as to keep out the sun, or drawn up to admit the air. But their way of living—though they eat and drink of the best—is rude, even compared with that of our farmers at home; and a thriving tradesman, say, of Taunton, would scorn to live in such a house as contenteth a wealthy planter of Barbadoes. Behind the house is always a spacious garden, in which grow all kinds of fruits and vegetables, and all round the buildings on every side stretched the broad fields of sugar-canes, which, when they are in their flower or blossom of grey and silver, wave in the wind more beautifully than even a field of barley in England.

On the approach of our party and hearing the voices of the overseers, a gentlewoman (so, at least, she seemed) came out of the house and stood upon the verandah, shading her eyes and looking at the gang of wretches. She was dressed splendidly in a silken gown and flowered petticoat, as if she was a very great lady, indeed; over her head lay a kerchief of rich black lace; round her neck was a gold chain; when she slowly descended the steps of the verandah and walked towards us I observed that she was of a darker skin than it is customary to find at home; it was, indeed, somewhat like the skin of the gipsy people; her features were straight and regular; her hair was quite black; her eyes were also black, and large, shaped like almonds. On her wrists were heavy gold bracelets, and her fingers were loaded with rings. She seemed about thirty years of age. She was a woman of tall and fine presence, and she stood and moved as if she was a queen. She presently came forth from the verandah and walked across the yard towards us.

'Let me look at them—your new batch,' she said, speaking languidly, and with an accent somewhat foreign. 'How many are there? Where do they come from? Who is this one, for instance?' She took the girl named Deb by the chin, and looked at her as if she were some animal to be sold in the market. 'A stout wench, truly. What was she over there?'

The overseer read the name and the crimes of the prisoner. Madam (this was the only name by which I knew her) pushed her away disdainfully.

'Well,' she said, 'she will find companions enough here. I hope she will work without the whip. Hark ye, girl,' she added with, I think, kindly intent, 'it goes still to my heart when I hear that the women have been trounced; but the work must be done. Remember that! And who are those—and those?' She pointed with contempt to the poor creatures covered with dirt and dust, and in the ragged, miserable clothes they had worn all the voyage. 'Street sweepings; rogues and thieves all. Let them know,' she said grandly, 'what awaits those who skulk and those who thieve. And whom have we here?'—she turned to me—'Is this some fine city madam fresh from Bridewell?'

'This prisoner,' said the overseer, 'is described as a rebel in the late Monmouth rising.'

'A rebel? Truly?' she asked with curiosity. 'Were Monmouth's soldiers women? We heard by the last ship something of this. Madam, I know not why you must needs become a rebel; but this, look you, is no place for gentlewomen to sit down and fold their arms.'

'Madam,' I replied, 'I look for nothing less than to work, being now a convict (though I was never tried) and condemned—I know not by whom—to transportation in his Majesty's Plantations.'

'Let me look at your hands,' she said sharply. 'Why, of what use are these little fingers? They have never done any work. And your face—prithee, turn back your hood.' I obeyed, and her eyes suddenly softened. Indeed, I looked not for this sign of compassion, and my own tears began to flow. "Tis a shame!' she cried. "Tis a burning shame to send so young a woman—and a gentlewoman, and one with such a face—to the Plantations! Have they no bowels? Child, who put thee aboard the ship?'

'I was brought on board by one Mr. Penne, who deceived me, promising that I should be taken to New England, where I have cousins.'

'We will speak of this presently. Meantime—since we must by the law find you some work to do—can you sew?'

'Yes, Madam, I can perform any kind of needlework, from plain sewing to embroidery.'

'What mean they,' she cried again, 'by sending a helpless girl alone with such a crew? The very Spaniards of whom they talk so much would blush for such barbarity. Well, they would send her to a convent where the good Nuns would treat her kindly. Madam, or Miss, thou art bought, and the master may not, by law, release you. But there is a way of which we will talk presently. Meanwhile, thou canst sit in the sewing-room, where we may find thee work.'

I thanked her. She would have said more; but there came forth from the house, with staggering step, the man who had bought us. He had now put off his wig and his scarlet coat, and wore a white dressing-gown and a linen nightcap. He had in his hand a whip, which he cracked as he walked.

'Child,' said Madam, quickly, 'pull down your hood. Hide your face. He hath been drinking, and at such times he is dangerous. Let him never set eyes upon thee save when he is sober.'

He came rolling and staggering, and yet not so drunk but he could speak, though his voice was thick.

'Oho!' he cried. 'Here are the new servants. Stand up, every man and woman. Stand up, I say!' Here he cracked his whip, and they obeyed, trembling. But Madam placed herself in front of me. 'Let me look at ye.' He walked along the line, calling the unhappy creatures vile and foul names. O shame! thus to mock their misery! 'What!' he cried. 'You think you have come to a country where there is nothing to do but lie on your backs and eat turtle and drink mobbie? What! You shall find out your mistake.' Here he cracked his whip again. 'You shall work all day in the field, not because you like it, but because you must. For your food, it shall be loblollie, and for your drink, water from the pond. What, I say! Those who skulk shall learn that the Newgate "cat" is tender compared with her brother of Barbadoes. Tremble, therefore, ye devils all; tremble!'

They trembled visibly. All were now subdued. Those of them who swaggered—the dare-devil reckless blades—when first we sailed, were now transformed into cowardly, trembling wretches, all half-starved, and some reduced with fevers, with no more spirit left than enabled them still to curse and swear. The feeblest of mortals, the lowest of human wretches, has still left so much strength and will that he can sink his immortal soul lower still—a terrible power, truly!

Then Madam drew me aside gently, and led me to a place like a barn, where many women, white and black, sat sewing, and a great quantity of little black babies and naked children played about under their charge. The white women were sad and silent; the blacks, I saw with surprise, were all chattering and laughing. The negro is happy, if he have enough to eat and drink, whether he be slave or free. Madam sat down upon a bench, and caused me to sit beside her.

'Tell me,' she said, kindly, 'what this means. When did[246] women begin to rebel? If men are such fools as to go forth and fight, let them; but for women'——

'Indeed,' I told her, 'I did not fight.'

Then nothing would do but I must tell her all, from the beginning—my name, my family, and my history. But I told her nothing about my marriage.

'So,' she said, 'you have lost father, mother, brothers, lover, and friends by this pretty business. And all because they will not suffer the King to worship in his own way. Well, 'tis hard for you. To be plain, it may be harder than you think, or I can help. You have been bought for sixty pounds, and that not for any profit that your work will bring to the estate, because such as you are but a loss and a burden; but only in the hope that your friends will pay a great sum for ransom.'

'Madam, I have indeed no friends left who can do this for me.'

'If so, it is indeed unfortunate. For presently the master will look for letters on your behalf, and if none come I know not what he may threaten, or what he may do. But think—try to find some one. Consider, your lot here must be hard at best; whereas, if you are released, you can live where you please; you may even marry whom you please, because beautiful young gentlewomen like yourself are scarce indeed in Barbadoes. 'Tis Christian charity to set you free. Remember, Child, that money will do here what I suppose it will do anywhere—all are slaves to money. You have six months before you in which to write to your friends and to receive an answer. If in that time nothing comes, I tell thee again, Child, that I know not what will happen. As for the life in the fields, it would kill thee in a week.'

'Perhaps, if the Lord so wills,' I replied helplessly, 'that may be best. Friends have I none now, nor any whom I could ask for help—save the Lord alone. I will ask for work in the fields.'

'Perhaps he may forget thee,' she said—meaning the master. 'But no; a man who hath once seen thy face will never forget thee. My dear, he told me when he came home that he had bought a woman whose beauty would set the island in flames. Pray heaven he come not near thee when he is in liquor. Hide that face, Child. Hide that face. Let him never see thee. Oh! there are dangers worse than labour in the fields—worse than whip of overseer!' She sprang to her feet, and clasped her hands. 'You talk of the Lord's will! What hath the Lord to do with this place? Here is nothing but debauchery and drinking, cruelty and greed. Why have they sent here a woman who prays?'

Then she sat down again and took my hand.

'Tender maid,' she said, 'thy face is exactly such as the face of a certain saint—'tis in a picture which hangs in the chapel of the convent where the good nuns brought me up long ago, before I came to this place—long ago. Yes, I forget the name of the saint; thou hast her face. She stood, in the picture, surrounded by soldiers who had red hair, and looked like devils—English[247] devils, the nuns said. Her eyes were raised to heaven, and she prayed. But what was done unto her I know not, because there was no other picture. Now she sits upon a throne in the presence of the Mother of God.'

The tears stood in her great black eyes—I take it that she was thinking of the days when she was young.

'Well, we must keep thee out of his way. While he is sober he listens to reason, and thinks continually upon his estate and his gains. When he is drunk no one can hold him, and reason is lost on him.'

She presently brought me a manchet of white bread and a glass of Madeira wine, and then told me that she would give me the best cottage that the estate possessed, and, for my better protection, another woman to share it with me. I thanked her again, and asked that I might have the girl called Deb, which she readily granted.

And so my first day of servitude ended in thus happily finding a protector. As for the cottage, it was a poor thing; but it had a door, and a window with a shutter. The furniture was a pallet with two thick rugs, and nothing more. My condition was desperate, indeed; but yet, had I considered, I had been, so far, most mercifully protected. I was shipped as a convict (it is true) by a treacherous villain; but on the ship I found a compassionate captain, who saved me from the company among whom I must otherwise have dwelt. I was sold to a drunken and greedy planter; but I found a compassionate woman who promised to do what she could; and I had for my companion the woman who had become a most faithful maid to me upon the voyage, and who still continued in her fidelity and her love. Greater mercies yet—and also greater troubles—were in store, as you shall see.

CHAPTER XXXVII.

BY THE WATERS OF BABYLON.

Thus delivered from the slavery of the fields, I began to work, an unprofitable servant, among those who made and mended the garments of the servants and negroes. On an estate so large as this there is always plenty to be done by the sempstresses and needlewomen. Thus, to every woman is given by the year four smocks, two petticoats, and four coifs, besides shoes, which are brought from England by the ships. Those who wait in the house have, in addition, six smocks and three waistcoats. To the men are given six shirts; and to every man and woman a rug or gown of thick stuff to cast about them when they come home hot, so that they may not catch cold—a thing which throws many into a fever. All these things have to be made and mended on the estate.

As for the children, the little blacks, they run about without clothing, their black skin sufficing. The women who are engaged upon the work of sewing are commonly those of the white servants, who are not strong enough for the weeding and hoeing in the fields, or are old and past hard work. Yet the stuff of which the smocks and shirts are made is so coarse that it tore the skin from my fingers, which, when Madam saw, she brought me fine work—namely, for herself. She was also so good as to provide me with a change of clothes, of which I stood sadly in need, and excused my wearing the dress of the other women. I hope that I am not fond of fine apparel, more than becomes a modest woman, but I confess that the thought of wearing this livery of servitude, this coarse and common dress of smock, petticoat, and coif, all of rough and thick stuff, like canvas, with a pair of shoes and no stockings, filled my very soul with dismay. None of the many acts of kindness shown me by Madam was more gratefully received than her present of clothes—not coarse and rough to the skin, nor ugly and common, befitting prisoners and criminals, but soft and pleasant to wear, and fit for the heat of the climate. 'Twas no great hardship, certainly, to rise early and to sit all day with needle and thread in a great room well-aired. The company, to be sure, was not what one would have chosen; nor was the language of the poor creatures who sat with me—prison and Bridewell birds, or negro slaves—such as my poor mother would have desired her daughter to hear. The food was coarse; but I was often at the house (when the master was away), and there Madam would constantly give me something from her own table, a dish of chocolata (rightly called the Indian nectar) made so thick and strong that a spoon stands upright in it, or a glass of Madeira, if my cheeks looked paler than ordinary. In this country, the great heat of the air seems to suck out and devour the heat of the body, so that those of European birth, if they are not nourished on generous diet, presently fall into a decline or wasting away, as is continually seen in the case of white servants, both men and women, who die early, and seldom last more than five or six years.

Briefly, Madam seemed to take great pleasure in my conversation, and would either seek me in the work-room, or would have me to the house, asking questions as to my former life. For herself, I learned that she was born in Cuba, and had been brought up by nuns in a convent; but how or why she came to this place, I knew not, nor did I ask. Other gentlewomen of the island I never saw, and I think there were none who visited her. Nor did she show kindness to the women servants (except to myself), treating them all, as is the fashion in that country, as if they were so many black negroes, not condescending to more than a word or a command; and if this were disobeyed, they knew very well what to expect from her. But to me she continued throughout to be kind and gracious, thinking always how she could lighten my lot.

In this employment, therefore, I continued with such contentment as may be imagined, which was rather a forced resignation to the will of the Lord than a cheerful heart. But I confess that I looked upon the lot of the other women with horror, and was thankful indeed that I was spared the miseries of those who go forth to the fields. They begin at six in the morning, and work until eleven, when they come home to dinner: at one o'clock they go out again and return at sunset, which, in this country, is nearly always about half-past six. But let no one think that work in the fields at Barbadoes may be compared with work in the fields at home; for in England there are cloudy skies and cold wintry days in plenty, but in Barbadoes, save when the rain falls in prodigious quantities, the skies have no clouds, but are clear blue all the year round: the sun burns with a heat intolerable, so that the eyes are well-nigh blinded, the head aches, the limbs fail, and, but for fear of the lash, the wretched toiler would lie down in the nearest shade. And a terrible thirst (all this was told me by the girl Deb) seizes the throat, all day long, which nothing can assuage but rest. For the least skulking the whip is laid on; and if there be a word of impatience or murmuring, it is called stark mutiny, for which the miserable convict, man or woman, is tied up and flogged with a barbarity which would be incredible to any were it not for the memory of certain floggings in our own country. Besides the lash, they have also the pillory and the stocks, and the overseers carry in addition to their whip a heavy cane, with which they constantly belabour the slaves, both white and black. I say 'slaves' because the white servants are nothing less, save that the negroes are far better off, and receive infinitely better treatment than the poor white creatures. Indeed, the negro being the absolute property of his master, both he and his children, to ill-treat him is like the wanton destruction of cattle on a farm; whereas there is no reason in making the convicts last out more than the ten years of their servitude, or even so long, because many of them are such poor creatures when they arrive, and so reduced by the miseries of the voyage, and so exhausted by the hard labour to which they are put, that they bring no profit to the master, but quickly fall ill and die like rotten sheep. Like rotten sheep, I say, they die, without a word of Christian exhortation; and like brute creatures, who have no world to come, are they buried in the ground! Again, the food served out to these poor people is not such as should be given to white people in a hot climate. There is nothing but water to drink, and that drawn from ponds, because in Barbadoes there are few springs or rivers. It is true that the old hands, who have learned how to manage, contrive to make plantain wine, and get, by hook or by crook, mobbie (which is a strong drink made from potatoes), or kill-devil, which is the new spirit distilled from sugar. Then for solid food, the servants are allowed five pounds of salt beef for each person every week, and this so hard and stringy that no boiling will make it soft enough for the teeth. Sometimes, instead of the beef, they have as much salt fish, for the most part stinking; with this a portion of ground Indian corn, which is made into a kind of porridge, and called loblollie. This is the staple of the food, and there are no rustics at home who do not live better and have more nourishing food.

I do not deny that the convicts are for the most part a horrid crew, who deserve to suffer if any men ever did; but it was sad to see how the faces of the people were pinched with hunger and wasted with the daily fatigues, and how their hollow eyes were full of despair. Whatever their sins may have been, they were at least made in God's own image: no criminal, however wicked, should have been used with such barbarity as was wreaked upon the people of this estate. The overseers were chosen (being themselves also convicts) for their hardness of heart. Nay, did they show the least kindness towards the poor creatures whom they drove, they would themselves be forced to lay down the whip of office and to join the gang of those who toiled. And over them was the master, jealous to exact the last ounce of strength from the creatures whom he had bought. Did the good people of Bristol who buy the sugar and molasses and tobacco of the Indies know or understand the tears of despair and the sweat of agony which are forced with every pound of sugar, they would abhor the trade which makes them rich.

The companion of my sleeping-hut, the girl Deb, was a great, strapping wench, who bid fair to outlast her ten years of servitude, even under the treatment to which, with the rest, she was daily subjected. And partly because she was strong and active, partly because she had a certain kind of beauty (the kind which belongs to the rustic, and is accompanied by good-humour and laughter), she would perhaps have done well, as some of the women do, and ended by marrying an overseer, but for events which presently happened. Yet, strong as she was, there was no evening when she did not return worn out with fatigue, her cheeks burning, her limbs weary, yet happy because she had one more day escaped the lash, and had the night before her in which to rest. If it is worth noting, the women were from the outset the most willing workers, and the most eager to satisfy their taskmasters; the men, on the other hand, went sullen and downcast, thinking only how to escape the overseer's whip, and going through the work with angry and revengeful eyes. I think that some great mutiny might have happened upon this estate—some wild revenge—so desperate were these poor creatures and so horrible were the scourgings they endured, and the shrieks and curses which they uttered. Let me not speak of these things.

There are other things which make residence in Barbadoes, even to the wealthy, full of annoyances and irritations. The place is filled with cockroaches, great spiders, horrid scorpions, centipedes, and lizards. There are ants which swarm everywhere, and there are clouds of flies, and at night there are moskeetos and merrywings, which by their bites have been known to drive new-comers into fever, or else into a kind of madness.

In the evenings after supper there reigned a melancholy silence in the village, the people for the most part taking rest with weary limbs. Sometimes there would be a quarrel, with horrid oaths and curses and perhaps some fighting; but these occasions were rare.

From the house there came often the noise of singing, drinking, and loud talking when other planters would ride over for a drinking bout. There was also sometimes to be heard the music of the theorbo, upon which Madam played very sweetly, singing Spanish songs; so that it seemed a pity for music so sweet to be thrown away upon this selfish crew. It made me think of Humphrey, and of the sweet and holy thoughts which he would put into rhymes, and then fit the rhymes with music which seemed to breathe those very thoughts. Alas! In the village of Bradford Orcas there would be now silence and desolation! The good old Squire dead, my father dead, the young men sent to the Plantations, no one left at all but the Rector and Madam his sister-in-law, and I, alas! a slave. Perchance at that moment the Rector might be slowly drawing his bow across the strings of his violoncello thinking of those who formerly played with him; or perhaps he would be sorrowfully taking out his cases and gazing for a little consolation upon the figures of his goddesses and his nymphs. Only to think of the place, and of those who once lived there, tore my poor heart to pieces.

One evening, when there was a great noise and talking at the house, while we were sitting upon our beds with no other light than that of the moon, Madam herself came to the cottage.

'Child,' she said, 'nothing will do but that the gentlemen must see thy beauty. Nay, no harm shall happen while I am there: so much they know. But he hath so bragged about thy beauty and the great price he will demand for ransom that the rest are mad to see thee. I swear that not the least rudeness shall be offered thee. They are drinking, it is true; but they are not yet drunk. Come!'

So I arose and followed her. First, she took me to her own room, where she took off my hood and threw over me a long white lace mantilla, which covered my head and fell over my shoulders and below the waist.

She sighed as she looked at me.

'Poor innocent!' she said. 'If money could buy that face, there is not a man in the room but would give all he hath and count it gain. Canst thou play or sing?'

I told her that I had some knowledge of the theorbo. Therefore she brought me hers, and bade me sing to the gentlemen and then retire quickly. So I followed her into the living or keeping room, where a dozen gentlemen were sitting round the table. A bowl of punch was on the table, and every man had his glass before him, and a pipe of tobacco in his hand. Some of their faces were flushed with wine.

'Gentlemen,' said Madam, 'our prisoner hath consented to sing one song to you, after which she will ask permission to bid you good-night.'

So they all clapped their hands and rapped the table, and I, being indeed terrified, but knowing very well that to show fear would be the worst thing I could do, touched the strings and began my song. I sang the song which Humphrey made, and which he sang to the officers at Taunton when the Duke was there.

When I finished, I gave back the theorbo to Madam, curtsied to the gentlemen, and quickly stepped back to Madam's room, while they all bellowed and applauded and roared for me to come back again. But I put on my hood and slipped out to the cottage, where I lay down beside Deb, and quickly fell asleep. (It is a great happiness, in these hot latitudes, that, when a new-comer[253] hath once got over the trouble of the merrywings, he falleth asleep the moment he lies down, and so sleeps through the whole night.)

But in the morning Madam came to see me while I was sewing.

'Well, Child,' she said, laughing, 'thou hast gotten a lover who swears that he will soon have thee out of this hell.'

'A lover!' I cried. 'Nay!—that may God forbid!'

"Tis true. Young Mr. Anstiss it is. While thou wast singing he gazed on thy pretty face and listened as one enchanted. I wonder—but no!—thou hast no eyes for such things.

And when thou wast gone he offered the master four times the sum he paid for thee—yea, four times—or six times—saying that he meant honourably, and that if any man dared to whisper anything to the contrary he would cut his throat.'

'Alas! Madam. I must never marry—either this Mr. Anstiss or any other.'

'Tut—tut. This is foolish maid's nonsense. Granted you have lost your old lover, there are plenty more. Suppose he hath lost his old sweetheart, there are plenty more—as I doubt not he hath already proved. Mr. Anstiss is a very pretty young gentleman; but the master would not listen, saying that he waited for the lady's friends.'

And so passed six weeks, or thereabouts, for the only count of time I kept was from Sunday to Sunday. On that day we rested; the negroes, who are no better than heathens, danced. The white servants lay about in the shade, and drank what they could; in one cottage only on that godless estate were prayers offered.

And then happened that great event which, in the end, proved to be a change in my whole life, and brought happiness out of misery, and joy out of suffering, though at first it seemed only a dreadful addition to my trouble. Thus is the course of things ordered for us, and thus the greatest blessings follow upon the most threatening juncture. What this was I will tell in a few words.

It was about the third week in September when I embarked, and about the third week in November when the ship made her port. Therefore, I take it that it was one day about the beginning of the year 1686, when Madam came to the work-room and told me that a ship had arrived carrying a cargo of two hundred rebels and more, sent out to work upon the Plantations, like myself, for the term of ten years. She also told me that the master was gone to the Bridge in order to buy some of them. Not, she said, that he wanted more hands; but he expected that there would be among them persons of quality, who would be glad to buy their freedom. He still, she told me, looked to make a great profit out of myself, and was thinking to sell me, unless my friends in England speedily sent proposals for my ransom, to the young planter who was in love with me. This did not displease me. I have not thought it necessary to tell how Mr. Anstiss came often to the estate, and continually devised schemes for looking at me, going to the Ingenio, whence he could see those who sat in the work-room, and even sending me letters, vowing the greatest extravagance of passion—I say I was not displeased, because there was in this young gentleman's face a certain goodness of disposition clearly marked; so that even if I became his property I thought I might persuade him to relinquish thoughts of love, even if I had to trust myself entirely to his honour and tell him all. But, as you shall hear, this project of the master's was brought to naught.

As for the rebels, I was curious to see them. Some I might recognise; to some I might perhaps be of a little use at the outset in guarding them against dangers. I did not fear, or think it likely, that there would be any among them whom I might know or who might know me. Yet the thing which I least suspected, and the least feared—a thing which one would have thought so unlikely as to make the event a miracle—nay, call it rather the merciful ordering of all—that thing, I say, actually happened.

The newly-bought servants arrived at about five in the evening.

I looked out of the work-room to see them. Why, I seemed to know their faces—all their faces! They were our brave West Country lads, whom I had last seen marching gallantly out of Taunton town to victory and glory (as they believed). Now—pale with the miseries of the voyage, thin with bad food and disease, hollow-cheeked and hollow-eyed, in rags and dirt, barefooted, covered with dust, grimy for want of washing, their beards grown all over their faces—with hanging heads, stood these poor fellows. There were thirty of them; some had thrown themselves on the ground, as if in the last extremity of fatigue; some stood with the patience that one sees in brute beasts who are waiting to be killed; and in a group together stood three—oh! merciful Heaven! was this misery also added to my cup!—they were Robin, Barnaby, and Humphrey! Robin's face, heavy and pale, betrayed the sorrow of his soul. He stood as one who neither careth for nor regardeth anything. My heart fell like lead to witness the despair which was visible in his attitude, in his eyes, in his brow. But Barnaby showed still a cheerful countenance and looked about him, as if he was arriving a welcome guest instead of a slave.

'Do you know any of them, Child?' Madam asked.

'Oh! Madam,' I cried; 'they are my friends—they are my friends. Oh! help them—help them!'

'How can I help them?' she replied coldly. 'They are rebels, and they are justly punished. Let them write home for money if they have friends, and so they can be ransomed. To make them write the more movingly, the master hath resolved to send them all to work in the fields. "The harder they work," he says, "the more they will desire to be free again."'

In the fields! Oh! Robin—my poor Robin!

CHAPTER XXXVIII.

HUMPHREY'S NARRATIVE.

With these words—'Oh! Robin! Robin!'—the history, as set down in my Mistress's handwriting, suddenly comes to an end. The words are fitting, because her whole heart was full of Robin, and though at this time it seemed to the poor creature a sin still to nourish affection for her old sweetheart, I am sure—nay, I have it on her own confession—that there was never an hour in the waking day when Robin was not in her mind, though between herself and her former lover stood the dreadful figure of her husband. I suppose that, although she began this work with the design to complete it, she had not the courage, even when years had passed away and much earthly happiness had been her reward, to write down the passages which follow. Wherefore (and for another reason—namely, a confession which must be made by myself before I die) I have taken upon myself to finish that part of Alice Eykin's history which relates to the Monmouth rising and its unhappy consequences. You have read how (thanks to my inexperience and ignorance of conspiracies, and belief in men's promises) we were reduced to the lowest point of disgrace and poverty. Alice did not tell, because till afterwards she did not know, that on Sir Christopher's death his estate was declared confiscated, and presently bestowed upon Benjamin by favour of Lord Jeffreys; so that he whose ambition it was to become Lord Chancellor was already (which he had not expected) the Lord of the Manor of Bradford Orcas. But of this hereafter.

I have called her my Mistress. Truly, all my life she hath been to me more than was ever Laura to Petrarch, or even Beatrice to the great Florentine. The ancients represented every virtue by a Goddess, a Grace, or a Nymph. Nay, the Arts were also feminine (yet subject to the informing influence of the other sex, as the Muses had Apollo for their director and chief). To my mind every generous sentiment, every worthy thought, all things that are gracious, all things that lift my soul above the common herd, belong not to me, but to my Mistress. In my youth it was she who encouraged me to the practice of those arts by which the soul is borne heavenwards—I mean the arts of poetry and of music: it was she who listened patiently when I would still be prating of myself, and encouraged the ambitions which had already seized my soul. So that if I turned a set of verses smoothly, it was to Alice[256] that I gave them, and for her that I wrote them. When we played heavenly music together, the thoughts inspired by the strain were like the Italian painter's vision of the angels which attend the Virgin—I mean that, sweet and holy as the angels are, they fall far short of the holiness and sweetness of her whom they honour. So, whatever my thoughts or my ambitions, amidst them all I saw continually the face of Alice, always filled with candour and with sweetness. That quality which enables a woman to think always about others, and never about herself, was given to Alice in large and plenteous measure. If she talked with me, her soul was all mine. If she was waiting on Madam, or upon Sir Christopher, or upon the Rector, or on her own mother, she knew their inmost thoughts and divined all their wants. Nay, long afterwards, in the daily exercise of work and study, at the University of Oxford, in the foreign schools of Montpellier, Padua, and Leyden, it was Alice who, though far away, encouraged me. I could no longer hear her voice; but her steadfast eyes remained in my mind like twin stars that dwell in heaven. This is a wondrous power given to a few women, that they should become as it were angels sent from heaven, lent to the earth a while, in order to fill men's minds with worthy thoughts, and to lead them in the heavenly way. The Romish Church holds that the age of miracles hath never passed; which I do also believe, but not in the sense taught by that Church. Saints there are among us still, who daily work miracles, turning earthly clay into the jasper and the precious marble of heaven!

Again, the great poet Milton hath represented his virtuous lady unharmed among the rabble rout of Comus, protected by her virtue alone. Pity that he hath not also shown a young man led by that sweet lady, encouraged, warned, and guarded along that narrow way, beset with quag and pitfall, along which he must walk who would willingly climb to higher place! And all this apart from earthly love, as in the case of those two Italian poets.

More, I confess, I would have had, and presumptuously longed for it—nay, even prayed for it with such yearnings and longings as seemed to tear my very heart asunder. But this was denied to me.

In September, 1685, ten weeks after the fight of Sedgemoor, we, being by that time well tired of Exeter Prison, were tried by Lord Jeffreys. It was no true trial, for we were all advised to plead guilty, upon which the Judge bellowed and roared at us, abusing us in such language as I never thought to hear from the bench, and finally sentenced us all to death. (A great deal has been said of this roaring of the Judge, but I am willing to excuse it in great measure, on the ground of the disease from which he was then suffering. I myself, who had heard that he was thus afflicted, saw the drops of agony upon his forehead, and knew that if he was not bawling at us he must have been roaring on his own account.) So we were marched back to prison and began to prepare for the last ceremony, which is, I think, needlessly horrible and barbarous. To cut a man open while he is still living is a thing not practised even by the savage Turk. At this gloomy time my cousin Robin set a noble example of fortitude, which greatly encouraged the rest of us. Nor would he ever suffer me to reproach myself (as I was continually tempted to do) with having been the cause of the ruin which had fallen upon the whole of our unfortunate house. Nay, he went further, and insisted, and would have it, that had I remained in Holland he himself would have joined the Duke, and that I was in no way to blame as an inciter to this unfortunate act. We knew by this time that Sir Christopher had been arrested and conveyed to Ilminster Jail, and that with him were Dr. Eykin, grievously wounded, and Barnaby; and that Alice, with her mother, was also at Ilminster. Mr. Boscorel, for his part, was gone to London in order to exert whatever interest he might possess on behalf of all. With him went Madam, Robin's mother; but she returned before the trial, much dejected, so that we were not encouraged to hope for anything from that quarter. Madam began to build some hopes at this time from Benjamin, because he, who had accompanied the Judges from London, was the boon companion every night of Lord Jeffreys himself. But it is one thing to be permitted to drink and sing with a great man at night, and another thing to procure of him the pardon of rebels (and those not the common sort, but leaders and captains). That Benjamin would attempt to save us, I did not doubt; because in common decency and humanity he must needs try to save his grandfather and his cousins. But that he would effect anything—that, indeed, I doubted. Whether he did make an attempt, I know not. He came not to the prison, nor did he make any sign that he knew we were among the prisoners. What he contrived, the plot which he laid, and the villainy with which he carried it out, you have already read. Well, I shall have much more to say about Benjamin. For the moment, let him pass.

I say, then, that we were lying in Exeter Jail, expecting to be called out for execution at any hour. We were sitting in the courtyard on the stone bench with gloomy hearts.

'Robin—Humphrey—lads both!' cried a voice we knew. It was the Rector, Mr. Boscorel himself, who called us. 'Courage, lads!' he cried (yet looked himself as mournful as man can look). 'I bring you good news—I have this day ridden from Ilminster (there is other news not so good)—good news, I say: for you shall live, and not die! I have so far succeeded that the lives are spared of Robin Challis, Captain in the Rebel Cavalry; Barnaby Eykin, Captain of the Green Regiment; and Humphrey Challis, Chyrurgeon to the Duke. Yet must you go to the Plantations—poor lads!—there to stay for ten long years. Well, we will hope to get your pardon and freedom long before that time is over. Yet you must, perforce, sail across the seas.'

'Lad,' cried Robin, catching my hand, 'cease to tear thy heart with reproaches! See! none of us will die, after all.'

'On the scaffold, none,' said Mr. Boscorel. 'On the scaffold, none,' he repeated.

'And what saith my grandfather, Sir?' Robin asked. 'He is also enlarged, I hope, at least. And how is the learned Dr. Eykin? and Alice—my Alice—where is she?'

'Young men,' said the Rector, 'prepare for tidings of the worst—yes; of the very worst. Cruel news I bring to you, boys; and for myself'—he hung his head—'cruel news, shameful news?'

Alas! you know already what he had to tell us. Worse than the death of that good old man, Sir Christopher; worse than the death of the unfortunate Dr. Eykin and his much-tried wife; there was the news of Alice's marriage and of her flight, and at hearing this we looked at each other in dismay, and Robin sprang to his feet and cried aloud for vengeance upon the villain who had done this thing.

'It is my own son,' said Mr. Boscorel; 'yet spare him not! He deserves all that you can call him, and more. Shameful news I had to tell you. Where the poor child hath found a retreat or how she fares, I know not. Robin, ask me not to curse my own son—what is done will bring its punishment in due time. Doubt it not. But of punishment we need not speak. If there were any way—any way possible—out of it! But there is none. It is a fatal blow. Death itself alone can release her. Consider, Humphrey, consider; you are not so distracted as your cousin. Consider, I say, that unhappy girl is Benjamin's lawful wife. If he can find her, he may compel her to live with him. She is his lawful wife, I say. It is a case in which there is no remedy; it is a wickedness for which there is no help, until one of the twain shall die.'

There was indeed no help or remedy possible. I will not tell of the madness which fell upon Robin at this news, nor of the distracted things he said, nor how he wept for Alice at one moment and the next cursed the author of this wickedness. There was no remedy. Yet Mr. Boscorel solemnly promised to seek out the poor innocent girl, forced to break her vows for the one reason which could excuse her—namely, to save the lives of all she loved.

'They were saved already,' Mr. Boscorel added. 'He knew that they were saved. He had seen me; he had the news that I brought from London; he knew it; and he lied unto her! There is no single particular in which his wickedness can be excused or defended. Yet, I say, curses are of no avail. The Hand of God is heavy upon all sinners, and will presently fall upon my unhappy son—I pray that before that Hand shall fall his heart may be touched with repentance.'

But Robin fell into a melancholy from which it was impossible to arouse him. He who, while death upon the scaffold seemed certain, was cheerful and brave, now, when his life was spared, sat heavy and gloomy, speaking to no one; or, if he spoke, then in words of rage and impatience.

Mr. Boscorel remained at Exeter, visiting us daily until the time came when we were removed. He brought with him one day[259] a smooth-tongued gentleman in sober attire, who was, he told us, a West Indian merchant of Bristol, named George Penne. (You have read, and know already, how great a villain was this man.)

'This gentleman,' said Mr. Boscorel, 'is able and willing, for certain considerations, to assist you in your exile. You have been given (among many others) by the King to one Mr. Jerome Nipho, who hath sold all his convicts to this gentleman. In his turn, he is under bonds to ship you for the Plantations, where you will be sold again to the planters.'

'Sirs,' Mr. Penne looked from one to the other of us with compassionate eyes, 'I have heard your melancholy case, and it will be to my great happiness if I may be able in any way to soften the rigours of your exile. Be it known to you that I have correspondents in Jamaica, Barbadoes, and Virginia, and that for certain sums of money these—my friends—will readily undertake to make your servitude one merely in name. In other words, as I have already informed his Reverence, I have bought you in the hope of being useful to you (I wish I could thus buy all unhappy prisoners), and I can, on paying my friends what they demand, secure to you freedom from labour, subject only to the condition of remaining abroad until your term is expired, or your friends at home have procured your pardon.'

'As for the price, Humphrey,' said Mr. Boscorel, 'that shall be my care. It is nearly certain that Sir Christopher's estates will be confiscated, seeing that he died in prison under the charge of high treason, though he was never tried. Therefore we must not look to his lands for any help. What this gentleman proposes is, however, so great a thing that we must not hesitate to accept his offer gratefully.'

'I must have,' said Mr. Penne, 'seventy pounds for each prisoner. I hear that there is a third young gentleman of your party now in the same trouble at Ilminster; I shall therefore ask for two hundred guineas—two hundred guineas in all. It is not a large sum in order to secure freedom. Those who cannot obtain this relief have to work in the fields or in the mills under the hot sun of the Spanish Main; they are subject to the whip of the overseer; they have wretched food; they are worse treated than the negroes, because the latter are slaves for life and the former for ten years only. By paying two hundred guineas only you will all be enabled to live at your ease. Meanwhile, your friends at home will be constantly endeavouring to procure your pardon. I myself, though but a simple merchant of Bristol City, can boast some influence, which I will most readily exert to the utmost in your behalf'——

'Say no more, Sir,' said Mr. Boscorel, interrupting him; 'the bargain is concluded. These young gentlemen shall not be subjected to any servitude; I will pay you two hundred guineas.'

'I would, Sir'—Mr. Penne laid his hand, which was large, white, and soft, the hand of a liar and a traitor, upon his treacherous heart—'I would to Heaven, Sir,' he said, 'that I could undertake this service for less. If my correspondents were men of tender hearts, the business should cost you nothing at all. But they are men of business; they say that they live not abroad for pleasure, but for profit; they cannot forego any advantage that may offer. As for me, this job brings me no profit. Upon my honour, gentlemen, profit from such a source I should despise: every guinea that you give me will be placed to the credit of my correspondents, who will, I am assured, turn a pretty penny by the ransom of the prisoners. But that we cannot help. And as for me—I say it boldly in the presence of this learned and pious clergyman—I am richly rewarded with the satisfaction of doing a generous thing. That is enough, I hope, for any honest man.'

The fellow looked so benevolent, and smiled with so much compassion, that it was impossible to doubt his word. Besides, Mr. Boscorel had learned many things during the journey to London; among others that it would be possible to buy immunity from labour for the convicts. Therefore, he hesitated not, but gave him what he demanded, taking in return a paper, which was to be shown to Mr. Penne's correspondents, in which he acknowledged the receipt of the money, and demanded in return a release from actual servitude. This paper I put carefully in my pocket, with my note-book and my case of instruments.

It was, so far as my memory serves me, about six weeks after our pardon was received when we heard that we were to be marched to Bristol, there to be shipped for some port or other across the ocean. At Taunton we were joined by a hundred poor fellows as fortunate as ourselves; and at Bridgwater by twenty more, whose lives had been bought by Colonel Kirke. Fortunate we esteemed ourselves; for everywhere the roads were lined with legs, heads, trunks, and arms, boiled and blackened in pitch, stuck up for the terror of the country. Well; you shall judge how fortunate we were.

When we reached Bristol, we found Mr. Penne upon the Quay, with some other merchants. He changed colour when he saw us; but quickly ran to meet us, and whispered that we were on no account to betray his goodness in the matter of ransom, otherwise it might be the undoing of us all, and perhaps cause his own imprisonment. He also told me that the ship was bound for Barbadoes, and we should have to mess with the other prisoners on the voyage, but that it would all be made up to us when we arrived. He further added that he had requested his correspondents to entertain us until money should arrive from England, and to become our bankers for all that we should want. And with that he clasped my hand tenderly, and with a 'God be wi' ye!' he left us, and we saw him no more.

CHAPTER XXXIX.

FOR TEN YEARS.

It was a numerous company gathered together on the deck of the ship. By their dress they were country lads; by their pale cheeks they were prison birds like ourselves; by their dismal faces they were, also, like ourselves, rebels condemned to the Plantations. Alas! how many of these poor fellows have returned to their homes, and how many lie in the graves of Jamaica, Virginia, and Barbadoes? As for preparations for a voyage, not one of us could make any, either of clothes or of provisions. There was not among the whole company so much as a change of clothes; nay, there was not even a razor, and our faces were already bristling horribly with the beards which before long made us look like so many Heyducs.

Among them I presently discerned, to my great surprise and joy, none other than Barnaby. His coat of scarlet was now so ragged and stained that neither colour nor original shape could be discerned, his ruffles and cravat of lace were gone, and the scarlet sash which had formerly carried his hanger was gone also. In a word, he was in rags and covered with the dust of the road. Yet his jolly countenance showed a satisfaction which contrasted greatly with the dejection of his companions. He sniffed the scent of tar and ropes with a joy which was visible to all, and he contemplated the ship and her rigging with the air of one who is at home.

Then he saw us and shouted to us while he made his way roughly through the rest.

'What cheer, ho! Humphrey, brave lad of boluses?'—never did any man grasp the hand of friend with greater vigour. 'This is better, I say, than the accursed prison, where one got never a breath of fresh air. Here one begins to smell salt water and tarred rope, which is a downright wholesome smell. Already I feel hearty again. I would willingly drink a tankard or two of black beer. What, Robin, what? We are not going to be hanged, after all. Lift up thy head, therefore: is this a time for looking glum? We shall live to hang Judge Jeffreys yet!—what? Thy looks are but poorly, lad. Is it the prison or is it thy disappointment? That villain, Benjamin! Hark ye, Robin'—some men's faces look black when they threaten, but Barnaby's grew broader, as if the contemplation of revenge made him the happier—'Hark ye, this is my business. No one shall interfere with me in this. Benjamin is my affair. No one but I myself must kill Benjamin: not you, Humphrey, because he is your cousin; not you, Robin, because you must not kill Alice's husband even to get back your own sweetheart.' Barnaby spoke wisdom here; in spite of Robin's vows he could not get Alice for himself by killing her husband, unworthy though he was. 'Benjamin,' he went on, 'may call her wife, but if he seek to make her his wife, if I know Sis aright, he will meet his match. As for her safety, I am certain that she is safe. For why? Wherever there are folks of her religious kidney, there will she find friends. Cheer up, Robin! Soon or late I will kill this fine husband of hers.'

But Robin shook his head.

Barnaby then asked if I knew whither we were bound. I told him Barbadoes, according to the information given me by Mr. Penne.

'Why,' said Barnaby, rubbing his hands, 'this is brave news, indeed. There is no place I would sooner choose. 'Tis a small island, to begin with: give me a small island, so that the sea runneth all round about and is everywhere within easy reach. Where there is the sea there are boats; where there are boats there are the means of escape. Cheer up, my lads! I know the Spanish Main right well. Give me a tight boat, I care not how small, and a keg of water, and I will sail her anywhere. Ha! we are bound to Barbadoes, are we? This is truly brave news!'

I asked him next what kind of place it was.

'It is a hot place,' he replied. 'A man is always thirsty, and there is plenty to drink except water, which is said to be scarce. But the merchants and the planters want none. They have wine of the best, of Spain and of France and of Madeira. Cider and strong ale they import from England. And drinks they make in the country—perino and mobbie—I remember—grippo and plantain wine and kill-devil. 'Tis a rare country for drink, and many there be who die of too much. Hold up thy head, Robin; we will drink damnation to Benjamin yet. But 'tis I who shall kill him. Courage, I say. What? Our turn will come!'

I told him, then, what had been done with Mr. George Penne—namely,[263] the ransom bought by the Rector for us all, and the letter which I carried to Mr. Penne's correspondent.

'Why,' he said, with some discontent, 'we shall not be long upon the island after all, and perhaps the money might have been better bestowed. But 'twas kindly done of the Rector. As for the banishment, I value it not a farthing. One place is as good as another; and, for my own part, I love the West Indies. We shall have our choice among them all, because, where there are boats and the open sea, a man can go whithersoever pleaseth him best. The voyage out'—he glanced round him—'will, I fear, be choking work—the rations will be short, there will be neither drink nor tobacco, and at nights we shall lie close. A more melancholy company I never saw. Patience, my lads; our turn will come.'

Well, 'twas a special mercy that we had with us one man, at least, who preserved his cheerfulness, for the rest of the company were as melancholy as King James himself could have desired. Indeed, to look back upon the voyage is to recall the most miserable time that can be imagined. First of all, as I have said, we were wholly unprepared for a voyage, having nothing at all with us. Then we had bad weather at the outset, which not only made our people ill, but caused the biscuit to be mostly spoiled, so that before the end of the voyage a few peas with the sweepings of the biscuit-room, and sometimes a little tough beef, was all our diet, and for drink nothing, not so much as a pannikin of beer, but water, and that turbid, and not too much of it.

As for me, I kept my health chiefly by the method common among physicians—namely, by watching the symptoms of others. But mostly was I concerned with the condition of Robin. For the poor lad, taking so much to heart the dreadful villainy which had been practised upon Alice, never once held up his head, and would talk and think of nothing else but of that poor maid.

'Where is she?' he asked a hundred times. 'Where hath she found a shelter and a hiding-place? How shall she escape the villain, who will now do what he pleases since we are out of his way? And no help for her—not any until she die, or until he dies! And we cannot even send her a letter to console her poor heart! Humphrey, it drives me mad to think that every day carries us further from her. If I could but be with her to protect her against her husband! Humphrey, Barnaby said well: I could not get her back to me over the dead body of her husband. But to protect her—to stand between her and the man she hath sworn to obey!'

There is no more dangerous condition of the mind than that which we call despair. It is, I take it, a disease, and that of the most dangerous kind. I have observed many men in that condition. With some, the devil enters into them, finding all the doors open and unguarded; nay, he even receives a warm welcome. With others it is as if the body itself was left without its armour—a cheerful and hopeful mind being certainly an armour against[264] disease, capable of warding off many of those invisible arrows which are always flying about the air and striking us down with fevers, agues, calentures, and other pains and grievous diseases.

I marvel that more of the men on board were not sick; for, to begin with, the water soon became thick and swarmed with wriggling creatures difficult to avoid in drinking; and then, though during the day we were allowed to be on deck (where the air was fresh even if the sun was hot), at night we were terribly crowded below, and lay too close for health or for comfort. However, we finally made Carlisle Bay and the port of St. Michael's or the Bridge. And I must say this for Barnaby, that he maintained throughout the whole voyage his cheerfulness, and that he never ceased to make his plans for escape, drawing on a paper, which he procured, a rough chart of the Spanish Main, with as many islands as he could remember. Of these there are hundreds, some desolate and safe for fugitives, some with neither water nor green trees, and some with springs and woods, wild fruit, land turtles on the shore, fish in the sea, and everything that man can desire.

We made the land, after I know not how many weeks, one day in the forenoon.

'Barbadoes,' said Barnaby, pointing to a little cloud far away on the horizon. 'Well; of this job I am wellnigh sick. To-morrow, if the wind holds, we shall have sailed round the island and shall beat up for Carlisle Bay. Well, it is lucky for us that we have this letter of Mr. Penne's. We will go—I know the place well—to the sign of the Rock and Turtle, kept by old Mother Rosemary, if she lives still, or, if she be dead, by one of her daughters—she had fifty daughters, at least, all buxom mulatto girls. There we will put off these filthy rags, have a wash in a tub of fresh water, get shaved, and then with smooth chins and clean shirts we will sit down to a dinner such as the old woman knows how to make, a potato-pudding and Scots collops with Rhenish wine, and afterwards a cool cup of beverage, which is nothing in the world but squeezed limes, with sugar and water, fit for such a womanly stomach as yours, Doctor. With this, and a pipe of tobacco, and perhaps a song and (when your Worship hath gone to bed) a dance from one of the girls—I say, my lad, with this I shall be ready to forget Sedgemoor and to forgive Judge Jeffreys. When we are tired of Barbadoes, we will take boat and sail away. I know one island, at least, where they care nothing for King James. Thither will we go, my lad.'

Well; what we found at our port, and how we fared, was not quite as Barnaby expected and hoped, as you shall hear. But I must admire the cunning of the man Penne, who not only took from Alice—poor child!—all her brother's money, amounting to two hundred and fifty pounds or thereabouts (which you have read), on the pretext of bestowing it for the advantage of all, but also received two hundred guineas from Mr. Boscorel on the same pretence. This made in all four hundred and fifty pounds. And not one penny—not a single penny—of this great sum did the man spend upon the purpose for which it was given him.

You have heard how the merchants and planters came aboard the ships which put in with servants and slaves, and how these are put up for sale one at a time. As was the sale described by Alice, just such was ours: though, I take it, our lads were not so miserable a company as were those on board her ship. Pale of cheek they looked, and dejected, and some were sick with various disorders, caused by the confinement of the prison or the sufferings of the voyage. They put us up one after the other and we were sold. I forget what I myself fetched, and, indeed, it matters not, save that many jests were passed at our expense, and that when one was put up—as Robin, for instance—who had been a Captain in the rebel army, the salesman was eloquent in praise of his rich and illustrious family, who would never endure that this unfortunate man should continue in servitude. But Barnaby put his tongue in his cheek and laughed.

When the sale was concluded, we were bundled into boats and taken ashore to the barracoon, of which you have heard from Alice. Here the same officer who read to her party the laws concerning servants and their duties, and the punishments which await transgressors, read them also to ourselves.

'Faith,' Barnaby whispered, 'there will be a great scoring of backs before many days are done, unless their bark is worse than their bite.'

This business despatched, I thought it was time to present my letter. Therefore I stepped forward, and informed the officer, who, by reason of his gown and wig and the beadles who were with him, I judged to be some lawyer, that, with my cousin and another, I held a letter which should hold us free from servitude.

'Ay, ay,' he said. 'Where is that letter?'

So I gave it to him. 'Twas addressed to one Jonathan Polwhele, and enjoined him to receive the three prisoners, named Humphrey Challis, Robin Challis, and Barnaby Eykin, to pay for them such sums as would reasonably be required to redeem them from servitude, and to advance them such moneys as they would want at the outset for maintenance, the whole to be accounted for in Mr. Jonathan Polwhele's next despatches to his obedient, much obliged servant, G. P.

'Sir,' said the officer, when he had read the letter through, 'this epistle is addressed to one Jonathan Polwhele. There is no merchant or planter of that name on the whole island.'

He gave me back the letter. 'If this,' he said, 'is all you have to show, there is no reason why you and your friends should not march with the rest.'

Truly, we had nothing else to show. Not only was there no one named Polwhele on the island, but there never had been any one of that name. Therefore it was plain that we had been tricked, and that the man George Penne was a villain. Alas! poor Barnaby. Where now were his cool cups and his pipe of tobacco? Then the officer beckoned to a gentleman—a sober and grave person—standing near, and spoke to him.

'Gentlemen,' said the merchant, 'permit me to read this letter. So, it is in the handwriting of Mr. George Penne, which I know well. There is here some strange mistake. The letter is addressed to Mr. Jonathan Polwhele; but there is no one of that name in the place. I am myself Mr. Penne's correspondent in this island. My name, gentlemen, is Sefton, not Polwhele.'

'Sir,' I said, 'do you know Mr. Penne?'

'I have never seen him. He consigns to my care once or twice a year a cargo of transported servants, being rogues and thieves, sent here, instead of to the gallows. He ships them to my care, I say, as he hath shipped the company arrived this morning; and I sell them for him, taking for my share a percentage, as agreed upon, and remitting to him the balance in sugar and tobacco.'

'Is there no letter from him?'

'There is a letter in which he advises me of so many rebels consigned to me in order to be sold. Some among them, he says, were captains and officers in Monmouth's army, and some are of good family, among whom he especially names Robin and Humphrey Challis. But there is not a word about ransom.'

'Sir,' I said, knowing nothing as yet of Alice and her money, 'two hundred guineas have been paid to Mr. Penne by the Rev. Philip Boscorel, Rector of Bradford Orcas, in the county of Somerset, for our ransom.'

'Nothing is said of this,' he replied gravely. 'Plainly, gentlemen, without despatches from Mr. Penne I cannot act for you. You have a letter; it is written by that gentleman; it is addressed to Mr. Polwhele; it says nothing about Barbadoes, and would serve for Jamaica or Virginia. So great a sum as two hundred guineas cannot have been forgotten. I exhort you, therefore, to patience until other letters arrive. Why, two hundred guineas would have gone far to redeem you all three, and to maintain you for a great while. Gentlemen, I am grieved for you, because there is for the present no help for it, but that you must go with the planter who hath bought you, and obey his orders. I will, however, send to Mr. Penne an account of this charge, and I would advise that you lose no time in writing to your friends at home.'

'Heart up, lad!' cried Barnaby, for I turned faint upon this terrible discovery, and would have fallen, but he held me up. 'Patience; our turn will come.'

'Write that letter,' said the merchant again. 'Write that letter quickly, so that it may go with the next vessel. Otherwise the work is hard and the heat is great.' So he turned and left us.

'Courage, man!' said Barnaby. 'To every dog his day. If now for five minutes only I could have my thumb on Mr. Penne's windpipe and my fingers round his neck! And I thought to spend the evening joyfully at Mother Rosemary's! Courage, lad! I have seen already,' he whispered, 'a dozen boats in the bay, any one of which will serve our turn.'

But Robin paid no heed, whatever happened. He stood up when his name was called, and was sold without showing any emotion. When we found that we had been tricked he seemed as if he neither heard nor regarded.

When all was ready we were marched, twenty in number, along a white and dusty road to our estate. By great good fortune—rather by Providence—we were all bought by the same master. He was, it is true, a bad man; but to be bought all together was a happiness which we could not expect. He bought us all because he understood that we belonged to the same family (and that one of position), in the hope of receiving substantial ransom. This man rode with us, accompanied by two overseers (these were themselves under the same sentence) who cracked their whips continually, and cursed us if we lagged. Their bark was worse, we afterwards found, than their bite, for it was only in the master's presence that they behaved thus brutishly, and in order to curry favour with him and to prevent being reduced again to the rank of those who served in the field. There was no doubt, from the very outset, that we were afflicted with a master whose like, I would hope, is not to be found upon the island of Barbadoes. Briefly, he was one whose appearance, voice, and manner all alike proclaimed him openly to all the world as a drunkard, a profligate, and a blasphemer. A drunkard he was of that kind who are seldom wholly drunk and yet are never sober; who begin the day with a glass and go on taking more glasses all day long, with small ale for breakfast, strong ale and Madeira for dinner, a tankard in the afternoon, and for supper more strong ale and Madeira, and before bed another tankard. As for compassion, or tenderness, or any of the virtues which a man who holds other men in slavery ought to possess, he had none of them.

Let me speak of him with no more bitterness than is necessary. We have, I think, all forgiven him, and he hath long since gone to a place where he can do no more harm to any, but awaiteth judgment—perhaps in the sure and certain hope of which the funeral service speaks—but this is open to doubt.

When we were arrived at the estate, the master dismounted, gave his horse to a negro, and ordered us to be drawn up in line.

He then made a short speech. He said that he had bought us, rebels and villains as we were, and that he meant to get his money's worth out of us or he would cut us all to pieces. Other things he told us, which I pass over because they were but repetitions of this assurance. He then proceeded to examine us in detail. When he came to me he cursed and swore because he said he had been made to pay for a sound, proper man, and had got a crookback for his bargain. I told him that, with submission, he might find the crookback,[268] who was a physician, a more profitable bargain than many a stronger man.

'What?' he roared. 'Thou art a physician, eh? Wouldst slink out of the field-work and sit idle among bottles and boluses? John'—he turned to one of the overseers—'pay particular attention, I command thee, to this learned physician. If he so much as turn round in his work, make his shoulders smart.'

'Ay, ay, Sir,' said the overseer.

'And what art thou, sirrah?' He turned next to Barnaby. 'Another learned physician, no doubt—or a Divine, a Bishop likely, or a Dean at the least?'

'As for what I was,' said Barnaby, 'that is neither here nor there. For what I am, I suppose I am your servant for ten years, or until our pardons are sent us.'

'Thou art an impudent dog, I dare swear,' returned the master. 'I remember now. Thou wast a Captain in the rebel army, once a sailor. Well, take care, lest thou taste the cat.'

'Gentlemen who are made to taste the cat,' said Barnaby, 'are apt to remember the taste of it when their time is up.'

'What?' he cried. 'You dare to threaten? Take that—and that!' and so began to belabour him about the head. I trembled lest Barnaby should return the blows. But he did not. He only held up his arm to protect his head, and presently, when the master desisted, he shook himself like a dog.

'I promise you I shall remember the taste of that wood,' he said quietly.

The master looked as if he would renew the cudgelling, but thought better of it.

Then, without more violence, we were assigned our quarters. A cottage or hut was given to us. We were served with a hammock, and a rug each; a pannikin, basin, spoon and platter for each; a Monmouth cap; two shirts, common and coarse; two pairs of canvas breeches, and a pair of shoes for each—so that we looked for all the world like the fellows who live by loading and unloading the ships in the port of Bristol. Yet the change after the long voyage was grateful. They served us next with some of the stuff they call loblollie, and then the night fell and we lay down in our hammocks, which were certainly softer than the planks of the ship, and then fell fast asleep in spite of the humming and the biting of the merrywings, and so slept till the break of day.

CHAPTER XL.

WITH THE HOE.

Before it was daylight we were aroused by the discordant clang of a bell: work was about to begin.

In these latitudes there is little twilight; the day begins, as it ends, with a kind of suddenness. I arose, being thus summoned, and looked out. Long rays of light were shooting up the sky from the East, and, though the stars were still visible, the day was fast breaking. In a few moments it became already so light that I could see across the yard—or what the Italians would call the piazza—with its ragged bonannow-leaves, the figures of our fellow-slaves moving about the huts, and hear their voices. Alas! sad and melancholy are the voices of those who work upon his Majesty's Plantations. Two old negresses went about among the new-comers, carrying a bucketful of their yellow mess, which they distributed among us, and giving us to understand that this bowl of yellow porridge, or loblollie, made out of Indian corn, was all we should have before dinner. They also gave us to understand in their broken English, which is far worse than the jargon talked by some of our country people, that we should have to prepare our own meals for the future, and that they would show us how to make this delectable mess.

'Eat it,' said Barnaby; 'a pig is better fed at home. Eat it, Robin, lest thou faint in the sun. Perhaps there will be something better for dinner. Heigho! only to think of Mother Rosemary's, where I thought to lie last night! Patience, lads!'

One would not seem to dwell too long on the simple fare of convicts: therefore I will say, once for all, that our rations consisted of nothing at all but the Indian meal and of salt beef or salt fish. The old hands and the negro slaves know how to improve their fare in many ways, and humane masters will give their servants quantities of the fruits such as grow here in great abundance—as plantains, lemons, limes, bonannows, guavas, and the like. And many of the black slaves have small gardens behind their huts, where they grow onions, yams, potatoes, and other things which they cultivate on Sundays. They are all great thieves also, stealing, whenever they can, poultry, eggs, and fruit, so that they grow fat and sleek, while the white servants daily grow more meagre, and fall into diseases by reason of the poorness of their[270] food. Then, as to drink, there are many kinds of drink (apart from the wines of Spain, Portugal, Canary, Madeira, and France) made in the country itself, such as mobbie, which is a fermented liquor of potatoes; and perino, from the liquor of chewed cassavy root; punch, which is water and sugar left to work for ten days; rum, which is distilled in every Ingenio, and is a spirit as strong as brandy, and said to be more wholesome. Those who have been long in the island, even the servants, though without a penny, know how and where to get these drinks; and, since there is no consoler, to the common sort, so good as strong drink, those who are able to drink every day of these things become somewhat reconciled to their lot.

'Come out, ye dogs of rebels and traitors!' It was the loud and harsh voice of the master himself, who thus disturbed us at our breakfast. 'Twas his custom thus to rise early, and to witness the beginning of the day's work. And 'twas his kindly nature which impelled him thus to welcome and encourage his newly-bought slaves. 'Come out, I say! Ye shall now show of what stuff ye are made. Instead of pulling down your lawful King, ye shall pull up your lawful master and make him rich. If ye never did a day's work in your lives, ye shall now learn the how by the must. Come forth, I say, ye lazy, guzzling skulkers!'

'Ay, ay,' said Barnaby, leisurely scraping his bowl, 'we are like, indeed, to be overfed here.' He rolled sailor fashion out of the hut.

'Barnaby,' I said, 'for God's sake, say nothing to anger the master! There is no help but in patience and in hope.'

So we, too, went forth. The master, red-faced as he was, looked as if he had been drinking already.

'So,' he cried, 'here is the learned physician. Your health, Doctor. And here is the gallant Captain, who was once a sailor. The air of the fields, Captain, will remind you, perchance, of the quarter-deck. This young gentleman looks so gallant and gay that I warrant he will ply the hoe with a light and frolick heart. Your healths, gentlemen. Hark ye, now. You are come of a good stock, I hear. Therefore have I bought you at a great price, looking to get my money back and more. Some planters would suffer you to lie at your ease cockered up with bonavist and Madeira till the money comes. As for me, I shall now show you what you will continue to do, unless the money comes. Therefore you will at once, I doubt not, ask for paper and pen and presently write. Sixty pounds a-piece, gentlemen—not one penny less—will purchase your freedom. Till then, the fields. And no difference between white and black; but one whip for both.'

We made no reply, but took the hoes which were given out to us and marched with the rest of the melancholy troop.

There were as many blacks as whites. We were divided into gangs; with every gang a driver armed with a whip; and over all the overseers, who, by their severity, showed their zeal for the master. The condition of slavery hath in it something devilish, both for those who are slaves and those who are masters. The former it drives into despair, and fills with cunning, dishonesty, treachery, and revenge. Why, the black slaves have been known to rise in rebellion, and while they had the power have inflicted tortures unheard-of upon their masters. The latter it makes cruel and unfeeling; it tempts them continually to sins of all kinds; it puts into their power the lives, the bodies—nay, the very souls—of the poor folk whom they buy. I do maintain, and conceal not my opinion, that no man ought, in a Christian country, to be a slave except for a term of years, and then for punishment. I have been myself a slave, and I know the misery and the injustice of the condition. But it is idle to hope that the planters will abandon this means of cultivating their estates, and it is certain that in hot countries no man will work except by compulsion.

The whip carried by the driver is a dreadful instrument, long, thick, and strongly plaited, with a short handle. It is coiled and slung round the shoulders when it is not being used to terrify or to punish, and I know well that its loud crack produces upon the mind a sensation of fear and of horror such as the thunder of artillery or the sight of the enemy charging could never cause even to a coward. The fellows are also extremely dexterous in the use of it; they can inflict a punishment not worse than the flogging of a schoolboy; or, with no greater outward show of strength, they will cut and gash the flesh like a Russian executioner with the cruel instrument which they call the knout.

For slight offences, such as laziness or carelessness in the field, the former is administered; but for serious offences, the latter. One sad execution (I cannot call it less) I myself witnessed. What the poor wretch had done I know not, but I can never forget his piercing shrieks as the whip cut into the bleeding flesh. This is not punishment: it is savage and revengeful cruelty. Yet the master and the overseers looked on with callous eyes.

They marched us to a field about half a mile from our village or camp, and there, drawing us up in line, set us to work. Our task was, with the hoe, to dig out square holes, each of the same depth and size, in which the sugar canes are planted, a small piece of old cane being laid in each. These holes are cut with regularity and exactness, in long lines and equally distant from each other. It is the driver's business to keep all at work at the same rate of progress, so that no one should lag behind, no one should stop to rest or breathe, no one should do less than his neighbours. The poor wretches, with bent bodies streaming with their exertions, speedily become afflicted with a burning thirst; their legs tremble; their backs grow stiff and ache; their whole bodies become full of pain; and yet they may not rest nor stand upright to breathe a while, nor stop to drink, until the driver calls a halt. From time to time the negroes—men and women alike—were dragged out of the ranks and laid on the ground three or four at a time, to receive lashes for not making the holes deep enough or fast enough. At home one can daily see the poor creatures flogged in Bridewell; every day there are rogues tied to the cart-wheel and flogged wellnigh to death; but a ploughman is not flogged for the badness of his furrow, nor is a cobbler flogged because he maketh his shoon ill. And our men do not shriek and scream so wildly as the negroes, who are an ignorant people and have never learned the least self-restraint. It was horrid also to see how their bodies were scarred with the marks of old floggings, and branded with letters to show by whom they had been bought. As for our poor fellows, who had been brave recruits in Monmouth's army, they trembled at the sight and worked all the harder; yet some of them with the tears in their eyes, to think that they should be brought to such a dismal fate and to herd with these poor, ignorant, black people.

'Twas the design of the master to set us to the very hardest work from the beginning, so that we should be the more anxious to get remission of our pains. For it must not be supposed that all the work on the estate was so hard and irksome as that with the hoe—which is generally kept for the strongest and hardest of the negroes, men and women. There are many other employments: some are put to weed the canes, some to fell wood, some to cleave it, some to attend the Ingenio, the boiling-house, the still-house, the curing-house; some to cut the maize, some to gather provisions, of bonavist, maize, yams, potatoes, cassavy, and the like. Some to the smith's forge; some to attend to the oxen and sheep; some to the camels and assinegoes, and the like: so that, had the master pleased, he might have set us to work better fitted to English gentlemen. Well, his greediness and cruelty were defeated, as you shall presently see. As for the domestic economy of the estate, there were on it five hundred acres of land, of which two hundred were planted with sugar, eighty for pasture, one hundred and twenty for wood, thirty for tobacco, five for ginger, and as many for cotton-wool, and seventy for provisions—viz. corn, potatoes, plantains, cassavy, and bonavist—with a few for fruit. There were ninety-six negroes, two or three Indian women with their children, and twenty-eight Christian servants, of whom we were three.

At eleven o'clock we were marched back to dinner. At one we went out again, the sun being at this time of the day very fierce, though January is the coldest month in the year. We worked till six o'clock in the evening, when we returned.

'This,' said Robin, with a groan, 'is what we have now to do every day for ten years.'

'Heart up, lads!' said Barnaby; 'our time will come. Give me time to turn round, as a body may say. Why, the harbour is full of boats. Let me get to the port and look round a bit. If we had any money now—but that is past praying for. Courage and patience! Doctor, you hoe too fast: no one looks for zeal. Follow the example of the black fellows, who think all day long how they shall get off with as little work as possible. As for their lash, I doubt whether they dare to lay it about us, though they may talk. Because you see, even if we do not escape, we shall some time or other, through the Rector's efforts, get a pardon, and then we are gentlemen again; and when that moment arrives I will make this master of ours fight, willy-nilly, and I will kill him, d'ye see, before I go home to kill Benjamin.'

He then went on to discourse (either with the hope of raising our spirits or because it cheered his mind just to set them forth) upon his plans for the means of escape.

'A boat,' he said, 'I can seize. There are many which would serve our purpose. But a boat without victuals would be of little use. One would not be accused of stealing, yet we may have to break into the store and take therefrom some beef or biscuit. But where to store our victuals? We may have a voyage of three or four hundred knots before us. That is nothing for a tight little boat when the hurricane season is over. We have no compass either—I must lay hands upon a compass. The first Saturday night I will make for the port and cast about. Lift up your head, Robin. Why, man, all bad times pass if only one hath patience.'

It was this very working in the fields, by which the master thought to drive us into despair, which caused in the long run our deliverance, and that in the most unexpected manner.

CHAPTER XLI.

ON CONDITIONS.

This servitude endured for a week, during which we were driven forth daily with the negroes to the hardest and most intolerable toil, the master's intention being so to disgust us with the life as to make us write the most urgent letters to our friends at home; since, as we told him two hundred guineas had been already paid on our account (though none of the money was used for the purpose), he supposed that another two hundred could easily be raised. Wherefore, while those of the new servants who were common country lads were placed in the Ingenio, or the curing-house, where the work is sheltered from the scorching sun, we were made to endure every hardship that the place permitted. In the event, however, the man's greed was disappointed and his cruelty made of none avail.

In fact, the thing I had foreseen quickly came to pass. When a man lies in a lethargy of despair, his body, no longer fortified by a cheerful mind, presently falls into any disease which is lurking in the air. Diseases of all kinds may be likened unto wild beasts: invisible, always on the prowl, seeking whom they may devour. The young fall victims to some, the weak to others; the drunkards and gluttons to others; the old to others; and the lethargic, again, to others. It was not surprising to me, therefore, when Robin, coming home one evening, fell to shivering and shaking, chattering with his teeth, and showing every external sign of cold, though the evening was still warm, and the sun had that day been more than commonly hot. Also, he turned away from his food, and would eat nothing. Therefore, as there was nothing we could give him, we covered him with our rugs; and he presently fell asleep. But in the morning, when we awoke, behold! Robin was in a high fever: his hands and head burning hot, his cheek flushed red, his eyes rolling, and his brain wandering. I went forth and called the overseer to come and look at him. At first he cursed and swore, saying that the man was malingering (that is to say, pretending to be sick, in order to avoid work); that, if he was a negro instead of a gentleman, a few cuts with his lash should shortly bring him to his senses; that, for his part, he liked not this mixing of gentlemen with negroes; and that, finally, I must go and bring forth my sick man or take it upon myself to face the master, who would probably drive him afield with the stick.

'Sir,' I said, 'what the master may do I know not. Murder may be done by any who are wicked enough. For my part, I am a physician, and I tell you that to make this man go forth to work will be murder. But indeed he is light-headed, and with a thousand lashes you could not make him understand or obey.'

Well, he grumbled, but he followed me into the hut.

'The man hath had a sunstroke,' he said. 'I wonder that any of you have escaped. Well, we can carry him to the sick-house, where he will die. When a new hand is taken this way he always dies.'

'Perhaps he will not die,' I said, 'if he is properly treated. If he is given nothing but this diet of loblollie and salt beef, and nothing to drink but the foul water of the pond, and no other doctor than an ignorant old negress, he will surely die.'

'Good Lord, man!' said the fellow. 'What do you expect in this country? It is the master's loss, not mine. Carry him between you to the sick-house.'

So we carried Robin to the sick-house.

At home we should account it a barn, being a great place with a thatched roof, the windows open, without shutter or lattice, the door breaking away from its hinges. Within there was a black lying on a pallet, groaning most piteously. The poor wretch, for something that he had done, I know not what, had his flesh cut to pieces with the whip. With him was an old negress mumbling and mouthing.

We laid Robin on another pallet, and covered him with a rug.

'Now, man,' said the overseer, 'leave him there, and come forth to your work.'

'Nay,' I said, 'he must not be left. I am a physician, and I must stay beside him.'

'If he were your son I would not suffer you to stay with him.'

'Man!' I cried. 'Hast thou no pity?'

'Pity!' The fellow grinned. 'Pity! quotha. Pity! Is this a place for pity? Why, if I showed any pity I should be working beside you in the fields. It is because I have no pity that I am overseer. Look here'—he showed me his left hand, which had been branded with a red-hot iron. 'This was done in Newgate seven years ago and more. Three years more I have to serve. That done, I may begin to show some pity. Not before. Pity is scarce among the drivers of Barbadoes. As well ask the beadle for pity when he flogs a 'prentice.'

'Let me go to the master, then.'

'Best not; best not. Let this man die and keep yourself alive. The morning is the worst time for him, because last night's drink is still in his head. Likely as not you will but make the sick man's case and your own worse. Leave him in the sick-house, and go back to him in the evening.'

The man spoke with some compassion in his eyes. Just then, however, a negro boy came running from the house and spoke to the overseer.

'Why,' he said, 'nothing could be more pat. You can speak to the master, if you please. He is in pain, and Madam sends for Dr. Humphrey Challis. Go, Doctor. If you cure him, you will be a lucky man. If you cannot cure him, the Lord have mercy upon you! Whereas, if you suffer him to die,' he added with a grin and a whisper, 'every man on the estate will fall down and worship you. Let him die! Let him die!'

I followed the boy, who took me to that part of the house which fronts the west and north. It was a mean house of wood, low and small, considering how wealthy a man was the master of it; on three sides, however, there was built out a kind of *loggia*, as the Italians call it, of wood instead of marble, forming a cloister or open chamber, outside the house. They call it a verandah, and part of it they hang with mats made of grass, so as to keep it shaded in the afternoon and evening, when the sun is in the west. The boy brought me to this place, pointed to a chair where the master sat, and then ran away as quickly as he could.

It was easy to understand why he ran away, because the master at this moment sprang out of his chair and began to stamp up and down the verandah, roaring and cursing. He was clad in a white linen dressing-gown and linen nightcap. On a small table beside him stood a bottle of beer, newly opened, and a silver tankard.

When he saw me he began to swear at me for my delay in coming, though I had not lost a moment.

'Sir,' I said, 'if you will cease railing and blaspheming I will examine into your malady. Otherwise I will do nothing for you.'

'What?' he cried. 'You dare to make conditions with me, you dog, you!'

'Fair words,' I said. 'Fair words. I am your servant to work on your plantation as you may command. I am not your physician; and I promise you, Sir, upon the honour of a gentleman, and without using the sacred name which is so often on your lips, that if you continue to rail at me I will suffer you to die rather than stir a little finger in your help.'

'Suffer the physician to examine the place,' said a woman's voice. 'What good is it to curse and to swear?'

The voice came from a hammock swinging at the end of the verandah. It was made, I observed, of a land of coarse grass loosely woven.

The man sat down and sulkily bade me find a remedy for the pain which he was enduring. So I consented and examined his upper jaw, where I soon found out the cause of his pain in a good-sized tumour formed over the fangs of a grinder. Such a thing causes agony even to a person of cool blood, but to a man whose veins are inflamed with strong drink the pain of it is maddening.

'You have got a tumour,' I told him. 'It has been forming for some days. It has now nearly, or quite, reached its head. It began about the time when you were cursing and insulting certain unfortunate gentlemen, who are for a time under your power. Take it, therefore, as a Divine judgment upon you for your cruelty and insolence.'

He glared at me, but said nothing, the hope of relief causing him to receive this admonition with patience, if not in good part. Besides, my finger was still upon the spot, and if I so much as pressed gently I could cause him agony unspeakable. Truly, the power of the physician is great.

'The pain,' I told him, 'is already grown almost intolerable. But it will be much greater in a few hours unless something is done. It is now like unto a little ball of red-hot fire in your jaw; in an hour or two it will seem as if the whole of your face was a burning fiery furnace; your cheek will swell out until your left eye is closed; your tortures, which now make you bawl, will then make you scream; you now walk about and stamp; you will then lie down on your back and kick. No negro slave ever suffered half so much under your accursed lash as you will suffer under this tumour—unless something is done.'

'Doctor,' it was again the woman's voice from the hammock, 'you have frightened him enough.'

'Strong drink,' I went on, pointing to the tankard, 'will only make you worse. It inflames your blood and adds fuel to the raging fire. Unless something is done the pain will be followed by delirium; that by fever, and the fever by death. Sir, are you prepared for death?'

He turned horribly pale and gasped.

'Do something for me!' he said. 'Do something for me, and that without more words!'

'Nay; but I will first make a bargain with you. There is in the sick-house a gentleman, my cousin—Robin Challis by name—one of the newly-arrived rebels, and your servant. He is lying sick unto death of a sunstroke and fever caused by your hellish cruelty in sending him out to work on the fields with the negroes instead of putting him to light labour in the Ingenio or elsewhere. I say, his sickness is caused by your barbarity. Wherefore I will do nothing for you at all—do you hear? Nothing! nothing!—unless I am set free to do all I can for him. Yea; and I must have such cordials and generous diet as the place can afford, otherwise I will not stir a finger to help you. Otherwise—endure the torments of the damned; rave in madness and in fever. Die and go to your own place. I will not help you. So; that is my last word.'

Upon this I really thought the man had gone stark, staring mad. For, at the impudence of a mere servant (though a gentleman of far better family than his own) daring to make conditions with him, he became purple in the cheeks, and, seizing his great stick which lay on the table, he began belabouring me with all his might about the head and shoulders. But I caught up a chair and used it for a shield, while he capered about, striking wildly and swearing most horribly.

At this moment the lady who was in the hammock stepped out of it and walked towards us slowly, like a Queen. She was without any doubt the most beautiful woman I had ever seen. She was dressed in a kind of dressing-gown of flowered silk, which covered her from head to foot; her head was adorned with the most lovely glossy black ringlets; a heavy gold chain lay round her neck, and a chain of gold with pearls was twined in her hair, so that it looked like a coronet; her fingers were covered with rings, and gold bracelets hung upon her bare white arms. Her figure was tall and full; her face inclined to the Spanish, being full and yet regular, with large black eyes. Though I was fighting with a madman, I could not resist the wish that I could paint her, and I plainly perceived that she was one of that race which is called Quadroon, being most likely the daughter of a mulatto woman and a white father. This was evident by the character of her skin, which had in it what the Italians call the *morbidezza*, and by a certain dark hue under the eyes.

'Why,' she said, speaking to the master as if he had been a petulant school-boy, 'you only make yourself worse by all this fury. Sit down, and lay aside your stick. And you. Sir'—she addressed herself to me—'you may be a great physician, and at home a gentleman; but here you are a servant, and therefore bound to help your master in all you can without first making conditions.'

'I know too well,' I replied, 'he bought me as his servant, but not as his physician. I will not heal him without my fee; and my fee is that my sick cousin be attended to with humanity.'

'Take him away!' cried the master, beside himself with rage. 'Clap him in the stocks! Let him sit there all day long in the sun! He shall have nothing to eat or to drink! In the evening he shall be flogged! If it was the Duke of Monmouth himself, he should be tied up and flogged! Where the devil are the servants?'

A great hulking negro came running.

'You have now,' I told him quietly, 'permitted yourself to be inflamed with violent rage. The pain will therefore more rapidly increase. When it becomes intolerable, you will be glad to send for me.'

The negro dragged me away (but I made no resistance), and led me to the courtyard, where stood the stocks and a whipping-post. He pointed to the latter with a horrid grin, and then laid me fast in the former. Fortunately, he left me my hat, otherwise the hot[279] sun would have made an end of me. I was, however, quite easy in my mind. I knew that this poor wretch, who already suffered so horribly, would before long feel in that jaw of his, as it were, a ball of fire. He would drink, in order to deaden the pain; but the wine would only make the agony more horrible. Then he would be forced to send for me.

This, in fact, was exactly what he did.

I sat in those abominable stocks for no more than an hour. Then Madam herself came to me, followed by the negro fellow who had locked my heels in those two holes.

'He is now much worse,' she said. 'He is now in pain that cannot be endured. Canst thou truly relieve his suffering?'

'Certainly I can. But on conditions. My cousin will die if he is neglected. Suffer me to minister to his needs. Give him what I want for him and I will cure your'—I did not know whether I might say 'your husband,' so I changed the words into—'my master. After that I will cheerfully endure again his accursed cruelty of the fields.'

She bade the negro unlock the bar.

'Come,' she said. 'Let us hear no more about any bargains. I will see to it that you are able to attend to your cousin. Nay, there is an unfortunate young gentlewoman here, a rebel, and a servant like yourself—for the last week she doth nothing but weep for the misfortunes of her friends—meaning you and your company. I will ask her to nurse the sick man. She will desire nothing better, being a most tender-hearted woman. And as for you, it will be easy for you to look after your cousin and your master at the same time.'

'Then, Madam,' I replied, 'take me to him, and I will speedily do all I can to relieve him.'

I found my patient in a condition of mind and body most dangerous. I wondered that he had not already fallen into a fit, so great was his wrath and so dreadful his pain. He rolled his eyes; his cheeks were purple; he clenched his fists; he would have gnashed his teeth but for the pain in his jaws.

'Make yourself easy,' said Madam. 'This learned physician will cause your pain to cease. I have talked with him and put him into a better mind.'

The master shook his head as much as to say that a better mind would hardly be arrived at without the assistance of the whipping-post; but the emergency of the case prevented that indulgence. Briefly, therefore, I took out my lancet and pierced the place, which instantly relieved the pain. Then I placed him in bed, bled him copiously, and forbade his taking anything stronger than small-beer. Freedom from pain and exhaustion presently caused him to fall into a deep and tranquil sleep. After all this was done I was anxious to see Robin.

'Madam,' I said, 'I have now done all I can. He will awake at noon, I dare say. Give him a little broth, but not much. There[280] is danger of fever. You had better call me again when he awakes. Warn him solemnly that rage, revenge, cursing, and beating must be all postponed until such time as he is stronger. I go to visit my cousin in the sick-house, where I await your commands.'

'Sir,' she said courteously, 'I cannot sufficiently thank your skill and zeal. You will find the nurse of whom I spoke in the sick-house with your cousin. She took with her some cordial, and will tell me what else you order for your patient. I hope your cousin may recover. But, indeed'——she stopped and sighed.

'You would say, Madam, that it would be better for him and for us all to die. Perhaps so. But we must not choose to die, but rather strive to live, as more in accordance with the Word of God.'

'The white servants have been hitherto the common rogues and thieves and sweepings of your English streets,' she said. 'Sturdy rogues are they all, who fear naught but the lash, and have nothing of tenderness left but tender skins. They rob and steal; they will not work, save by compulsion; they are far worse than the negroes for laziness and drunkenness. I know not why they are sent out, or why the planters buy them, when the blacks do so much better serve their turn, and they can without reproach beat and flog the negroes, while to flog and beat the whites is by some accounted cruel.'

'All this, Madam, is doubtless true: but my friends are not the sweepings of the street.'

'No, but you are treated as if you were. It is a new thing having gentlemen among the servants, and the planters are not yet accustomed to them. They are a masterful and a wilful folk, the planters of Barbadoes; from childhood upwards they have their own way, and brook not opposition. You have seen into what a madness of wrath you threw the master by your opposition. Believe me, Sir, the place is not wholesome for you and for your friends. The master looks to get a profit, not from your labour, but by your ransom. Sir'—she looked me very earnestly in the face—'if you have friends at home—if you have any friends at all—entreat them—command them—immediately to send money for your ransom. It will not cost them much. If you do not get the money you will most assuredly die, with the life that you will have to live. All the white servants die except the very strongest and lustiest. Whether they work in the fields, or in the garden, or in the Ingenio, or in the stables, they die. They cannot endure the hot sun and the hard fare. They presently catch fever, or a calenture, or a cramp, and so they die. This young gentlewoman who is now with your cousin will presently fall into melancholy and die. There is no help for her, or for you—believe me, Sir—there is no hope but to get your freedom.' She broke off here, and never at any other time spoke to me again upon this subject.

In three weeks' time, indeed, we were to regain our freedom, but not in the way Madam imagined.

Before I go on to tell of the wonderful surprise which awaited me, I must say that there was, after this day, no more any question about the field-work for me. In this island, then, there was a great scarcity of physicians; nay, there were none properly qualified to call themselves physicians, though a few quacks; the sick servants on the estates were attended by the negresses, some of whom have, I confess, a wonderful knowledge of herbs—in which respect they may be likened to our countrywomen, who, for fevers, agues, toothache, and the like, are as good as any physicians in the world. It was, therefore, speedily rumoured abroad that there was a physician upon my master's estate, whereupon there was immediately a great demand for his services; and henceforth I went daily, with the master's consent, to visit the sick people on the neighbouring estates—nay, I was even called upon by his Excellency the Lieutenant-Governor himself, Mr. Steed, for a complaint from which he suffered. And I not only gave advice and medicines, but I also received a fee just as if I had been practising in London. But the fees went to my master, who took them all, and offered me no better diet than before. That, however, mattered little, because wherever I went I asked for, and always received, food of a more generous kind, and a glass or two of wine, so that I fared well and kept my health during the short time that we remained upon the island. I had also to thank Madam for many a glass of Madeira, dish of cocoa, plate of fruit, and other things, not only for my patient Robin, but also for myself, and for another, of whom I have now to speak.

When, therefore, the master was at length free from pain and in a comfortable sleep, I left him, with Madam's permission, and sought the sick-house in a most melancholy mood, because I believed that Robin would surely die, whatever I should do. And I confess that, having had but little experience of sunstroke and the kind of fever which followeth upon it, and having no books to consult and no medicine at hand, I knew not what I could do for him. And the boasted skill of the physician, one must confess, availeth little against a disease which hath once laid hold upon a man. 'Tis better for him so to order the lives of his patients while they are well as to prevent disease, just as those who dwell beside an unruly river (as I have seen upon the great river Rhone) build up a high levée, or bank, over which it cannot pass.

In the sick-house the floor was of earth, without boards; there was no other furniture but two or three wooden beds, on each a coarse mattress with a rug; and all was horribly filthy, unwashed, and foul. Beside the pallet where Robin lay there knelt, praying, a woman with her head in her hands. Heavens! there was, then, in this dark and heathenish place one woman who still remembered her Maker!

Robin was awake. His restless eyes rolled about; his hands clutched uneasily at his blanket; and he was talking. Alas! the poor brain, disordered and wandering, carried him back to the old village. He was at home again in imagination, though we were so far away. Yea; he had crossed the broad Atlantic, and was in fair Somerset, among the orchards and the hills. And, only to hear him talk, the tears rolled down my cheeks.

'Alice,' he said. Alas! he thought that he was again with the sweet companion of his youth. 'Alice; the nuts are ripe in the woods. We will to-morrow take a basket and go gather them. Benjamin shall not come to spoil sport. Besides, he would want to eat them all himself. Humphrey shall come, and you, and I. That will be enough.'

Then his thoughts changed again. 'Oh! my dear,' he said—in a moment he had passed over ten years, and was now with his mistress, a child no longer. 'My dear, thou hast so sweet a face. Nowhere in the whole world is there so sweet a face. I have always loved thy face; not a day but it has been in my mind—always my love, my sweetheart, my soul, my life. My dear, we will never leave the country; we want no grandeur of rank, and state, and town; we will always continue here. Old age shall find us lovers still. Death cannot part us, oh! my dear, save for a little while—and then sweet Heaven will unite us again to love each other for ever, and for ever'——

'Oh! Robin! Robin! Robin!'

I knew that voice. Oh! Heavens! was I dreaming? Was I, too, wandering? Were we all back in Somerset?

For the voice was none other than the voice of Alice herself!

CHAPTER XLII.

ALICE.

'Alice!' I cried.

She rose from her knees and turned to meet me. Her face was pale; her eyes were heavy and they were full of tears.

'Alice!'

'I saw you when you came here, a week ago,' she said. 'Oh! Humphrey, I saw you, and I was ashamed to let you know that I was here.'

'Ashamed? My dear, ashamed? But how—why—what dost thou here?'

'How could I meet Robin's eyes after what I had done?'

'It was done for him, and for his mother, and for all of us. Poor child, there is no reason to be ashamed.'

'And now I meet him, and he is in a fever, and his mind wanders; he knows me not.'

'He is sorely stricken, Alice; I know not how the disease may end; mind and body are sick alike. For the mind I can do nothing; for the body I can do but little: yet with cleanliness and good food we may help him to mend. But tell me, Child, in the name of Heaven, how camest thou in this place?'

But before anything she would attend to the sick man. And presently she brought half-a-dozen negresses, who cleaned and swept the place, and sheets were fetched and a linen shirt, in which we dressed our patient, with such other things as we could devise for his comfort. Then I bathed his head with cold water, continually changing his bandages so as to keep him cool; and I took some blood from him, but not much, because he was greatly reduced by bad food and hard work.

When he was a little easier we talked. But, Heavens! to think of the villainy which had worked its will upon this poor child! As if it was not enough that she should be forced to fly from a man who had so strangely betrayed her, and as if it was not enough that she should be robbed of all her money—but she must also be put on board, falsely and treacherously, as one, like ourselves, sentenced to ten years' servitude on the Plantations! For, indeed, I knew and was quite certain that none of the Maids of Taunton were thus sent abroad. It was notorious, before we were sent away, that, with the exception of Susan Blake, who died of jail-fever at Dorchester, all the Maids were given to the Queen's ladies, and by them suffered to go free on the payment by their parents of thirty or forty pounds apiece. And as for Alice, she was a stranger in the place, and it was not known that she had joined that unfortunate procession. So that, if ever a man was kidnapper and villain, that man was George Penne.

It behoves a physician to keep his mind under all circumstances calm and composed. He must not suffer himself to be carried away by passion, by rage, hatred, or even anxiety. Yet, I confess that my mind was clean distracted by the discovery that Alice herself was with us, a prisoner like ourselves; I was, I say, distracted, nor could I tell what to think of this event and its consequences. For, to begin with, the poor child was near those who would protect her. But what kind of protection could be given by such helpless slaves?

Then was she beyond her husband's reach; he would not, it was quite certain, get possession of her at this vast distance. So far she was safe. But then the master, who looked to make a profit by her, as he looked to make a profit by us—through the ransom of her friends! She had no friends to ransom her. There was but one, the Rector, and he was her husband's father. The time would come when the avarice of the master would make him do or threaten something barbarous towards her. Then she had found favour with Madam, this beautiful mulatto woman, whom Alice innocently supposed to be the master's wife. And there was the young planter, who wished to buy her with the honourable intention of marrying her. In short, I knew not what to think or to say, because at one moment it seemed as if it was the most Providential thing in the world that Alice should have been brought here, and the next moment it seemed as if her presence only magnified our evils.

'Nay,' she said, when I opened my mind to her, 'seeing that the world is so large, what but a special ruling of Providence could have brought us all to this same island, out of the whole multitude of isles—and then again to this same estate out of so many? Humphrey, your faith was wont to be stronger. I believe—nay, I am quite sure—that it was for the strengthening and help of all alike that this hath been ordained. First, it enables me to nurse my poor Robin—mine, alas! no longer! Yet must I still love him as long as I have a heart to beat.'

'Love him always, Child,' I said. 'This is no sin to love the companion of thy childhood, thy sweetheart, from whom thou wast torn by the most wicked treachery'—but could say no more, because the contemplation of that sweet face, now so mournful, yet so patient, made my voice to choke and my eyes to fill with tears. Said I not that a physician must still keep his mind free from all emotion?

All that day I conversed with her. We agreed that for the present she should neither acknowledge nor conceal the truth from Madam, upon whose good-will we now placed all our hopes. That is to say, if Madam questioned her she was to acknowledge that we were her former friends; but, if Madam neither suspected anything nor asked her anything, she should keep the matter to herself. She told me during this day all that had happened unto her since I saw her last, when we marched out of Taunton. Among other things I heard of the woman called Deb, who was now working in the canefields (she was one of a company whose duty it was to weed the canes). In the evening this woman, when the people returned, came to the sick-house. She was a great strapping woman, stronger than most men. She was dressed, like all the women on the estate, in a smock and petticoat, with a thick coif to keep off the sun, and a pair of strong shoes.

She came to help her mistress, as she fondly called Alice. She wanted to sit up and watch the sick man, so that her mistress might go to sleep. But Alice refused. Then this faithful creature rolled herself up in her rug and laid herself at the door, so that no one should go in or out without stepping over her. And so she fell asleep.

Then we began our night watch, and talked in whispers, sitting by the bedside of the fevered man. Presently I forgot the wretchedness of our condition, the place where we were, our hopeless, helpless lot, our anxieties and our fears, in the joy and happiness of once more conversing with my mistress. She spoke to me after the manner of the old days, but with more seriousness, about the marvellous workings of the Lord among His people; and presently we began to talk of the music which we loved to play, and how the sweet concord and harmony of the notes lift up the soul; and of pictures and painting, and Mr. Boscorel's drawings and my own poor attempts, and my studies in the schools, and so forth, as if my life was, indeed, but just beginning, and, instead of the Monmouth cap, and the canvas breeches, and common shirt, I was once more arrayed in velvet, with a physician's wig and a gold-headed cane.

Lastly she prayed, entreating merciful Heaven to bestow health of mind and enlargement of body to the sick man upon the bed, and her brother, and her dear friend (meaning myself), and to all poor sufferers for religion; and she asked that, as it had been permitted that she should be taken from her earthly lover by treachery, so it might now be granted to her to lay down her life for his, so that he might go free and she die in his place.

Through the open window I saw the four stars which make the constellation they call the 'Crucero,' being like a cross fixed in the heavens. The night was still, and there was no sound save the shrill noise of the cigala, which is here as shrill as in Padua. Slave and master, bondman and free, were all asleep save in this house, where Robin rolled his heavy head, and murmured without ceasing, and Alice communed with her God. Surely, surely, I thought, here was no room for doubt! This my mistress had been brought here by the hand of God Himself, to be as an angel or messenger of His own, for our help and succour—haply for our spiritual help alone, seeing that no longer was there any help from man.

CHAPTER XLIII.

BARNABY HEARS THE NEWS.

The master, my patient, got up from his bed in a few days, somewhat pale and weak after his copious blood-letting and the drastic medicines with which I purged the grossness of his habit and expelled the noxious humours caused by his many intemperances. These had greatly injured what we call—because we know not what nor what else to call it—the pure volatile spirit, and, so to speak, turned sour the *humor radicalis*—the sweet oil and balsamical virtues of the body. I gave him such counsel as was fitting for his case, admonishing him urgently to abstain from strong liquors, except in their moderate use; to drink only after his meals; to keep his head cool and sober, and above all things to repress and govern his raging temper, which would otherwise most certainly catch him by the throat like some fierce and invisible devil and throw him into a fit, and so kill him. I told him also what might be meant by the Wise Man (who certainly thought of all the bearings which his words could have) when he said that one who is slow to wrath is of great understanding—namely, that many men do throw away their lives by falling into excessive fits of rage. But I found that the words of Holy Scripture had little authority over him, for he lived without prayer or praise, trampled on the laws of God, and gave no heed at all to the flight of time and the coming of the next world.

For a day or two he followed my injunctions, taking a tankard of small ale to his breakfast, the same quantity with his dinner, a pint of Madeira for his supper, and a sober glass or two before going to bed. But when he grew well, his brother planters came round him again, the drinking was renewed, and in the morning I would find him again with parched throat, tongue dry, and shaking hand, ready to belabour, to curse, and to rail at everybody. If one wanted an example for the young how strong drink biteth like a serpent and stingeth like an adder, here was a case the sight of which might have caused all young men to forswear drunkenness. Alas! there are plenty of such examples to be seen in every part of England; yet the younger men still continue to drink, and that, I think, worse than their fathers. This man, however, who was not yet five-and-thirty, in the very prime of strong and healthy manhood, had his finger-joints swollen and stony from taking much wine; he commonly ate but little meat, craving continually for more drink, and his understanding, which was by nature, I doubt not, clear and strong, was now brutish and stupid. Thinking over this man, and of the power, even unto death, which he possessed over his servants and slaves, the words came into my mind: 'It is not for Kings, O Lemuel, it is not for Kings to drink wine; nor for Princes strong drink.'

Nay, more (and this I say, knowing that many godly men will not agree with me): I am fully persuaded that there is no man in the whole world so good and so strong in virtue and religion that he should be suffered to become the master or despot over any other man, even over a company of poor and ignorant blacks, or a gang of transported thieves. When I think of those unhappy people, driven forth in the morning, heavy-eyed and downcast, to the hard day's work; and when I remember how they crept home at night, after being driven, cursed, and beaten all day long; and when I think upon their drivers, overseers, and masters, and of their hard and callous hearts, I am moved to cry aloud (if any would hear me) that to be a slave is wretched indeed; but that to own and to drive slaves should be a thing most dangerous for any who would continue members of Christ's Church.

When I told Barnaby the surprising news that his sister was not only safe, but a servant like ourselves upon the same estate, I looked that he would rejoice. On the contrary, he fell into a strange mood, swearing at this ill stroke as he called it. He said that he never had the least doubt as to her safety, seeing there were so many in the West Country who knew and respected her father, and would willingly shelter her. Then he dwelt upon certain evils—of which, I confess, I had thought little—which might befall her. And, lastly, he set forth with great plainness the increased dangers in escaping when one has to carry a woman or a wounded man—a thing, he pointed out, which had caused his own capture after Sedgemoor.

Then he opened up to me the whole business of our escape.

'Last Saturday night,' he said, 'while you were sleeping, I made my way to the port, and, having a shilling or so left, I sought out a tavern. There is one hard by the Bridge, a house-of-call for sailors, where I had the good fortune to find a fellow who can do for us all we want—if his money hold out, which I doubt. He is a carver by trade, and a convict, like ourselves; but is permitted by his master to work at his trade in the town. He hath been, it is true, branded in the hand; but, Lord! what signifies that? He was once a thief—well—he is now an honest lad again, who asks for nothing but to get home again. John Nuthall is his name.'

'Go on, Barnaby. We are already in such good company that another rogue or two matters little.'

'This man came here secretly last night, while you were in the sick-house. He is very hot upon getting away. And because I am a sailor and can navigate a craft (which he cannot do) he will take with him not only myself, but also all my party. Now listen, Humphrey. He hath bought a boat of a Guinea man in the harbour; and because, to prevent the escape of servants, every boat is licensed and her owner has to give security to the Governor's officers, he hath taken this boat secretly up a little creek of which he knows, and hath there sunk her three feet deep. The masts, the sails, the oars, and the other gear he hath also safely bestowed in a secret place. But we cannot sail without water, provisions, nor without a compass at least. If our party is to consist of Sister, Robin, you, John Nuthall, and myself—five in all—we shall have to load the boat with provisions, and I must have a compass. I looked for a boatful with ourselves and John Nuthall. Now we have Sis as well; and the boat is but small. Where shall we get provisions? and where shall we lay our hands upon the money to buy what we want?'

He could talk of nothing else, because his mind was full of his plan. Yet it seemed to me a most desperate enterprise, thus to launch a small boat upon the wide ocean, and in this cockle-shell to brave the waves which are often fatal to the tallest ships.

'Tut, man,' said Barnaby. 'We are not now in the season of the tornadoes, and there is no other danger upon these seas. I would as lief be in an open boat as in a brigantine. Sharks may follow us, but they will not attack a boat; calamaries they talk of, big enough to lay their arms round the boat and so to drag it under; but such monsters have I never seen, any more than I have seen the great whale of Norway or the monstrous birds of the Southern Seas. There is only one danger, Humphrey, my lad.' Here he laid his hand upon mine and became mighty serious. 'If we are taken we shall be flogged—all of us. Thirty-nine lashes they will lay on, and they will brand us. For myself, I value not their thirty-nine lashes a brass farthing, nor their branding with a hot iron, which can but make a man jump for a day or two. To me this risk against the chance of escape matters nothing. Why, when I was cabin-boy I got daily more than thirty-nine lashes—kicks, cuffs, and rope's-endings. Nay, I remember, when we sat over the Latin syntax together my daily ration must have been thirty-nine, more or less, and Dad's arm was stronger than you would judge, to look at him. If they catch me, let them lay on their thirty-nine and be damned to them! But you and Robin, I doubt, think otherwise.'

'I would not willingly be flogged, Barnaby, if there were any way of escape—even by death.'

'So I thought! So I thought!'

'And as for Robin, if he recovers—which I doubt—he too, if I know him, would rather be killed than be flogged.'

'That comes of Oxford!' said Barnaby. 'And then there is Sis. Humphrey, my lad, it goes to my heart to think of that poor girl, stripped to be lashed like a black slave or a Bristol drab.'

'Barnaby, she must never run that dreadful risk.'

'Then she must remain behind, and here she runs that risk every day. What prevents yon drunken sot—the taste of that cudgel still sticks in my gizzard!—I say, what prevents him from tying her up to-day, or to-morrow, or every day?'

'Barnaby, I say that she must never run that risk, for if we are caught——' I stopped.

'Before we are caught, you would say, Humphrey. We are of the same mind there. But who is to kill her? Not Robin, for he loves her; not you, because you have too great a kindness for her. Not I, because I am her brother. What should I say to my mother when I meet her after we are dead, and she asks me who killed Alice?'

'Barnaby, if she is to die, let us all die together.'

'Ay,' he replied, 'though I have, I confess, no great stomach for dying; yet, since we have got her with us, it must be done. 'Tis easy to let the water into the boat, and so, in three minutes, with no suspicion at all, and my mother never to know anything about it, she would have said her last prayers, and we should be all sinking together with never a gasp left.'

I took him after this talk to the sick-house, where Alice was beginning her second night of nursing. Barnaby saluted his sister as briefly as if her presence was the thing he most expected.

The room was lit by a horn lanthorn containing a great candle, which gave enough light to see Robin on the bed and Alice standing beside him. The woman called Deb was sitting on the floor, wrapped in her rug.

'Sis,' said Barnaby, 'I have heard from Humphrey how thou wast cozened out of thy money and enticed on board ship. Well, this world is full of villains, and I doubt whether I shall live to kill them all. One I must kill and one I must cudgel. Patience, therefore, and no more upon this head. Well, Sis, dost love to be a servant?'

'Surely not, Barnaby.'

'Wouldst like to get thy freedom again?'

'I know not the meaning of thy words, brother. Madam says that those who have interest at home may procure pardons for their friends in the Plantations. Also that those whose friends have money may buy their freedom from servitude. I am sure that Mr. Boscorel would willingly do this for Robin and for Humphrey; but for myself—how can I ask him? How can I ever let him know where I am and in what condition?'

'Ay, ay, but I meant not that way, child; wilt thou trust thyself to us?'

She looked at Robin. 'I cannot leave him,' she said.

'No, no; we shall wait until he is dead—or, perhaps, better.' But he only added this to please his sister. 'When he is better, Sis, thou wilt not be afraid to trust thyself with us?'

'I am not afraid of any danger, even of death, with you, if that is the danger in your mind, Barnaby.'

'Good! Then we understand each other. There are other dangers for a young and handsome woman—and, maybe, worse dangers. Hast any money at all, by chance?'

'Nay; the man Penne took all my money.'

Barnaby, for five or six minutes without stopping, spoke upon this topic after the manner of a sailor. 'My turn will come,' he added. 'No money, child? 'Tis a great pity. Had we a few gold pieces, now! Some women have rings and chains. But of course——'

'Nay, brother; chains I never had, and as for rings, there were but two that ever I had— one from Robin, the day that I was plighted to him; and one from the man who made me marry him, and put it on in the church. The former did I break and throw away when I agreed—for your dear lives—Barnaby, oh! for the lives of all'——

'I know, I know,' said Barnaby. 'Patience—patience. Oh! I shall get such a chance some day!'

'The other I threw away when I fled from my husband at the church door.'

'Ay, ay! If we only had a little money! 'Tis pity that we should fail for want of a little money.'

'Why,' said Alice, 'I had quite forgotten. I have something that may bring money.' She pulled from her neck a black ribbon on which was a little leathern bag. ''Tis the ring the Duke gave me at Ilchester long ago. I have never parted with it. "God grant," he said, when he gave it to me, "that it may bring thee good luck!" Will the ring help, Barnaby?'

I took it first from her hand.

'Why,' I said, 'it is a sweet and costly ring. Jewels I know and have studied. If I mistake not, these emeralds must be worth a great sum. But how shall we dispose of so valuable a ring in this place, and without causing suspicion?'

'Give it to me.' Barnaby took it, looked at it, and laid it, bag and all, in his pocket. 'There are at the port merchants of all kinds, who will buy a ship's cargo of sugar one minute and the next will sell you a red herring. They will also advance money upon a ring. As for suspicion, there are hundreds of convicts and servants here. 'Tis but to call the ring the property of such an one, and no questions will be asked. My friend John Nuthall, the carver, shall do this for us. And now, Sis, I think that our business is as good as done. Have no fear; we shall get away. First get Robin well, and then'——Here Barnaby gazed upon her face with affection and with pity. 'But, sister, understand rightly: 'tis no child's play of hide and seek. 'Tis life or death!—life or death! If we fly, we must never come back again! Understand that well.'

'Since we are in the Lord's hands, brother, why should we fear? Take me with you; let me die, if you must die; and if you live I am content to live with you, so that my husband never find me out.'

CHAPTER XLIV.

A SCARE.

There is between the condition of the mind and that of the body an interdependence which cannot but be recognised by every physician. So greatly has this connection affected some of the modern physicians, as to cause doubts in their minds whether there be any life at all hereafter, or if, when the pulse ceases to beat, the whole man should become a dead and senseless lump of clay. In this, they confuse the immortal soul with the perishable instruments of brain and body, through which in life it manifests its being and betrays its true nature, whether of good or ill.

Thus, the condition in which Robin now lay clearly corresponded, as I now understand, with the state of his mind induced by the news that Alice, to save his life, had been betrayed into marrying his cousin. For at the hearing of that dreadful news he was seized with such a transport of rage (not against that poor innocent victim, but against his cousin) as threatened to throw him into madness; and on recovering from this access, he presently fell into a kind of despair, in which he languished during the whole voyage. So also in a corresponding manner, after a fever, the violence of which was like to have torn him to pieces, he fell into a lethargy, in which, though his fever left him, he continued to wander in his mind, and grew, as I could not fail to mark, daily weaker in his body, refusing to eat, though Alice brought him dainty broth of chicken, delicate panadas of bread and butter, fruit boiled with sugar, and other things fit to tempt a sick man's appetite, provided by the goodness of Madam. This lady was in religion a Romanist; by birth she was a Spanish Quadroon. To escape the slavery to which the colour of her grandmother doomed her, she escaped from Cuba and found her way to Jamaica, where she met with our master. And whether she was lawfully married unto him I will not, after her kindness to Alice and her faithfulness to myself as regards Robin, so much as ask.

Robin, therefore, though the fever left him, did not mend. On the contrary, as I have said, he grew daily weaker; so that I marvelled at his lasting so long, and looked to see him die, as so many die, in the early morning, when there is a sharpness or eagerness in the air, and the body is exhausted by long sleep. Yet he died not.

And now you shall hear how, through the Duke of Monmouth's ring, we escaped from our servitude. 'God grant,' said the Duke, 'that it bring thee good luck!' This was a light and unconsidered prayer, forgotten as soon as uttered, meant only to please the ear[292] of a child. And yet, in a manner most marvellous to consider, it proved the salvation of us all. What better luck could that ring cause than that we should escape from the land of Egypt—the House of Bondage?

'I have disposed of the ring,' Barnaby told me a few days later. 'That is to say, John Nuthall has secretly pledged it with a merchant for twenty guineas. He said that the ring belongs to a convict; but many of them have brought such precious things with them in order to buy their freedom. He owns that the stones are fine, and very willingly gave the money on their security.'

'Then nothing remains,' I said, 'but to get away.'

'John Nuthall has bought provisions and all we want, little by little, so as to excite no suspicion. They are secretly and safely bestowed, and half the money still remains in his hands. How goes Robin?'

'He draws daily nearer to his grave. We cannot depart until either he mends or dies. 'Tis another disaster, Barnaby.'

'Ay; but of disaster we must not think. Robin will die. Yet our own case may be as bad if it comes to scuttling the ship. Cheer up, lads; many men die, but the world goes on. Poor Robin! Every man for himself and the Lord for us all. Sis will cry; but even if Robin recovers he cannot marry her: a consideration which ought to comfort her. And for him—since nothing else will serve him—it is best that he should die. Better make an end at once than go all his life with hanging head for the sake of a woman, as if there are not plenty women in the world to serve his turn.'

'I know not what ails him that he does not get better. The air is too hot for him; he hath lost his appetite. Barnaby,' I cried, moved to a sudden passion of pity such as would often seize me at that time, 'saw one ever ruin more complete than ours? Had we been fighting for Spain and the accursed Inquisition we could not have been more heavily punished. And we were fighting on the Lord's side!'

'We were—Dad was with us too. And see how he was served! The Lord, it seems, doth not provide His servants with arms, or with ammunition, or with commanders. Otherwise, the Duke this day would be in St. James's Palace wearing his father's crown, and you would be a Court physician with a great wig and a velvet coat, instead of a Monmouth cap and a canvas shirt. And I should be an admiral. But what doth it profit to ask why and wherefore? Let us first get clear of the wreck. Well; I wish we were to take Robin with us. 'Twill be a poor business going back to Bradford Orcas without him.'

We waited, therefore, day after day, for Robin either to get better or to die, and still he lingered, seemingly in a waste or decline, but such as I had never before seen; and I know not what would have happened to him, whether he would have lived or died, but then there happened a thing which caused us to wait no longer. It was this.

The master having, according to his daily custom, gone the round of his estate—that is to say, having seen his servants all at work under their drivers; some planting with the hoe, some weeding, some cutting the maize, some gathering yams, potatoes, cassavy, or bonavist for provisions, some attending the ingenio or the still-house—did unluckily take into his head to visit the sick-house. What was more unfortunate, this desire came upon him after he had taken a morning dram, and that of the stiffest: not, indeed, enough to make him drunk, but enough to make him obstinate and wilful. When I saw him standing at the open door, I perceived by the glassiness of his eyes and the unsteadiness of his shoulders that he had already begun the day's debauch. He was now in a most dangerous condition of mind. Later in the day, when he was more advanced in drink, he might be violent, but he would be much less dangerous, because he would afterwards forget what he had said or done in his cups.

'So, Sir Doctor,' he said, 'I have truly a profitable pair of servants!—one who pretends to cure everybody, and so escapes work; and your cousin, who pretends to be sick, and so will do none! A mighty bargain I made, truly, when I bought you both!'

'With submission, sir,' I said, 'I have within the last week earned for your honour ten guineas' worth of fees.'

'Well, that is as it may be. How do I know what hath gone into your own pocket? Where is this malingering fellow? Make him sit up! Sit up, I say, ye skulking dog; sit up!'

'Sir,' I said, still speaking with the greatest humility, 'nobody but the Lord can make this man sit up.' And, indeed, Robin did not comprehend one word that was said.

'I gave fifty pounds for him only a month ago. Am I to lose all that money, I ask? Fifty pounds! because I was told that he was a gentleman and would be ransomed by his family. Hark ye, Doctor, you must either cure this man for me—or else, by the Lord! you shall have his ransom added to your own. If he dies, I will double your price! Mark that!'

I said nothing, hoping that he would depart. As for Alice, she had turned her back upon him at his first appearance (as Madam had ordered her to do), so that he might not notice her.

Unfortunately he did not depart, but came into the room, looking about him. Certainly he was not one who would suffer his servants to be negligent, even in the smallest things.

'Here is fine work!' he said. 'Sheets of the best—a pillow; what hath a servant to do with such luxuries?'

'My cousin is a gentleman,' I told him, 'and accustomed to lie in linen. The rug which is enough for him in health must have a sheet to it as well, now that he is sick.'

'Humph! And whom have we here! Who art thou, madam, I wish to know?'

Alice turned.

'I am your honour's servant,' she said. 'I am employed in this sick-house when I am not in the sewing-room.'

'A servant? Oh! madam, I humbly crave your pardon. I took you for some fine lady. I am honoured by having such a servant. All the rest of my women servants go in plain smock and petticoat. But,' here he smiled, 'to so lovely a girl as Alice Eykin—fair Alice, sweet Alice—we must give the bravest and daintiest. To thee, my dear, nothing can be denied. Those dainty cheeks, those white hands, were never made to adorn a common coif. Mistress Alice, we must be better acquainted. This is no fit place for you. Not the sick-house, but the best room in my house shall be at thy service.'

'Sir, I ask for nothing but to sit retired, and to render such service as is in my power.'

'To sit retired? Why, that cannot be longer suffered. 'Twould be a sin to keep hidden any longer this treasure—this marvel, I say, of beauty and grace. My servant! Nay; 'tis I—'tis the whole island—who are thy servants. Thou to render service! 'Tis for me, madam, to render service to thy beauty.' He took off his hat and flourished it, making a leg.

'Then, sir,' said Alice, 'suffer me, I pray, to go about my business, which is with this sick man, and not to hear compliments.'

He caught her hand and would have kissed it, but she drew it back.

'Nay, coy damsel,' he said; 'I swear I will not go without a kiss from thy lips! Kiss me, my dear.'

She started back, and I rushed between them. At that moment Madam herself appeared.

'What do you here?' she cried, catching his arm. 'What has this girl to do with you? Come away! Come away, and leave her in peace!'

'Go back to the house, woman!' he roared, breaking from her and flourishing his stick, so that I thought he was actually going to cudgel her. 'Go back, or it will be the worse for you. What? Am I master here or you? Go back, I say.'

Then a strange thing happened. She made no reply, but she turned upon him eyes so full of authority that she looked like a queen. He shifted his feet, made as if he would speak, and finally obeyed, and went out of the place to his own house with the greatest meekness, soberness, and quietness.

Presently Madam came back.

'I blame thee not, child,' she said. 'It is with him as I have told thee. When he begins to drink the Devil enters into him. Dost think he came here to see the sick man? No, but for thy fair eyes, inflamed with love as well as with drink. At such times no one can rule him but myself, and even I may fail. Keep snug, therefore. Perhaps he may forget thee again. But, indeed, I know not.'

She sighed, and left us.

CHAPTER XLV.

BARNABY THE AVENGER.

The man did not come back. During the whole day I remained with Alice in fear. But he molested us not.

When the sun set, and the field hands returned, I was in two minds whether to tell Barnaby what had happened, or not. But when I saw his honest face, streaked with the dust of the day's work, and watched him eating his lump of salt beef and basin of yellow porridge with as much satisfaction as if it had been a banquet of all the dainties, I could not bear, without greater cause, to disturb his mind.

'To-night,' he told me, when there was no more beef and the porridge was all eaten, 'there is a great feast at the Bridge. I would we had some of their Sherris and Madeira. The Governor of Nevis landed yesterday, and is entertained to-day by our Governor. All the militia are feasting, officers and men; nobody will be on the look-out anywhere; and it is a dark night, with no moon. What a chance for us, could we make our escape to-night! There may never again happen such a chance for us! How goes Robin?'

And so after a little more talk we lay down in our hammocks, and I, for one, fell instantly asleep, having no fear at all for Alice; first, because the Master would be now at the Bridge, feasting and too drunk for anything but to sleep; and next, because she had with her the woman Deb, as stout and lusty as any man.

The Master was not at the Bridge with the rest of the planters and gentlemen. Perhaps the drink which he took in the morning caused him to forget the great banquet. However that may be, he was, most unluckily for himself, drinking at home and alone, yet dressed in his best coat and wig, and with his sword, all of which he had put on for the Governor's banquet.

After a while the Devil entered into him, finding easy admission, so to speak, all doors thrown wide open, and even a welcome in that deboshed and profligate soul. About eight o'clock, therefore, prompted by the Evil One, the Master rose and stealthily crept out of the house.

It was a dark night, but he needed no light to guide his footsteps. He crossed the court and made straight for the sick-house.

He pushed the door open and stood for a little, looking within. By the light of the horn lanthorn he saw the girl whose image was in his mind. The sight might have caused him to return, repentant and ashamed. For she was on her knees, praying aloud beside the bedside of the sick man.

As he stood in the door the woman named Deb, who lay upon the floor asleep, woke up and raised her head. But he saw her not. Then she sat up, watching him with suspicion. But his eyes were fixed on the figure of Alice. Then she sprang to her feet, for now she knew that mischief was meant, and she stood in readiness, prepared with her great strong arms to defend her mistress. But he thought nobody was in the house but Alice and the sick man. He saw nothing but the girl at the bedside.

I say that I was sleeping. I was awakened at the sound of a shriek—I knew the voice—I sprang from the hammock.

'God of mercy!' I cried, 'it is Alice! Barnaby, awake!—awake, I say! It is the cry of Alice!'

Then I rushed to the sick-house.

There I saw Alice—shrieking and crying for help. And before her the Master struggling and wrestling with the woman Deb. She had her arms round his neck and made as if she was trying to throttle him. Nay, I think that she would have throttled him, so strong she was and possessed of such a spirit, and by the light of the lanthorn gleaming upon the blade I saw that his sword had either fallen from his hand or from the scabbard, and now lay upon the floor.

'Stand back,' cried Barnaby, pushing me aside. 'Leave go of him, woman. Let me deal with him.'

The thing was done in a moment. Merciful Heavens! To think that thus suddenly should the soul of man be called to its account! I had seen the poor fellows shot down and cut to pieces on Sedgemoor; but then they knew that they were going forth to fight, and so might be killed. There was time before the battle for a prayer. But this man had no time—and he was more than half drunk as well.

He lay at our feet, lifeless, Barnaby standing over him with a broken sword in his hand.

For a while no one spoke or moved. But the woman called Deb gasped and panted and even laughed, as one who is well pleased because she hath had her revenge.

Then Madam herself, clad in a long white night-dress and with bare feet, suddenly pushed us aside and fell upon her knees beside the wounded man.

She lifted his head. The face was pale and the eyes closed. She laid it gently down and looked round.

'You have killed him,' she said, speaking not in a rage or passion, but quietly. 'You have killed him. To-morrow you will hang! you will all hang!'

We said nothing.

'Doctor,' she turned to me, 'tell me if he is dead or living.'

She snatched the lanthorn and held it while I made such examination as was possible. I opened his waistcoat and laid back his shirt. The sword had run straight through him and broken off short, perhaps by contact with his ribs. The broken point remained in the wound and the flesh had closed around it, so that, save for a drop of blood or two oozing out, there was no flow.

It needs no great knowledge to understand that when a man hath six inches of steel in his body which cannot be pulled out, and when he is bleeding inwardly, he must die.

Still, as physicians use, I did not tell her so.

'Madam,' I said, 'he is not dead; he is living. While there is life, there is hope.'

'Oh!' she cried; 'why did he buy you when he could have had the common sort? You will hang—you will hang, every one!'

'That shall we presently discover,' said Barnaby. 'Humphrey, we have now no choice left—what did I tell thee about the chances of the night? We must go this night. As for this villain, let him bleed to death.'

'Go!' said Madam. 'Whither, unhappy men, will you go? There is no place in the island where you can hide but with bloodhounds they will have you out. You can go nowhere in this island but you will be found and hanged, unless you are shot like rats in a hole.'

'Come, Humphrey,' said Barnaby, 'we will carry Robin. This poor woman must go too; she will else be hanged for trying to throttle him. Well, she can lend a hand to carry Robin. Madam, by your leave we will not hang, nor will we be shot. In the—in the—the cave—cave that I know of, your bloodhounds will never find us.'

'Madam,' I said, 'it is true that we shall attempt to escape. For what hath happened I am truly sorry; yet we may not suffer such a thing as was this night attempted without resistance, else should we be worse than the ignorant blacks. The Master will perhaps live, and not die. Listen, and take heed therefore.'

'Doctor,' she said, 'do not leave me. Stay with me, or he will die. Doctor, stay with me, and I will save your life. I will swear that you came at my call. Stay with me—I will save Alice as well. I will save you both. You shall be neither flogged nor hanged. I swear it. I will say that I called you for help when it was too late. Only this man and this woman shall hang. Who are they? A rogue and——'

Barnaby laughed aloud.

'Doctor,' she said, 'if you stay he will perhaps recover and forgive you all.'

Barnaby laughed again.

'Madam,' I told her, 'better death upon the gallows than any further term of life with such a man.'

'Oh!' she cried; 'he will die where he is lying!'

'That may be, I know not.' I gave her certain directions, bidding her, above all, watch the man, and cause him to lie perfectly quiet and not to speak a word, even in a whisper, and to give him a few drops of cordial from time to time.

'Come,' said Barnaby, 'we lose time, which is precious. Madam, if your husband recover—and for my part I care nothing whether he recover or whether he die—but if he should recover, tell him from me, Captain Barnaby Eykin, that I shall very likely return to this island, and that I shall then, the Lord helping, kill him in fair duello, to wipe out the lash of the cudgel which he was good enough once to lay about my head. If he dies of this trifling thrust with his own sword he must lay that to the account of my sister. Enough,' said Barnaby, 'we will now make our way to the woods and the cave.'

This said, Barnaby went to the head of Robin's bed and ordered Deb to take the foot, and so between them they carried him forth with them, while Alice followed and I went last.

We heard, long afterwards, through one Mr. Anstiss—the same young gentleman who loved Alice and would have married her—what had happened when we were gone. An hour or thereabouts afterwards, Madam woke up one of the overseers, telling him what had happened, and bidding him be ready at daybreak, with the bloodhounds, horses, and loaded guns, to follow in pursuit and bring us back.

There would be, they thought, no difficulty at all in catching us, because we were encumbered by a sick man and two women.

There was, however, more difficulty than they expected. For the footsteps led the bloodhounds to the seashore; and here the trace was lost, nor could it ever be afterwards recovered. And though the hue and cry was out over all the island, and the woods and the ravines and caves where runaway negroes hide were searched, we were never found. Therefore, since no boat at all was missing (the Guineaman had sailed away), it was certain that we could not have escaped by sea. It was fortunate, indeed, that Barnaby dropped no hint about the sea; otherwise there would have been despatched some of the boats of the port in search of us, and in that case the scuttling of the ship might have been necessary. For, had we been caught, we should certainly have been hanged for murder, after being flogged for attempted escape. For the Master died. He lay speechless until the day broke. Then he became conscious, and presently breathed his last in great anguish of body and terror of mind. What hath since become of Madam, and of that miserable family of servants and slaves, I know not. Certain it is that they could not find a more barbarous or a more savage master in place of him whom Barnaby slew if they were to search the whole of the Spanish Main and the islands upon it

CHAPTER XLVI.

A PERILOUS VOYAGE.

I n this way, unexpected and tragical, arrived our chance of escape. We walked to Carlisle Bay by way of the sea-shore, so that we might be met by none, and in order that the bloodhounds (if they should use them) in the morning might be thrown off the track. On the march that stout and lusty wench who carried one end of the bed neither called for a halt nor complained of the burden she carried all the way. It was nigh unto midnight when we arrived at the creek in which the boat lay sunk. This was within a stone's throw of John Nuthall's cottage, where were bestowed the mast, sails, oars, and gear, with such provisions as he had gotten together for the voyage. The man was sleeping when Barnaby called him, but he quickly got up, and in less than an hour we had the boat hauled out of the water, the provisions hastily thrown in, the mast stepped, our sick man and the women placed in the bows, the stern and middle of the boat being encumbered with our provisions, we had pushed down the muddy and stinking creek, we had hoisted sail, and we were stealing silently out of Carlisle Bay under a light breeze. Three or four ships were lying in the bay; but either there was no watch kept aboard, or (which is more probable) it was no one's business to hail a small sail-boat going out, probably for fishing at dawn. Besides, the night was so dark that we may very well have escaped notice. However that might be, in a quarter of an hour we were well out at sea, beyond the reach of the guns of Carlisle Bay, no longer visible to the ships in port, and without any fear of being seen until daybreak. The wind, which sometimes drops altogether in the night, still continued favourable, though very light.

'My lads,' said Barnaby presently, drawing a long breath, 'I verily believe that we have given them the slip this time. In the morning they may go forth, if they please, with their bloodhounds to hunt for us. Let them hunt. If any inquiry is made for us at the Bridge, no boat will be missing, and so no suspicion will be awakened. They will then, I suppose, search for us among the caves and ravines of which I have heard, where there are hiding-places in plenty, but no water to drink, so that the poor devils who run away and seek a refuge there are speedily forced to come out for water, and so are caught or shot down. Well, they will hunt a long time before they find us. This boat makes a little water, but I think not much. If she proves watertight, and the breeze holds, by daylight we should be well to the south of the island. Courage, therefore! All will be well yet! How goes Robin?'

He was lying as easily as we could manage for him—one rug over him and another under him. Alice sat on one side of him, and the woman they called Deb on the other. Then, because the boat sometimes shipped a little water when she dipped in the waves, Barnaby rigged a tarpaulin round the bows to prevent this; and (but this was not till next day) over the tarpaulin he made, out of a rug and a spare spar, a low tilt which, unless the weather grew bad, should shelter those three by night from dew and spray, and by day from the sun overhead and the glare and heat of the water.

'Deb,' he said softly, 'art afraid?'

'No, sir—not while my mistress is here.' (Meaning Alice.)

'If we are taken, we shall all be flogged well nigh unto death, and very likely hanged as well.'

'I am not afraid, sir.'

'We may spring a leak,' said Barnaby, 'and so go all to the bottom and be devoured. Art not afraid to die?'

'No, sir—not if I may hold my mistress by the hand, so that she may take me whither she goeth herself.'

'Good,' said Barnaby. 'As for me, I expect I shall have to go alone or with John Nuthall here. Well, there will be a goodly company of us. Go to sleep, my girl! In the morning we will serve around the first ration, with perhaps, if all be well, a dram of cordial.'

In the dim light of the stars I watched all night the three figures in the bow. Robin lay white and motionless; Alice sat, covered with her hood, bending over him; and Deb, from whose head her coif had fallen, lay, head on arm, sound asleep. She had no fear, any more than a common soldier has when he goes into action, because he trusts his captain.

Thus began our voyage: in an open boat twenty feet long, with a company of three sound men, two women, and a sick man. For arms, in case we needed them, we had none at all. If any ship crossed our track and should call upon us to surrender we could not deny that we were escaped convicts, because the dress of all but one proclaimed the fact. Who, in such a climate, would choose to wear a coarse shirt and canvas breeches, with a Monmouth cap, except it was a servant or a slave who had no choice, but must take what is given him?

But we should not surrender, come what might. If we could neither fight nor fly, we could sink. Said Barnaby, in the dead of night, whispering in my ear, 'Lad, 'tis agreed between us, we will have that clear; sooner than be taken, we will scuttle the ship, and so sink all together. If 'tis accounted murder, the blame shall lie between us.'

A little before daybreak the breeze freshened, and the waves began to rise; but not so high as to threaten the boat, which proved, indeed, a most gallant little craft, dancing over the waters as if she enjoyed being driven by the breeze. Some boats, as sailors will tell you (being always apt to compare these craft with living creatures), come thus, frolic and sprightly, from their makers' hands; while others, built of the same material and on the same lines, are, on the contrary, and always remain, heavy and lumpish; just as some children are lively and gay, while others, born of the same parents, are dull and morose.

Then the sun rose, seeming to leap out of the water, a most glorious ball of fire, which instantly warmed the cool air and began to burn and scorch our hands and faces. In these hot latitudes one understands what the ancients meant when they spoke of the dreadful Sun-God, who both gives and destroys life, and is so beneficial and yet so terrible. We, who live in a cold country, are sometimes greatly comforted by the sun, but are never burned; we feel his warmth, but understand not his power.

Then Barnaby began to gaze curiously all round the horizon. We had no glass or telescope; but his eyes were to him as good as any telescope is to most men.

'Thank the Lord!' he said, drawing breath (it was rare for Barnaby thus openly to give praise), 'there is no sail in sight. To be sure, we have the day before us. But yet'—here he began to talk as some men use when they desire to place before their own minds clearly the position of affairs. 'Very well, then—Barbadoes laying thirty miles and more nor'-east by north—vessels bound for the island from Bristol commonly sailing round the north—very well, then—we are out of their track. Yet—then again—some are driven south by stress of weather. Ay, there is our danger. Yet again, if one should see us, would she bear down upon us? I greatly doubt it. The wind will continue—that is pretty sure. If they were to discover that we had gone by boat, would they sail after us? Why, what boat could they send? And whither would they steer? And what boat have they that can sail faster than this little craft? Yet we are pretty low down in the water. Humphrey, lad'—he turned upon me his broad and sunburnt face, full of cheerfulness—'we are not within many hours of scuttling yet. A tight boat, a fair wind, a smooth sea—let us hope for the best! How goes Robin?'

There was no change in Robin, either for better or for worse.

'Sis,' said Barnaby; 'art sleeping still, Sis? Wake up, and let us eat and drink, and be jolly! What! Alice, I say! Why—we have escaped! We are far away at sea! Let us laugh and sing. If there were room in this cockle, I would dance also!'

She lifted her head, and threw back her hood. Ah! what a mournful face was there!

'Oh, brother!' she said, 'canst thou laugh and sing? Hast thou forgotten last night?'

'Why, no,' he replied. 'One must not forget last night, because it was the night of our escape. All else, I own, I can forget. Let it not stick in thy gizzard, my dear, that the man frightened thee. Rejoice rather that he thus afforded me a chance of giving him a taste of his own cold iron.'

'Nay, brother,' she said, shaking her head; then she looked round her. 'We are a long way from the land,' she said. 'When will they send out a ship to bring us back?'

'Why, d'ye see,' Barnaby replied, 'give us twelve hours more, and they may send out all their fleet, if they have one, and sail the wide world round for us, and yet not capture us. And now let us overhaul the provisions, and examine the ship's stores.' Alice pulled her hood down again, and said no more. The woman they called Deb was now wide awake, and staring about her with the greatest satisfaction.

'Come, John Nuthall,' Barnaby went on, 'we are hungry and thirsty. Where is the list I made for thee? Thou art our purser, our supercargo, our cook, and our steward; thou art also bo's'n and carpenter, and half the crew. Where is my list, I say? Give it me, and we will examine our stores. Look up, Sis; never cry over what is done and over. What? A villain hath received a lesson, and thou hangest thy head therefor? Look up, I say. There is now hope for all; thou shalt merrily dance at my wedding yet.'

Then he read the list, and examined each parcel or box with great care.

'A hundred and a half of bread, a soft cheese, plantains, a keg of water (nine gallons), six bottles of Canary (not one broken), a compass, a half-hour glass, a spare rug ('tis over Robin's legs), flint and steel, a bit of tarpaulin, a hatchet and hammer, a saw, some nails, a spar or two, a coil of rope and yarn, a lump of tobacco (we can chew it, though I would rather put it into a pipe), candles—faugh! they are run together in a lump; they will serve to caulk something presently.'

We had, in fact, no light during our voyage, but the tallow proved useful when—I think it was the next day—the boat started a leak.

This was all our store. 'Twas not much for six people, but Barnaby hoped that the voyage would be short. If he should be disappointed, who would not put up with short rations for a day or two for the sake of freedom?

'And now,' he said, when everything was stowed according to his mind, 'we will have breakfast. Our provisions are no great things; but, after the accursed loblollie, a bit of bread and cheese will be a feast.'

A feast indeed it was, and our captain gratified us further by opening a flask of Canary, which raised all our hearts. Strange that men should be able to recover their spirits, which should be independent of the creature comforts, by a dram of wine. As for Barnaby, I thought he would have kissed the bottle.

'It is now three months and more,' he said, 'that we have had nothing save a sup of kill-devil fresh from the still, and now we are mercifully permitted to taste again a glass of Canary. 'Tis too much!' he sighed, drinking his ration. 'Well, we have but a few bottles, and the voyage may be longer than we hope; therefore we must go upon short allowance. But fear not, Sis; there shall always be enough for Robin, poor lad.'

He then proceeded to tell us what he intended, and whither he would steer.

'We have no chart,' he said. 'What then? I can draw one as good as they are made to steer by in these seas.' He could not draw one, because he had no paper or pencil; but he carved one with the point of his knife on the seat, and marked out our course upon it day by day. 'See,' he said, 'here is Barbadoes. Our course all night hath been sou'-west. She now makes five knots an hour. It is now eight, I take it; and we must therefore be about forty miles from Barbadoes. To-morrow morning we should make the Grenadilloes, which are a hundred and fifty miles from Carlisle Bay. Hark ye! There may be a Bristol vessel sailing from Great Grenada to Barbadoes, or the other way. That would be the devil. But such ships are rare, and there is no trade between the two islands. Well, we shall give Grenada as wide a berth as may be.' Here he considered a little. 'Therefore, 'twill be our wiser plan to bear more to the south. Once south of Grenada, I take it, there will be no more danger. Off the main of South America the sea is covered with islands. They are No Man's Land; inhabitants have they none; navigators, for the most part, know them not; English, French, and Spanish ships come never to these islands. My purpose, therefore, is to put in at Great Margaritos or Tortuga for rest and fresh water, and so presently make the Dutch island of Curaçao.'

'And after that?'

'Then, my lad, we shall take ship to some country where a sailor may get a berth and a physician may find patients. It must be to Holland first; but, never fear, we shall get back to England some time; and perhaps fight another battle with a different tale to tell afterwards.'

As the day advanced, the coast of Barbadoes continually receded, until, before sunset, the island lay like a purple cloud low down in the horizon. The north-east breeze blew steadily, but the sun caused a most dreadful heat in the air, and our eyes smarted from the glare of the water and the spray that was blown upon us. It was at this time that Barnaby constructed the tilt of which I have spoken. The sea lay spread out round us in a broad circle, of which we were the centre, and the cloudless blue sky lay over us like unto a roof laid there for us alone. It is only in a ship one doth feel thus alone, in the centre of creation; even as if there were nothing but the sea around, the sky above, and our boat in the centre. Thus must the Patriarch Noah have felt when his ark floated upon the vast face of the water, and even the tops of the[304] high hills were hidden and covered over. All day Barnaby scanned the horizon anxiously; but there came into sight no sail or ship whatever. To us, who sometimes see the vessels lying in a crowded port, and hear how they bring argosies from every land, it seems as if every part of the ocean must be covered with sails driving before the wind from whatever quarter it may blow. But he who considers the 'Mappa Mundi' will presently discover that there are vast expanses of sea where never a sail is seen, unless it be the fugitive sail of the pirate or the bark canoe of the native. We were now nearing such a lonely sea or part of the ocean. Barnaby knew, what these planters did not, how to steer across the unknown water to a port of safety beyond.

At midday our captain served out another drink of water, and to Robin I gave a sop of bread in Canary, which he seemed to suck up and to swallow with readiness.

In such a voyage, where there is nothing to do but to keep the ship on her course and to watch the horizon for a strange sail, one speedily falls into silence, and sits many hours without speech; sometimes falling asleep, lulled by the ripple of the water as the boat flies through it.

I have said nothing about the man John Nuthall. He was a plain, honest-looking man, and we found him throughout all this business faithful, brave, and patient, obedient to Barnaby, and of an even temper and contented with his share. That he had formerly been a thief in his native country cannot be denied, but I hope that we shall not refuse to any man the right of repentance.

Barnaby divided the crew—namely, himself, John Nuthall, and me—into three watches of eight hours each, of which each man kept two at a stretch. Thus, beginning the day at noon, which was the only time we knew for certain, Barnaby would himself (but this was after the first two days) lie down and sleep till sunset or a little later. Then John Nuthall lay down and took his turn of sleep till Barnaby thought it was two o'clock in the morning, when he woke him and I took his place. But for the first day or two Barnaby slept not at all, and the whole of the voyage he slept as a good watch-dog sleeps—namely, with one eye open.

At sunset he gave out another pannikin of cold water to each of us, a ration of bread and cheese, and a dram of wine. Then he commanded John Nuthall to lie down and sleep, while I took the tiller and he himself held the ropes. Then the night fell once more upon us.

Presently, while we sat there in silence, Alice rose up from her seat and came aft and sat down beside me.

'Humphrey,' she whispered, 'think you that he is truly dead?' She was speaking, not of Robin, but of the Master.

'I know not, my dear.'

'I can think of nothing but of that man's sudden end, and of what may happen to us. Say something to comfort me, Humphrey! You always had some good word to say, like manna for refreshment. My soul is low in the dust—I cannot even pray.'

'Why, my dear?' What could I say? ''Tis true that the man was struck down, and that suddenly. And yet——'

'To think that my brother—that Barnaby—should have killed him!'

'Why,' said Barnaby, 'if some one had to kill him, why not I as well as another? What odds who killed him?'

'Oh!' she said, 'that a man should be called away at such a moment, when his brain was reeling with wine and wicked thoughts!'

'He was not dead,' I told her (though I knew very well what would be the end), 'when we came away. Many a man recovers who hath had a sword-thrust through the body. He may now be on the mend—who can tell?' Yet I knew, I say, very well how it must have ended. 'Consider, my dear: he tempted the wrath of God, if any man ever did. If he is destroyed, on his own head be it—not on ours. If he recover, he will have had a lesson which will serve him for the rest of his life. If he doth not recover, he may have time left him for something of repentance and of prayer. Why, Alice, if we get safely to our port we ought to consider the punishment of this sinner (which was in self-defence, as one may truly say) the very means granted by Providence for our own escape. How else should we have got away? How else should we have resolved to venture all, even to carrying Robin with us?' All this, I repeat, I said to encourage her, because, if I know aught of wounds, a man bleeding inwardly of a sword-thrust through his vitals would have short time for the collecting of his thoughts or the repentance of his sins, being as truly cut off in the midst of them as if he had been struck down by a thunderbolt. A man may groan and writhe under the dreadful torture of such a wound, but there is little room for meditation or for repentance.

Then I asked her if she was in fear as to the event of the voyage.

'I fear nothing,' she told me, 'but to be captured and taken back to the place whence we came, there to be put in prison and flogged. That is my only fear. Humphrey, we have suffered so much that this last shame would be too great for me to bear. Oh! to be tied up before all the men, and flogged like the black women—'twould kill me, Humphrey!'

'Alice,' I said very earnestly, 'art thou, indeed, brave enough to endure death itself rather than this last barbarity?'

'Oh! Death!—death!' she cried, clasping her hands. 'What is death to me, who have lost everything?'

'Nay, but consider, my dear. To die at sea—it means to sink down under the cold water out of the light of day; to be choked for want of air; perhaps to be devoured quick by sharks; to lie at the bottom of the water, the seaweed growing over your bones; to be rolled about by the troubled waves——'

'Humphrey, these are old wives' tales. Why, if it had been lawful I would have killed myself long ago. But I must not lose heaven as well as earth. A brief pang it is to die, and then to be happy for ever. What do I care whether the seaweed covers my bones, or the cold clay? Oh, Humphrey, Humphrey, why should I care any longer to live?'

'My dear,' I said, 'if we escape in safety there may yet be happiness in store. No man knoweth the future.' She shook her head. 'Happiness,' I told her, 'doth not commonly come to man in the way which he most desires and prays. For, if he doth obtain the thing for which he hath so ardently prayed, he presently finds that the thing bringeth not the joy he so much expected. Or it comes too late, as is the case often with honours and wealth, when one foot is already in the grave. I mean, my dear, that we must not despair because the thing which most we desired is taken from us. Perhaps we ought not to desire anything at all, except what the Lord shall provide. But that is a hard saying, and if men desired nothing it is certain they would no longer work.' I talked thus at length to divert her mind from her troubles. 'To thee, poor child,' I said, 'have been given afflictions many and great—the loss of godly parents, a husband whom thou must avoid, and the deprivation of earthly love. Yet, since thou art so brave, Alice, I will tell thee—I thought not to tell thee anything of this——'

'What, Humphrey? What?'

'Briefly, Alice, thou shalt not be taken alive.'

'How—unless you kill me?'

'We are agreed, my dear—Barnaby and I—that if we cannot escape any boats which may pursue us the boat shall be sunk, and so we shall all drown together. Indeed, Alice, I confess that I am not myself so much in love with life as to return to that captivity and intolerable oppression from which we have gotten away. Therefore, be assured, we will all drown rather than go back.'

'Oh!' she sighed, but with relief, 'now shall I fear nothing. I have not lost everything, since I have thee still—and Barnaby. Alas! my head has been so full of what Madam said—that we should be certainly caught, and all of us flogged. To be flogged! Who would not rather die?'—she shivered and trembled. 'To be flogged!—Humphrey, I could not bear the shame!' She trembled and shivered as she repeated this confession of fear.

'Fear not, my dear,' I said; 'there are those on the boat who love thee too well to suffer that extreme of barbarity. Put that fear out of thy mind. Think only that we may have to die, but that we shall not be taken. To die, indeed, is very likely our fate: for we have but a quarter of an inch of frail wood between us and the seas. If a storm should arise, we fill with water and go down; if the wind should drop we should be becalmed, and so perish miserably of hunger and thirst; if Barnaby steer not aright——'

'Humphrey,' said Barnaby, 'fill not her innocent head with rubbish. 'Tis not the time of tornadoes, and there will be no storm. The wind at this season never drops, therefore we shall not lie becalmed. And as for my steering aright, why, with a compass—am I a lubber?'

'Brother,' she said, 'if I am not to be flogged, the rest concerns me little. Let us say no more about it. I am now easy in my mind. Robin sleeps, Humphrey. He hath slept since the sun went down, and this afternoon he looked as if he knew me. Also, he took the bread sopped in Canary eagerly, as if he relished it.'

'These seas,' said Barnaby, 'are full of sharks.'

I knew not what he meant, because we were speaking of Robin.

'Sharks have got their senses, as well as humans,' he went on.

Still I understood him not.

'When a man on board a ship is going to die, the sharks find it out, and they follow that ship until he does die and is flung overboard. Then they devour his body and go away, unless there is more to follow. I have looked for sharks, and there are none following the boat; wherefore, though I am not a doctor, I am sure that Robin will not die.'

'I know not at all,' I said, 'how that may be. There are many things believed by sailors which are superstitions—fond beliefs nourished by the continual presence of perils. On the other hand, the senses of man are notoriously as far below those of creatures as his intellect is above them (yet a skilful man may read the premonition of death in a sick man's face). Therefore I know not but a shark may have a sense, like unto the eye of a hawk or the scent of a hound, with which to sniff the approach of death afar off. Let us comfort ourselves, Alice, with Barnaby's assurance.'

"Tis a well proved and tried thing,' said Barnaby; 'and sailors, let me tell thee, Master Doctor, have no superstitions or idle beliefs.'

'Well, that may be. As to Robin's disease, I can pronounce nothing upon it. Nay, had I the whole library of Padua to consult, I could learn nothing that would help me. First, the mind falls into a languishing and spiritless condition. That causeth the body to lie open to attacks of any disease which may be threatening. Then, the body, being ill at ease, works upon the mind, and causes it to wander beyond control. So that the soul, which is bound up with body and mind, cannot show herself or manifest her will. It is the will which shows the presence of the soul: the will which governs body and mind alike. But if I know aught of disease, if a change comes upon Robin it will either swiftly cure or swiftly kill.'

'Humphrey,' she whispered, 'if he recover, how shall I meet his face? How shall I reply when he asks me concerning my faith?'

'My dear, he knows all. 'Twas that knowledge, the pity of it,[308] and the madness of it, believe me, which threw him into so low a condition.'

'I have looked daily for reproaches in thy kind eyes, Humphrey. I have found none, truly. But from Robin—oh! I dare not think of meeting those eyes of his.'

'Reproach thee will he never, Alice. Sorrow and love, I doubt not, will lie in his eyes all his life. What thou hast done was for him and for thy father and thy brother and for all of us. But, oh! the pity—and the villainy! Fear not to meet the poor lad's eyes, Alice.'

'I long to see the light of reason in those dear eyes—and yet I fear. Humphrey, I am married; but against my will. I am a wife, and yet no wife; I am resolved that, come what may, I will never, never go to my husband. And I love my Robin still—oh!' she sobbed, 'I love my Robin still!'

'If we die,' I told her, 'you shall go down with your arm round his neck, and so you shall die together.'

Then we sat silent a while.

'My dear,' I said, 'lie down and take some sleep.'

'I cannot sleep, Humphrey, for the peace of mind which hath fallen me upon. If Robin now come to his senses again I shall not fear him. And the night, it is so peaceful—so cool and so peaceful;' the wind had dropped, till there was barely enough to fill the sail, and only enough way on the boat to make a soft murmur of the water along her sides. 'The sea is so smooth; the sky is so bright and so full of stars. Can there be, anywhere, a peace like this? Alas! if we could sail still upon a silent and peaceful ocean! But we must land somewhere. There will be men, and where there are men there is wickedness, with drink and wrath and evil passions—such as we have left behind us. Humphrey—oh! my brother Humphrey!—it would be sweet if the boat would sink beneath us now, and so, with Robin's hand in mine, we could all go together to the happy land, where there is neither marrying nor giving in marriage.'

From beneath the tilt there came a voice—I verily believe it was an answer sent straight from heaven to comfort this poor faithful soul. 'Alice'—it was the voice of Robin, in his right mind at last. 'Alice,' he said, 'we will continue to love each other, yet without sin.'

'Oh, Robin! Robin!' she moved quickly to his side and fell upon her knees. 'Robin, thou wilt recover?'

'Stay!' I interposed. 'Robin will first have a cup of cordial.'

'I have been sleeping,' he said; 'I know not what hath happened. We are in a boat, it seems, and on the open sea. Unless I am still dreaming, we are slaves to a planter in Barbadoes! And this is Alice—who was in England! And I know not what it means.'

'You have been ill, Robin,' I told him. 'You have been nigh unto death. Many things have happened of which we will speak, but not now. Alice is at your side, and Barnaby is navigating the boat. Drink this cup of wine—so—sleep now; and in the morning, if it please Heaven, you shall be so strong that you shall hear everything. Ask no more questions, but sleep. Give him your hand, Alice.'

She obeyed me, sitting at his side and taking his hand in hers, and so continued for the rest of the night, Robin sleeping peacefully.

In a word, he was restored. The fresh sea-breeze brought him back to life and reason; and, though he was still weak, he was now as sound in his mind as any man could desire to be. And in the morning we told him all that had been done, whereat he marvelled.

Alice might love him still. That was most true, yet between them stood her husband. Why, there was another man in the boat who also loved a girl he could never wed. His passion, I swear, was full of constancy, tenderness, and patience. Would Robin be as patient?

When the day broke again we were still sailing over a lonely sea, with never a sail in sight, and never a sign of land.

And now Robin was sitting up, his face pale, and his hands thin. But the light of reason was in his eyes, and on his lips such a smile of tenderness as we were wont to see there in the days of old.

'Said I not,' cried Barnaby, 'that he would recover? Trust the sharks for common-sense. And again an open sea, with never a sail in sight. Praise the Lord, therefore!'

But Alice, when the sun rose above the waves, threw back her hood and burst forth into singing:—

O Lord, how glorious is Thy grace, And wondrous large Thy love! At such a dreadful time and place, To such as faithful prove.

The tears came into my eyes only to see the change that had fallen upon her gracious, smiling countenance. It was not, truly, the sweet and happy face that we remembered before her troubles fell upon her, but that face graver with the knowledge of evil and of pain. And now it was like unto such a face as one may see in many an altar-piece in Italy, glorified with gratitude and love.

Then the woman called Deb fell to weeping and blubbering for very joy that her mistress looked happy again. 'Twas a faithful, loving creature.

'Humphrey,' said Alice, 'forgive me that I murmured. Things that are done cannot be undone. Robin is restored to us. With three such brothers, who should not be content to live? I hope, now, that we shall get safely to our port; but if we die, we shall die contented in each other's arms. Going through the Vale of Misery,' she added softly, 'we will use it as a well.'

CHAPTER XLVII.

TORTUGA.

'I take it,' said Barnaby, on the third morning—the weather continuing fine and the sea clear of ships—'that we are now clear out of the track of any British vessels. We may fall into the hands of the Spaniard; but he is mild and merciful of late compared with his temper a hundred years ago. 'Tis true we have given him many lessons in humanity. We should now before nightfall make the islands of Testigos; but I think they are only rocks and sandy flats, such as they call Keys, where we need not land, seeing that we should get nothing by so doing, except to go out of the way, and so make the rations shorter. Robin'—'twas at breakfast, when he served out a dram of wine to every one—'I drink to thy better health, lad. Thou hast cheated the Devil. Nay, Sis, look not so angry!—I meant, thou wilt not go to heaven this bout. Up heart, then, and get strong! We will find thee another sweetheart, who shall make thee lift up thine head again. What? Is there but one woman in the world?

'I was saying then,' he went on, 'that we shall presently make the islands of Testigos. There followeth thereafter, to one who steereth west, a swarm of little islands. 'Twas here that the pirates used to lie in the good old days, snug and retired, with their girls and their drink. Ay, and plenty of both! A happy time they had!' Barnaby wagged his head and sighed. 'South of this archipelago (which I will some day visit, in order to search for treasure) there lieth the great and mountainous island of Margaritos. This great island we shall do well to keep upon our south, and so bear away to the desert island of Tortuga, where we shall find water for certain—and that, I have been told, the best spring-water that flows; turtles we may also find, and fish we may catch; and when we have recovered our strength, with a few days' rest ashore, we will once more put to sea and make for the island of Curaçao and the protection of the Dutchmen.'

It needs not to tell much more about the voyage, in which we were favoured by Heaven with everything that we could desire—a steady breeze from the best quarter, a sea never too rough, provisions in sufficiency, the absence of any ships, and, above all, the recovery of Robin.

I say, then, that we sighted (and presently passed) the group of islets called the Testigos; that we coasted along the great island of Margaritos, where we landed not, because Barnaby feared that certain smoke which we saw might betoken the presence of the Spaniard, whom, in spite of his new character for mildness, he was anxious to avoid. 'Tis strange thus to sail along the shore of a great island whereon are no inhabitants, or, if any, a few sailors put in for water, for turtle, and for cocoanuts; to see afar off the forests climbing round the mountain sides, the waterfalls leaping over the precipices, and to think of the happy life one might lead in such a place, far from men and their ways. I confess (since my Mistress will never see this page) that my thoughts for a whole day, while we sailed along the shores of Margaritos, turned upon those pirates of whom Barnaby spoke. They lived here at ease, and in great happiness. 'Tis of such a life that a man sometimes dreams. But if he were suffered so to lie in sloth, farewell Heaven! Farewell future hopes! Farewell our old talk of lifting the soul above the flesh! Let us henceforth live the lives of those who are content (since they can have no more) with a few years of love and wine and revelry! It is in climates like that of the West Indies that such a temptation seizes on men the most strongly: for here everything is made for man's enjoyment; here is no cold, no frost, no snow or ice; here eternal summer reigns, and the world seems made for the senses and for nothing else. Of these confessions enough. 'Twas impossible that in such a luxurious dream the image of Alice could have any part.

We landed, therefore, on the desert island of Tortuga, where we remained for several days, hauling up our boat and covering her with branches to keep off the sun. Here we lived luxuriously upon turtle, fresh fish, the remains of our bread, and what was left of our Canary; setting up huts in which we could sleep, and finding water of the freshest and brightest I ever saw. Here Robin mended apace, and began to walk about with no more help from his nurses.

We were minded, as I have said, to sail as far as the island of Curaçao, but an accident prevented this.

One day, when we had been ashore for ten days or thereabouts, we were terrified by the sight of a small vessel rigged in the fashion of a ketch—that is, with a small mizzen—beating about outside the bay which is the only port of Tortuga.

'She will put in here,' said Barnaby. 'That is most certain. Now, from the cut of her she is of New England build, and from the handling of her she is under-manned; and I think that we have nothing to fear from her, unless she is bound for Barbadoes, or for Grenada, or Jamaica.'

Presently the vessel came to anchor, and a small boat was lowered, into which three men descended. They were unarmed.

'She is certainly from New England,' said Barnaby. 'Well, they are not from Barbadoes in quest of us, otherwise they would not send ashore three unarmed men to capture four desperate men. That is certain. And as we cannot hide our boat, though we might hide ourselves, I will e'en go forth and parley with these strangers.'

This he did, we watching from a safe place. The conversation was long and earnest, and apparently friendly. Presently Barnaby returned to us.

'There offers,' he said, 'a chance which is perhaps better than to make for Curaçao, where, after all, we might get scurvy treatment. These men, in a word, are privateers; or, since we are at war with none, they are pirates. They fitted out a brigantine, or bilander (I know not which), and designed to sail round Cape Horn to attack the Spaniard on the South Seas. On the way they took a prize, which you now see in the bay. Ten men were sent aboard to navigate her as a tender to their ship. But they fell into bad weather off Brazil, and their ship went down with all hands. Now they are bound for Providence, only seven hands left, and they will take us aboard and carry us to that island for our services. Truly, I think we should go. They have provisions in plenty, with Madeira wine; and Providence is too far for the arm of King James to reach. What say ye all? Alice, what sayest thou?'

'Truly, brother, I say nothing.'

'Then we will agree, and go with them.'

We went on board, taking with us a good supply of turtle, clear water, and cocoanuts (being all that the isle afforded). Honest fellows we found our pirates to be. They belonged to the island of Providence, in the Bahamas, which has long been the rendezvous of English privateers. Ten years before this the Spaniards plucked up courage to attack and destroy the settlement, when those who escaped destruction found shelter in some of the adjacent islands, or on the mainland of Virginia. Now some of them have come back again, and this settlement, or colony, is re-established.

Thither, therefore, we sailed. It seemed as if we were become a mere shuttlecock of fortune, beaten and driven hither and thither upon the face of the earth.

CHAPTER XLVIII.

THE ISLAND OF PROVIDENCE.

It was some time in the month of March, A.D. 1686, that we landed in Providence. The settlement—from which the Spaniards had now nothing to fear—then consisted (it is now, I learn, much larger) of no more than one hundred and fifty people in all, the men being all sailors, and ready to carry on again the old trade of privateer or pirate, as you please to call it, when they should be strong enough to buy or hire a ship and to equip her.

We stayed on the island for two years and a quarter, or thereabouts. It is one of an archipelago, for the most part, I believe, desert. The settlement was, as I have said, but a small one, living in scattered houses; there were plenty of these to spare (which had belonged to the former settlement), if one only took the trouble to clear away the creeping plants and cut down the trees which had grown up round them since the Spaniards came and destroyed the colony. Such a house, built of wood, with a shingle roof, we found convenient for us; and after we had cleared the ground round it and repaired it, we lived in it. Some of the people helped us to a porker or two and some chickens. They also gave us some salt beef and maize to start with. That we had little money (only what was left over from the sale of Alice's ring) made no difference to us here, because no one had any at all, and at this time there was neither buying nor selling on the island—a happy condition of things which will not, I take it, last long. So great is the fertility of the ground here, and such is the abundance which prevails, that we very shortly found ourselves provided with all that we wanted to make life pleasant. Work there was for us, but easy and pleasant work—such as weeding our patches of vegetables and fruit in the early mornings; or going to fish; or planting maize; or attending to our pigs, poultry, and turkeys; and for the rest of the time, sitting in the shade conversing. It is none too hot in this place, though one would not in the summer walk abroad at noon; nor is it ever too cold. All the fruits which flourish under the tropics grow here, with those also which belong to the temperate zone. Here are splendid forests, where you can cut the mahogany-tree, and build your house, if you please, of that lovely wood. Here we ourselves grew, for our own use, maize, tobacco, coffee, cocoa, plantains, pines, potatoes, and many other fruits and vegetables.

Barnaby soon grew tired of this quiet life, and went on board a schooner bound for New England, promising that we should hear from him. After two years we did receive a letter from him, as you shall immediately learn. When he was gone we carried on a quiet and peaceful life. Books, paper, and pen there were none upon this island. Nor were there any clothes, so that the raggedness of our attire (we were dressed in the sailors' clothes our friends the privateers gave us) became incredible. I made some kind of guitar on which we played, and in the evening we would have very good playing and singing together of such pieces and songs as we could remember. I made verses, too, for amusement, and Alice learned them. We found our brother-settlers a rough but honest folk, to whom we taught many arts: how to procure sea-salt, how to make wine from pineapples, how to cure the tobacco-leaf—things which greatly added to their comfort; and, seeing that there was no church on the island, we every Sabbath held a meeting for prayer and exhortation.

Seeing, then, that we had all that man could desire, with perfect freedom from anxiety, our liberty, a delightful climate, plenty to eat and drink—ay, and of the very best—and that at home there was nothing for us but prison again, and to be sent back to the place whence we had escaped, we ought, every one will acknowledge, to have felt the greatest contentment and gratitude for this sure and quiet refuge. We did not. The only contented members of our household were John Nuthall and the woman Deb, who cheerfully cultivated the garden and fed the poultry and the pigs (for we had now everything around us that is wanted to make life pleasant). Yet we were not contented. I could read the signs of impatience in the face whose changes I had studied for so long. Other women would have shown their discontent in ill-temper and a shrewish tongue; Alice showed hers in silence, sitting apart, and communing with herself. I daresay I also showed my discontent; for I confess that I now began to long vehemently for books. Consider, it was more than two years since I had seen a book! There were no books at all on the island of Providence—not one book, except a Bible or two, and, perhaps, a Book of Common Prayer. I longed, therefore, for the smell of leather bindings, the sight of books on shelves, and the holy company of the wise and the ingenious. No one, again, could look upon Robin without perceiving that he was afflicted with a constant yearning for that which he could not have. What that was I understood very well, although he never opened his mind unto me.

Now I confess that at this time I was grievously tormented with the thought that, Alice's marriage having been no true marriage—because, first, she was betrayed and deceived; and, next, she had left her husband at the very church porch—there was no reason in the world why she should not disregard that ceremony altogether, and contract a marriage after her own heart. I turned this over in my mind a long while; and, indeed, I am still of the opinion that there would have been nothing sinful in such an act. But the law of the country would not so regard it. That is quite true. If, therefore, I had advised these unhappy lovers in such a sense they would have been compelled to live for the rest of their lives on this island, and their offspring would have been illegitimate. So that, though the letter of the law caused a most cruel in justice—*summum jus summa injuria*—it was better that it should be obeyed. In the end, it was a most happy circumstance that it was so obeyed.

I have presently to relate the means by which this injustice was removed. As for my own share in it, I shall neither exaggerate nor shall I extenuate it. I shall not defend it. I will simply set it down, and leave judgment to a higher Court than the opinion of those who read these pages. I must, however, acknowledge that, partly in Barbadoes and partly in Providence, I learned from the negresses, who possess many secrets and have a wonderful knowledge of plants and their powers, the simple remedies with which they treat fevers, agues, rheumatisms, and other common disorders. I say simple, because they will, with a single cup of liquor boiled with certain leaves, or with a pinch of some potent powder gotten from a plant, effect a speedier cure than our longest prescriptions, even though they contain more than fifty different ingredients. Had I possessed this knowledge, for example, while we lay in Exeter Jail, not one prisoner (except the old and feeble) should have died of the fever. This said, you will understand presently what it was I did.

It was, then, about the month of March, in the year 1688, that a ship, laden with wine, and bound from New York to Jamaica, put in at the port of Providence. Her captain carried a letter for me, and this was the first news of the world that came to us since our flight.

The letter was from Barnaby. It was short, because Barnaby had never practised the art of letter-writing; but it was pertinent. First, he told us that he had made the acquaintance at Boston (I mean the little town Boston of New England) of his cousins, whom he found to be substantial merchants (so that here, at least, the man George Penne lied not), and zealous upholders of the Independent way of thinking; that these cousins had given him a hearty welcome for the sake of his father; that he had learned from them, first, that the Monmouth business was long since concluded, and, so great was the public indignation against the cruelties of the Bloody Assize, that no one would again be molested on that account, not even those who had been sent abroad should they venture to return. He also said—but this we understood not—that it was thought things would before long improve.

'And now,' he concluded, 'my cousins, finding that I am well skilled and have already navigated a ship with credit, have made me captain of their own vessel, the *Pilgrim*, which sails every year to Bristol and back again. She will be despatched in the month of August or September. Come, therefore, by the first ship which will set you ashore either at New York or at Boston, and I will give you all a passage home. Afterwards, if you find not a welcome there, you may come back with me. Here a physician may find practice, Robin may find a farm, and sister will be safe from B. B.'

At this proposal we pricked up our ears, as you may very well believe. Finally we resolved to agree to it, promising each other to protect Alice from her husband, and to go back to Boston with Barnaby if we found no reason to stay in England. But the woman Deb, though she wept at leaving her mistress, would not go back to the place where her past wickedness might be remembered, and John Nuthall was also unwilling, for the same reason, to return; and, as this honest couple had now a kindness for each other, I advised them to marry and remain where they were. There was on the island no minister of religion, nor any magistrate or form of government whatever (yet all were honest); therefore I ventured to hear their vows of fidelity, and prayed with them while I joined their hands—a form of marriage, to my mind, as binding and as sacred as any wanting the assistance of a priest. So we handed over to them all our property (which was already as much theirs as ours), and left them in that sunny and delightful place. If the man was a repentant thief, the woman was a repentant magdalen, and so they were well matched. I hope and believe that, being well resolved for the future, they will lead a godly and virtuous life, and will be blessed with children who will never learn the reason why their parents left their native country.

There is little trade at Providence, but many vessels touch at the port, because it lies between the English possessions in America and those in the West Indies. They put in for water, for fruit, and sometimes, if they are short-handed, for men, most of them in the place being sailors. Therefore we had not to wait long before a vessel put in, bound from Jamaica to New York. We bargained with the captain for a passage, agreeing that he should find us provisions and wine, and that we would pay him (by means of Barnaby) on our reaching Boston (which is but a short distance from New York). Strange to say, though we had been discontented with our lot, when we sailed away Alice fell to weeping. We had murmured, and our murmuring was heard. We should now be permitted to live out what was left to us of life in England, and we should die and be buried among our own folk. Yet there are times when I remember the sweet and tranquil life we led in the island of Providence, its soft and sunny air, the cool sea-breeze, the shade of its orange groves, and the fruits which grew in such abundance to our hands.

CHAPTER XLIX.

HOME.

I n one thing alone the villain Penne spoke the truth. The Eykin family of Boston (I say again of New England) was one of the most considerable in the place—great sticklers for freedom and for religion (but, indeed, it is a most God-fearing town, and severe towards transgressors). They received us with so much kindness that nothing could surpass it; we were treated as Christian martyrs at the least, and towards Alice, of whose cruel lot they had heard from Barnaby, they showed (but that no one could help) an affection quite uncommon. They generously furnished us all with apparel becoming our station, and with money for our daily occasions; they approved of our going with Barnaby; but, in the event of our finding no welcome or means of a livelihood at home, and if Alice should be molested by her husband, they engaged us to return to New England. Here, they said, Robin might become a farmer, if he had no inclination for trade; they would joyfully receive Alice to live with them; and I myself would certainly find practice as a physician; while Barnaby should continue to command their ship. When I considered the many conveniences which exist in Boston (it is already, though young, better provided with everything than Barbadoes), the excellence of the climate, the books which are there, the printing press which hath already been established, the learned ministers, the college, the schools, and the freedom of religion, I should have been nothing loth to remain there. But I was constrained first to go home. I found also, which astonished me, so great a love of liberty that the people speak slightingly of the English at home who tamely suffer the disabilities of the Nonconformists and the prerogative of the Crown; and they ask why, when the country had succeeded in establishing a Commonwealth, they could not keep it? It certainly cannot be denied, as they argue, that Israel acted against the declared will of the Lord in seeking a king.

So we left them. But in how changed a condition did we now cross the ocean! Instead of huddling in a noisome and stinking dungeon, unclean for want of water, ill fed, and with no change of raiment, we had now comfortable cabins, clothes such as become a gentleman, and food of the best. And Barnaby, who had then sat humbly in the waist, where the prisoners were confined, now walked the quarterdeck—a laced kerchief round his neck, lace ruffles at his wrist, a scarlet coat on his back, a sword at his side, and gold lace in his hat: the captain of the ship.

The winds were contrary, and it was not until the last days of October that we arrived at Bristol. Here we lay for a few days, while Barnaby transacted his business, resolving to remain in retirement, for fear of accidents, until our captain should be ready to ride with us to Bradford Orcas.

The first news we learned was joyful indeed. It was that the Prince of Orange himself was about to invade England, with intent to drive his father-in-law from the throne. (He had indeed already sailed, but his fleet was driven back by a storm.) It was also stated that he had with him a great army of Dutch and English, and such preparations of arms and ammunition as (it was hoped) would make such a failure as that of our unhappy Duke impossible.

We also confirmed Barnaby's information that Monmouth's men could now go about without fear or molestation.

As to the position of affairs at Bradford Orcas, we could learn nothing.

There was one point on which I was curious—namely, as to what Barnaby would do in the matter of the villain Penne. On the one hand it was certain that Barnaby would not forget this man, nor was he likely to sit down with his arms folded after he had been robbed of so great a sum.

Therefore, I was not surprised when, the evening before we rode out of Bristol, he brought a big bag of blue stuff in his hands and poured out the contents—a vast shower of gold pieces—into the lap of his astonished sister.

'Alice,' he said, 'I bring you back your money. You will find it all here, and Mr. Boscorel's money to boot. He hath disgorged.'

With that he sat down and laughed, but as one who hath a joke in secret and would tell us no more.

For a day or two after this he would (on the road to Bradford Orcas) begin to laugh at intervals, rolling about in his saddle, shaking his sides, choking with laughter; insomuch that I presently lost patience with him, and, as a physician, ordered him instantly to make full confidence, or I would not answer for it but he would have a fit.

Then he told us what he had done.

Towards five in the afternoon, when the autumn day is ended, he repaired to the man Penne's counting-house (a place easily found on inquiry), having with him one of those fellows who bawl at fairs, selling medicines and charms, drawing teeth, letting blood, and so forth. At the sight of a sea captain, many of whom came to this place, the worthy merchant's servant, without suspicion, opened the door of the private office, or chamber, where Mr. Penne transacted his affairs. Barnaby found him dozing by the fire, his wig on the table, a silk handkerchief over his head, and the candles already lighted.

He awoke, however, on the opening of the door.

'Friend,' said Barnaby, 'I am Captain Barnaby Eykin, commanding the ship *Pilgrim*, from Boston—at your service. I am also brother to the young woman Alice Eykin, whom you robbed ('twas my money) of two hundred and fifty pounds, and afterwards kidnapped.'

Mr. Penne looked about him, and would have cried out for assistance; but Barnaby clapped a pistol to his forehead. Then he sank in his chair and gasped.

'Stir not,' said his enemy, 'I am also one of the three rebels for whose ransom the Reverend Philip Boscorel, Rector of Bradford Orcas, paid the sum of two hundred and ten pounds—which you have also stolen.'

'Sir,' said Mr. Penne, 'upon my honour those moneys were sent to Barbadoes. Upon my honour, sir.'

'You will therefore,' said Barnaby, taking no heed of this assurance, 'pay over to me the sum of four hundred and sixty pounds, with interest at five per cent. for three years, which I have calculated; the whole amount is five hundred and twenty-nine pounds. Begin by paying this.' Well, to make a long story short, though the man protested that he had not so much in the world, yet he presently opened his strong box and counted out the money, all in gold. This done, he hoped to be let off.

'There now remains,' said Barnaby, 'the punishment—and I forgot sister's ring: I ought to have added fifty pounds for that. But time presses. Perhaps I shall come back. I did intend to kill thee, brother, for thy great villany. However——'

He then beckoned the man with him, who lugged out of his pocket an instrument which made Mr. Penne shake and quake with terror. Barnaby then informed his victim that, as he had been the means of inflicting grievous bodily suffering upon four undeserving people, it was meet and right that he himself should experience something which, by its present agony, should make him compassionate for the future, and by its permanence of injury should prevent his ever forgetting that compassion for the rest of his life.

He therefore, he told him, intended to draw from his head four of his stoutest and strongest grinders.

This, in a word, he did; the man with him dragging them out with the pincers; Barnaby holding the pistol to the poor wretch's head, so that he should not bellow and call for assistance.

His laughter was caused by the remembrance of the twisting of the man's features in this agony, and by his moanings and groanings. The grinders he had brought away with him in his pocket, and showed them in triumph.

It was late in the afternoon when we rode into Bradford Orcas. The November sun, now setting, lay upon the woods, yellow and red with the autumn leaves not yet fallen. As we neared the village the sun went down, and a mist began to rise. All the doors were closed, and no one looked forth to greet us; the old cottage where Alice was born and where she lived so long was empty still; the door was open, the shutter hung upon one hinge; the honey hives were overturned, the thatch was broken; the garden was neglected.

'Why, Sis,' said Barnaby, 'thy mother is not there; nor Dad,—is he?—poor old Dad!'

We rode up the village till we came to the church, and the Manor House beside it. Alas! the house itself was closed, which had formerly stood open to all. There was no smoke from its chimneys, and the grass grew in the courtyard. We dismounted and opened the door, which was not locked. We went into the house: all was cold, and empty, and deserted. The twilight falling outside made the rooms dark. Beside the fireplace stood Sir Christopher's great chair, empty! his tankard was on the table and his tobacco-pipe, and—strange!—there lay, forgotten, the unhappy Duke's Proclamation.

Then a truly wonderful thing happened. Barnaby says that I must have dreamed it, for he saw nothing. Suddenly Sir Christopher himself appeared sitting in the chair; on his knees lay the Bible open. Beside him stood, with upraised forefinger, as if commenting on some knotty point, the Rev. Dr. Comfort Eykin. I declare that I saw them plainly, as plainly as I now behold the paper on which I write. They were but as shadows in the dark shadows of the empty room, and they appeared but for a moment, and then vanished, and I saw them no more.

'Come to the Rectory,' said Robin; 'it chokes us to be here.'

'Listen,' said Alice, outside the house.

From the Rectory there came the sound of a violoncello. Then was the good Rector himself there, comforting his soul.

We opened the garden-gate and walked softly across the lawn and looked in at the window ('twas made after the foreign fashion, to open upon the lawn). Beside the fire sat Madam, her hands clasped, thin, pale, and prematurely aged. Thus had she sat for three long years, still waiting for news of her son.

The Rector laid down his bow, crossed the room and sat down to the spinnet (on which he played prettily, but not with such command as he possessed over the other instrument). He played—I caught Alice's hand—an air of my own making to which I had set certain words, also of my own.

Then, while he played, we began to sing outside the window, Alice singing treble, or first, I the second part, and Robin the bass, as I had taught him in Providence Island the words of that little song. We sang it *piano*, or softly, at first, and then *crescendo*, or louder:—

As rides the moon in azure skies The twinkling stars beside; As when in splendour she doth rise, Their lesser lights they hide. So beside Celia, when her face we see, All unregarded other maidens be.

When we began, softly as I said, the Rector looked round him, playing still and listening. He thought the voices were in his own brain—echoes or memories of the past. Madam heard them too, and sat up listening as one who listens in a dream. When we sang louder Madam sprang to her feet, and held out her arms—but the Rector played the verse quite through. Then he opened the window for us.

'My son! my son!' cried Madam.

CHAPTER L.

THE GREAT LORD CHANCELLOR.

But the Prince of Orange had already landed.

We learned this news next day, and you may be sure that we were in the saddle again and riding to Exeter, there to join his standard.

This we did with the full consent of Madam and of Alice. Much as we had suffered already, they would not deter us, because this thing would have been approved by Sir Christopher and Dr. Eykin. Therefore we went. As all the world knows, this expedition was successful. Yet was not Barnaby made an Admiral, nor was I made a Court physician; we got, in fact, no reward at all, except that for Barnaby was procured a full pardon on account of the homicide of his late master.

My second campaign, as everybody knows, was bloodless. To begin with, we had an army, not of raw country lads armed indifferently and untrained, but of veteran troops, fifteen thousand strong, all well equipped, and with the best General in Europe at their head. At first, indeed, such was the dread in men's minds caused by Lord Jeffreys' cruelties, few came in; yet this was presently made up by what followed, when, without any fighting at all, the King's regiments melted away, his priests fled, and his friends deserted him. This was a very different business from that other, when we followed one whom I now know to have been a mere tawdry pretender, no better fitted to be a King than a vagabond actor at a fair is fit to be a Lord. Alas! what blood was wasted in that mad attempt!—of which I was myself one of the most eager promoters. I was then young, and I believed all that I was told by the conspirators in Holland; I took their list of well-wishers for insurgents already armed and waiting only for a signal; I thought that the roll of noble names set down for sturdy Protestants was that of men already pledged to the Cause; I believed that the whole nation would rise at the first opportunity to turn out the priests; I even believed in the legitimacy of the Duke, and that against the express statement of his father (if King Charles was in reality his father); and I believed what they told me of his princely virtues, his knowledge of the art of war, and his heroic valour. I say that I believed all these things and that I became a willing and zealous tool in their hands. As for what those who planned the expedition believed, I know not; nor will any one now ever learn what promises were made to the Duke, what were broken, and why he was, from the outset, save for a few days at Taunton, so dejected and disappointed. As for me, I shall always believe that the unhappy man—unwise and soft-hearted—was betrayed by those whom he trusted.

It is now an old tale, though King Monmouth will not speedily be forgotten in the West Country, nor will the memory of the Bloody Assize. The brave lads who followed him are dead and buried; some in unhonoured graves hard by the place where they were hanged, some under the burning sun of the West Indies. The Duke himself hath long since paid the penalty of his rash attempt. All is over and ended, except the memory of it.

It is now common history, known to everybody, how the Prince of Orange lingered in the West Country, his army inactive, as if he knew (doubtless he was well informed upon this particular) that the longer he remained idle the more likely was the King's Cause to fall to pieces. There are some who think that if King James had risked an action he could not but have gained, whatsoever its event—I mean that, the blood of his soldiers once roused, they would have remained steadfast to him, and would have fought for him. But this he dared not to risk; wherefore the Prince did nothing, while the King's regiments fell to pieces and his friends deserted him. It was in December when the Prince came to Windsor, and I with him, once more Chyrurgeon in a rebel army. While there I rode to London—partly with the intention of judging for myself as to the temper of the people; partly because, after so long an absence, I wished once more to visit a place where there are books and pictures; and partly because there were certain notes and herbs which I desired to communicate to the College of Physicians in Warwick Lane. It happened to be the very day when the King's first flight—that, namely, when he was taken in the Isle of Sheppey—became known. The streets in the City of London I found crowded with people hurrying to and fro, running in bands and companies, shouting and crying, as if in the presence of some great and imminent danger. It was reported and currently believed that the disbanded Irish soldiers had begun to massacre the Protestants. There was no truth at all in the report; but yet the bells were ringing from all the towers, the crowds were exhorting each other to tear down and destroy the Romish chapels, to hunt for and to hang the priests, and especially Jesuits (I know not whether they found any), and to shout for the Prince of Orange. I stood aside to let the crowds (thus religiously disposed) run past, but there seemed no end to them. Presently, however (this was in front of the new Royal Exchange), there drew near another kind of crowd. There marched six or eight sturdy fellows bearing stout cudgels and haling along a prisoner. Round them there ran, shrieking, hooting, and cursing, a mob of a hundred men and more; they continually made attacks upon the guard, fighting them with sticks and fists; but they were always thrust back. I thought at first that they had caught some poor, wretched priest whom they desired to murder. But it proved to be a prize worth many priests. As they drew nearer, I discerned the prisoner. He was dressed in the garb of a common sailor, with short petticoats (which they call slops), and a jacket; his cap had been torn off, leaving the bare skull, which showed that he was no sailor, because common sailors do not wear wigs; blood was flowing down his cheek from a fresh wound; his eyes rolled hither and thither in an extremity of terror; I could not hear what he said for the shouting of those around him, but his lips moved, and I think he was praying his guards to close in and protect him. Never, surely, was seen a more terror-stricken creature.

I knew his face. Once seen (I had seen it once) it could never be forgotten. The red and bloated cheeks, which even his fear could not make pale; the eyes, more terrible than have been given to any other human creature: these I could not forget—in dreams I see them still. I saw that face at Exeter, when the cruel Judge exulted over our misery and rejoiced over the sentence which he pronounced. Yea, he laughed when he told us how we should swing, but not till we were dead, and then the knife—delivering his sentence so that no single point of its horror should be lost to us. Yes; it was the face of Judge Jeffreys—none other—this abject wretch was that great Judge. Why, when we went back to our prison there were some who cast themselves upon the ground, and, for terror of what was to come, fell into mere *dementia*. And now I saw him thus humbled, thus disgraced, thus threatened, thus in the last extremity and agony of terror.

They had discovered him, thus disguised and in hiding, at a tavern in Wapping, and were dragging him to the presence of the Lord Mayor. It is a long distance from Wapping to Guildhall, and they went but slowly, because they were beset and surrounded by these wolves who howled to have his blood. And all the way he shrieked and trembled for fear!

Sure and certain is the vengeance of the Lord!

This Haman, this unjust Judge, was thus suffering, at the hands of the savage mob, pangs far worse than those endured by the poor rustics whom he had delivered to the executioner. I say worse, because I have not only read, but have myself proved, that the rich and the learned—those, that is, who live luxuriously and those who have power to imagine and to feel beforehand—do suffer far more in disease than the common, ignorant folk. The scholar dies of terror before ever he feels the surgeon's knife, while the rustic bares his limb, insensible and callous, however deep the cut or keen the pain. I make no doubt, therefore, that the great Lord Chancellor, while they haled him all the way from Wapping to Guildhall, suffered as much as fifty ploughboys flogged at the cart-tail.

Many thousands there were who desired revenge upon him—I know not what revenge would satisfy the implacable; because revenge can do no more than kill the body, but his worst enemy should be satisfied with this, his dreadful fate. Even Barnaby, who was sad because he could get no revenge on his own account (he wanted a bloody battle, with the rout of the King's armies and the pursuit of a flying enemy, such as had happened at Sedgemoor), was satisfied with the justice which was done to that miserable man. It is wonderful that he was not killed amidst so many threatening cudgels; but his guards prevented that, not from any love they bore him; but quite the contrary (more unforgiving faces one never saw); for they intended to hand him over to the Lord Mayor, and that he should be tried for all his cruelties and treacheries, and, perhaps, experience himself that punishment of hanging and disembowelling which he had inflicted on so many ignorant and misled men.

How he was committed to the Tower, where he shortly died in the greatest torture of body as well as mind, everybody knows.

CHAPTER LI.

THE CONFESSION.

Now am I come to the last event of this history, and I have to write down the confession of my own share in that event. For the others—for Alice and for Robin—the thing must be considered as the crown and completion of all the mercies. For me—what is it? But you shall hear. When the secrets of all hearts are laid open, then will Alice hear it also:

what she will then say, or what think, I know not. It was done for her sake—for her happiness have I laid this guilt upon my soul. Nay, when the voice of conscience doth exhort me to repent, and to confess my sin, then there still ariseth within my soul, as it were, the strain of a joyful hymn, a song of gratitude that I was enabled to return her to freedom and the arms of the man she loved. If any learned Doctor of Divinity, or any versed in that science which the Romanists love (they call it casuistry), should happen to read this chapter of confession, I pray that they consider my case, even though it will then be useless as far as I myself am concerned, seeing that I shall be gone before a Judge who will, I hope (even though my earthly affections do not suffer me to separate my sin from the consequences which followed), be more merciful than I have deserved.

While, then, I stood watching this signal example of God's wrath, I was plucked gently by the sleeve, and, turning, saw one whose countenance I knew not. He was dressed as a lawyer, but his gown was ragged, and his bands yellow; he looked sunk in poverty; and his face was inflamed with those signs which proclaim aloud the habit of immoderate drinking.

'Sir,' he said, 'if I mistake not, you are Dr. Humphrey Challis?'

'The same, Sir; at your service,' I replied with some misgivings. And yet, being one of the Prince's following, there needed none.

'I have seen you, Sir, in the chambers of your cousin, Mr. Benjamin Boscorel, my brother learned in the law. We drank together, though (I remember) you still passed the bottle. It is now four or five years ago. I wonder not that you have forgotten me. We change quickly, we who are the jolly companions of the bottle; we drink our noses red, and we paint our cheeks purple; nay, we drink ourselves out of our last guinea, and out of our very apparel. What then, Sir? a short life and a merry. Sir, yonder is a sorry sight. The first Law Officer of the Crown thus to be haled along the streets by a howling mob. Ought such a thing to be suffered? 'Tis a sad and sorry sight, I say!'

'Sir,' I replied hotly, 'ought such villains as Judge Jeffreys to be suffered to live?'

He considered a little, as one who is astonished and desires to collect his thoughts. Perhaps he had already taken more than a morning draught.

'I remember now,' he said. 'My memory is not so good as it was. We drink that away as well. Yes, I remember—I crave your forgiveness, Doctor. You were yourself engaged with Monmouth. Your cousin told me as much. Naturally you love not this good Judge, who yet did nothing but what the King, his master, ordered him to do. I, Sir, have often had the honour of sitting over a bottle with his Lordship. When his infirmities allowed (though not yet old, he is grievously afflicted) he had no equal for a song or a jest, and would drink so long as any were left to keep him company. Ha! they have knocked him down—now they will kill him. No; he is again upon his feet; those who protect him close in. So—they have passed out of our sight. Doctor, shall we crack a flask together? I have no money, unhappily; but I will with pleasure drink at your expense.'

I remembered the man's face now, but not his name. 'Twas one of Ben's boon companions. Well; if hard drinking brings men so speedily to rags and poverty, even though it be a merry life (which I doubt), give me moderation.

'Pray, Sir,' I said coldly, 'to have me excused. I am no drinker.'

'Then, Doctor, you will perhaps lend me, until we meet again, a single guinea?'

I foolishly complied with this request.

'Doctor, I thank you,' he said. 'Will you now come and drink with me at my expense? Sir, I say plainly, you do not well to refuse a friendly glass. I could tell you many things, if you would but drink with me, concerning my Lord Jeffreys. There are things which would make you laugh. Come, Doctor; I love not to drink alone. Your cousin, now, was always ready to drink with any man, until he fell ill'—

'How? is my cousin ill?'

'Assuredly; he is sick unto death. Yesterday I went to visit him, thinking to drink a glass with him, and perhaps to borrow a guinea or two, but found him in bed and raving. If you will drink with me, Doctor, I can tell you many curious things about your cousin. And now I remember, you were sent to the Plantations; your cousin told me so. You have returned before your time. Well, the King hath run away; you are, doubtless, safe. Your cousin hath gotten his grandfather's estate. Lord Jeffreys, who loved him mightily, procured that grant for him. When your cousin wakes at night he swears that he sees his grandfather by his bedside looking at him reproachfully, so that he drinks the harder;[327] 'tis a merry life. He hath also married a wife, and she ran away from him at the church door, and he now cannot hear of her or find her anywhere, so that he curses her and drinks the harder. Oh! 'tis always the jolliest dog. They say that he is not the lawyer that he was, and that his clients are leaving him. All mine have left me long since. Come and drink with me, Doctor.'

I broke away from the poor toper who had drunk up his wits as well as his money, and hurried to my cousin's chambers, into which I had not thought to enter save as one who brings reproaches—a useless burden.

Benjamin was lying in bed: an old crone sat by the fire, nodding. Beside her was a bottle, and she was, I found, half drunk. Her I quickly sent about her business. No one else had been attending him. Yet he was laid low, as I presently discovered, with that kind of fever which is bred in the villainous air of our prisons—the same fever which had carried off his grandfather.

Perhaps, if there were no foul and stinking wards, jails, and clinks, this kind of fever would be banished altogether, and be no more seen. So, if we could discover the origin and cause of all diseases, we might once more restore man to his primitive condition, which I take to have been one free from any kind of disease or infirmity, designed at first by his Creator so to live for ever, and, after the Fall, enabled (when medicine shall be so far advanced) to die of old age after such prolongation of life and strength as yet we cannot even understand.

'Cousin,' I said, 'I am sorry to find thee lying in this condition.'

'Ay,' he replied, in a voice weak and low, not like his old blustering tones. 'Curse me and upbraid me, if thou wilt. How art thou come hither? Is it the ghost of Humphrey? Art thou dead like my grandfather? Are we on the Plantations of Barbadoes?'

'Indeed, I am no ghost, Benjamin. As for curses, I have none; and as for reproaches, I leave them to thy conscience.'

'Humphrey, I am sore afflicted. I am now so low that I cannot even sit upright in my bed. But thou art a doctor—thou wilt bring me back to health. I am already better only for seeing thee here.'

I declare that as yet I had no thought, no thought at all, of what I was to do. I was but a physician in presence of a sick man, and therefore bound to help him if I could.

I asked him first certain questions, as physicians use, concerning his disorder and its symptoms. I learned that, after attending at the Court, he was attacked by fits of shivering and of great heat, being hot and cold alternately, and that in order to expel the fever he had sat drinking the whole evening—a most dangerous thing to do. Next, that in the morning he had been unable to rise from his bed, and, being thirsty, had drunk more wine—a thing enough of itself to kill a man in such a fever. Then he lost his head, and[328] could tell me no more what had happened until he saw me standing by his bedside. In short, he had been in delirium, and was now in a lucid interval, out of which he would presently fall a-wandering again, and, perhaps, raving, and so another lucid interval, after which he would die, unless something could be done for him.

I liked not his appearance nor the account which he gave me, nor did I like his pulse, nor the strange look in his eyes—death doth often show his coming by such a prophetic terror of the eyes.

'Humphrey,' he said pitifully. 'It was no fault of mine that thou wast sent to the Plantations.'

'That I know full well, Cousin,' I answered him. 'Be easy on that score.'

'And as for Alice,' he went on. 'All is fair in love.'

I made no reply, because at this point a great temptation assailed my soul.

You have heard how I learned many secrets of the women while I was abroad. Now, while we were in Providence Island I found a woman of the breed they call half caste—that is, half Indian and half Portuguese—living in what she called wedlock with an English sailor, who did impart to me a great secret of her own people. I obtained from her not only the knowledge of a most potent drug (known already to the Jesuits), but also a goodly quantity of the drug itself. This, with certain other discoveries and observations of my own, I was about to communicate to the College in Warwick Lane.

As for this drug, I verily believe it is the most potent medicine ever yet discovered. It is now some years since it was first brought over to Europe by the Jesuits, and is therefore called *Pulvis Jesuiticus,* and sometimes Peruvian Bark. When administered at such a stage of the fever as had now been reached by my unhappy cousin, it seldom fails to vivify the spirits, and so to act upon the nerves as to restore the sinking, and to call back to life a man almost moribund.

Remembering this, I lugged the packet out of my pocket and laid it on the table.

'Be of good cheer, Cousin,' I said; 'I have a drug which is strong enough, with the help of God, to make a dying man sit up again. Courage, then!'

When I had said these words my temptation fell upon me. It came in the guise of a voice which whispered in my ear.

'Should this man die,' it said, 'there will be freedom for Alice. She can then marry the man she loves. She will be restored to happiness. While he lives, she must still continue in misery, being cut off from love. Let him die therefore.'

'Humphrey,' said Ben; 'in this matter of Alice: if she will come to me, I will make her happy. But I know not where she is hidden. Things go ill with me since that unlucky day. I would to God I had not done it! Nothing hath gone well since; and I drink daily to hide her face. Yet at night she haunts me—with her father, who threatens, and her mother, who weeps, and my grandfather, who reproaches. Humphrey—tell me—what is it, man? What mean thy looks?'

For while he spoke that other voice was in my ears also.

'Should he die, Alice will be happy again. Should he live, she will continue in misery.' At these words (which were but my own thoughts, yet involuntary), I felt so great a pity, such an overwhelming love for Alice, that my spirit was wholly carried away. To restore her freedom! Oh! what price was too great for such a gift? Nay—I was seized with the thought that to give her so great a thing, even my own destruction would be a light price to pay. Never, until that moment, had I known how fondly and truly I loved her. Why, if it were to be done over again—but this matters not. I have to make my confession.

'Humphrey, speak!' I suppose that my trouble showed itself in my face.

'Thou art married to Alice,' I said slowly. 'That cannot be denied. So long as thou livest, Benjamin, so long will she be robbed of everything that she desires, so long will she be unhappy. Now, if thou shouldst die'——

'Die? I cannot die; I must live.' He tried to raise himself, but he was too weak. 'Cousin, save my life.'

'If thou shouldst die, Benjamin,' I went on, regardless of his words, 'she will be set free. It is only by thy death that she can be set free. Say then to thyself: "I have done this poor woman so great an injury that nothing but my death can atone for it. Willingly, therefore, will I lay down my life, hoping thus to atone for this abominable wickedness."'

'Humphrey, do not mock me. Give me—give me—give me speedily the drug of which you spoke. I die—I die!—Oh!—give me of thy drug.'

Then I took the packet containing the *Pulvis Jesuiticus* and threw it upon the fire, where in a moment it was a little heap of ashes.

'Now, Benjamin,' I said, 'I cannot help thee. Thou must surely die.'

He shrieked, he wept, he implored me to do something—something to keep him alive. He began to curse and to swear.

'No one can now save thee, Benjamin,' I told him. 'Not all the College of Physicians; not all the medicines in England. Thou must die. Listen and heed: in a short time, unless thy present weakness causeth thee to expire, there will fall upon thee another fit of fever and delirium, after which another interval of reason: perhaps another—but yet thou must surely die. Prepare thy soul, therefore. Is there any message for Alice that thou wouldst send to her, being now at the point of death?'

His only answer was to curse and weep alternately.

Then I knelt beside his bed, and prayed aloud for him. But incessantly he cried for help, wearing himself out with prayers and curses.

'Benjamin,' I said, when I had thus prayed a while, but ineffectually, 'I shall take to Alice, instead of these curses, which avail nothing, a prayer for pardon, in order to touch her heart and cause her to think of thee with forgiveness, as of one who repented at the end. This I shall do for her sake. I shall also tell thy father that thy death was repentant, and shall take to him also a prayer for forgiveness as from thee. This will lighten his sorrow, and cause him to remember thee with the greater love. And to Robin, too, so that he may cease to call thee villain, I will carry, not these ravings, but a humble prayer (as from thyself) for forgiveness.'

The sick man, when he found that prayers or curses would not avail, fell to moaning, rolling his head from side to side. When he was thus quiet I prayed again for him, exhorting him to lift up his soul to his Judge, and assuring him of our full forgiveness. But, indeed, I know not if he heard or understood. It was then about four of the clock, and growing dark. I lit a candle, and examined him again. I think that he was now unconscious. He seemed as if he slept. I sat down and watched.

I think that at midnight, or thereabouts, I must have fallen asleep.

When I awoke the candle was out, and the fire was out. The room was in perfect darkness. I laid my hand upon my cousin's forehead. He was cold and dead.

Then I heard the voice of the watchman in the street: 'Past two o'clock, and a frosty morning!'

The voice I had heard before whispered again in my ear.

'Alice is free —Alice is free! Thou—thou—thou alone hast set her free! Thou hast killed her husband!'

I threw myself upon my knees and spent the rest of that long night in seeking for repentance; but then, as now, the lamentation of a sinner is also mingled with the joy of thinking that Alice was free at last, and by none other hand than mine.

This I repeat is my confession: I might have saved my cousin, and I suffered him to die. Wherefore I have left the profession in which it was my ambition to distinguish myself, and am no longer anything but a poor and obscure person, living on the charity of my friends in a remote village.

Two days afterwards I was sitting at the table, looking through the dead man's papers, when I heard a footstep on the stair.

It was Barnaby, who broke noisily into the room.

'Where is Benjamin?' he cried. 'Where is that villain?'

'What do you want with him?'

'I want to kill him. I am come to kill him.'

'Look upon the bed, Barnaby.' I laid back the sheet and showed him the pale face of the dead man.

'The hand of the Lord—or that of another—hath already killed him. Art thou now content?'

CHAPTER THE LAST.

In the decline of years, when the sixtieth birthday is near at hand and one looks not to live much longer, and the future hath no fresh joy to bring with it (but only infirmities of age and pain), it is profitable and pleasant to look back upon the past, to observe the guidance of the Unseen Hand, to repent one's sins, and to live over again those seasons, whether of sorrow or of joy, which we now perceive to have been Providentially ordered.

This have I done, both in reading the history of our lives as related by my Mistress, and in writing this latter part. To the former have I added nothing, nor have I subtracted anything therefrom, because I would not suffer the sweet and candid soul of her whom I have always loved to be tarnished by any words of mine, breaking in upon her own, as jarring notes in some lovely harmony. It is strictly laid upon me to deliver her words just as she hath written them down.

Now, after the death of Benjamin, I took it upon myself, being his cousin, in the absence of his father, to examine the papers which he had left. Among them I found abundance of songs, chiefly in praise of wine and women, with tavern bills. Also, there were notes of legal cases, very voluminous, and I found notes of payment made to various persons engaged in inquiring after his wife, in those towns of the West Country where her father's name would procure friends for her. But there was no will; Benjamin had died (never looking for so early an end) without making any will. Therefore the estate of Bradford Orcas, with the old house, became the property of the Rector, Benjamin's father. And he, being moved to make reparation for his son's sin, and out of the great love which he bore to Alice, conveyed the whole to Robin on the day of his marriage. Thus the confiscated estate returned to the ancient family who had always held it, and promise to hold it still, so long as the good old stock shall last.

It is thirty years ago and more. King William III. is dead; Queen Anne is dead; King George (who cannot, they say, speak English, but is a stout Protestant) sits upon our throne; the Nonconformists are free , save that they cannot enter the Universities, and are subject to other disabilities, which will, doubtless, be removed in the course of years. But English people, I think, love power beyond all earthly things; and so long as the Church is in a majority the Churchmen will exercise their power and will not part with it. To us of Bradford Orcas it matters little. We worship at the parish church. Every Sunday I contemplate, as I did fifty years ago, the monument of Filipa kneeling apart, and of her husband and his second wife kneeling together. There is a new tablet in the chancel put up to the memory of Sir Christopher, and another to that of Dr. Comfort Eykin. Their bodies lie somewhere among the mounds on the north side of Ilminster Church.

Forty years ago, as you have seen, there stood three boys in the garden of the Manor House discoursing on their future. One wished never to go anywhere, but to remain always a country gentleman, like his grandfather; one would be a great lawyer, a Judge, even the Lord Chancellor; the third would be a great Physician. Lo! the end of all! The first, but after divers miseries, perils, and wanderings, hath attained to his desire; the second lies buried in the churchyard of St. Andrew's, Holborn, forgotten long since by his companions (who, indeed, are now with him in the pit), and remembered only among his own kin for the great wickedness which he wrought before the Lord. And, as for the third and last, no illustrious physician is he; but one who lives obscure (but content) in a remote village (in the very cottage where his Mistress was born), with books and music, and the society of the sweetest woman who ever graced this earth for his solace. She was always gracious: she was gracious in her childhood; gracious as a maiden; more gracious still is she in these latter days when her hair is grey, and her daughters stand about her, tall and comely.

Now, had I administered that powder—that sovereign remedy, the *Pulvis Jesuiticus*—what would have been her lot?

'Humphrey,' said Robin, 'a penny for thy thoughts.'

'Robin, I was thinking—it is not a new thing, but twenty years old and more—that Cousin Benjamin never did anything in his life so useful as to die.'

'Ay, poor Benjamin! That he had at the end the grace to ask our forgiveness and to repent hath in it something of a miracle. We have long forgiven him. But consider, Cousin. We were saved from the fight; we were saved from the sea; we were saved from slavery; we were enabled to strike the last blow for the Protestant religion—what were all these blessings worth if Benjamin still lived? To think, Humphrey, that Alice would never have been my wife and never a mother; and all these children would have remained unborn! I say that, though we may not desire the death of a sinner, we were not human if we rejoiced not at the death of our poor cousin.'

Yes; that is the thought which will not suffer me to repent. A single pinch of the *Pulvis Jesuiticus*, and he might have been living unto this very day: then would Alice have lost the crowning blessing of a woman's life.

Yet—I was, it is true, a physician—whose duty it is to save life, always to save life, even the life of the wretched criminal who is afterwards to die upon the gallows.

Yet, again, if he had been saved! As I write these lines I see my Mistress walking down the village street. She looks over my garden-gate; she lifts the latchet and enters, smiling gravely and tenderly. A sober happiness sits upon her brow. The terror of her first marriage has long been forgotten.

Why, as I watch her tranquil life, busy with her household and her children, full of the piety which asks not (as her father was wont to ask) how and where the mercy of Heaven is limited, and if, indeed, it will embrace all she loves; as I mark the tender love of husband and of children, which lies around her like a garment and prevents all her doings, there comes back to me continually a bed-room in which a man lies dying. Again in memory, again in *intention*, I throw upon the fire that handful of *Pulvis Jesuiticus* which should have driven away his fever and restored him to health again. A great and strong man he was, who might have lived till eighty years: where then would have been that love? where those children? where that tranquil heart and that contented mind? '*I WILL NOT SAVE HIS LIFE.*' I say again in my mind: '*I WILL NOT SAVE HIM; HE SHALL DIE.*'

'Humphrey,' my Mistress says, 'leave thy books awhile and walk with me: the winter sun is warm upon the hills. Come, it is the day when Benjamin died—repentant—what better could we wish? What greater blessing could have been bestowed upon him and upon us than a true repentance and to die? Oh! dear Brother, dear Humphrey, let us walk and talk of these blessings which have been showered upon my undeserving head.

Printed in the USA
CPSIA information can be obtained
at www.ICGtesting.com
LVHW071317201223
766878LV00072B/1094